LUCY CROWN

Lucy Crown

IRWIN SHAW

NEW ENGLISH LIBRARY
TIMES MIRROR

First published in Great Britain by Jonathan Cape Ltd.
© Irwin Shaw 1964

*

FIRST NEL PAPERBACK EDITION SEPTEMBER 1977

*

NEL Books are published by
New English Library Limited from Barnard's Inn, Holborn, London EC1N 2JR
Made and printed in Great Britain by Hunt Barnard Printing Ltd., Aylesbury, Bucks.

45003246 9

To Saxe Commins

Chapter One

AT that moment, in a good many of the bars and night-clubs of the city, people were singing 'I love Paris in the Springtime, I love Paris in the Fall . . .' It was two o'clock in the morning, in the month of July, champagne was being sold at eight thousand francs a bottle, and the singers were working hard to convince the tourists that being in Paris was worth eight thousand francs a bottle.

It was a coloured man, with a broad, industrious Harlem face, who was singing it as though he meant it, sitting at the yellowish piano at the back of the long narrow room, when the woman came in through the door. She hesitated a moment, checked by the blare of sound and the stares of the drinkers at the bar near the entrance. Then the owner came over, smiling, because the woman was clearly an American, and well dressed and not drunk.

'Good evening,' he said in English. He spoke English because his bar was in the eighth arrondissement and a high proportion of his clientele, at least in the summertime, was American. 'Madame is alone?'

'Yes,' the woman said.

'Would you like to sit at the bar or at a table, Madame?'

The woman glanced quickly at the bar. There were three or four men of various ages, two of them looking frankly at her, and a girl with long yellow hair, who was saying, 'Sharlee, Darling, I 'ave told you three times, thees night I am with George.'

'A table, please,' the woman said.

The owner led her towards the centre of the room, making a quick professional estimate of her as he threaded his way between the tables. He decided to put her next to three other Americans, two men and a woman, a little noisy, but harmless, who kept requesting the pianist to play 'St. Louis Woman' and who might be inclined to offer the lady a drink, seeing that it was so late at night and she was alone and they didn't speak the language.

I bet that was a beautiful one, the owner was thinking, when

7

that was younger. Even now. In this light, the hair looks truly blonde, and the big, soft grey eyes. And hardly any of the wrinkles showing. And she knows how to dress and carry herself, with those long legs. Wedding ring, but husband not present. Husband probably a victim of *tourisme* and over-eating, collapsed back in the hotel, and the wife still full of energy and out on her own to see the *real* Paris and maybe have something interesting happen that could never happen to a woman her age back home in the Midwest of America or wherever.

The owner pulled the table out for her and bowed, approving of the square shoulders, the firm throat and bosom, the neat, smart black dress, the pleasant, almost girlish smile of thanks as the woman sat down. He revised his estimate downwards. No more than forty-three, forty-four, he thought, at the outside. Maybe the husband isn't here at all. Maybe she is one of those executive types of women the Americans are turning out, who travel all over, always stepping in and out of planes, giving statements to the newspapers and running things, and never a hair out of place, no matter what.

'A half-bottle of champagne, Madame?' the owner said.

'No, thank you.' The owner didn't wince at the voice. He was sensitive and a great many American and English voices gave him an uncomfortable scraping sensation in the armpits. But not this one. It was low, direct and musical, but not fancy. 'I'd just like a ham sandwich and a bottle of beer, please.'

The owner wrinkled his nose, indicating surprise, a mild displeasure. 'Actually, Madame, there is a minimum charge which covers the price of several drinks and I suggest . . .'

'No, thank you,' the woman said firmly. 'At my hotel they said I could get something to eat here.'

'Of course, of course. We have a *specialité*, onion soup, gratinée, cooked . . .'

'Just the sandwich, thank you.'

The owner shrugged, bowed slightly, gave the order to a waiter, and walked back to his station at the bar, thinking, A ham sandwich, what is she doing out at this hour?

He watched her after that, in between greeting new guests and bowing others out of the door. A woman alone in his night-club at two o'clock in the morning was no novelty, and he knew, almost every time, just what they were there for. There were the drunks who couldn't afford to buy their own liquor and the wild young American girls who were crowding in everything they could get before Papa closed the cheque book down on them and made them get on the boat, and there were the hungry ones, usually divorced and feeling older every minute and stretching the alimony, who were afraid they'd commit suicide if they went back to their single hotel rooms alone one more night. A club, of course, was supposed to be a gay place, and the owner did everything he could to give it that appearance, but he knew better.

The woman sitting at her little table, quietly eating her sandwich and drinking her beer, wasn't any wild American girl and she certainly wasn't a drunk and with those clothes she wasn't stretching any alimony. And if she was lonely, she didn't show it. He watched the Americans at the next table turn towards her and talk to her, as he had known they would, their voices booming over the music, but she smiled politely and shook her head, refusing whatever it was they were offering, and after that they left her alone.

It was a slow night and the owner had time to speculate about her. Studying her through the cigarette smoke, as she sat back on the banquette, listening to the Negro at the piano, the owner decided that she reminded him of the two or three women in his life who, he had known from the beginning, were too good for him. The women had known it, too, and for that reason the owner remembered them romantically and still sent flowers on her birthday to the last of them, who had later married a colonel in the French Air Force. She is that rare combination, the owner thought; she has sweetness and she is confident of herself at the same time. Why couldn't she have walked in here ten years ago?

Then he had to go into the kitchen. He passed her table and smiled at her and made a careful check on the whiteness and slight irregularity of the teeth and the healthy texture of the skin, as the woman smiled back. He shook his head as he went through the kitchen door, puzzled, thinking, Now really, what is a woman like that doing in a joint like mine? He resolved to stop at her table on the way back and offer her a drink, and perhaps find out.

Then, when he came out of the kitchen, he saw that two American college boys had moved from the end of the room and were sitting at her table, and they were all talking, all very lively, and the woman was smiling, first at one of them and then at the other, and her hands were on the table and she was leaning over

9

and touching the arm of the better-looking of the boys momentarily as she said something to him.

The owner didn't stop at the table. That's it, he thought, it's as simple as that. The young ones, she likes the young ones. He felt obscurely betrayed, as though the memory of the two or three women who had been too good for him had somehow been damaged.

He went back to the bar and tried not to look at her again. College boys, he thought. And one of them with glasses, besides. To the owner, all Americans under thirty-five who cut their hair short were college boys, but these were the real, authentic, tall, slouchy, skinny models, with big hands and feet twice the size of any Frenchman's. Sweet and confident, he thought, disappointed in his own judgment. I bet.

There was a flurry of arrivals and departures and the owner was busy for almost a half hour. Then there was a little lull and he looked over at the woman again. She was still with the two college boys and the boys were talking as much as ever, but she didn't seem to be listening closely any more. She was leaning on the table between the boys, staring hard at the bar. At first, the owner thought she was staring at him and he essayed a little smile, to make a polite connection. But there was no answering flicker on the woman's face, and he realized that she wasn't looking at him, but at a man two places down the bar from him

The owner turned and looked at the man and thought, with a faint touch of bitterness, Well, of course. The man was an American, by the name of Crown, young, about thirty, with a little touch of grey in his hair, tall, but not outsize like the college boys. He had big, grey, guarded eyes, with heavy black lashes, and a reckless, soft, curly kind of mouth that looked as though it probably got him into trouble. The owner knew him as he knew perhaps a hundred other people who came into his place for a drink a few times a week. Crown lived nearby, the owner knew, and had been in Paris for a long time, and usually came in late at night, alone. He didn't drink much, maybe two whiskies a night, and he spoke good French, and when he noticed it, he merely seemed mildly amused by the fact that women invariably stared at him.

The owner moved down the bar and greeted Crown, shaking his hand, remarking that Crown was deeply tanned from the

10

sun. 'Good evening,' he said. 'I haven't seen you in some time. Where've you been?'

'Spain,' Crown said. 'I only came back three days ago.'

'Ah, that's why you're so brown,' the owner said. He touched his jaw regretfully. 'I myself am a deep green.'

'It's the proper colour for a night-club owner. Don't complain,' Crown said gravely. 'It'd make the clients uneasy if they came in and saw you rosy and healthy-looking. They'd suspect something sinister about the place.'

The owner laughed. 'Maybe you're right,' he said. 'Let me buy you a drink.' He waved to the bartender.

'There *is* something sinister about this place,' Crown said. 'Be careful that it isn't reported back to the police that you have been known to offer something for nothing to an American.'

Uh-uh, the owner thought, he has been drinking more than I thought tonight, and he signalled, with his eyes, to the bartender, to make the drink a light one. 'You went to Spain on business?' he asked.

'No,' Crown said.

'Oh. Pleasure.'

'No.'

The owner grinned conspiratorially. 'Ah—a lady . . .'

Crown chuckled. 'I do like coming in here and talking to you, Jean,' he said. 'How intelligent of you to separate the ideas of lady and pleasure.' He shook his head. 'No—no lady. No, I merely went down there because I don't speak the language. I needed refreshment, and there's nothing so refreshing as being some place where nobody understands you and you understand nobody.'

'Everybody goes there,' the owner says. 'Everybody likes Spain these days.'

'Of course,' said Crown, sipping at his drink. 'It's dry, mismanaged and underpopulated. How can you avoid liking a country like that?'

'You're full of fun tonight, Mr. Crown, aren't you?'

Crown nodded soberly. 'Full of fun,' he said. He finished his drink quickly and threw down a five-thousand-franc note for the whiskies he had had before the owner joined him. 'If I ever have a bar, Jean, you come to it and I'll buy *you* a drink,' he said.

While Crown was waiting for his change, the owner looked down the room and saw that the woman sitting between the two

11

college boys was still staring at the bar, past him, at Crown.

Not for you, Madame, the owner thought with a flavour of sour satisfaction. Stick to your college boys tonight.

He walked Crown to the door and went outside with him to get a breath of air. Crown stood there for a moment, looking up at the dark buildings against the starred sky. 'When I was a boy in college,' he said, 'I was firmly convinced that Paris was gay.' He turned to the owner and they shook hands and said good night.

The street was dark and empty and the air cool and the owner stood in front of the door watching the man walk slowly away. In the stillness of the sleeping city, with his heeltaps echoing faintly against the shuttered buildings, Crown gave the impression of a man who was irresolute and sad. It's a funny hour, the owner thought, watching the diminishing figure crossing under the pale light of a lamp; it's a bad time to be alone. I wonder if he would look the same way on a street in America.

After a while, the owner went back into the bar, wrinkling his nose at the staleness of the smoky room. As soon as he came up to the bar, he saw the woman stand up. She walked hurriedly towards him, leaving the college boys, surprised, half-standing, behind her.

'I wonder if you could help me,' she said. Her voice was tight, as though she was having difficulty controlling it, and her face looked queer, drained and excited at the same time, and marked by the night.

I was all wrong, the owner thought as he bowed politely to her. She'll never see forty-five again. 'Anything I can do, Madame,' the owner said.

'That man who was standing here,' the woman said. 'The one who just went out with you . . .'

'Yes?' The owner put on his cautious, non-understanding, waiting face, thinking, Good God, at her age.

'Do you know his name?'

'Well . . . let me see . . .' The owner pretended to search for it, tantalizing her, displeased with this naked and unseemly pursuit, out of respect for the memory of the women of whom the lady had reminded him earlier in the evening. 'Yes, I think I do,' he said. 'Crown. Tony Crown.'

The woman closed her eyes and put out her hand towards the bar, as though to steady herself. As the owner watched her, puzzled, she opened her eyes and pushed away, with a little

12

impatient movement, from the bar. 'Do you happen to know where he lives?' the woman asked. Her voice was flat now, and the owner had a curious, momentary impression that she would be relieved if he said no.

He hesitated. Then he shrugged, and told her the address. He wasn't there to make people behave themselves. He was in the business of running a bar and that meant pleasing his customers. And if that included humouring ageing ladies who came around asking for the addresses of young men, that was their affair.

'Here,' he said, 'I'll write it out for you.' He scribbled it quickly on a pad and ripped off the sheet and gave it to her. She held it stiffly and he noticed that the paper rattled a little, because her hands were trembling.

Then he couldn't help being nasty. 'Let me advise you, Madame, to telephone first,' he said. 'Or even better, write. Mr. Crown is married. To a beautiful and charming lady.'

The woman looked at him as though she didn't quite believe that he had said what he had said. Then she laughed. Her laugh was real, unforced, musical. 'Why, you silly man,' the woman said, laughing. 'He's my son.'

Then she folded the paper with the address on it, after looking at it carefully, and put it into her bag. 'Thank you,' she said. 'And good night. I've already paid the bill.'

He bowed, and watched her, feeling foolish, as she went out.

Americans, he thought. The most mysterious people in the world.

Chapter Two

When we look back into the past, we recognize a moment in time which was decisive, at which the pattern of our lives changed, a moment at which we moved irrevocably off in a new direction. The change may be a result of planning or accident; we may leave happiness or ruins behind us and advance to a different happiness or more thorough ruin; but there is no going back. The moment may be just that, a second in which a wheel is turned, a look exchanged, a sentence spoken—or it may be a long afternoon, a week, a season, during which the issue is in doubt, in which the wheel is turned a hundred times, the small, accumulating accidents permitted to happen.

For Lucy Crown it was a summer.

It began like other summers.

There was the sound of hammering from the cottages around the lake as screens were put into place, and the rafts were floated out into the water in time for the first bathers. At the boys' camp at one end of the lake, the baseball diamond was weeded and rolled, the canoes arranged on their racks, and a new gilt ball put on top of the flag-pole in front of the mess hall. The owners of the two hotels had had their buildings repainted in May, because it was 1937 and it looked, finally, even in Vermont, as though the Depression was over.

At the end of June, when the Crowns drove up to the same cottage they had rented the year before, all three of them, Oliver, Lucy, and Tony, who was thirteen years old that summer, sensed with pleasure the air of drowsy, pre-holiday anticipation that hung over the place. The pleasure was intensified by the fact that since they had been there last, Tony had nearly died and had not died.

Oliver only had two weeks to spend at the lake before he had to go back to Hartford, and he devoted most of that time to Tony, fishing with him, swimming a little, going on leisurely walks through the woods, trying, as delicately as possible, to make Tony feel that he was leading an active and normal thirteen-year-old life, while keeping his exertions down to the level that Sam Patterson, their family doctor, had prescribed as being safe.

Now the two weeks were over and it was Sunday afternoon and one of Oliver's bags was standing, packed, on the cottage porch. All around the lake there was a little extra traffic and bustle of departure, as husbands and fathers, lethargic from the Sunday dinner and peeling from the week-end sun, got into their cars and started back to the cities where they worked, leaving their families behind, according to the American custom which decrees that those who need them the least get the longest vacations.

Oliver and Patterson were lounging in canvas deck chairs on the lawn, under a maple tree, facing out towards the lake. They had glasses of Scotch and soda in their hands and occasionally one of them would shake his drink to enjoy the sound of ice against the glass.

14

They were both tall men, approximately the same age, and obviously of the same class and education, but they were marked by wide differences of temperament. Oliver still had the body and movements of an athlete, precise, quick and energetic. Patterson seemed to have let himself go somewhat. A slouch seemed natural to him and even when you saw him sitting down you had the feeling that when he stood he would stoop over a little. He had shrewd eyes, which he kept half-veiled almost all the time by a lazy droop of the eyelids, and there were habitual wrinkles from laughter cut into the skin at their corners. His eyebrows were thick and unruly and overhanging and his hair was coarse, unevenly cut, with a good deal of rough grey in it. Oliver, who knew Patterson very well, once told Lucy that he was sure that Patterson had looked in a mirror one day and decided quite coldly that he had a choice between appearing rather conventionally good-looking, like a second leading man in the movies, or letting himself go a little and being interestingly grizzled. 'Sam's a clever man,' Oliver had said approvingly, 'and he opted for the grizzle.'

Oliver was already dressed for the city. He wore a seersucker suit and a blue shirt and his hair was a little long because he hadn't bothered to go to a barber on his holiday and his skin was evenly tanned from the hours on the lake. Looking at him, Patterson thought that Oliver was at his best at this moment, when all the advantages of his vacation were so clearly marked on him, but at the same time wearing clothes that in this setting gave him an air of urban formality. He ought to wear a moustache, Patterson thought idly; he would look most impressive. He looks like a man who ought to be doing something complicated, important and rather dangerous; he looks like the portraits of young Confederate cavalry commanders you used to see in histories of the Civil War. If I looked like that, Patterson thought, and all I did was run a printing business that my father left me, I think I would be disappointed.

Across the lake, where a slanting outcropping of granite dipped into the water, they could see Lucy and Tony, minute sunny figures floating quietly in a small boat. Tony was fishing. Lucy hadn't wanted to take him, because it was Oliver's last afternoon, but Oliver had insisted, not only for Tony's sake but because he felt that Lucy had an unhealthy tendency to sentimentalize arrivals and farewells and anniversaries and holidays.

15

Patterson was dressed in corduroy trousers and a short-sleeved shirt, because he still had to go up to the hotel, which was about two hundred yards away, on the same estate, and pack his bag and get dressed. The cottage was too small for guests.

When Patterson had volunteered to come up for the week-end to check up on Tony, which would save Lucy and the boy a long trip down to Hartford later in the summer, Oliver had been touched by this evidence of thoughtfulness on his friend's part. Then he saw Patterson with a Mrs. Wales who was staying at the hotel, and he had been less touched. Mrs. Wales was a handsome brunette, with a small, full figure and avid eyes, who came from New York, a place that Patterson found an excuse to visit, without his wife, at least twice a month. Mrs. Wales, it turned out, had arrived on Thursday, the day before Patterson had stepped off the train, and was due to leave for New York again, discreetly, the following Tuesday. She and Patterson made a point of being most formal and correct with each other, even to the extent of not calling each other by their first names. But after twenty years of friendship with the doctor, who had always been ambitious, as Oliver put it, with women, Oliver was not to be fooled. He was too reticent to say anything, but he tempered his gratitude for Patterson's long trip to Vermont with a touch of fond though cynical amusement.

From the boys' camp a half mile away across the lake came the thin music of a bugle. The two men listened in silence, sipping their drinks, while the sound died echoing away on the water.

'Bugles,' Oliver said. 'They have an old-fashioned sound, don't they?' He stared drowsily at the distant boat in which his wife and son floated, just on the edge of the shadow of the granite shelf. 'Reveille, Assembly, Retreat, Lights out.' He shook his head. 'Preparing the younger generation for the world of tomorrow.'

'Maybe they'd be better off using a siren,' Patterson said. 'Take Cover. Enemy Overhead. All Clear . . .'

'Aren't you cheerful?' Oliver said good-naturedly.

Patterson grinned. 'Actually, I am. It's just that a doctor always sounds so much more intelligent when he's gloomy. I can't resist the temptation.'

They sat in silence for a moment, remembering the bugle, vaguely thinking of old, enjoyable wars. There was a telescope which belonged to Tony, lying on the lawn beside Oliver, and he

16

idly picked it up. He put the telescope to his eye and focused it across the water. The distant skiff became clearer and larger in the round blur of the lens and Oliver could see Tony slowly reeling in his line and Lucy begin to row towards home. Tony had a red sweater on, even though it was hot in the sun. Lucy was wearing a bathing suit and her back was deep brown against the blue-grey of the distant granite. She rowed steadily and strongly, the oars making an occasional small white splash in the still water. My ship is coming in, Oliver thought, smiling inwardly at the large saltwater image for such a modest arrival.

'Sam,' Oliver said, still with the telescope to his eye. 'I want you to do something for me.'

'Yes?'

'I want you to tell Lucy and Tony exactly what you told me.'

Patterson seemed almost asleep. He was slumped in his chair, his chin down on his chest, his eyes half-closed, his long legs stretched out. He grunted. 'Tony, too?'

'Most important of all, Tony,' Oliver said.

'You're sure?'

Oliver put the telescope down and nodded decisively. 'Absolutely,' he said. 'He trusts us completely . . . so far.'

'How old is he now?' Patterson asked.

'Thirteen.'

'Amazing.'

'What's amazing?'

Patterson grinned. 'In this day and age. A boy thirteen years old who still trusts his parents.'

'Now, Sam,' Oliver said, 'you're going out of your way to sound intelligent again.'

'Perhaps,' Patterson said agreeably, taking a sip of his drink and staring at the boat, still far out on the sunny surface of the water. 'People're always asking doctors to tell them the truth,' he said. 'Then when they get it . . . the level of regret is very high in the truth department, Oliver.'

'Tell me, Sam,' said Oliver, 'do you always tell the truth when you're asked for it?'

'Rarely. I believe in another principle.'

'What's that?'

'The principle,' Patterson said, 'of the soft, healing lie.'

'I don't think that there is such a thing as a healing lie,' said Oliver.

'You come from the North,' said Patterson, smiling. 'Remember, I'm from Virginia.'

'You're no more from Virginia than I am.'

'Well,' Patterson said, 'my father came from Virginia. It leaves its marks.'

'No matter where your father came from,' Oliver said, 'you must tell the truth *sometime*, Sam.'

'Yes,' said Patterson.

'When?'

'When I think people can stand it,' Patterson said, keeping his tone light, almost joking.

'Tony can stand it,' said Oliver. 'He has a lot of guts.'

Patterson nodded. 'Yes, he has. Why not—at the age of thirteen.' He took another drink and held up his glass, turning it in his hand, inspecting it. 'What about Lucy?' he asked.

'Don't worry about Lucy,' Oliver said stiffly.

'Does she agree with you?' Patterson persisted.

'No.' Oliver made an impatient gesture. 'If it was up to her, Tony would reach the age of thirty believing that babies came out of cabbage patches, that nobody ever died, and that the Constitution guaranteed that everyone had to love Anthony Crown above everything else on earth, on pain of imprisonment for life.'

Patterson grinned.

'You smile,' Oliver said. 'Before you have a son, you think that what you're going to do with him is raise him and educate him. That isn't what you do at all. What you do is struggle inch by inch for his immortal soul.'

'You should have had a few others,' Patterson said. 'The debate gets less intense that way.'

'Well, we don't have a few others,' said Oliver, flatly. 'Are you going to tell Tony or not?'

'Why don't you tell him yourself?'

'I want it to be official,' said Oliver. 'I want him to get used to the verdict of authority, unmodified by love.'

'Unmodified by love,' Patterson repeated softly, thinking, What a curious man he is. I don't know another man who would use a phrase like that. The verdict of authority, he thought. *My boy, do not expect to live to a ripe old age*. 'All right, Oliver,' he said. 'On your responsibility.'

'On my responsibility,' Oliver said.

'Mr. Crown . . . ?'

Oliver turned around in his chair. A young man was approaching across the lawn from the direction of the house. 'Yes?' Oliver said.

The young man came around in front of the two men and stopped. 'I'm Jeffrey Bunner,' he said. 'Mr. Miles, the manager of the hotel, sent me down here.'

'Yes?' Oliver looked at him puzzledly.

'He said you were looking for a companion for your son for the rest of the summer,' the young man said. 'He said you planned to leave this evening, so I came right down.'

'Oh, yes,' Oliver said. He stood up and shook hands with the young man, examining him briefly. Bunner was slender, a little above medium height. He had thick, black hair that was cut short and naturally dark skin that had been made even darker by the sun, giving him an almost Mediterranean appearance. His eyes were a profound, girlish blue, approaching violet, and they had the shining clarity of a child's. He had a thin lively face which gave an impression of endless youthful energy and a high, bronzed forehead. In his faded grey sweatshirt and his unpressed flannels and his grass-stained tennis shoes he seemed like an intellectual oarsman. There was an air about him, too, as he stood there easily, unembarrassed but respectful, of the privileged but well-brought-up son of a polite family. Oliver, who believed in having handsome people around him whenever possible (their coloured maid at home was one of the prettiest girls in Hartford), decided immediately that he liked the young man.

'This is Dr. Patterson,' Oliver said.

'How do you do, Sir?' Bunner said.

Patterson lifted his glass lazily. 'Forgive me for not getting up,' he said. 'I rarely get up on Sundays.'

'Of course,' Bunner said.

'Do you want to grill this young man in private?' Patterson asked. 'I suppose I could move.'

'No,' Oliver said. 'That is, if Mr. Bunner doesn't mind.'

'Not at all,' Bunner said. 'Anybody can listen. Anything embarrassing I'll lie about.'

Oliver chuckled. 'That's a good start. Cigarette?' He offered the pack to Bunner.

'No, thanks.'

Oliver took a cigarette and lit it and tossed the pack to Patterson. 'You're not one of those young men who smokes a pipe, are you?'

'No.'

'Good,' Oliver said. 'How old are you?'

'Twenty,' Bunner said.

'When I hear the word twenty,' Patterson said, 'I feel like reaching for a pistol.'

Oliver peered out at the lake. Lucy was rowing steadily and already the boat seemed much larger and the red of Tony's sweater had grown brighter. 'Tell me, Mr. Bunner,' he said, 'were you ever sick?'

'Forgive him, Boy,' Patterson said. 'He's one of those people who's never been sick in his life and he regards illness as a wilful sign of weakness.'

'That's all right,' Bunner said. 'If I were hiring somebody to hang around with my son I'd want to know whether he was healthy or not.' He turned to Oliver. 'I had a broken leg once,' he said. 'When I was nine. Sliding into second base. I was tagged out.'

Oliver nodded, liking the young man more and more. 'Is that all?'

'Just about.'

'Do you go to college?' Oliver asked.

'Dartmouth,' said Bunner. 'I hope you have no objection to Dartmouth.'

'I am neutral on the subject of Dartmouth,' Oliver said. 'Where is your home?'

'Boston,' Patterson said.

'How do you know?' Oliver looked over at Patterson, surprised.

'I have ears, don't I?' Patterson said.

'I didn't know I gave myself away so easily,' Bunner said.

'That's all right,' said Patterson. 'It's not unpleasant. It's just Boston.'

'How is it,' Oliver asked, 'that you didn't go to Harvard?'

'Now I think you've gone too far,' Patterson said.

Bunner chuckled. He seemed to be enjoying the interview. 'My father said I'd better get away from home,' he said. 'For my own good. I have four sisters and I'm the baby of the family and my father felt I was getting more than my share of loving kindness. He said he wanted me to learn that the world was not a place

20

where you have five devoted women running interference for you all the time.'

'What do you expect to do when you get out of college?' Oliver asked. He was obviously feeling friendly towards the boy, but he wasn't going to skip any information that might have a bearing on his capabilities.

'I expect to go into the Foreign Service,' Bunner said.

'Why?' Oliver asked.

'Travel,' Bunner said. 'Foreign lands. Reading *Seven Pillars of Wisdom* at the age of sixteen.'

'I doubt that you'll be called upon to lead any camel charges,' Patterson said, 'no matter how high you rise in the Department.'

'Of course, it's not only that,' Bunner said. 'I have a feeling that a lot of important things are going to happen in the next few years and I like the idea of being on the inside when they do happen.' He laughed self-deprecatingly. 'It's hard to talk about what you want to do with your life without sounding like a stuffed shirt, isn't it? Maybe I just fancy the picture of myself in a morning coat sitting at a conference table, saying, "I refuse to give up Venezuela." '

Oliver looked at his watch and decided to lead the conversation into more practical lines. 'Tell me, Mr. Bunner,' he said, 'are you an athlete?'

'I play a little tennis, swim, ski . . .'

'I mean on any of the teams,' Oliver said.

'No.'

'Good,' Oliver said. 'Athletes are so busy taking care of themselves, they never can be relied upon to take care of anyone else. And my son may need a great deal of care . . .'

'I know,' Bunner said. 'I saw him.'

'Oh?' Oliver asked, surprised. 'When?'

'I've been up here for a few days now,' Bunner said. 'And I was here most of last summer. My sister has a place a half mile down the lake.'

'Are you staying with her now?'

'Yes.'

'Why do you want this job?' Oliver asked suddenly.

Bunner grinned. 'The usual reason,' he said. 'Plus being out in the open air for the summer.'

'Are you poor?'

21

The boy shrugged. 'My father survived the Depression,' he said. 'But he's still limping.'

Oliver and Patterson nodded, remembering the Depression.

'Do you like children, Mr. Bunner?' Oliver asked.

The boy hesitated, as though he had to think this over carefully. 'About the same as people,' he said. 'There're several children I'd gladly wall up in cement.'

'That's fair enough,' Oliver said. 'I don't think you'd want to wall Tony up in cement. You know what was wrong with him?'

'I think somebody told me he had rheumatic fever last year,' Bunner said.

'That's right,' said Oliver. 'His eyes have been affected and his heart. I'm afraid he'll have to take it easy for a long time.' Oliver stared out at the lake. The boat was well in towards shore by now and Lucy was rowing steadily. 'Because of his trouble,' Oliver said, 'he's been kept away from school for the last year and he's been around his mother too much . . .'

'Everybody's been around his mother too much,' Patterson said. 'Including me.' He finished his drink.

'The problem is,' Oliver said, 'to permit him to behave as much like a normal boy as possible—without letting him overdo anything. He mustn't strain himself or tire himself too much—but I don't want him to feel as though he's an invalid. The next year or two are going to be crucial—and I don't want him to grow up feeling fearful or unlucky . . .'

'Poor little boy,' Bunner said softly, staring out at the approaching boat.

'That's exactly the wrong tack,' Oliver said quickly. 'No pity. No pity at all, please. That's one of the reasons I'm glad I can't stay up here for the next few weeks with Tony myself. That's why I don't want him left alone with his mother. And why I've been looking for a young man as a companion. I want him to be exposed to some normal, youthful, twenty-year-old callousness. I imagine you can manage that. . . . ?'

Bunner smiled. 'Do you want some references?'

'Do you have a girl?' Oliver asked.

'Now, Oliver,' Patterson said.

Oliver turned to Patterson. 'One of the most important things you can know about a twenty-year-old boy is whether he has a girl or not,' he said mildly. 'Whether he's had one, whether he's between girls at the moment.'

22

'I have one,' Bunner said, then added, 'approximately.'

'Is she here?' Oliver asked.

'If I told you she was here,' Bunner said, 'would you give me the job?'

'No.'

'She's not here,' Bunner said promptly.

Oliver bent down, hiding a smile, and picked up the telescope, collapsing it against his palm. 'Do you know anything about astronomy?'

Patterson grunted. 'This is the damnedest set of questions,' he said.

'Tony is sure he wants to be an astronomer when he grows up,' Oliver explained, playing with the telescope. 'And it would help if . . .'

'Well,' Bunner said doubtfully, 'I know a little bit . . .'

'What time tonight,' Oliver asked, like a schoolteacher, 'do you think the constellation Orion will be visible?'

Patterson shook his head and heaved himself to his feet. 'I certainly am glad *I'll* never have to ask you for a job,' he said.

Bunner was grinning at Oliver. 'You're very devious, aren't you, Mr. Crown?'

'Why do you say that?' Oliver asked innocently.

'Because you know that Orion can't be seen in the Northern Hemisphere until September,' Bunner said cheerfully, 'and you were waiting for me to make a fool of myself.'

'The job pays thirty dollars a week,' Oliver said. 'It includes teaching Tony how to swim, going fishing with him, watching stars with him, and preventing him, as much as possible, from listening to those damned serials on the radio.' Oliver hesitated and then spoke in a lower and graver tone of voice. 'It also includes winning him away—diplomatically—a certain distance from his mother, because their relationship, as of this moment . . .' He stopped, conscious that he was on the verge of sounding harsher than he wanted to sound. 'What I mean,' he said, 'is that for the good of both of them it would be better if they weren't quite so dependent upon each other. Do you want the job?'

'Yes,' Bunner said.

'Good,' Oliver said, 'you can start tomorrow.'

Patterson sighed in mock relief. 'I'm exhausted,' he said. He sank into the chair again.

'I turned down three other young men, you know,' Oliver said.

'I heard,' said Bunner.

'Young men today seem to be either vulgar or cynical and the worst ones are both,' said Oliver.

'You should have tried a Dartmouth man sooner,' Bunner said.

'I believe one of them *was* a Dartmouth man,' said Oliver.

'He must have gotten in on an athletic scholarship.'

'I suppose I ought to warn you about a troublesome little wrinkle in Tony's . . . uh . . . character,' Oliver said. 'I guess you can talk about a thirteen-year-old boy's character, can't you? When he was sick and had to stay in bed for so long he developed a tendency towards—well—fantasy. Tall stories, fibs, lies, inventions. Nothing serious,' Oliver said, and Patterson could see how painful it was for Oliver to make such an admission about his son, 'and my wife and I haven't made an issue of it, considering the circumstances. Although I've spoken to him about it and he's promised to put a rein on his—imagination. Anyway, if it comes up, I don't want you to be surprised—and at the same time, I'd like to see it discouraged before it grows into a habit.'

Listening, Patterson had a sudden, chilly insight into Oliver. He *must* be disappointed, Patterson thought, he must feel that his own life is somehow empty, if he is working so hard on his son's. Then Patterson rejected the idea. No, he thought, it's just that he's used to running things. It's easier for him to run things than to let other people do it. His son is just another thing that he automatically runs.

'Oh . . .' Oliver was saying. 'One more thing . . . Sex.'

Patterson waved his hand warningly. 'Now, Oliver, now I think you've really gone too far.'

'Tony has no brothers or sisters,' Oliver explained, 'and as I say—for the most natural reasons in the world, he's been rather overprotected. And I'm afraid both his mother and myself have ducked the question up to now. If all goes well, he'll be going to school this autumn and I'd rather he heard about sex from a bright young man who is studying to be a diplomat anyway than from the thirteen-year-old lechers of a fashionable private school.'

Bunner pulled gravely at his nose. 'Where would you like me to begin?'

'Where did *you* begin?' Oliver asked.

'I'm afraid I'd have to begin later than that,' Bunner said. 'Remember, I told you I have four older sisters.'

'Use your discretion,' Oliver said. 'After six weeks I'd like him to have a calm . . . uh . . . understanding of the theory, without a violent desire to plunge into the . . . uh . . . practice—immediately.'

'I'll do my best to be explicit,' the boy said, 'without being lascivious. Everything in grave scientific language. No word under three syllables. And play down the more . . . uh . . . pleasurable aspects as much as possible?'

'Exactly,' Oliver said. He looked out over the lake. The boat was nearly into the shore by now and Tony was standing in the stern waving at him, over his mother's shoulder, the sun reflecting off his smoked glasses. Oliver waved back. Still staring at his wife and his son, he said to Bunner, 'I suppose I sound a little like a crank on the subject of the boy but I hate the way most children are being brought up these days. Either they're given too much freedom and they grow up into undisciplined animals—or they're clamped down and they become secretly vicious and vindictive and turn on their parents as soon as they can find some place else to get their meals. The main thing is—I don't want him to grow up frightened . . .'

'How about you, Oliver?' Patterson asked curiously. 'Aren't you frightened?'

'Terribly,' Oliver said. 'Hi, Tony,' he called and walked down to the water's edge to help beach the boat.

Patterson stood up and he and Bunner watched Lucy drive the boat up on to the shingle with two last strong sweeps of the oars. Oliver held the bow steady as Lucy gathered a sweater and a book and stepped out. Tony balanced himself, then jumped off, disdaining help, into a few inches of water.

'The Holy Family,' Patterson murmured.

'What's that, Sir?' Bunner asked, surprised, not sure that he'd heard what the doctor had said.

'Nothing,' said Patterson. 'He certainly knows what he wants, doesn't he?'

Bunner grinned. 'He certainly does.'

'Do you think it's possible for a father to get what he wants in a son?' Patterson asked.

Bunner glanced at the doctor, looking for a trap. 'I haven't thought about it,' he said carefully.

'Has your father got what he wanted from *his* son?'

Bunner almost smiled. 'No.'

Patterson nodded.

They watched Oliver approach, flanked by Lucy on one side and Tony, carrying his fishing rod, on the other. Lucy was putting on a loose white sweater over her bathing suit. There was a slight gleam of perspiration on her upper lip and forehead, from the long row, and the wooden clogs on her bare feet fell noiselessly on the short grass. The group passed in and out of the sunlight between the trees and Lucy's long, naked thighs shone, briefly and goldenly, when she emerged from the shadow of the trees. She walked very straight, keeping her hips in a strict line, as though trying to minimize her womanliness. At one point she stopped and put her hand against her husband's shoulder and lifted her foot to dislodge a pebble from her clog and the group was posed there, immobile for one midsummer moment in slanting leafy sunlight.

Tony was talking as the group approached Patterson and Bunner. 'This lake is all fished out,' he was saying. His voice was a clear, high childish alto, and although he was tall for his age, he seemed frail and undeveloped to Bunner, with a head too big for his body. 'It's too close to civilization. We ought to go to the North Woods. Except for the mosquitoes and the moose. You have to be careful of the moose. And you have to carry the canoe in on your head, Bert says. There're so many fish, Bert says, they splinter the paddles.'

'Tony,' Oliver said gravely, 'do you know what a grain of salt is?'

'Sure,' the boy said.

'That's what you need for Bert.'

'Do you mean he's a liar?' Tony asked.

'Not exactly,' said Oliver. 'Just that he should be taken salted, like peanuts.'

'I've got to tell him that,' Tony said. 'Like peanuts.'

They stopped in front of Patterson and Bunner. 'Mr. Bunner,' Oliver said, 'my wife. And Tony.'

'How do you do?' Lucy said. She nodded briefly and buttoned her sweater up to the neck.

Tony went over to Bunner and politely shook hands.

'Hullo, Tony,' Bunner said.

'Hullo,' said Tony. 'Boy, your hand is calloused.'

'I've been playing tennis.'

'I bet in four weeks I can beat you,' Tony said. 'Maybe five weeks.'

'Tony . . .' Lucy said warningly.

'Is that boasting?' Tony turned towards his mother.

'Yes,' she said.

Tony shrugged and turned back to Bunner. 'I'm not allowed to boast,' he said. 'I have a hot forehand, but my backhand has flaws. I don't mind telling you,' he said candidly, 'because you'd find it out anyway, in the first game. I once saw Ellsworth Vines play.'

'What did you think of him?' Bunner asked.

Tony made a face. 'Overrated,' he said carelessly. 'Just because he comes from California and he can play every day. You've been swimming.'

'Yes, I have,' Bunner said, puzzled and amused. 'How do you know?'

'Easy. I can smell the lake on you.'

'That's his one parlour trick,' Oliver said, coming over and ruffling the boy's hair. 'He had his eyes bandaged when he was sick and he developed the nose of a bloodhound.'

'I can swim, too. Like a streak,' Tony said.

'Tony . . .' It was Lucy again, with the tone of warning.

Tony smiled, caught out. 'But only for ten strokes. Then I go under. I don't know how to breathe.'

'We'll work on that,' Bunner said. 'You can't go through life not knowing how to breathe.'

'I have to put my mind to it,' Tony said.

'Jeff'll teach you, Tony,' Oliver said. 'He's going to stay with you until the end of the summer.'

Lucy glanced sharply at her husband, then dropped her eyes. Tony, too, stared at Oliver, carefully, with guarded suspicion, remembering nurses, medicines, regimes, pain, captivity. 'Oh,' he said. 'Is he going to take care of me?'

'Not exactly,' Oliver said. 'Just help you catch up on a couple of things.'

Tony examined Oliver for a long moment, trying to discover just how candid his father was being. Then he turned and silently inspected Bunner, as though now that their connection had been announced it was necessary to start the process of judgment immediately.

'Jeff,' Tony said finally, 'how are you as a fisherman?'

'When the fish see me coming,' Bunner said, 'they roar with laughter.'

27

Patterson looked at his watch. 'I think we'd better be going, Oliver. I have to pay my bill and throw on some clothes and I'm ready.'

'You said there was something you wanted to tell Tony,' Oliver said.

Lucy glanced from his face to Patterson's, distrustfully.

'Yes,' Patterson said. Now that the moment had come he was sorry he had given in to Oliver's demand. 'Still,' he said, conscious that he was being cowardly, 'don't you think it could wait for another time?'

'I think this is the very best time, Sam,' Oliver said evenly. 'You're not going to see Tony for another month, at least, and Tony after all is the one who's finally responsible for taking care of himself and I think it'd be better if he knew just what he has to expect and why. . . .'

'Oliver . . .' Lucy began.

'Sam and I have talked all this out already, Lucy,' Oliver said, touching her hand.

'What do I have to do now?' Tony asked, eyeing Patterson distrustfully.

'You don't have to do anything, Tony,' Patterson said. 'I just want to tell you how things are with you.'

'I feel fine.' Tony sounded sullen as he said this and he looked unhappily at the ground.

'Of course,' Patterson said. 'And you're going to feel a lot better.'

'I feel good enough,' Tony said stubbornly. 'Why do I have to feel better?'

Patterson and Oliver laughed at this, and, after a moment, Bunner joined in.

'*Well* enough,' Lucy said. 'Not good enough.'

'*Well* enough,' Tony said obediently.

'Of course you do,' Patterson began.

'I don't want to stop anything,' Tony said warningly. 'I stopped enough things already in my life.'

'Tony,' said Oliver, 'let Dr. Patterson finish what he has to say.'

'Yes, Sir,' said Tony.

'All I want to tell you,' Patterson said, 'is that you mustn't try to read for a while yet, but aside from that, you can do almost anything you want—in moderation. Do you know what moderation means?'

'It means not asking for a second ice-cream soda,' Tony said promptly.

They all laughed at that and Tony looked around him, shrewdly, because he had known it was going to make them laugh.

'Exactly,' Patterson said. 'You can play tennis and you can swim and . . .'

'I want to learn to play second base,' said Tony. 'I want to learn to hit curves.'

'We can try,' Bunner said, 'but I don't guarantee anything. I haven't hit a curve yet and I'm a lot older than you. You're either born hitting curves or you're not.'

'You can do all that, Tony,' Patterson went on, noting somewhere at the back of his mind that Bunner was a pessimist, 'on one condition. And the condition is that as soon as you feel yourself getting the least bit tired, you quit. The least bit . . .'

'And if I don't quit?' the boy said sharply. 'What happens then?'

Patterson looked inquiringly at Oliver.

'Go ahead and tell him,' Oliver said.

Patterson turned back to Tony. 'Then you might have to go back to bed and stay there again for a long time. You wouldn't want that, would you?'

'You mean I might die,' Tony said, ignoring the question.

'Tony!' Lucy said. 'Dr. Patterson didn't say that.'

Tony looked around him with hostility and Patterson had the impression, for a moment, that the boy was regarding the people who surrounded him not as his parents and friends, but as the instigators and the representatives of his illness.

'Don't worry,' Tony said. He smiled and the hostility vanished. 'I won't die.'

'Of course not,' said Patterson, resenting Oliver for having put him through a scene like that. He took a step forward to the boy and leaned over him a little, coming closer to his level.

'Tony,' he said, 'I want to congratulate you.'

'Why?' Tony asked, a little guardedly, suspecting teasing.

'You're a model patient,' Patterson said. 'You recovered. Thank you.'

'When can I throw away these?' Tony asked. He put his hand up with a quick movement and took off his glasses. His voice suddenly seemed mature and bitter. Without his glasses his eyes looked deep-set, peering, full of melancholy and judgment, alarming in the thin, boyish face.

'Maybe in a year or two,' Patterson said. 'If you do the exercises every day. One hour each morning, one hour each night. Will you remember that?'

'Yes, Sir,' Tony said. He put on the glasses and they made him seem boyish again.

'Your mother knows all the exercises,' Patterson said, 'and she's promised she won't skip a minute . . .'

'You can show them to me, Doctor,' said Bunner, 'and we can spare Mrs. Crown.'

'There's no need of that,' Lucy said quickly. 'I'll do it.'

'Of course,' Jeff said. 'Whatever you say.'

Tony went over to Oliver. 'Daddy,' he said, 'do you have to go home?'

'I'm afraid so,' Oliver said. 'But I'll try to come up on a weekend later in the month.'

'Your father has to go back to the city and work,' Patterson said, 'so that he can afford to pay me, Tony.'

Oliver smiled. 'I think you should have allowed me to make that joke, Sam.'

'Sorry.' Patterson went over and kissed Lucy on the cheek. 'Bloom,' he said, 'bloom like the wild rose.'

'I'm walking past the hotel,' Bunner said. 'Do you mind if I tag along with you, Doctor?'

'My pleasure,' Patterson said. 'You can tell me what it's like to be twenty.'

'So long, Tony,' said Bunner. 'What time should I arrive tomorrow? Nine o'clock?'

'Ten-thirty,' Lucy said quickly. 'That's early enough.'

Bunner glanced at Oliver. 'Ten-thirty it is,' he said.

He and Patterson started up the path towards the hotel, a big, gravely moving, bulky man and an agile, slender, dark boy in grass-stained canvas shoes. Lucy and Oliver watched them for a moment in silence.

That boy is too sure of himself, Lucy thought, watching the graceful, retreating figure. Imagine coming asking for a job wearing a sweatshirt. For a moment she thought of turning on Oliver and complaining about Bunner. At least, she thought, he might have let me be here when he interviewed him. Then she decided not to complain. It was done, and she knew Oliver too well to believe that she could change his mind. She would have to try to handle the young man by herself, her own way.

She hunched her shoulders and rubbed her bare thighs. 'I'm cold,' she said. 'I'm going to put on some clothes. Are you all packed, Oliver?'

'Just about,' he said. 'There're a couple of things I have to collect. I'll go in with you.'

'Tony,' Lucy said. 'You'd better put some pants on, too, and some shoes.'

'Oh, Mother.'

'Tony,' she said, thinking, He never talks back to Oliver.

'Oh, all right,' Tony said, and he led the way, shuffling his feet luxuriously in the cool thick grass of the lawn, into the house.

Chapter Three

ALONE in the bedroom with Lucy, Oliver finished packing his bags. He was not a fussy man and he never took long, but when he finished with a bag it was always rigidly neat, almost as though it had been done by a machine. To Lucy, who had to pack and repack bags in bursts of inefficient energy, it seemed that Oliver had some brisk, inborn sense of order in his hands. While Oliver was packing she took off her sweater and bathing suit and looked at her naked body in the long glass. I'm getting old, she thought, staring at herself. There are the little secret marks of time on the flesh of my thighs. I must walk more. I must sleep more. I must not think about it. Thirty-five.

She brushed her hair. She wore it down a little past her shoulders, because Oliver liked it that way. She would have preferred it shorter, especially in the summer.

'Oliver,' she said, brushing her hair, looking at his reflection in the mirror as he quickly and neatly put an envelope full of papers, a pair of slippers, a sweater into the bag on the bed.

'Yes?' He snapped the bag shut, crisply, like a man cinching a horse.

'I hate the idea of your going home.'

31

Oliver came over to her and stood behind her, putting his hands around her. She felt his hands on her and the cool stuff of his suit against her back, and fought down a sudden quiver of distaste. He owns me, she thought, he must not behave as though he owns me. Oliver kissed the back of her neck, under her ear.

'You have a wonderful belly,' he said, moving his hands, kissing her.

She turned in his arms and held on to him. 'Stay another week,' she said.

'You heard what Sam said about earning enough to pay for his bill,' Oliver said. Gently, he stroked her shoulder. 'He wasn't kidding.'

'But all those people at the plant . . .'

'All those people at the plant are out at the first tee by two o'clock in the afternoon, if I'm not there,' Oliver said good-naturedly. 'You're turning a marvellous colour.'

'I hate being alone,' Lucy said. 'I'm not good at being alone. I'm too stupid to be alone.'

Oliver laughed and held her tighter. 'You're not stupid at all.'

'Yes, I am,' Lucy said. 'You don't know me. When I'm alone my brain is like an old washrag. I hate the summers,' she said. 'I'm in exile in the summertime.'

'I admire the colour you turn in the summertime,' Oliver said.

Lucy felt a little touch of anger because he was treating her lightly. 'Exile,' she repeated stubbornly. 'Summertime is my Elba.'

Oliver laughed again. 'See,' he said, 'you're not so stupid. No stupid woman would have thought of that.'

'I'm literary,' Lucy said, 'but I'm stupid. I'm going to be so lonesome.'

'Now, Lucy . . .' Oliver moved away and started walking around the room, opening drawers and looking in closets to make sure he had left nothing behind. 'There're hundreds of people around the lake.'

'Hundreds of horrors,' Lucy said. 'Women whose husbands can't stand them. You look at them congregated together on the porch of the hotel and you can almost see the ghosts of their husbands, in the cities, roaring with delight.'

'I promise,' Oliver said, 'not to roar with delight in the city.'

'Or perhaps you'd like me to cultivate Mrs. Wales,' Lucy said. 'To improve my mind and pick up some interesting facts to amuse the company with when we play bridge with the Pattersons next winter.'

Oliver hesitated. 'Oh,' he said lightly, 'I wouldn't take that so seriously. It's just Sam . . .'

'I just wanted to let you know that I knew about it,' Lucy said, with an unreasonable desire to make Oliver uncomfortable. 'And I don't like it. And you might tell Sam about it on the way home, since everybody's being so damned candid this afternoon.'

'Very well,' Oliver said. 'I'll mention it. If you want.'

Lucy began to dress. 'I'd like to go home with you,' she said. 'Right now.'

Oliver opened the bathroom door and looked in. 'What about Tony?' he asked.

'Take Tony with us.'

'But it's so good for him here.' Oliver came back into the room, satisfied that he had left nothing behind him. He never left anything behind him, in any room, but he never neglected this final, swift check-up. 'The lake. The sunshine.'

'I know all about the lake and the sunshine,' Lucy said. She bent over and put on a pair of moccasins, the leather feeling cool and pleasantly tight against her bare feet. 'I think his father and mother, all together, will do him more good.'

'Darling,' Oliver said gently, 'do me a favour.'

'What?'

'Don't insist.'

Lucy put on a blouse. The blouse had a long row of buttons up the back and she went up to Oliver and turned around so that he could do them up for her. Automatically, he began, at the bottom, his hands neat and quick.

'I hate the idea of you rattling around all by yourself in that big, empty house. And you always overwork when I'm not there.'

'I promise not to overwork,' Oliver said. 'I'll tell you what . . . Try it for a week. See how you feel. How Tony's getting along. Then if you still want to come home . . .'

'Yes?'

'We'll see,' Oliver said. He finished the buttons and tapped her lightly on the small of her back.

'We'll see,' Lucy repeated. 'Every time you say we'll see, it means no. I know you.'

Oliver laughed and kissed the top of her head. 'This time it means we'll see.'

Lucy moved away from him, back to the mirror, to put on lipstick. 'Why is it,' she asked coldly, 'that we always do what you want to do?'

'Because I'm an old-fashioned husband and father,' Oliver said, amused at it as he said it.

Lucy put the lipstick on heavily, because she knew Oliver didn't like it and she wanted to punish him, even by that little bit, for denying her. 'What if one day I decided to turn into a new-fashioned wife?'

'You won't,' Oliver said. He lit a cigarette, and noticing the lipstick, crinkled his brow a little, which he did when he was annoyed. 'You won't,' he said, keeping his tone playful. 'That's why I married you so young. To catch you before you became set in your ways.'

'Don't make me sound so malleable. It's insulting,' Lucy said.

'I swear,' Oliver said with mock gravity, consciously avoiding an argument, 'that I find you absolutely unmalleable. Do you like that better?'

'No,' Lucy said. She made a big, garish bow of red on her lips, pouting her lips, using her little finger. Oliver had never said anything about it, but she knew that he disliked the moment at the mirror when her lips were in that vain, self-satisfied posture and the tip of the finger shiny with the red grease, and she prolonged it spitefully.

'We know a lot of modern couples,' Oliver said. He turned away, pretending to be looking for an ashtray, so that he wouldn't have to watch her. 'With both parties making decisions all the time. Every time I see a woman with a dissatisfied expression on her face I know her husband is letting her make decisions for herself.'

'If I weren't married to you, Oliver,' said Lucy, 'I think I'd hate you.'

'Think of the couples we know,' Oliver said. 'Am I right or wrong?'

'Right,' Lucy said. 'Right. Always right.' She turned and made a mock bow in his direction. 'I bend the neck because you are always right.'

Oliver laughed and then Lucy had to laugh, too.

'It's funny,' Oliver said, coming close to her again.

'What's funny?'

'When you chuckle,' Oliver said. 'Even when you were a young girl. It's as though there's somebody else in there'—he touched her throat—'who does your laughing for you.'

'Somebody else,' Lucy said. 'What's she like?'

'Husky-voiced,' Oliver said softly, 'with a swaying walk and wild red hair . . .'

'Maybe I'd better stop laughing,' Lucy said.

'Never,' said Oliver. 'I love it.'

'I was waiting to hear that word.'

'Love?'

'Uhuh. I haven't heard it in a long time.' Lucy held the lapels of his coat and pulled him gently towards her.

'None of the present crop of writers would ever dream of using it,' Oliver said gravely.

'Go ahead.'

'Go ahead what?'

'Go ahead and use it. Nobody's looking.'

'Mother . . . Dad . . .' It was Tony calling from the living room. 'I'm all dressed. Are you ready yet?'

'In a minute, Tony,' Oliver called, trying to pull away. 'We'll be right out.'

'Oh, Oliver,' Lucy murmured, still holding on to him. 'It's so terrible.'

'What's terrible?' Oliver asked, puzzled.

'I depend on you so much.'

'Daddy . . .' It was Tony again, calling politely from the other side of the door.

'Yes, Tony?'

'I'll go up to the hotel and wait for you. I want to ride to the gate with you.'

'Okay, Tony,' Oliver said. 'Tell Dr. Patterson I'll be there in five minutes.'

'Righteo,' Tony said.

Oliver winced. 'Where did he pick that up?' he whispered.

Lucy shrugged. There was a little smudge of lipstick from her finger on the shoulder of Oliver's jacket and she guiltily decided to say nothing about it. They heard Tony going out of the house and his footsteps receding on the gravel outside the window.

'Well . . .' Oliver looked once more around the room. 'That just about does it.' He picked up the two bags. 'Open the door please, Lucy,' he said.

Lucy opened the door and they went out through the living

room on to the porch. The living room was filled with flowers, to take the curse off the shabby rented furniture, and they mingled their fragrance with the constant fresh smell of the lake.

On the porch, Lucy stopped. 'I'd love a drink,' she said. She didn't really want one, but it would delay Oliver's departure for another ten minutes. She knew that Oliver understood this and that he usually was annoyed, or at best impatiently amused, at what he considered her rattled postponements of farewells, but she couldn't bear to face up to the moment when the sound of the car would diminish down the driveway and she would be left alone.

'All right,' Oliver said, after a tiny hesitation, putting down his bags. He, himself, made efficient departures, said good-bye once, meaning it, and promptly left. He stood staring out at the lake while Lucy went over to the table against the wall and poured some whisky from the bottle there and some ice water into two glasses.

A hawk wheeled up from the lakeside trees and circled slowly, its wings unmoving, above the water, and from the camp on the other shore, came the faint call of the bugle again, the soldiers' signals with their echo of gunfire and defeat and victory, calling the children to swimming period or a ball game. The hawk slipped calmly across the wind, waiting for the small, fatal events of the world below him, the movement of grass, the lift of a branch, to disclose the presence of his supper.

'Oliver,' Lucy was saying, coming up to him with the two glasses in her hands.

'Yes?'

'How much are you paying that boy? The Bunner boy?'

Oliver shook his head, dissolving the confused images raised in his mind by the bird and the bugle and the imminence of departure. 'Thirty dollars a week,' he said, taking one of the glasses.

'Isn't that a lot?'

'Yes.'

'Can we afford it?' Lucy asked.

'No,' Oliver said, irritated by her question. Lucy ordinarily was haphazard about money and in his eyes was given to outlandish bursts of extravagance, not from greed or a love of luxury, but because of an infirm conception of the value and difficulty of money. But when she was opposed to something he

36

wished to do, as he knew she was opposed to the hiring of Bunner, she showed an argumentative housewifely parsimoniousness.

'Do you really think we need him?' Lucy asked, standing at his side, watching the slow circling of the hawk over the water.

'Yes,' Oliver said. He lifted his glass ceremoniously. 'To the small boy with the telescope.'

Lucy lifted her glass, almost absently, and took a small sip. 'Why?'

'Why what?'

'Why do we need him?'

Oliver touched her arm gently. 'To give you some time to enjoy yourself.'

'I love being with Tony.'

'I know,' Oliver said. 'But I think, for these few weeks, to have a bright, lively young man around him, somebody who can be a little rough with him . . .'

'You think I'm making him too soft,' Lucy said.

'It's not that. It's just that . . .' Oliver tried to find the most moderate and innocent reasons for his argument. 'Well, only children, especially ones who've had a serious illness and who've had to be around their mothers a lot . . . When they grow up you're liable to find them in the ballet.'

Lucy laughed. 'Aren't you silly?'

'You know what I mean,' Oliver said, annoyed at himself because he felt he was sounding stuffy. 'Don't think it isn't a problem. Read any work on psychoanalysis.'

'I don't have to read anything,' Lucy said, 'to tell me how to bring up my son.'

'Just common sense,' Oliver began.

'I suppose you want to say I'm doing everything wrong,' Lucy said bitterly. 'Say it and . . .'

'Now, Lucy,' Oliver said soothingly, 'I don't want to say anything of the kind. It's just that maybe I see a different set of problems than you do, that I see things that I want to prepare Tony for that you don't recognize.'

'Like what?' Lucy asked stubbornly.

'We live in chaotic times, Lucy,' Oliver said, feeling the words ringing hollow and grandiose, but not knowing how else to phrase what he wanted to say. 'Changeable, dangerous times. You've got to be a giant to face them.'

'And you want to make a giant out of poor little Tony.' Lucy's voice was sardonic.

'Yes,' Oliver said defensively. 'And don't call him poor little Tony. He's only seven or eight years away from being a man.'

'A man is one thing,' Lucy said. 'A giant is another.'

'Not any more,' Oliver said. 'You've got to be a giant first these days. Then, after that, maybe you can manage to be a man.'

'Poor little Tony,' Lucy said. 'And a snippy little college junior can make a giant out of a son, but a mother can't.'

'I didn't say that,' said Oliver. He felt himself getting angry and controlled himself consciously, because he didn't want to leave on the bitter end of an argument. He made himself speak calmly. 'First of all, Bunner isn't a snippy little college boy. He's intelligent and poised and humorous . . .'

'And I, of course,' Lucy said, 'am dull and shy and sad.' She walked away from him, towards the house.

'Now, Lucy.' Oliver followed her. 'I didn't say that, either.'

Lucy stopped and turned and faced him, angrily. 'You don't have to,' she said. 'For months, I manage to forget it. Then you say something . . . or I see another woman my age who has managed to escape. . . .'

'For God's sake, Lucy,' Oliver said, his irritation overcoming his resolution to avoid a quarrel, 'don't go into that song and dance.'

'Please, Oliver.' She lapsed suddenly into pleading. 'Leave Tony alone with me this summer. It's only for six more weeks. I've given in on the school—you can give in on this. He'll be away so long, surrounded by all those little ruffians . . . I can't bear to let him out of my sight yet. After what we've gone through with him. Even now, even when I know all he's doing is walking up to the hotel and riding to the gate with you—it's all I can do to keep myself from running down to make sure he's all right.'

'That's exactly what I was talking about, Lucy,' Oliver said.

Lucy stared at him, her eyes suddenly cold. She put the drink down on the grass with a kind of awkward curtsy. Then she stood up and made a mocking little inclination of her head. 'I bend the neck,' she said, 'because you're always right. As usual.'

With a sharp movement of his hand, Oliver took her chin and jerked her head up. Lucy didn't try to pull away. She stood there, smiling crookedly, staring at him. 'Don't ever do that to me again, Lucy,' Oliver said. 'I mean it.'

Then she wrenched her head away and turned and went into the house. The screen door slammed lightly behind her. Oliver looked after her for a moment, then drained his drink and picked up his bags and went to the side of the house, where the car was parked under a tree. He put the bags into the car, hesitated a moment, then said, under his breath, 'The hell with it.' He got into the car and started the motor. He was backing out when Lucy came out of the house and over to the car. He cut the engine and waited.

'I'm sorry,' she said in a low voice, standing against the car, her hand on the door.

Oliver took her hand and patted it. 'Let's forget it,' he said gently.

Lucy leaned over and kissed his cheek. She touched his tie with a flutter of her hand. 'Buy yourself some new ties,' she said. 'All your ties look as though you got them for Christmas, 1929.' She looked at him, smiling uncertainly, pleading. 'And don't be angry with me.'

'Of course not,' Oliver said, relieved that the afternoon and the departure were healed. Or almost healed. Or at least healed on the surface.

'Call me up during the week,' Lucy said. 'And use the forbidden word.'

'I will.' Oliver leaned over and kissed her. Then he started the motor once more. Lucy stepped back. They waved at each other as Oliver drove the car up towards the hotel.

Lucy stood in the shade of the tree, watching the car disappear around a turn, hidden by the grove of trees. She sighed and went back into the living room. She sat down heavily on a dark wooden chair. She looked around her, thinking, No matter how many flowers you put in here, this room is impossible. She sat there, remembering the sound of the car, moving away up the narrow, sandy road. She sat there, in the ugly, fragrant room, thinking, Defeat, defeat. I always lose. I am always the one who says, I'm sorry.

Chapter Four

SITTING beside Oliver in the sedate Buick as they drove through the white Vermont towns, Patterson settled back comfortably in the front seat, pleased with everything, pleased with the neat, efficient way Oliver drove, pleased with the weather, with the week-end, with the memory of Mrs. Wales, with his friendship with the Crowns, with the recovery of Tony, pleased with the image of Lucy, bare-legged, with her white sweater loose over her bathing suit, stopping in the sunlight, leaning on Oliver's shoulder, to shake out a pebble that had been caught between her toes and the sole of her wooden clog.

He looked across at Oliver, sitting easily at the wheel, his face severe and intelligent, modified subtly by that touch of useless daring, that obsolete and almost military recklessness that Patterson had remarked when they were drinking their whiskies on the lawn. God, thought Patterson, if he were interested in other women, it would be a holy parade! If I looked like that . . . He grinned inwardly. He half-closed his eyes, and thought again of Lucy, caught in the sunlight, on the path up from the lake, her hair falling loose over her face as she bent over her bare, long leg.

Well, he thought, if I were married to Lucy Crown I wouldn't look at anyone else, either.

Sometimes, when he had drunk too much or was feeling sad, he told himself that if he had permitted it, he would have fallen in love with Lucy Crown, who at that time was Lucy Hammond, the first evening he saw her, a month before she married Oliver. And there had been one night, at a dance at the country club, when he nearly had told her so. Or perhaps he *had* told her so. It had been confused and quick and the band was playing loudly, and Lucy had been in his arms one moment and out of them the next and there had been no doubt about it, *that* night he had drunk too much.

The first time Patterson had met Lucy was in the early 1920s, when Oliver brought her back to Hartford to introduce her to his family. Patterson was older than Oliver and had already been married more than a year and had just begun to practice in Hartford. The Crowns had lived in Hartford for four generations and old man Crown had a printing business that had come down in the family and had kept the Crowns comfortably rich for fifty years. There were two daughters in the family, both older than Oliver and already married, and there had been a brother who had been killed in a plane accident during the war. Oliver had trained to be a pilot, too, but had arrived in France very late and had never flown in combat.

After the war and after France, Oliver had settled in New York and started a small, experimental aeroplane business with two other veterans. Old man Crown had put up Oliver's share of the money, and the three young men had set up a factory near Jersey City and some years they almost broke even.

Patterson had known Oliver ever since Oliver had been a freshman trying to make the baseball team when Patterson was a senior in high school. Even then, when Oliver couldn't have been more than fourteen or fifteen years old, Patterson had envied the tall, mannerly boy the dignity and quiet self-assurance with which he conducted himself and the ease with which he came off with the highest marks in his class, made all the teams and attracted the prettiest girls in the school. After that, Patterson envied him the war, envied him France, New York, the aeroplane business, the large, drunken gay young men who were his partners, and when he met Lucy, he envied him Lucy. If anyone had asked either Patterson or Crown about their relationship, they would both have said, unhesitatingly, that they were each other's best friends. Crown, as far as Patterson could tell, envied no one anything.

Lucy at that time was about twenty years old, and from the moment Oliver introduced her, Patterson began to feel a vague and sorrowful sense of loss. She was a tall girl with soft blonde hair and wide grey, speckled eyes. There was something curiously Oriental about her face. The nose was flat and very straight and the bridge blended smoothly into her broad, low forehead. There was the hint of a slant about her eyes, and her upper lip turned up strangely in a flat plane and seemed to be cut off squarely and abruptly at the corners. In trying to describe her long after he knew her, Patterson said that she looked as though she came

41

from a family of blondes among whom had slipped, secretly, and perhaps only for one night, a Balinese dancing-girl grandmother. Lucy had a full, hesitant mouth and a breathy, low, slightly disconnected way of talking, as though she never was sure that people were willing to listen to what she had to say. Her clothes were never quite stylish, but since the style that year was so hideous, that was all to the good. She seemed to be aiming at immobility, especially with her hands, keeping them folded in her lap when she was seated, and straight at her sides, like a polite and well-schooled child, when she stood. Her father and mother were dead, and she had no family except for a shadowy aunt in Chicago, of whom Patterson never found out more than that she was the same size as Lucy and sent her disastrous clothes when she had finished with them. When he was considerably older and given more closely to reflection, Patterson realized that the slightly bizarre dowdiness that her aunt's clothes lent to Lucy gave her an added attraction, by making her different from the other girls around her, none of whom were as beautiful as she, and by introducing a warm, protective note of pity for her poverty and her youthful awkwardness.

Lucy was working then as an assistant to a research biologist at Columbia University, who was, according to Oliver, deeply involved with single-celled marine plants. It was an unlikely thing for a girl who looked like that to be doing, and what was more unlikely, she had made it plain to Oliver that she intended to continue, marriage or no marriage, and take her Ph.D. and try to get a job as an instructor, with research projects of her own. Oliver had been tolerantly amused at the idea of having a wife who was so stubbornly scientific and who messed around all day long with what he insisted upon calling algae, but as long as she looked the way she did, and as long as it meant that she stayed in New York, for the moment he made no protest.

As far as Patterson could tell, they were very much in love with each other, although Lucy was modest and undemonstrative in public, again the polite child into whom it has been drilled that it is bad manners to draw attention to oneself. As for Oliver, he had always been humorously off-hand and reserved, an attitude which had been intensified by the rituals of the pilots among whom he had been thrown, and it was only because Patterson knew him so well that he could see in the way he behaved towards Lucy a steady tenderness and delight.

All in all, they were tall, shining, innocent young people, and if, later on, looking back at it, it had turned out that they had not been as shining as all that, seeing them standing gravely together at the altar (in New York—Oliver said he didn't want to blight his marriage by starting it off in Hartford) made Patterson feel that of all the marriages taking place on that June day in the nation, this certainly must be numbered among the fairest.

At the reception, at which Patterson got a little drunk on the champagne that old man Crown had put away before Prohibition, Patterson had said, looking a little maliciously around the room, 'This is a damned peculiar wedding. There isn't a guest here who has slept with the bride.' The people who heard him laughed, and it added to his reputation as a wit and as a man in whom it was dangerous to confide too much.

When Patterson took the train home for Hartford the next day, with Catherine, his wife, he sat, leaning against the window, conscious of his head, and conscious, too, that his own marriage, now thirteen months old, was a mistake. There was nothing to be done about it, and it wasn't Catherine's fault, and Patterson knew that he wasn't going to do anything about it, and that he was going to make Catherine suffer as little as possible from it. Sitting there, closing his eyes against the last fumes of the wedding champagne, he knew that it was going to be a long, quiet, submerged mistake. At that period he was a cynic and a pessimist, and he felt that it was quite normal to realize, about the age of twenty-seven, that you had made a mistake that you would have to live with for the rest of your life.

When they got back from their honeymoon, Oliver and Lucy Crown lived, for a while, exactly as they had planned. They had an apartment on Murray Hill, with a large living room, which, more often than not, was full of the kind of ambitious young people who were flooding into New York at the time. Oliver went every morning to the little factory outside Jersey City and crashed occasionally in meadows and salt flats in the planes that he and his partners manufactured and Lucy took the subway five days a week to the laboratory and the algae on Morningside Heights and came home to prepare dinner or give a party or go to the theatre, or, more rarely, to work on the thesis she was preparing for her Ph.D. She no longer wore her aunt's clothes, but it turned out that her own taste was uncertain, or perhaps deliberately plain, out of some adolescent concept of modesty,

43

and she never really looked as though she belonged in New York.

Patterson came to the city as often as he could. He came without Catherine when he could manage it, and always made the Crown apartment his headquarters, adding to the long list of things he envied Oliver Crown, the place he lived in and the friends he saw. It occurred to Patterson at that time that although Lucy looked quietly happy, she seemed almost to be visiting the marriage rather than being a full partner in it. This was in some measure due to her shyness, which had not yet left her, and Oliver's quality of dominating and directing, cheerfully, without effort and often without desiring it, whatever company he was in.

After one of Patterson's visits to New York, Catherine asked him if he thought Lucy was happy. Patterson hesitated, and then said, 'Yes, I think so. Or almost happy. But she expects to be happier later on. . . .'

Oliver's father was drowned off Watch Hill and Lucy gave birth to a son in the same year. Oliver went up to Hartford, looked at the books of the printing company, talked to his mother and the plant manager, then came home and told Lucy to start packing. They were going to have to live in Hartford, for a long time. Whatever regrets he had about giving up the aeroplane business, and giving up New York, he swallowed on the trip back in the train and never mentioned them either to Lucy or to Patterson, or, as far as Patterson knew, to anyone else. Lucy packed the notes that she had collected for the thesis that she was never going to write, had a farewell lunch with the researcher in single-celled marine life, closed the apartment and followed her husband to the big Crown house in Hartford in which he had been born and in which he had grown up and which he had tried, for so long, to leave.

Selfishly, Patterson was pleased to have Lucy and Oliver living just a half-dozen streets away from him. They were a centre of gaiety and life in a way that Patterson and his wife never could be, and in his role of old friend and then family doctor, Patterson was in and out of the house three or four times a week, sharing impromptu meals, invited to all parties, acting not only as a doctor to the little boy, but appointed uncle, the recipient of confidences, giver of advice (to Lucy only; Oliver never asked anyone for advice), planner of vacations and week-ends, bridge partner and privileged philosopher around the family fire. The Crown house became the centre for a good many of the more

44

attractive younger married people of the city, and it was at their dinner table that Patterson met, in different years, two pretty ladies with whom he later had affairs.

Whether Oliver and Lucy knew about the two ladies or about the other liaisons, secret and not so secret, that were inevitable in a circle like that in the 1920s and early 1930s, Patterson never knew. Neither of them gossiped or encouraged gossip and neither of them, in all that time, ever showed, for a moment, any interest in anybody else. It was a little surprising in Oliver, who before his marriage had been an easy and equal companion to the pilots and other jovial thugs with whom he had come out of the war. But with each passing year, he seemed to become more singly and happily devoted to his wife, not sentimentally or cloyingly, but with a frank gift of virility and confidence that made Patterson's marriage, when he thought of it, which was as seldom as possible, seem barren and without purpose.

As for Lucy, the move to a smaller city and the preoccupation with the child made her seem more adult and at ease, and it was only at rare moments, at big parties, when Oliver would be, as usual, the centre of a group and she found herself half-neglected in a corner, that the old impression that Patterson had had of her —that she was a visitor to the marriage, not a half-owner of it— would occur to him again.

They only had the one child. Tony was a bright and handsome little boy with very good manners, whose only disability from being an only child seemed to be a too nervous attachment to his mother. When Lucy was not in the house when he came home from school, or was late in returning from shopping, the boy developed the habit of waiting for her, sitting on her bed, and calling, on the bedside telephone table, the various friends at whose houses he felt his mother might be found. His grave, soft voice, saying, 'Hullo, this is Tony Crown. I wonder if my mother happens to be with you. Thank you. No, there's no emergency,' became familiar over the telephones of ten different houses. Oliver, who, naturally, was displeased with the habit, spoke of him, half-fondly, half-annoyed, as 'The Caller.'

As Patterson pointed out, there was nothing wrong with the little boy that a few brothers and sisters wouldn't cure, but for some reason Lucy never conceived again, and by the time Tony was ten, the Crowns had given up hope of ever having any more children.

Those years Patterson was to regard as being the best of his life. The reason for that was not of course only the Crowns, or even primarily the Crowns. It was in that period that Patterson was establishing himself and prospering and feeling horizons opening out steadily ahead of him. But the background of the home of the Crowns, with its open door, its easy freedom, with the friendship of Oliver, and the shy warmth of Lucy and the devotion of the little boy, doubly valuable since he was himself childless, made a brightly coloured setting to Patterson's other successes that he could find nowhere else. And the feeling that he had towards Lucy, which at one time or another he described, but only to himself, and then only with a little laugh, as love, gave a new flicker of expectation and secret pleasure to him whenever he stood at their door and pressed the bell.

Sitting in the Buick, moving through the late Sunday traffic at a comfortable fifty miles an hour, he looked across again at Oliver. I wonder what he would say, Patterson thought wryly, if he knew what I was thinking at this moment. What a marvellous thing it is that we can't read our friends' minds.

'Sam . . .' Oliver said, without taking his eyes off the road.

'Yes?'

'Do you think you can get up to the lake again during the summer?'

'I'm going to try,' Patterson said.

'Will you do me a favour?'

'What's that?'

'Leave Mrs. Wales home,' Oliver said.

'What in the world are you talking about . . .' Patterson began, with what he thought was an accurate imitation of surprise.

Oliver smiled at the wheel. 'Now, Sam . . .' he said mildly.

Patterson laughed. 'Okay,' he said. 'Farewell, Mrs. Wales.'

'I don't give a damn,' Oliver said. 'But Lucy fired a shot.'

'Lucy,' Patterson said. 'Oh.' He felt a warm flush of embarrassment and he knew, instantaneously, that he wasn't going to come up to the lake again that summer, with or without Mrs. Wales.

'The wives' benevolent association,' Oliver said, 'protecting the other members.'

They drove without speaking for a few more miles. Then Oliver spoke again. 'Sam, what did you think of that boy? Bunner?'

'Okay,' Patterson said. 'I think he'll be good for Tony.'

'If he lasts,' Oliver said.

'What do you mean?'

'Lucy'll make his life hell.' Oliver chuckled. 'I bet a week from now I get a letter saying he nearly let Tony drown or he taught him a dirty word and she had to fire him.' Oliver shook his head. 'God, bringing up an only child is a touchy job. And a sick boy, to boot. Sometimes I look at him and a shiver goes over me when I think of the way he's liable to turn out.'

'He'll turn out all right,' Patterson said, defending Tony, but believing it, too. 'You're too nervous.'

Oliver only grunted an answer.

'What do you want?' Patterson demanded. 'Do you want a guarantee that he'll be elected governor of the state or win the heavyweight championship of the world? What do you want him to do?'

Oliver hunched thoughtfully over the wheel. 'Well,' he said, slowing the car down a bit, 'I don't want him to do anything particularly.' Then he grinned. 'I just want him to turn out lucky.'

'Don't worry,' Patterson said. 'With his mother and father, he'll be lucky. It runs in the family.'

Oliver smiled, and Patterson was sure that there was irony and bitterness in the smile. 'I'm glad you think so,' Oliver said.

Well, what do you know about that, Patterson thought, suddenly remembering the intuition he had had on the lawn several hours before, that Oliver was a disappointed man. With everything he has, he doesn't think he's lucky. What the hell does he expect out of this life?

Chapter Five

AFTER the first week, Lucy wrote Oliver that young Bunner was turning out very well, that he had won Tony by intelligently allowing Tony to make all the overtures in his own time. Young Bunner was very gay, she had written, and ingenious in keeping Tony from tiring himself. He had even managed to keep Tony happy on rainy days, she wrote.

At the end of the second week, Lucy was not sure what to write because Jeff had by that time told her that he was in love with her.

At first she had laughed at him, self-consciously playing the part of the amused older woman, something she had never had the occasion to do before. Then she had decided to write Oliver and ask him what to do about it, but had put it off because she was afraid that Oliver would make fun of her for taking something like that so seriously. Then almost patronizingly she had permitted Jeff to kiss her, to show him that it didn't mean anything to either of them. After that she knew that whatever happened, she wasn't going to write Oliver.

For three days she had avoided being left alone with Jeff and ten times during the three days she almost told him that he had better leave, but she didn't do that, either.

Lucy was one of those women who achieve innocence in marriage. As desirable as she was, and she never realized the full power of her beauty or the real effect she had on men, she was so clearly unapproachable that she had rarely been approached.

The only notable exception had been Sam Patterson, one night at a country-club dance, when he had been rather drunk and had found himself alone with her on the terrace and had taken her into his arms, which she had permitted, momentarily mistaking amorousness for friendliness.

'Lucy, dearest,' he had whispered, 'there's something I have to tell you that I . . .'

She had caught on then, from the tone of his voice, and she knew that whatever he had to tell her it would be better not to hear.

She had twisted away and laughed good-naturedly, and said, 'Now, Sam, how many drinks have you had?'

He had stood there, ashamed, defiant, almost tragic. 'It's not the drink,' he said. But then he had turned away and walked swiftly back into the club, and she had thought, It's only Sam, everybody knows about *him*, and when she had gone inside she had entertained herself by looking around the room and taking a count of the women that Sam Patterson had had affairs with, and there were three that she was sure of, two that she was almost sure of, and one that she guessed. She had never said anything to Oliver about it, because what was the use, and Oliver would be certain to be harsh about it and stop seeing Patterson, and everybody would lose by the whole thing. Patterson had never mentioned the night on the terrace again and neither had she and it had been long ago, when she and Oliver had only been married for five years, and sometimes now she had the feeling that it had never happened.

Her fidelity was not so much a matter of morality as a mixture of love, gratitude and fear of Oliver. It was her conviction that Oliver had rescued her from an uncertain and tormented youth and the memory of that escape, as she regarded it, made her reject almost automatically whatever fleeting desires she might have felt through the years for other men.

Despite his debonair manner, Jeff was inexperienced enough so that to him most women were equally approachable or unapproachable. And rather surprisingly, considering his good looks, he was completely humble, and had blurted it all out one afternoon, while they were seated on the lawn after lunch. They were alone for an hour because Tony was taking the daily nap which was a fixed part of his regime.

There was a mid-day hush over the lake and the morning's wind had died down and even the insects seemed to have drowsed off. Lucy, in a flowered cotton dress, was seated leaning against a tree, her legs stretched out in front of her, her ankles crossed, a book, open and face-down, on her lap. Jeff was kneeling on one knee a few feet away from her, like a football-player resting during a time out. He had a piece of grass in his mouth and he kept his eyes down and from time to time plucked a clover stem and examined it and threw it away. It was cool in the shade of the tree and Lucy felt, sitting there, with her skin still remembering the soft touch of lake water from the morning's swim, that she was at one of those perfect silent moments of her life that she would have wished to prolong unchanged indefinitely.

Jeff was wearing faded blue denim trousers and a white collarless T shirt with short sleeves. In the flickering shadow of the foliage above them, his skin looked mahogany against the white of his shirt. His arms were smooth but muscular, and when he plucked at the grass, Lucy noticed how the tendons moved delicately under the dark skin above his wrists. He was barefooted and his feet were squarish and much lighter in colour than the rest of him and somehow they seemed to Lucy to be childishly vulnerable. Somewhere along the line, Lucy thought, I've forgotten what young men look like.

4

Jeff was squinting at a leaf in his hand. 'All my life,' he said, 'I've been on the hunt and I haven't found one yet.'

'Found what yet?' Lucy asked.

'A four-leaf clover.' He tossed the leaf aside. 'Do you think it's significant?'

'Profoundly,' Lucy said.

'That's what I think, too,' said Jeff. He sat down in a neat, economical, folding movement, holding his knees.

The narrow, flexible waists of young men, Lucy thought. She shook her head and picked up her book and stared at the page. 'Everything turned out badly,' she read. 'There were mosquitoes at Arles and when they got to Carcassonne they discovered the water was turned off for the afternoon.'

'I want to know the conditions,' Jeff said.

'I'm reading,' said Lucy.

'Why've you avoided me for the last three days?' Jeff asked.

'I can't wait to see how this book comes out,' said Lucy. 'They are rich and young and beautiful and they travel all over Europe and their marriage is going on the rocks.'

'I asked you a question.'

'Have you ever been to Arles?' Lucy said.

'No,' said Jeff. 'I haven't been anywhere. Do you want to go to Arles with me?'

Lucy turned the page. 'That's why I've been avoiding you for three days,' she said. 'If you keep saying things like that, I really think it might be better if you leave.' But even as she said it she knew she was thinking, Isn't this pleasant, sitting here under a tree, listening to a young man talking foolishly like that, *Do you want to go to Arles with me?*

'I'm going to tell you something about yourself,' Jeff said.

'I'm trying to read,' Lucy said. 'Don't be rude.'

'You are letting yourself be wiped out,' Jeff said.

'What?' Lucy put down her book, surprised.

'By your husband,' he said. He stood up and talked down at her. 'He's got you locked in, stowed down, vaulted, stifled . . .'

'You don't know what you're talking about,' Lucy said, all the more vehemently because from time to time she had said almost the same thing to Oliver in practically the same words. 'You hardly even know him.'

'I know him, I know him,' Jeff said. 'And if I didn't know him, I'd know the type. My father has ten like him for friends and they've been in and out of my house since I was born. The holy, superior, soft-voiced, all-knowing, Ivy-League owners of the earth.'

'You haven't the faintest idea what you're talking about,' Lucy said.

'Don't I, though?' Jeff began to stride restlessly back and forth in front of her. 'I watched you all last August. I sat behind you in the movie house, I hung around the soda fountain when you came for ice cream. I pretended to be buying a magazine in the bookshop when you came into the circulating library. I rowed past here three times a day. I had my eye on you, I had my eye on you,' he chanted wildly. 'Why do you think I came back here this summer?'

'Sssh,' Lucy said. 'You're making too much noise.'

'Nothing escaped me,' Jeff said melodramatically. 'Nothing. Didn't you even notice me?'

'No,' Lucy said.

'You see!' Jeff said loudly, as though he'd scored a point. 'He's put blinkers on you! Blinded you! You don't even *see* anything except through those cold, filing-cabinet eyes.'

'Well, now,' Lucy said reasonably, hoping to calm Jeff down, 'I don't think it's so unusual for a married woman of my age not to notice nineteen-year-old boys in drug-stores.'

'Don't call me a nineteen-year-old boy,' Jeff shouted in anguish. 'And don't call yourself a married woman of your age.'

'You *are* the most difficult boy,' Lucy said. She picked up her book again. 'Now I'm going to read,' she said firmly.

'Go ahead and read.' Jeff crossed his arms and glared down at her. 'I don't care whether you hear what I have to say or not. But I'm going to say it anyhow. I watched you because I thought you were the most magnificent woman I had ever seen in my whole life . . .'

'After Carcassonne,' Lucy read aloud, her voice clear and melodious, 'they were stopped by floods and they decided that Spain would probably be boring anyway, so they turned north in the direction of . . .'

With a choked sound, Jeff leaned over and grabbed the book. Then he threw it, with all his strength, far out across the lawn.

'All right.' Lucy stood up. 'That's enough. It's one thing to be an irresponsible and amusing boy. It's quite another to be an insulting and overconfident boor. . . . Now, please leave.'

51

Jeff faced her, his lips tight. 'Forgive me,' he said huskily. 'I'm not overconfident. I'm the least overconfident man in the world. I keep remembering what it was like to kiss you and I . . .'

'You must forget that completely,' said Lucy crisply. 'I let you kiss me because you begged like a puppy and it was like kissing a nephew good night.' Even as she said it she was pleased with herself for the intelligent way she was handling him.

'Don't lie,' he whispered. 'Whatever else you do, don't lie.'

'I asked you to leave,' Lucy said.

Jeff glared at her. Anybody watching us, Lucy thought, would be certain that he had just finished telling me he hated me. Suddenly he turned, and strode, bare-footed and straight-backed, over to where he had thrown the book. He picked it up and smoothed out a crumpled page and walked slowly back to her, under the tree.

'I return the book,' he said, giving it to her. 'I admit I am a fool. I admit everything.' He grinned at her tentatively. 'I even admit I was nineteen years old last summer. I don't remember anything you don't want me to remember. I don't remember that I ever said that you were a magnificent woman and I don't remember that I ever did anything but praise Oliver Crown as a paragon among men. And above all, I don't remember that I ever kissed you. I am abject in the most Eastern, Oriental, abject way and I promise to remain abject from this date until Labour Day.'

He waited for her to smile, but she didn't smile. She found her place again in the book.

'I am as humble as the worm,' Jeff said, watching her closely, 'I am as respectful as a millionaire's butler, I am as sexless as a seventy-year-old eunuch in a home for aged Turks . . . There,' he said triumphantly. 'You laughed.'

'All right,' Lucy said, seating herself again. 'You can stay. On one condition.'

'What condition?' He looked down at her suspiciously.

'You must promise not to be serious.'

'I will be so frivolous,' he said gravely, 'that little children will turn from me in disgust.'

Across the lake the bugle from the boys' camp blew, and as if this were a signal for him, he made a stiff, wide salute, and turned, with military precision, on his heel, saying, 'I leave you now. I go to devote my life to the pursuit of the three-leaf clover.'

He walked off slowly, head down, staring at the ground and

started a methodical, quartering course over the lawn, stopping from time to time to bend over and pick one of the small plants. Lucy sat there, against the tree, her eyes half-closed, conscious of the white-shirted figure moving across the sunlit grass with the lake shining behind him and the mountains pale blue in the mid-day heat. *He watched me all summer*, she thought drowsily, *now what about that?*

Chapter Six

'Now look, Lucy, you must remember where you put it,' Oliver was saying over the phone, his voice loaded with the weary patience which Lucy knew so well and which always froze her into a state of near-amnesia, because she knew what exasperated impatience it disguised. 'Think hard.'

'I *am* thinking hard,' Lucy said, and she knew she sounded sullen and childish, but she couldn't help it. 'I'm sure I left all the bills in my desk.'

She was standing in the living room in the cottage as she spoke, watching Tony and Jeff playing chess under the light of a lamp at the big table in the middle of the room. Both of them were concentrating, heads close together over the board, Tony because he was determined to win and Jeff because he was being polite and did not want to seem to be listening to the conversation on the phone being conducted six feet away from him.

'Lucy, darling,' Oliver's voice now compounded both the weariness and the patience, 'I've looked twice in your desk. It's not there. You've got bills from 1932 there and recipes for fish soup and an invitation to the wedding of two people who were divorced three years ago—but the bill from the garage is not there. I repeat,' he said slowly, in that maddening voice, 'the bill for the garage is not there.'

She felt like crying. Whenever Oliver got after her for the in-efficiency with which she ran the household accounts, she had a flustered, tragic sense that the modern world was too complicated for her, that unknown people came into her room when she was absent and maliciously rifled her papers, that Oliver was sure she was an idiot and regretted marrying her. If Tony and Jeff hadn't been there she would have cried, which would have had the advantage of making Oliver relent and say, 'The hell with it. It isn't that important. I'll straighten it out somehow.'

But even though neither Tony nor Jeff were watching her she couldn't cry, of course. All she could say was, 'I'm sure I paid it. I'm absolutely sure.'

'Jenkins says no,' Oliver said. Jenkins was the owner of the garage and Lucy despised him because he had a trick of turning from the warmest affability to whining protest when people made him wait for his money past the fifth of the month.

'Whose word are you going to take?' Lucy asked. 'Jenkins' or mine?'

'Well, it's not in the cheque book,' Oliver said, and she could have screamed at the thin, distant persistence of the voice on the phone, 'and I can't find the receipted bill and he was most obnoxious about it today when I stopped in for gas. It's very embarrassing, Lucy, to have a man come up to you and say you've owed him seventy dollars for three months, when you've thought you've paid it.'

'We *have* paid it,' Lucy said stubbornly, not remembering anything.

'Lucy, I repeat,' Oliver said, 'we must have the bill.'

'What do you want me to do?' she cried, her voice rising, despite herself. 'Come down and look for it myself? If that's what you want, I'll take the train tomorrow morning.'

Jeff looked up quickly at this, then returned to the game.

'Guard your queen,' he said to Tony.

'I have a deadly plan,' Tony said. 'Watch.'

'No, no,' Oliver said wearily. 'I'll talk to him myself. Forget it.'

When he said, Forget it, Lucy knew that it was a sentence on her, a small, recurrent, punitive, mounting sentence.

'How are things up there?' Oliver asked, but coolly, disciplining her. 'How's Tony?'

'He's playing chess with Jeff,' said Lucy. 'Do you want to talk to him?'

'Yes, please.'

Lucy put the phone down. 'Your father wants to talk to you, Tony,' she said. She started out of the room, as Tony said, 'Hi, Dad.'

She was conscious that Jeff was watching her as she went out on to the porch and she had a feeling that she looked tense and humiliated.

'We saw a deer today,' Tony was saying. 'He came down to the lake to drink.'

Lucy moved off across the lawn towards the shore of the lake because she didn't want to have to talk to Oliver again. The moon was full and it was a warm night and a slight milky mist was rising from the water. From the opposite shore came the sound of the bugle. Every night at the camp there, the bugler gave a short concert. Tonight he was playing French cavalry calls, very well, and the strange, quick music made the whole scene, with the borders of the lake softened and almost obscured by the rising mist, seem unfamiliar and melancholy.

Lucy stood there, holding her bare arms because of the little chill along the edge of the water, allowing her irritation to be soothed by the moonlight and the bugle calls into self-pity.

She heard the steps behind her, but she didn't turn around and when Jeff put his arms around her she had the feeling not of a woman being pursued by a young man, but of a child taken under mature protection. And when she turned around and he kissed her, although it soon changed into something else, she had the feeling that she had been bruised and that her hurt was being assuaged. She felt his hands, smooth and hard, on the bare flesh of her back, gentle, searching, demanding. She pulled her head away and, still embraced, put her face against his shoulder.

'Oh, Lord . . .' Jeff whispered. He put his hand under her chin and tried to pull her head up, but she resisted and pushed deeper into the loose flannel of his shirt.

'No,' she said. 'No. No more . . .'

'Later,' he whispered. 'I have the house all to myself. My sister's in town for the week.'

'Stop it.'

'I've been so good,' Jeff said. 'I can't any more. Lucy . . .'

'Mother . . .' It was Tony's voice, high and childish, carrying across the lawn from the house. 'Mother . . .'

Lucy broke away and hurried across the lawn.

'Yes, Tony,' she called, as she reached the porch.

'Daddy wants to know if you want to talk to him again.'

Lucy stopped and leaned against the pillar of the porch, trying to breathe properly. 'Not unless he has something he particularly wants to say to me,' she said, through the open window.

'Mother says only if you have something you particularly want to say to her,' Tony said into the phone.

She waited. There was silence for a moment and then Tony said, 'Okay. I will. So long,' and she heard the click of the phone as he hung up. He poked his head out through the window, lifting the screen.

'Mother,' he called.

'I'm here,' she said, from the shadows of the porch.

'Daddy said to tell you he can't come up this week-end,' he said. 'There's a man coming in from Detroit he has to see.'

'All right, Tony,' she said, watching Jeff coming slowly through the moonlight across the lawn towards the house. 'Now, if you're going to sleep out here, you'd better start getting your bed ready.'

'We haven't finished the chess game yet,' Tony said. 'I have him in a gruesome position.'

'Finish it tomorrow,' said Lucy. 'You'll still have him in a gruesome position.'

'Righteo,' Tony said, and pulled his head inside the house, letting the screen fall with a bang.

Jeff came on to the porch and stood in front of her. He started to put out his arms towards her, but she moved off and switched on the lamp that stood on the rattan table near the big glider on which Tony was going to sleep.

'Lucy,' Jeff whispered, following her. 'Don't run away.'

'It didn't happen,' she said. Nervously, she pushed one of Tony's shirts, on which she had been sewing buttons that afternoon, into a sewing basket that was on the table. 'Nothing happened. Forget it. I beg you. Forget it.'

'Never,' he said, standing close to her. He put out his hand and touched her mouth. 'Your lips . . .'

She heard herself moan and even as the sound came from her she was surprised at it. She had the feeling that she was losing control of the simplest mechanical gestures, the movement of her arms, the voice in her throat. 'No,' she said and pushed past Jeff, scraping harshly at her mouth with the back of her hand.

Tony came out, loaded with bedclothes, and dumped them on the glider. 'Listen, Jeff,' he said. 'You're not to study the board until tomorrow morning.'

'What? What's that?' Jeff turned slowly towards the boy.

'No unfair advantages,' Tony said. 'You promise?'

'I promise,' Jeff said. He smiled stiffly at Tony, then bent over and picked up Tony's telescope, which was lying under a chair, and seemed to become absorbed in polishing the lens with the sleeve of his shirt.

Lucy watched Tony as he began to arrange the sheets and the blankets on the glider. 'You're sure you want to sleep out here tonight?' she asked, thinking, I will be motherly, that will bring me back. 'You won't be too cold?'

'It's not cold,' Tony said cheerfully. 'Millions of people sleep out in the summertime, don't they, Jeff?'

'Millions,' Jeff said, still polishing the lens of the telescope. He was seated now and he was bent over and Lucy couldn't see his face.

'Soldiers, hunters, mountain climbers,' said Tony. 'I'm going to write Daddy and ask him to bring me a sleeping bag. Then I can sleep out in the snow, too.'

'You'll have plenty of time for that,' Jeff said. He stood up and Lucy, watching him, saw that his face was quiet, unchanged, and that his expression was once more the usual one of friendly and sceptical indulgence that he displayed to Tony.

I have to be careful of him, Lucy thought. He is too resilient for me. It is not only the waists of young men that are flexible.

'Plenty of time, Tony,' Jeff said carelessly. 'In World War Twelve.'

'That isn't funny,' Lucy said sharply. She went over and started helping Tony make up the glider for the night.

'Pardon,' Jeff said. 'World War Fifteen.'

'Don't be sore at him, Mummy,' Tony said. 'We have a deal. He talks to me just as though I was twenty years old.'

'There won't be any World War Twelve or Fifteen or World War Anything,' Lucy said. She was frightened of the idea of war and she refused to read any of the news from Spain, where the Civil War had been going on for a year, and she had successfully prevented Oliver from buying tin soldiers or air-rifles for Tony when he was younger. Actually, she would not have been so touchy on the subject if somehow she could have been guaranteed that whatever war took place would come at a time when Tony was either too young or too old to be involved in it. If she had been forced to state her position she would have said that

57

patriotism was only for people with large families. 'Talk about something else,' she said.

'Talk about something else, Tony,' Jeff said obediently.

'Did you look at the moon tonight, Jeff?' Tony asked. 'It's nearly full. You can see just about everything.'

'The moon,' said Jeff. He lay down on his back on the floor of the porch and took one of the wooden chairs and up-ended it, holding it steady between his knees. He used the crossbar as a rest for the telescope and squinted off into the sky.

'What're you doing there?' Lucy asked, almost suspiciously.

'Tony showed me this,' Jeff said, adjusting the telescope. 'You've got to have a steady field, haven't you, Tony?'

'Otherwise,' Tony said, working busily on the glider, 'the stars blur.'

'And one thing we won't have around here,' said Jeff, 'is blurred stars.' He made a final quarter turn on the tube. 'Consider the unblurred moon,' he said professorially. 'An interesting place to visit, if you like travelling. Sail on a stone boat across the Mare Crisium . . . In English, Tony?'

'Sea of Crises,' Tony said automatically.

'Crises,' Jeff said. 'Even on the cold, dead moon.'

He couldn't have meant what he said before, Lucy thought resentfully, he was just trying it on, if he can play like this with Tony now. . . .

'And to the south,' Jeff was saying, 'a more pleasant place. The Mare Foecunditas.'

'The Sea of Fertility,' Tony said promptly.

'We will dip you in that two or three times, just to make sure.' Jeff grinned, lying there on his back, with the telescope pointed towards the stars.

'Jeff,' Lucy said, warningly.

'The Sea of Tranquillity, the Marsh of Sleep, the Lake of Dreams,' Jeff went on, as though he hadn't heard her, his deep youthful voice with its pleasant, educated touch of Boston making a trance-like music out of the names. 'Maybe the moon is the place to move to this century, after all. When were you born, Tony?'

'March twenty-sixth,' Tony said. He was making an elaborate hospital corner with the sheets and the blankets on the lower edge of the glider mattress.

'Aries,' Jeff said. He put the telescope down and lay with his head back on the wooden flooring of the porch. His eyes were closed now, as though he were searching for visions, listening to unworldly voices, waiting for omens from the heavens. 'The sign of the Ram, the horned beast in the heavens. Do you know how the Ram got there, Tony?'

'Do you believe in that stuff?' Tony stopped his work on the bed for a moment and looked at Jeff.

'I believe in everything,' Jeff said, still with his eyes closed, his voice liturgical and solemn. 'I believe in the Zodiac and luck and transmigration of souls and sacrifice and secret diplomacy, secretly arrived at.'

'Human sacrifice,' Tony said incredulously. 'Did people ever really do that?'

'Of course,' Jeff said.

'Until when?' Tony asked sceptically.

'Until yesterday at three-fifteen P.M. It's the only kind of sacrifice that ever does any good,' Jeff said. 'Wait until you've tried it two or three times, Tony, and you'll see what I mean.'

'All right, Jeff, that's enough of that,' Lucy said, thinking, He's deliberately provoking me, he's revenging himself on me. 'Tony, pay attention here.'

'Phrixus and Helle,' Jeff said, almost as if she hadn't spoken, 'sons of the King of Thessaly, were badly treated by their stepmother . . .'

'Is this educational?' Lucy said, determined to show nothing.

'Enormously,' Jeff said.

'What was her name?' Tony asked.

'Who?'

'The stepmother.'

'That's in the next lesson,' Jeff said. 'So Mercury took pity on the boys and sent a ram with golden fleece to help them escape. The ram carried them on his back, high above the earth, and everything was going fine until they came to the strait that separates Europe from Asia. Then Helle fell and was drowned and they call the water the Hellespont to this day. And when Phrixus reached Colchis, which was a lively town when the weather was right, he sacrificed the ram in gratitude and Jupiter set the poor dead flying beast among the stars in recognition of his service to the king's son . . .'

Lucy looked down curiously at Jeff. 'Did you know all this before you met Tony?' she asked.

'Not a word,' Jeff said. 'I go home and study every night so that Tony will think I'm the smartest man that ever lived.' He smiled. 'I want him to be disappointed with every teacher he has from now on and get disgusted with education and never listen to any one of them again. It's the least I can do for him.' He sat up suddenly, his face naïve and open, his eyes shining candidly in the light of the lamp. 'Tony,' he said, 'show your mother how you breathe when you swim.'

'Like this,' Tony said, ducking his head and making a swimming motion with his arms. 'Kick, one, two, three, four, BREATHE!' He put his head to one side and opened his mouth wide at one corner, as though it was half in and half out of the water, and sucked in air with a loud, wet sound.

'Isn't there a more gentlemanly way to breathe?' Lucy asked, thinking, The danger is over, everything is back to normal.

'No,' Jeff said, 'I taught him that, too.' Sitting crosslegged on the floor now, he addressed Tony. 'Do you think your father is getting his money's worth out of me?'

'Well,' Tony said, teasing him, 'almost.'

'Lie a little in your next letter,' Jeff said. 'For friendship's sake.' He stood up, picking up the telescope. He put the telescope to his eye and regarded Tony, at a distance of ten feet. 'You will have to shave,' he said solemnly, 'in exactly three years, two months, and fourteen days.'

Tony laughed and rubbed his chin.

'I have a question to ask you, young man.' Jeff came over to the glider and leaned against the chain, making it swing a little. 'Don't you think it would be a good idea if I went home with you after Labour Day and stayed with you this winter to smarten you up some more?'

'Do you think you could do that?' Lucy could see that Tony was deeply pleased with the idea.

'Don't stop, Tony,' Lucy said sharply. 'Jeff was joking. He has to go back to college and be sensible again until next summer. Stop swinging on the chain, please, Jeff, it's hard enough to make this up as it is.'

'One thing I don't like about summers,' Tony said, 'towards the end, they go too fast. Will I really see you this winter, Jeff?'

'Of course,' Jeff said. 'Get your mother to bring you up to Dartmouth. For the football games and the winter carnival.'

'Mother, do you think we can go?'

'Maybe,' Lucy said, because she didn't want to make an issue of it. 'If Jeff remembers to invite us.'

'Tomorrow, Tony,' said Jeff, 'I'll stab myself in the hand and print the invitation in blood and that constitutes a holy contract. We'll pull wires and get your mother elected Queen of the Carnival and they'll take her picture sitting on top of a snowball and everybody'll say, "By gum, there's never been anything like that in New Hampshire before." '

Lucy glanced uneasily at Tony. If he were a year older, she thought, he would catch on. Maybe even now . . . 'Stop it,' she said to Jeff, risking alerting Tony. 'Don't make fun of me.'

'I'm not making fun of you,' Jeff said slowly. He walked to the edge of the porch and looked once more at the sky through the telescope. 'Mars,' he said, making his voice throaty and dramatic. 'The low, baleful, red, unwinking planet. That's your ruling planet, Tony, because you're Aries. Favourable to slaughter and the arts of war. Become a soldier, Tony, and you'll take a hundred towns and be at least a lieutenant-colonel by the age of twenty-three.'

'Now, really, Jeff,' Lucy said, 'that's enough of that nonsense.'

'Nonsense?' Jeff said, sounding surprised. 'Tony, do you think it's nonsense?'

'Yes,' Tony said judiciously. 'But it's interesting.'

'People have been guiding their lives by the stars for five thousand years. The Kings of Egypt . . .' Jeff said. 'Lucy,' and his voice was like a mischievous boy's now, 'when were you born?'

'A long time ago.'

'Tony, what's your mother's birthday?'

'August twenty-fifth.' Tony was enjoying this and he appealed to Lucy. 'It can't do any harm.'

'August twenty-fifth,' Jeff repeated. 'The sign of Virgo. The Virgin . . .'

'Mother . . .' Tony looked inquiringly at Lucy.

'I'll explain some other time.'

'In the region of the Euphrates,' Jeff went on, now pretending to be a lecturer and speaking rapidly and with no inflection, 'it was identified with Venus, who was sad and perfect and was worshipped by lovers. The ruling planet is Mercury, the brightest star, which always keeps the same side turned to the sun and is frozen on one side and burning on the other. Virgoans are shy and fear to be brilliant . . .'

61

'Now,' said Lucy, feeling he had gone far enough, 'where did you pick up all this foolishness?'

'Madame Vietcha's *Book of the Stars*,' Jeff said, grinning. 'Thirty-five cents at any good bookstore or at your druggist's. Virgoans fear impurity and disorder and are liable to peptic ulcers. When they love, they love passionately and place a high premium on fidelity . . .'

'And how about you?' Lucy interrupted, almost with hostility, forgetting Tony for the instant, challenging Jeff. 'What about your horoscope?'

'Aaah . . .' Jeff put the telescope down and wagged his head. 'Mine is too sad to relate. I'm in opposition to my stars. They sit up there'—he waved sadly at the sky—'winking, defying me, saying, "Not a chance, not a chance . . ." I want to lead and they advise me to follow. I want to be brave and they say, Caution. I want to be great and they say, Perhaps in another life. I say, Love, and they say, Disaster. I'm a hero in the wrong twelfth of the Zodiac.'

There were footsteps on the gravel path alongside the porch and a moment later Lucy saw a young girl in blue jeans and a loose sweater come into view. For a moment Lucy didn't recognize her, then saw that it was the daughter of a Mrs. Nickerson whom she had met at the hotel that afternoon. Tony halted work on the glider to stare at her.

'Hullo,' the Nickerson girl said, coming on to the porch. She was a plump and prematurely developed girl and the blue jeans were stretched tight across her solid little behind. Her hair was streaked and Lucy noted disapprovingly that it had almost certainly been touched up. 'Hullo,' she repeated, standing with her legs widespread and her hands plunged into the pockets of the blue jeans. She looked around her with the unabashed self-possession of an animal trainer. 'I'm Susan Nickerson,' she said, and if you closed your eyes you would have been sure it was a mature and rather unpleasant woman speaking. 'We were introduced this afternoon.'

'Of course, Susan,' Lucy said. 'This is my son Tony.'

'Delighted,' Susan said crisply. 'I've heard a great deal about you.' Jeff made a face.

'My mother sent me over, Mrs. Crown,' Susan said, 'to ask if you'd like to make a fourth at bridge tonight.'

Jeff glanced swiftly across at Lucy, then leaned over and picked up the chair that he had up-ended on the floor to observe the stars.

Lucy hesitated. She thought of the veranda of the hotel and the seared ranks of seasonal widows there. 'Not tonight, Susan,' she said. 'Tell your mother thank you, but I'm tired and I'm going to bed early.'

'Okay,' Susan said flatly.

'Bridge,' said Jeff, 'has put this country further back than Prohibition.'

Susan inspected him coldly. She had bright, cold, blue, coin-like eyes. 'I know about you,' she said. She had the trick of making the simplest statement sound like an accusation. It will come in very handy, Lucy thought, noticing it, if she later decides to become a policewoman.

Jeff laughed. 'Maybe you'd better keep it to yourself, Susan,' he said.

'You're the Dartmouth boy,' she said. 'My mother thinks you're very handsome.'

Jeff nodded gravely, agreeing. 'And what do you think?' he asked.

'You're all right.' She shrugged, a small, plump movement under the loose sweater. 'They'd never take you in the movies, though.'

'I was afraid of that,' Jeff said. 'And how long are you going to be here?'

'I hope not long,' the girl said. 'I like Nevada better.'

'Why?' Jeff asked.

'There was more happening,' Susan said. 'This place is dead. It's got the wrong age groups. They don't even have movies, except on Saturdays and week-ends. What do you do here at night?'

'We look at the stars,' said Tony, who had been watching her, fascinated.

'Ummn,' Susan said, not impressed.

She may be only fourteen years old, Lucy thought, repelled and amused at the same time, but she sounds as though only the most extreme forms of vice could hold her interest for more than five minutes at a time.

Tony went over to Susan and offered her the telescope. 'You want to take a look?'

Susan shrugged again. 'I don't care.' But she took the telescope and put it languidly to her eye.

'You ever look through one of those before?' Tony asked.

'No,' Susan said.

'You can see the mountains of the moon with this one,' said Tony.

Susan looked critically and without favour at the moon.

'How do you like that?' Tony asked, the moon's proprietor.

'It's okay,' Susan said, returning the telescope. 'It's the moon.'

Jeff chuckled, shortly, once, and Susan raked him with her policewoman's eyes. 'Well,' she said, 'I must be off. My mother will want to know about the bridge.' She raised her hand with terrible grace, as though dispensing a blessing. 'Ta,' she said.

'See you tomorrow,' Tony said, and his effort to be nonchalant made Lucy feel she was going to break into a sweat in sympathy.

'Maybe,' Susan said wearily.

Poor Tony, Lucy thought. The first girl he's ever looked at.

'Delighted to have made your acquaintance, everybody,' Susan said. 'Ta, again.'

They watched her walk down the path, her buttocks like two solidly pumped-up beach balls under the tight cloth of the jeans.

Jeff shuddered elaborately as she disappeared around the corner of the house. 'I bet her mother is something,' he said. 'I'll give you three guesses why that lady was in Nevada last summer.'

'Don't gossip,' Lucy said. 'Tony, stop lingering.'

Tony slowly came back to the adult world. 'She looks funny in pants, doesn't she? Kind of lumpy.'

'You'll find they get lumpier and lumpier in pants as you go along, Tony,' Jeff said.

The moment, with its joke about sex, and the memory of the girl's dry and effortless rejection of her son, made Lucy uncomfortable. Another night, she thought, resenting Jeff, and I would have laughed. Not tonight.

'Tony,' she said, 'inside with you. Get into your pyjamas. And don't forget to brush your teeth.'

Tony slowly started in. 'Jeff,' he said, 'will you read to me when I get into bed?'

'Sure.'

'I'll read to you tonight,' Lucy said, almost automatically.

'I like the way Jeff reads better.' Tony stopped at the door. 'He skips the descriptions.'

'Jeff's had a long day,' Lucy said, stubbornly, sorry that she

64

had started this, but committed now. 'He probably has a date or something.'

'No,' Jeff began, 'I . . .'

'Anyway, Tony,' Lucy said, in a tone of sharp command she almost never used with him, 'go in and get your pyjamas on. Quickly.'

'All right,' Tony said, sounding hurt. 'I didn't mean . . .'

'Go ahead!' Lucy said, almost hysterically.

Puzzled, and a little frightened, Tony went into the house. Lucy moved quickly, in little jerky movements around the porch, throwing some magazines together, closing the sewing basket, standing the telescope on the chair next to the glider, conscious that Jeff was watching her closely, humming tunelessly to himself.

She stopped in front of him. He was leaning against the porch pillar, his head in darkness, only a faint gleam showing where his eyes were.

'You,' she said. 'I don't like the way you behave with Tony.'

'With Tony?' Jeff straightened up, surprised, and came into the light of the lamp. 'Why? I just behave naturally.'

'Nobody behaves naturally with children,' Lucy said, conscious that her voice was strained and artificial. 'There is no such thing. All those sly jokes. All that pretence . . .'

'What pretence?'

'That you're so fond of him,' Lucy said. 'That you're really just about the same age. That you want to see him again after the summer . . .'

'But I do,' Jeff said.

'Don't lie to me. By Thanksgiving you won't remember his name. And you'll raise a lot of hopes in him . . . and all that it'll mean to him is a long, disappointed autumn. Do your job,' she said. 'And that's all.'

'As I understood it,' Jeff said, 'my job was to try to make him feel like a normal, healthy boy.'

'You've made him morbidly attached to you.'

'Now, Lucy . . .' Jeff said angrily.

'What for? Why?' She was almost shouting now. 'Out of vanity? What's so gratifying about getting a poor lonely little sick boy to cling to you? Why is it worth all the tricks? The Sign of the Ram, the Sea of Fecundity, human sacrifice, the Virgin, the Winter Carnival . . .' She was gasping, as though she had been running for a long time, and the words seemed to be pushed out past sobs. 'Why don't you go home? Why don't you leave us both alone?'

Jeff took her arms and held them. She didn't try to break away. 'Is that what you want?' he asked.

'Yes,' she said. 'You're the wrong age. You're too old for him and you're too young for me. Go find someone who's twenty years old.' With a sharp movement, she pulled her arms out of his grasp. 'Someone you can't damage,' she said. 'Someone for the summer. Someone you'll forget in September just the way you're going to forget us.'

'Lucy,' he whispered. 'Stop it.'

'Go away.' She almost wept.

But he held her again, this time high up on her arms, close to her shoulders, his hands digging into her. 'What do you think it's been like for me?' he demanded, his voice still low, modified by the necessity of keeping Tony from hearing him. 'Being so close to you, day after day? Going home and lying awake, remembering how your hand felt when I helped you out of the boat, remembering the sound your dress made as you brushed past me on the way down to dinner. Remembering what your laugh sounded like . . . And never being able to touch you, tell you . . . Damage!' he whispered harshly. 'Don't talk to me about damage!'

'Please,' she said, 'if this is the way you talk to everybody, if this is the technique you've worked out, if this is how you've been successful with all your girls . . . spare me. Spare me.'

His hands tightened momentarily on her arms and she thought he was going to shake her. Then he let go of her. They stood there close to each other and he spoke wearily, without force. 'You had a big straw hat last summer,' he said, his voice flat. 'When you wore it in the sunlight, your face was all rosy and soft. Now, whenever I see a woman in a red straw hat like that, it's as though someone has grabbed me by the throat . . .'

'Please,' Lucy said, 'for the last time . . . go find yourself some other girl. There're dozens of them. Young, unattached, who have no one to answer to when the summer is over.'

He stared at her, then nodded, as though agreeing. 'I'll tell you something,' he said. 'But you must promise not to laugh.'

'All right,' Lucy said, puzzled. 'I won't laugh.'

Jeff took a deep breath. 'There are no other girls,' he said. 'There never have been.'

Lucy lowered her head. She noticed that one of the middle

buttons of her blouse was undone. She closed it carefully. Then she began to laugh, helplessly.

'You promised,' Jeff said, hurt.

'I'm sorry,' she said. She raised her eyes, trying to control her mouth. 'I'm not laughing at you. I'm laughing at myself.'

'Why?' he asked suspiciously.

'Because we're both so clumsy,' she said. 'Because we're both so hopeless. Because neither of us knows how to do this.' Now she was looking at him squarely and soberly. 'Because we're going to do it,' she said.

They stood that way in silence for a second. Jeff made an uncertain movement with his hands. She took a step towards him and kissed him, hard.

'Lucy,' he whispered. He touched the back of her neck lightly with his hand.

'Now, little boy,' Lucy said, sounding motherly, almost jocular, pushing him away, 'go to your nice, dark, empty sister's house and sit on the porch and look at the moon and think of all the younger, prettier women you might have made love to tonight—and wait for me.'

Jeff made no move. 'You . . . you'll come there?' he asked warily, disturbed by her strange switch in attitude. 'You're not joking now? It's not a trick?'

'It's not a trick,' Lucy said lightly. 'I'll come along, never fear.'

Jeff tried to kiss her again, but she held him off, smiling, shaking her head. Then he wheeled and went quickly across the lawn, his shoes making no sound in the dewy grass. Lucy watched him disappear. Then she shook her head again and moved absently over to the glider. She was sitting there, her hands quiet in her lap, looking out at the misted lake, when Tony came out a few minutes later, in his pyjamas and bathrobe, carrying a book.

'I brought the book,' Tony said as he came through the door.

'Good.' Lucy stood up. 'Get into bed.'

Tony looked around him as he took off his robe. 'Where's Jeff?'

Lucy took the book and seated herself next to the glider, where the light of the lamp was strongest. 'He had to go,' she said. 'He remembered he had a date.'

'Oh,' Tony said, disappointed. He got into bed after moving the telescope so that he could reach it easily. 'That's funny. He didn't tell me.'

'You mustn't expect him to tell you everything,' Lucy said calmly. She opened the book. It was *Huckleberry Finn*. Oliver had made a list of books that were to be read to Tony during the summer and this was the third on the list. The next book to be read was a biography of Abraham Lincoln. 'Is this the place?' Lucy asked.

'Where the leaf is,' said Tony. He was using a maple leaf as a bookmark.

'I see,' said Lucy.

She read the first few lines silently to orient herself and there was silence except for the busy sounds of crickets in the woods around them.

Tony took off his glasses and put them on the floor next to the telescope. He wriggled under the bedclothes and stretched luxuriously. 'Isn't this great?' he said. 'Wouldn't it be great if it was summertime all year long?'

'Yes, Tony,' said Lucy, and began to read. '*So we went over to where the canoe was,*' she read, '*and while he built a fire in a grassy open place amongst the trees, I fetched meal and bacon and coffee, and a coffee-pot and frying pan, and the nigger was set back considerable, because he reckoned it was all done with witchcraft. . . .*'

Chapter Seven

SHE lay on the narrow bed with his head on her breast, holding him lightly, watching him sleep. He had said, when she saw his eyelids drooping, 'No, how could I sleep on a night like this?' Then he had sighed and moved his head gently against her breast, and had drifted off. He had a triumphant expression on his face, like a small boy who has accomplished something difficult and praiseworthy in the presence of his elders, and she smiled, seeing it, and touched his forehead with her fingertips.

He had also murmured, 'Forever,' once, his lips against her throat, and she remembered it now and thought, How young you have to be to say forever.

He had been hesitant and uncertain in the very beginning, but after the first violent awkwardness, he had found, almost as if it had been locked always in him, needing only her touch to free it, a delicacy and gentleness that had moved Lucy profoundly and in a manner in which she had never been moved before.

Now, lying with the sleeping boy pressed against her, her limbs feeling light and powerful, Lucy thought calmly of the moment of passion as though it were already far in the past, something that had happened once, long ago, and would never happen again. They would make love from time to time, perhaps, but it would never again be like this.

The sign of Virgo, she remembered. In the region of the Euphrates, she remembered, almost hearing again Jeff's youthful, playful voice, it was identified with Venus . . . Virgoans are shy and fear to be brilliant. Virgoans fear impurity and disorder and are liable to peptic ulcers.

She chuckled softly and the boy moved in her arms. A frown came over his face and he threw his head back on the pillow fearfully, as though he were trying to escape a blow. Lucy stroked his shoulder, which was dry and warm, and seemed still to be giving off the heat of the sun that had fallen on it during the day. The obscure look of terror slowly flowed out of his face and his lips relaxed and he slept steadily again.

The time, she thought. I ought to get up and see what time it is. It must be nearly dawn. But she lay there quietly, feeling somehow that even to be thinking about the hour was a form of betrayal of the boy beside her.

She had no desire to sleep. Sleep, she felt, would subtract from the completeness of the night. She wanted to lie there serenely, conscious of every sound—Jeff's steady breathing, the peeping of young frogs at the lake's edge, the call of an owl in the pine forest, the occasional rustle of the wind against the curtains of the bare room, the faraway resonance of an automobile horn on the highway leading to the mountains. She wanted to lie there conscious, above all, of herself. The thought struck her that she felt infinitely more valuable now at three o'clock in the morning than she had felt even so recently as ten the night before or at any other time in her life. Valuable. She smiled at the word.

Examining herself with the critical pleasure of a woman before a mirror, she realized that tonight she felt finally grown-up. She had the feeling that before this a great deal of her life had been devoted to those activities that a child might engage in if the child were anxious to pretend that she was an adult. And there had always been, too, the complementary anxiety that the masquerade would be discovered at any moment. She remembered her mother, dying at the age of sixty, and knowing she was dying, lying in her bed, yellowed and wasted, after a life of pain, trouble, poverty, disappointment, saying, 'I can't believe it. The hardest thing to believe is that I'm an old woman. Somehow, unless I catch sight of myself in a mirror, I still have the same feeling about myself that I had when I was sixteen years old. And even now, when the doctor comes in and pulls a long face, and I know he thinks I'm not going to last through the month, I want to tell him, "No, there's been a misunderstanding. Dying is much too sophisticated for someone who feels sixteen years old."'

Oliver had been no help, Lucy thought. Secure in his strength and forgiving and even approving of her timidity, he had made all decisions, protected her, kept his troubles to himself, only occasionally scolding her, and even then with a quick, fatherly indulgence, for such mistakes as the lost garage bill. At parties, she remembered, where he seemed always at home, where, at ease, ceremonious, never embarrassed, he was always the centre of a group, he would suddenly sense that she was off somewhere in a corner, lost in the social flood, backed to the wall by a bore or desperately pretending to be studying the pictures on the walls or the books on the shelves while hoping that it would soon be time to leave. Then, he would break away from whomever he was talking to and come over to her, smiling and interested, and lead her skilfully back with him, into the middle of things.

She had recognized what he had done through the years and she had been grateful. Now, she thought, perhaps it was wrong to be grateful. Now, she thought, feeling that because what she had done that night was different from anything she had ever done before, everything that came after would also be different, now nobody has to protect me any more.

She wondered what Oliver would do if he found out. Probably, she thought, he would forgive her with the same mannerly, overpowering condescension with which he was no doubt forgiving her for the lost garage bill. Thinking this, she resented him in advance, then could not help being amused at herself for her contrariness.

She remembered a conversation that she and Oliver and

Patterson had had about a woman they all knew, who was having an affair with a colonel on Governor's Island. 'That,' Sam had said, 'is unpermissible adultery.'

'Wait a minute, Sam,' Oliver had said. 'What's your idea of *permissible* adultery?'

Sam had put that solemn, close-mouthed expression on his face that he used when he was preparing to say something clever, and had said, 'Permissible adultery is when you enjoy it.'

Oliver had laughed heartily then. She wondered if he would laugh now. It had never occurred to her that he might be unfaithful to her just as she was sure that it had never occurred to him to doubt her. Maybe, she thought, that's what has been missing in our marriage.

Still, there was no reason to make any changes. There was no need for Oliver to know anything. She was so practised in innocence that now, when she was innocent no longer, the habit and impetus of the years would sustain her. Also, she had lied from time to time to Oliver, always successfully. The lies, certainly, had not been very grave, fibs about overdrafts at the bank, purposely misplaced invitations to parties she did not wish to attend, forgotten appointments. But great or small, they had always gone undiscovered, and Lucy had forgiven and justified them to herself as part of the necessary lubrication to keep their marriage going smoothly. Now, if the lie to be told was more serious in nature, she was confident she could bring it off unhesitatingly and with even greater justification. Tonight, she felt, with a delicious tingle of power, she was capable of handling anything.

It couldn't be too difficult. After all, she thought, look at all the women who manage it. Mrs. Wales, with her discreet weekend in the mountains and the two or three afternoons a month in New York. Claudia Larkin, with her golf pro, and the pro giving lessons, besides, every Saturday afternoon to Bill Larkin. Edith Brown, who was one of the silliest women alive, but even so appearing serenely on all occasions with her husband, despite the fact that everyone but her husband was certain about her and a chemistry professor in New Haven.

One thing she was sure of, Lucy thought righteously. She would never expose Oliver to anything like that. Her reticence would be complete, and she would make certain, too, of Jeff's discretion. Whatever happened, Oliver would lose nothing, tangible or intangible. If anything, she felt, although she was a

71

little vague in her own mind about the reasoning that went into the reflection, she would make a better wife than ever to Oliver. Oh, she thought comfortably, it doesn't pay to make too much out of this. Fifteen years are a long time. There probably isn't a single marriage we know of that's lasted half that long without some kind of excursion on somebody's part. . . .

As for Jeff . . . She looked down at the thick, dark youthful hair crushed against her breast. *Forever*, he had said. Well, she thought indulgently, time will take care of that.

She lay still, pleased with herself. I've never figured out anything as completely and intelligently as this, she thought. I've never been in such control.

And, she thought, luxuriating in a new-found delight in mischief, the next time a young man watches me all summer, I certainly will notice him.

Jeff stirred in her arms, tensed, trembled. His head moved spasmodically against her and his lips opened as though he were trying to scream. She kissed him on the cheek and woke him.

'What is it?' she whispered. 'What's the matter?'

He stared at her. For the moment he didn't seem to know where he was or to recognize her. 'What is it, Baby?' she repeated softly, holding him tighter.

Then he relaxed. 'Nothing.' He smiled and moved and lay back against the pillow, staring at the ceiling. 'I guess I was dreaming.'

'What about?'

He hesitated. 'Nothing,' he said. He ran his fingers slowly through her hair. 'Anyway, thanks for waking me.'

'What about?' she asked again, curiously.

'The war,' he said, looking up at the dark ceiling.

'What war?' Lucy asked, puzzled, because Jeff couldn't have been more than two years old when the war ended.

'The war in which I'm going to be killed,' he said flatly.

'Oh, no,' she said. Is that what young men dream about these days? she thought. While I was lying here, congratulating myself.

'I keep having the same damned dream,' Jeff said. 'It's in a city I've never seen and the signs on the shop windows are in a language I can't quite recognize, and I run and run along the street and I can't tell where the bullets are coming from and they keep coming closer and closer and I know that if I don't wake up fast they're going to hit me. . . .'

'That's horrible,' said Lucy.

'Oh, it's not so bad,' he said. 'I always manage to wake up in time.' He smiled in the darkness.

Suddenly the whole night seemed changed for Lucy, touched by premonitions, clouded by dreams, and the boy on the pillow seemed strange to her and sorrowfully necessary. She bent over and kissed him. 'You mustn't dream any more,' she said, and then she made her first great claim on him. 'It's disloyal.'

He chuckled, and for a little while, at least, she felt that she had rescued him. 'You're right,' he said. 'I shall refrain from dreaming.'

She sat up. 'I must see what time it is,' she said. 'Where's your watch?'

'On the table,' he said, 'near the window.'

She got out of bed, and walked barefooted across the cold wood floor through the diffuse light of the moon. She found the watch and held it close. It had a radium dial and she could see that it was nearly four o'clock.

'I must go,' she said, bending for her shoes.

He was sitting up in bed now, watching her.

'Not yet,' he said. 'Not just yet.'

'I must,' she said.

'Do something for me,' he said.

'What?' She stood, waiting.

'Walk once more,' he said softly, 'through the moonlight.'

She put her shoes down, without noise, stood still for a moment, then walked slowly, her body tall and naked and glistening palely, across the room.

Chapter Eight

THE call of an owl awakened Tony. He had kicked the blankets off, because he slept restlessly, and he was cold, too. He reached down and pulled the blankets up on to the glider and lay there, with the blankets in a disorderly pile on top of him, shivering,

73

waiting to get warm again, listening to the owl. Now there were two owls. One nearby, right behind the house, and one somewhere along the lake, maybe a hundred and fifty yards away. They were hooting to each other, over and over again in the darkness, monotonous and threatening, like Indians signalling to each other before making the final dash at the house.

He didn't like owls. He didn't like things that made noises at night. And if they had so much to say to each other, why didn't they just fly across to each other and meet halfway? But they didn't. They just sat there, hidden in the trees, making that sneaky noise to each other. He didn't like the way they flew, either. They had a fat, suspicious way of flying, he thought, and he bet they smelled bad, too, when you got up close to them.

The moon was down by now and it was very dark. He was a little sorry now that he hadn't slept inside, in his own room. It wasn't that he was afraid of the dark. If it hadn't been for the owls, he wouldn't give it another thought. It was just that lying there, with everything black around, the way they sounded made you feel as though something bad was preparing to happen to you.

He thought of getting up and going into the house to see what time it was. It had to be after four o'clock, because he knew the moon was due to set at three-fifty-seven this morning. He bet there wasn't a single boy in that whole camp across the lake that knew that the moon set at three-fifty-seven this morning.

If he went in to look at the time he could go in and look at his mother. Except she might wake up, and then what would he say? That the owls scared him? That he was afraid of the dark? It would be all right with her, but she'd be liable to write it to his father and his father'd probably write him a long letter, joking about it. He didn't mind joking, but there were certain things he'd just rather people didn't joke about.

Of course, his mother might not wake up. There was the time he had gone into her room in the middle of the night and she had been sleeping so soundly that he couldn't hear her breathe. She just lay there, and the blankets hadn't even gone up and down. A terrible thought had hit him. She's not asleep, he had thought. She's dead. He couldn't bear it and he had gone over to the bed and leaned over and raised one of her eyelids with his fingers. She never moved. She just lay there and it wasn't her eye at all. It was something blank, that didn't see anything, that didn't

74

have any light in it. It was the worst thing he'd ever seen. It was deader than anything he'd ever imagined. It had frightened him and he'd let go of her eyelid and it had closed again and she had moved and begun to breathe more heavily and she was his mother again. He had gone out of the room quietly and got into his own bed, knowing he would never do anything like that again. And he hadn't told her about it, either. There were a lot of things he didn't tell anybody about. The idea of being dead, for example. Whenever he came into the room and they happened to be talking about it, like the time old man Watkins died next door, they shut up and began talking about the weather or about school or about any darn thing. He pretended he didn't catch on, but he caught on all right. When he was four years old his grandmother died in his aunt's house in Haverford. He had been taken up there to say good-bye to her in the big, old house with the greenhouse out back. He remembered two smells from the house. The smell before his grandmother was dying, which was the smell of all the apple and pumpkin and pineapple pies that had been baked in the house, and the smell of his grandmother dying, medicine and people smoking downstairs and people being afraid. At the last minute, his grandmother had decided to die in a hurry and they didn't have time to take him to a hotel and the house was crowded and they put him in a little room off the hall and he heard people going past all night and whispering and crying, and he remembered somebody saying, 'She is at peace.'

He'd thought about it a lot, although he didn't say anything about it, because he knew people wouldn't like the idea of his talking about something like that. He'd come to the conclusion that his grandmother had decided to die in the middle of the night because she didn't want to do it in daylight, when people could see her and make her ashamed. For a long time he thought that's what you did—you decided to die and you died. If you didn't decide to do it, you stayed alive. It was yourself, he'd thought, and you did what you wanted with yourself. Then a funny thing changed his mind. He broke his finger trying to catch a baseball. He must have been about eight. The finger was crooked after that. The top joint bent over in a queer way. After a while, the finger didn't feel bad, but it still was bent over at the end. He could straighten it out by pushing it against a table, but when he took it away from the table, it went back being crooked again. He'd looked at it and he'd said to himself, It's my finger, if I say, 'Straighten up,' it would have to straighten up. But it stayed twisted, just the same. That's when he'd begun to realize that if you told your body, 'Don't die,' it wouldn't make any difference, you'd die just the same.

There were a lot of things you didn't tell anybody. For instance, school. His father had asked him how he would like to go away to school next autumn and he'd said he'd like to, because he knew that was what his father wanted him to say and he didn't want to disappoint him. His father didn't say anything when he was disappointed, but you could tell just the same. It was almost like a smell or somebody whispering in the next room, and you couldn't hear exactly what was being said, but you could get the idea all right. And it was worse than if he said anything. And he'd disappointed his father enough by being so sick. The way Tony knew that was by watching his father when his father was looking at other boys his age.

He knew his father wanted him to be something big when he grew up. So when people asked him what he wanted to be when he grew up, he said, 'Astronomer,' because nobody else ever thought of that. Everybody else said a doctor or a lawyer or a baseball player and his father always laughed when he said it and Tony knew his father thought it showed how original he was and still didn't take it too seriously, so there was no business of practising anything or worrying about getting good marks in school so you could go to Harvard.

About the school, though. He would have to do something about that. He didn't mind school, but he didn't want to go away from his mother. If he said that to his father, his father would look that way again, and start to talk about how when people grew up they didn't hang around their mothers all the time. Maybe, Tony thought, just about the end of the summer, when it's too late to keep me in bed much up here, I can have an attack. A little attack. I can say I can't breathe very well and I see dots in front of my eyes. And if I stay out in the sun one whole day, I can be pretty hot and it would look an awful lot like a fever.

Being sick wasn't altogether bad, except in the beginning, when everything hurt and they put bandages on his eyes and they kept coming in every ten minutes. After that, his mother had stayed with him almost all day, every day, reading to him, playing spelling games, singing to him, having lunch with him in his room. And when the other kids came in to visit him, he had it all over them, because he told them he'd nearly died and none of them had ever nearly died.

Albert Barker had tried to make up for not having nearly died, like him, by telling him about babies. According to Albert Barker a lady and a man got into bed with no clothes on and the man climbed on top of the lady and said, 'Move your legs,' and the lady made a funny sound (Albert Barker had tried to imitate it—it was a kind of low grunt, like somebody picking up a heavy box) and sometime after that the lady got very big and the baby was born. He was pretty sure Albert Barker was making most of this up, but he couldn't question him more closely because his mother had come into the room with milk and cookies and he had a feeling this was one of the things, like dying, not to talk about in front of grownups.

Albert Barker had never come back to visit him. The kids had visited him once or twice, in the beginning, but then they'd stopped because there wasn't anything much to do, just sitting around the room like that. But his mother had said they were waiting for him to get better and be able to come out and play with them again and then they'd be just as good friends as ever.

He didn't really mind their not coming to see him, because his mother was around all the time, but he'd have liked to see Albert Barker once more and get *that* straight.

He wondered if Susan Nickerson knew about it. She seemed to know a lot about a lot of things. Only she didn't pay much attention to him. Every once in a while she would go swimming with him or she'd come around and talk to him, but she always seemed to be looking for something else or waiting for a telephone to ring, and if somebody else showed up, she'd go right off.

He wished the summertime would last longer. He'd figure out some way of making Susan Nickerson pay attention to him if the summertime lasted long enough. Summertime was better than winter. People were together more in the summertime. In the winter everybody was in a hurry. In the winter everybody separated and became absent-minded.

Jeff was going to college and he wouldn't see him for months. Maybe forever. Forever. It was a bad word, but sometimes you had to face words like that. And even if he did see him, it wouldn't be the same thing. People were one way if you saw them all the time, every day, and they were another thing if you only saw them every couple of months. They really were thinking about something else after a couple of months.

That was one of the reasons he didn't want to go away to school—when he got back his mother would be thinking about something else. Grownups didn't seem to mind that. When they left each other, they said good-bye and shook hands and they didn't care if they didn't see each other for months—for years—forever. Grownups didn't really know how to be friends. Even when his grandmother had died and they'd buried her, his father hadn't changed much. His father had read the paper at breakfast the next morning and the day after the funeral he'd gone off to work as usual and after a week or so he was playing bridge at night, just as though nothing had happened.

Tony shivered a little and pulled the blankets up around him. He was sorry he had started thinking about things like that. Still, if his mother died, he'd guarantee he wouldn't be playing bridge a week later.

Maybe the thing to be was a doctor, a scientist. Then you could work on a serum to keep people alive forever. You could start with monkeys. You would keep it very quiet and then one day you would take the monkey to the auditorium of a college, and everybody would be sitting there, wondering, waiting to hear what you had to say, and you'd lead the monkey on to the stage and you'd say, 'Gentlemen, forty years ago I injected this monkey with my secret serum, Number Qy zero seven. You will notice that he has no grey hairs and he can swing from the highest trees.'

Then you'd be very strict about who got any of the serum. You'd start with your mother and father and Jeff and Dr. Patterson, but there'd be a lot of people to whom you'd say, 'No, I'm sorry, there isn't enough to go around.' No matter what they offered you. You wouldn't give your reasons, but you'd have darn good reasons, every time.

He chuckled to himself, under the blankets, as he thought of what people's faces would look like when he said, 'No, there isn't enough to go around.'

He turned over on his side and he was just about to close his eyes, thinking of the immortal old monkey, when he saw someone coming across the lawn towards the house. He stopped breathing for a moment, and didn't move, watching. Then he saw that it was his mother, in a loose, open coat, coming across the grass. There was a light mist, close to the ground, and his mother seemed to be floating towards him over a grey lake. He didn't say anything until she reached the porch. She stopped then and turned around and looked out over the mist for a few seconds. It was very dark, just one little light coming through the curtains from inside the house, on the other side of the porch, but he could tell that his mother was smiling.

'Mummy,' he said, whispering, because it was so late and so dark.

Even though he spoke in a low voice, she jumped a little. She came over to him and leaned over him and kissed his forehead. 'What're you doing up?' she asked.

'I was listening to the owls,' he said. 'Where were you?'

'Oh,' she said, 'I just took a little walk.'

'You know what I'm going to be when I grow up?' he said.

'What, darling?'

'A doctor. I'm going to experiment with monkeys.'

She laughed and touched his hair with her fingers. 'When did you decide that?'

'Tonight.' But he didn't tell her his reasons. The reasons could wait.

'Well,' she said, 'this has been a very important night, hasn't it?'

'Yes,' he said.

She leaned over and kissed him. She smelled warm and her coat smelled of pine needles, as though she had brushed against saplings in the woods. 'Good night, now, Doctor,' she said. 'Sleep tight.'

She went into the house and he closed his eyes. He heard her moving around softly inside the house, and then the light was put out and it was quiet. It was lucky, he thought, that I didn't go in to see if she was there when I woke up. I wouldn't have found her and I'd've been scared.

The owls stopped hooting, because the dawn was coming up, and he slept.

Chapter Nine

TONY came home in the middle of the afternoon, much earlier than he had expected. The hayride was supposed to have taken all day with a picnic lunch at Lookout Rock at the end of the lake and an expedition into the caves there. They'd had the lunch all right and they had taken a quick look at the caves, but Tony had been glad when it began to rain a little bit and Bert, who was driving the team, had rounded them all up and started back at two o'clock. All the other children on the ride had been much younger than Tony and there had been a confusion of mothers and nurses and Tony had spent the day feeling alternately superior and deserted. He wouldn't have gone on the ride at all except that Jeff had taken the day off to go into Rutland to the dentist. His mother had said that she was going to be busy and he could tell that she wanted him to go. But now it was only about four o'clock and here he was back at the cottage, alone. He looked through the house for his mother but she wasn't there. There was a note on the kitchen table from her, saying that she had gone into town to the movies and that she would be back by five o'clock.

He took an apple and went out on the porch, eating it, and looked at the lake. It was a cold day and the lake looked grey and mean. He wished the sun would come out so he could go swimming. He finished the apple and wound up carefully and threw it at a tree. He missed the tree. Apple cores didn't have enough weight for accurate pitching, he decided. He thought of trying to get a lift into town with the hotel bus to look for his mother. Then he decided against that. Whenever he went looking for her and found her she would smile at first and seem very glad to see him and then she'd say, 'Now, Tony, you mustn't tag after me all the time.'

He went in and looked at the clock in the living room. It hardly paid to go into town to look for her in the movies if she was going to be back by five. Anyway he had no money and he wouldn't know how to get into the theatre. He had never been to the movies. First he was too young, his father said. And then it was bad for his eyes. His father disapproved of the movies. His father disapproved of a lot of things. His father kept saying; 'When you're older, Tony. When you're older.' Tony had the feeling that when he was twenty years old he would be so busy catching up on all the things his father disapproved of now that he'd never have any time to sleep.

He went on to the porch again and put a record on the gramophone that Jeff had lent him. The record was 'I Get a Kick Out of You.' He listened critically to the words for a while and turned the volume up good and high so that it sounded as though he had a party going on the porch. Then he went into his mother's room and picked up the long mirror on a stand that she had against the wall and carried it out to the porch. When he was younger and his mother wasn't home and he was waiting for her he would very often go into her room and sit on her bed, refusing to move until he heard her coming into the house. But he was too old for that now.

There was a baseball bat leaning against the wall of the porch and he picked it up and rubbed his hand along it. Then he took up a stance in front of the mirror, his left leg out in front of him the way Jeff had shown him and a good distance between his feet. He waved the bat gently and menacingly over his shoulder, waiting for the pitch, staring at himself in the mirror with cold, alert eyes. He stepped in, in a nice clean movement, the way Jeff had showed him, and swung at a waist-high ball, bending his knees a little, watching himself closely in the mirror. He let two balls go past, twitching his bat a little, but they were wide. Then he swung four or five more times, remembering to snap his wrists and get his shoulders behind the ball and remembering not to step in the bucket. When he had enough of batting he went over and picked up the fielder's glove and ball. He and Jeff had a game that they played. They threw pickups and backhand catches to each other and the one who missed ten first, lost. They kept the score with a pencil on one of the shingles of the porch. Jeff had won twenty-two times and Tony had won twice. With the ball, in front of the mirror, Tony practised pickups and backhands and a funny catch with the glove held close to his belly for high pop flies that Jeff called a basket catch and which he said was a specialty of a shortstop called Rabbit Maranville who played for Boston. It wasn't as easy as it looked, especially if at the same time you had to watch yourself in the mirror. While he was in the middle of it he heard someone come up behind him. He didn't turn around and a moment later he saw that it was Susan Nickerson. She was dressed in the blue jeans and sweater which seemed to be her uniform. He had seen her earlier in the day at the hotel, just before the hayride. He'd asked her if she was going but she had said, 'No. Hayrides are for kids.'

He threw the ball up two or three more times, not too hard, making sure that he would catch it each time that it came down, conscious of Susan watching him. Finally she was the one to talk

6

first. 'Hi,' she said and he had a small sensation of victory 'Hi,' he said, continuing to toss and catch the ball.

Susan came up closer to him and looked at him suspiciously. 'What are you doing there?'

'Developing my hands,' Tony said. 'One thing an infielder has to have is sure hands.'

'What do you need the mirror for?' Susan asked. She looked into the glass above Tony's shoulder and pushed delicately at her hair. Her hair was long for a girl her age and was cut in a way that made her look much older than she was.

'To correct my form,' Tony said. 'All the big ones use mirrors.' Susan sighed as if this subject, like all others, proved, upon examination, to be instantaneously boring. For a moment she peered closely at Tony with her animal trainer's expression, as though she were figuring out just how to handle this particular beast at this particular moment. Then she began to prowl slowly around the porch, picking up books, staring at them coldly, letting them drop, touching a magazine with her fingertips, standing in front of the gramophone and listening without pleasure to the music that was blaring out of the loudspeaker. 'Are you alone?' she asked.

'Yeah.'

'This place sure is dead,' Susan said. 'Isn't it?'

Tony shrugged and turned away from the mirror, making a pocket in the glove with his other fist. 'I don't know,' he said. 'Maybe for girls.'

'Where's Jeff?' Susan asked flatly.

'He went into Rutland,' Tony said. 'He had a bad tooth.'

'Uh-huh,' Susan said, in her policewoman's voice. 'Rutland.' She turned the volume of the gramophone down a little. 'Where's your mother?' she asked, in the tone of a hostess politely making conversation on a subject which was of no interest to her, for the benefit of an awkward guest.

'She went to the movies,' Tony said. 'I'll be able to go to the movies myself in about another month.'

'She went to the movies,' Susan said, putting only a fraction of a question mark at the end of the phrase.

'Yeah.'

'What's playing?'

'I don't know,' Tony said.

'Ask her when she gets back.' Susan turned the gramophone down even lower.

'Why?'

'Just curious,' Susan said. 'Maybe I'll ask my mother to take me tonight. Where did you get the gramophone?'

'It's Jeff's,' Tony said. 'He got it from an aunt as a present when he went away to college. She's rich and she's always giving him presents. He has a library of eight hundred and forty-five records. He's an expert on swing.'

'He thinks he's something,' Susan said. 'Doesn't he?'

'He *is* something,' said Tony.

'He talks as though he's fifty years old,' said Susan. From the tone in which she said it, it was clear that she considered this one of the gravest charges possible to make against a man.

'He's the smartest man you're ever likely to know,' said Tony combatively.

'That's what you think,' said Susan.

Tony would have liked to say something crushing and final. But nothing crushing came to his mind. 'Yeah,' he said lamely, and knowing that it sounded lame, 'that's what I think.'

Susan went over to the gramophone and switched it off. The music ended with a sliding, unpleasant sound.

'What did you do that for?' Tony asked.

'I hate jazz,' said Susan. 'I only listen to the classics. I play three instruments.'

Tony went over to the gramophone and started it again. 'Well, I like it,' he said. 'And this is my house.'

'It's your father's house,' Susan said, like a lawyer. 'He pays the rent.'

'If it's my father's,' said Tony, 'it's mine.'

'That doesn't necessarily follow,' said Susan. 'Still, if that's the way you feel, I'll leave.'

'Go ahead,' said Tony, but with no conviction in his voice.

'Okay,' said Susan. 'I only came around because this place is so dead.' She started off the porch slowly, with her little, bumpy, beach-balloon walk. Tony watched her obliquely, glumly. Then with a sudden movement he picked the playing arm off the record and stopped the machine. 'Aaah . . .' he said, 'I'm not crazy about this record anyway.'

A bleak, swift smile of satisfaction crossed the girl's face, the policewoman at the moment of confession. 'That's better,' she said. She came back on to the porch.

'What three instruments do you play?' Tony asked.

'The piano, the trombone and the 'cello.'

Impressed despite himself and determined not to show it, Tony competed with her by picking up the telescope and staring up with an expert air at the sky. 'The sky,' he said, 'is full of *cirrus* cumulus clouds. The ceiling is about a thousand feet and visibility is less than a mile.'

'Who wants to know stuff like that?'

'And at Mount Wilson, that's in California, they got a telescope so strong they can see the stars in the daytime. I bet you didn't know that either.'

'Who wants to know about that?'

Gently, triumphantly, Tony closed the trap. 'Who wants to know how to play the 'cello?' he asked.

'I do,' said Susan. 'I show a lot of promise.'

'Who told you?' Tony asked sceptically. He had discovered that a mixture of scepticism and hostility served to bridge the gap in age and sex between them and put him, at least for the moment, on a footing of approximate equality with her.

'Mr. Bradley told me,' Susan said. 'He's the music teacher at school. He conducts the orchestra and the band. I play the trombone in the band at football games because you can't carry a 'cello around with you. Mr. Bradley says I have great natural ability. He tried to kiss me in the auditorium last winter. He tries to kiss all the girls. He kissed three of the first violinists last year.'

'What did he want to do that for?' Tony asked, trying not to show how fascinating he found the conversation.

Susan shrugged. 'He likes it.'

'What did you do when he tried to kiss you?'

'I let him,' Susan said flatly.

'Why?'

'Why not?' Susan said. 'But when he tried to rub me I told him I would go to the principal and he stopped. He's very artistic, Mr. Bradley. When he plays the violin he closes his eyes. In the movies when they kiss they always close their eyes too. Your mother,' she said, 'she's at the movies now?'

'I told you.'

'I just wanted to make sure,' Susan said. She took a slow

84

deliberate turn around the porch, going up on her toes like a ballet dancer on each step. 'Did you ever kiss a girl?' she asked.

'I . . . I . . . sure,' Tony said.

'How many?'

Tony hesitated, searching for a reasonable number. 'Seventeen,' he said finally.

Susan came up to him and stood in front of him. He noticed uncomfortably that she was at least two inches taller than he was. 'Let me see,' she said coldly.

'What do you mean?' Tony said, stalling for time and trying to make his voice low and gruff.

'Let me see.' A weary flicker of a smile twitched across Susan's face without making a change in her cold, coin-like, mistrustful blue eyes. 'I bet,' she said, 'you never kissed a girl in your whole life.'

'I did so,' Tony said, feeling cornered and wishing he was at least two inches taller.

'I dare you,' said Susan.

'Okay,' Tony said. He felt as if he had a fever and he wished that somebody would come in quickly and interrupt them. But nobody came. He advanced warily and kissed Susan. His aim was off for the first kiss and he landed more or less on her chin. She bent her knees a little and this time he found her mouth. He kissed her quickly, just long enough to show that he wasn't afraid to do it. 'There,' he said, his arm still around her.

'Take your glasses off,' Susan said.

Tony took off his glasses and put them carefully on the gramophone. Then he kissed her again. She tasted pleasantly of spearmint chewing gum and he began to enjoy it.

Satisfied in her experiment, Susan stepped back. 'This place is dead,' she said. She took a pocket mirror and a lipstick out of her blue jeans and did her mouth, making Tony wish that he didn't feel so feverish and that he was at least five years older. 'If there were any boys of my age group around,' said Susan, 'I wouldn't even be here.'

Tony stared at her, puzzled. He knew that he was hurt but he didn't know why he should feel that way. Distractedly he picked up his telescope and stared at the sky. 'The ceiling is lifting,' he said.

Susan studied him bleakly, the animal trainer deciding to try one last turn before closing the cage for the night. 'Do you know what grownups do when they go to sleep together?' Susan asked.

'Sure,' Tony said falsely.

'What do they do?' Susan asked.

Tony remembered what young Barker had told him on this subject. But it was all so confused in his mind and Barker had been so vague about actual details that to try to repeat what he had heard to Susan would only show her how hopelessly ignorant he was. 'Well,' he said uncomfortably, 'I only know kind of . . .'

'Do you or don't you?' Susan asked implacably.

Tony reached down and got his glasses and put them on again, fighting for time. 'Jeff started to tell me something the other day,' he mumbled. 'He said my father wanted him to. Something about . . . about seeds.'

'Seeds,' Susan snorted disdainfully. 'That shows how much you know.'

'How do *you* know so much?' Tony asked, hoping to save himself by attack.

'I watched my mother and father one night,' said Susan. 'My second father. They came home late and they thought I was sleeping and they forgot to close the door. Didn't you ever watch your father and mother?'

'No,' said Tony. 'They never do anything.'

'Sure they do,' said Susan.

'They do not.'

'Don't be a kid,' Susan said wearily. 'Everybody does.'

'Not my mother and father.' His voice was very high now. He didn't know why he felt he had to deny it so hotly, but it had something to do with the grunting pig-like noise Albert Barker had made.

'Stop saying that,' said Susan.

He felt himself on the verge of tears and he hated her for being there and talking like that. 'You're dirty,' he said. 'You're a dirty girl.'

'Don't call me names,' Susan said warningly.

'You're a dirty girl,' Tony repeated.

'Go see for yourself,' said Susan. 'And not with your father either.'

'You're a liar,' Tony said.

'The movies!' Susan made a contemptuous gesture with her hand. 'There are no movies except on Saturday and Sunday.

They can tell you anything, can't they, and you'll believe it? What a kid!' She made a savage, pointing gesture behind her. 'You go down to his sister's house and look through the window the way I did and you'll see whether I'm a liar or not.'

Tony swung at her with the telescope, clumsily, but she was very quick and stronger than he was. They wrestled for the telescope for a moment and she tore it from his hands and tossed it on to the floor. They stood there facing each other, panting. 'Don't you hit me,' Susan said. She pushed him away disdainfully. 'Baby,' she said. 'Stupid little baby. And don't forget to take your glasses.' She turned on her heel and went off, her hips swinging under the tight blue jeans.

Tony stared after her, biting back tears. Then, without knowing why he did it, he went into the house, into his mother's room and sat down on his mother's bed. The room smelled of his mother's perfume and the special soap she used that she had sent up from New York. Then he jumped up and went out on the porch again. It was quiet and the clouds had come even lower and the lake looked meaner and greyer than before. He stood there in the silence for a moment, then jumped off the porch and began to run through the woods, along the lakeshore, in the direction of Jeff's sister's house.

Chapter Ten

It was almost dark as Lucy and Jeff approached the cottage. Through a break in the clouds the sun could be seen setting behind the mountains, its level rays without heat turning the lake into a leaden rose colour. Across the water a bugle blew. It sounded much farther away than usual, wavery and muffled and saddened by the thick weather. Lucy was wearing a raincoat draped like a cape across her shoulders and it fell in stiff archaic folds around her body as she walked slowly, with Jeff a pace behind her, across the lawn towards the cottage. She climbed the two steps to the porch and stopped, listening to the bugle. She started to take the coat off and Jeff reached out and lifted it from her shoulders and put it down on a chair and turned her round slowly. She ducked a little and smiled up at him, her head tilted to one side. His face seemed to be fragmented in the oblique sunset light into four or five different expressions, as though he were not quite sure whether he was, at the moment, the conqueror or the conquered, whether he was happy remembering the afternoon or in despair because it was over. The brass notes from across the lake died away and Lucy went over to a table and picked up a package of cigarettes that was lying on it.

'No matter where I am,' Jeff said, lighting her cigarette, 'whenever I hear a bugle call from now on, it will make me remember.'

'Shh . . .' Lucy said.

Jeff tossed the match away and stared at her, at the long, grey, half-closed, smiling eyes, with their incongruous hint of the Orient and their look of guarding a secret she would never disclose, at the full soft lips that now, without any lipstick on them blending into the tan skin of her face, seemed almost colourless. 'Oh, Lord,' he said softly. Without embracing her he ran one hand slowly and lightly down her side and then made a slow, caressing movement across her belly. 'What an excellent place,' he whispered.

Lucy chuckled. 'Shh . . .' she said.

She captured his hand, raised it to her mouth and kissed the inside of the palm.

'Tonight,' Jeff began.

Lucy kissed his fingertips with a light brisk smack of the lips, as one might kiss a child's hand. 'That's all,' she said. She dropped his hand and opened the door of the cottage. 'Tony,' she called into the house. 'Tony, where are you?' There was no answer and she turned back to Jeff. He had picked up the glove and ball that Tony had dropped an hour before and was tossing the ball up and making fancy little backhand catches.

'He's probably still on the hayride,' Jeff said. 'Don't worry. He'll be back in time for dinner.'

'I want to go in and change my clothes,' said Lucy.

Jeff put the glove and ball down. 'Please don't,' he said to her. 'Stay here. You don't have to change. I'm crazy about this dress.' He touched the cotton where it flounced out at the hip. 'I'm cruelly attached to this dress.'

'All right,' she said. 'We do anything you want because . . .' She paused.

'Because why?' Jeff asked.

'Because you're twenty years old,' said Lucy.

'That's a hell of a reason,' Jeff said.

'There are no better ones, little boy,' Lucy said lightly. She lay back on the glider against the pillows, her legs over the edge, her feet on the floor. Jeff stood looking down at her as she let her head fall back, the smoke of the cigarette making her close her eyes.

'Oh, Lord,' Jeff murmured.

'You must stop saying "Oh, Lord," ' Lucy said.

'Why?'

'Because it brings in an entirely new concept. You'll end up by making me feel guilty and I don't want to feel guilty. And sit down. You mustn't loom over me all the time.'

Jeff sat on the floor, his back against the glider, his head near her waist. 'I like to loom over you.'

'Only at carefully specified hours,' said Lucy. She touched his head with her fingertips, on the back of his neck. 'Delicious,' she said. 'You must never let your hair grow long.'

'Okay,' said Jeff.

Lucy ran her hand over his head. 'You have a hard, persistent skull,' she said.

'Okay.'

'Your hair smells like Tony's,' said Lucy. 'Like summertime. Dry and sunshiny. When men get older their hair smells different. Cigarettes, worry, fatigue, barber shops.'

'What does fatigue smell like?' Jeff asked.

Lucy considered this. 'The way aspirin tastes,' she said finally. 'If I were a man I'd only make love to seventeen-year-old girls, glossy, plump, brand new.'

'If I were a man,' Jeff said, 'I would only make love to you.'

Lucy chuckled. 'What nice manners you have! Tell the truth. How many girls have you had?'

'One.'

'Oh,' Lucy said. 'That makes two, including me.'

'That makes one, including you.'

'You really do have nice manners. Of course I don't believe you.'

'All right,' Jeff said. 'I'll confess. I'm a dazzler. Half a dozen women have committed suicide for me since I was fifteen. I'm a bigamist. I'm wanted in ten different states by other names. I seduced my grandmother's best friend at the age of four and I've been busy ever since. I'm barred from the campuses of all the leading women's colleges in the East. My book, "How to Win, Hold and Get Rid of Women" has already been printed in a dozen countries, including several where the people only speak languages that have been dead two thousand years.'

'Enough. I get the idea,' said Lucy, laughing. 'You're funny. I thought young men today were terribly—well, you know, loose.'

'I'm the opposite of loose,' said Jeff.

Lucy lifted her head and examined him curiously. He didn't turn around. 'I believe you are,' said Lucy.

'I was waiting.'

'For what?'

'For you,' Jeff said.

'Be serious.'

'I am serious,' said Jeff. 'I was waiting for something'—he hesitated—'something overwhelming. I don't believe in anything casual or unimportant or imperfect. The girls I knew. They were pretty or cute or they were amusing. Never overwhelming.'

'My,' said Lucy. 'You *are* a romantic boy.'

'Love is either romantic,' Jeff said didactically, 'or you might just as well go to a gymnasium.'

Lucy chuckled. 'You *are* peculiar.' She sat up and spoke more seriously. 'And you thought I was overwhelming?'

'Yes.'

'That's the first time anybody ever thought anything like that about me,' Lucy said.

'How about your husband?' Jeff asked.

'I don't know,' Lucy said carefully. 'I imagine he thinks I'm comfortable.'

'It's not enough,' said Jeff.

'No?' Lucy's tone was guarded now. 'It has been up to now.'

'And now?'

Lucy tossed her cigarette away and straightened the folds of her dress with two or three efficient movements of her hand. 'And now,' she said, 'I think I'd like to go down to the bar and get a drink.' She stood up.

Without turning around, Jeff threw his arm back, to push her down gently again. 'What's it like—your marriage?'

'Why do you want to know?'

'I have to know,' Jeff said. 'I want to know everything about you. I want to see pictures of you when you were a little girl. I want to know what your maiden name was.'

'Hammond,' said Lucy.

'Hammond,' Jeff repeated. 'Lucy Hammond. Excellent. I want to know what books you read when you were fourteen years old.'

'*Wuthering Heights*,' said Lucy. '*Das Kapital* and *Little Women*.'

'Excellent,' said Jeff. 'I want to know what you expected to do with your life before you got married. I want to know what you talk about at dinner, at home with your husband.'

'Why?' Lucy asked.

'Because I want to own you. I want to own your past, and all the time you are away from me, and your future.'

'Be careful,' Lucy warned him.

'And I don't want to be careful,' he said, 'What about your marriage? The fundamental marriage?'

'I always thought,' Lucy said, speaking soberly, 'that it was satisfactory.'

'And now?'

'From the middle of September on I'll think it is satisfactory—again.'

Jeff stood up and walked towards the edge of the porch and leaned against the pillar, staring out at the lake.

'Lucy,' he said.

'Yes?'

'When he comes up here,' Jeff said in a low voice. 'Crown. Are you going to go to bed with him?' He turned and faced her.

Lucy stood up briskly and picked up her raincoat. 'I think it's time we went and got me that drink,' she said.

'Answer me,' said Jeff.

'You mustn't be silly.' There was a warning note in Lucy's voice now.

'Answer me.'

'It has nothing to do with us.' Lucy put on the raincoat and started to button it.

'I want you to promise me something,' Jeff said, not moving from the front of the porch, still leaning against the pillar.

'What?'

'I want you to promise not to have anything to do with your husband while . . .'

'While what?' Lucy asked.

'While we're together.'

Lucy finished buttoning the coat and put the collar up against her ears. 'And just how long will that be?'

Jeff swallowed miserably. 'I don't know,' he said.

'Give me a figure,' said Lucy. 'Two days? A week? A season? Five years?'

Jeff came over to her but didn't touch her. 'Don't be angry.' He spoke brokenly. 'It's just that I can't bear the thought . . . Listen, we can see each other all the time. I can come down to the city at least once a month. And the holidays—Thanksgiving, the Christmas vacation. And almost every week-end I can get into Boston.'

Lucy nodded as though she were taking this very seriously. 'Uhuh. Boston. What hotels do you propose I stop at? The Ritz? The Copley? Or perhaps one of the travelling-salesmen hotels. The Touraine? The Statler? And should I wear my wedding ring?'

Jeff put up his hands as though to ward off blows. 'Lucy,' he said, tortured. 'Don't.'

'And how should I introduce you in Boston?' Lucy went on. 'As my son? My nephew? An old friend?'

'Don't make it ugly,' Jeff said angrily.

'What do you propose I tell my husband? A person who shall be nameless has raised certain objections to . . .'

'Stop it,' Jeff said. 'There are a lot of ways of doing things like that.'

'Are there?' Lucy said, sounding agreeably surprised. 'Perhaps you'll write me a note. As a budding diplomat. It'll be good practice for you later on, when you have to send a protest to the Prime Minister of Iran or a sharp reminder to the Hungarian Foreign Office. Dear Sir: It has come to the attention of this office that there are several conflicting claims on the body of your wife . . .'

'Don't make fun of me,' said Jeff. He was sullen now. 'What do you expect me to do?' he pleaded. 'Lucy, darling, it's been perfect up to now. Are you going to blame me because I want to keep it that way?'

'Perfect.' Lucy nodded in ironic agreement. 'They loved each other perfectly—on school holidays, in various inexpensive hotel rooms—and the young man always managed to get to his first class on Monday on time. Is that your idea of perfect?'

'Oh, God,' Jeff said. 'I feel so trapped. If I were older, settled, with some money of my own . . .'

'Then what?' Lucy challenged him.

'Then we could go off together,' Jeff said. 'Get married. Live together.'

Lucy hesitated for a moment. Then she spoke in a low, assuaging voice. 'Be glad,' she said, 'that you're not older, settled, with money of your own.'

'Why?'

'Because I wouldn't go with you.'

'Don't say that.'

'And then,' Lucy said, 'you'd blame yourself instead of your youth or your poverty. And it would hurt a lot more. This way you can go back in the autumn and boast in the dormitories on the cold nights about the lively summer you had at your sister's house in the mountains. I can just hear you say it now and I forgive you in advance and half envy you the pleasure you're going to have in saying it. "I don't know what it is about me," you can say, "but married women of a certain age"—you can wink at the other boys here—"just throw themselves at me." '

'What are you trying to do?' Jeff asked.

'I'm trying to tell you,' Lucy said, 'that summertime is summertime. That the hotels close. That the cottages are shuttered against the snow. That the lake freezes over. That the birds fly south. That the children go back to school and the grownups go back to . . . to shopping lists, bridge games, imperfection, security, reality . . .'

Now Jeff's face looked stricken in the last cold rays of the sun. 'You don't love me,' he said.

Lucy came over to him, smiling gently. 'Even that isn't quite true,' she said. Lightly she took his chin in her hand and kissed him. Then she relinquished him. 'Don't look so sad, little boy,' she said, turning away. 'The summertime still has two weeks to go.'

Jeff took a step after her and then stopped because he saw Tony coming out of the shade of the trees, walking slowly towards the house across the lawn. Lucy saw him at the same time and stepped off the porch to greet the boy. Tony stopped and regarded his mother and Jeff without expression. He looked tired and, in the grey light, pale.

'Hullo, Tony,' Lucy said. 'Where have you been until now?'

'No place much,' Tony said. He carefully avoided going close to his mother as he stepped on the porch.

'How was the hayride?' Jeff asked.

'Okay,' said Tony. He leaned against the wall of the porch and examined Jeff. 'How's your tooth?'

'Okay,' said Jeff.

'Did you have a good time at the movies?' Tony asked his mother. 'What was playing?'

'I . . . I didn't go,' Lucy said. 'I found out that they only showed them on week-ends.'

'Oh,' said Tony politely. 'Where did you go?'

'I did a little shopping,' Lucy said. 'For antiques.'

'Did you buy anything?' Tony asked.

'No,' said Lucy. 'Everything is too expensive. I just looked around. Jeff and I are going down to the hotel for a drink. Do you want to join us? You can have a Coke.'

'I'm not thirsty,' Tony said.

'Even so,' Lucy said.

'I'm not thirsty,' Tony repeated.

Lucy went over to him and felt his forehead. 'Are you all right?'

The boy twisted away. 'I'm fine,' he said. 'I'm just a little tired,' he explained vaguely. 'The hayride. I missed my nap. I think I'll just lie down for fifteen minutes.' Then, afraid that his mother would bustle over him, he smiled widely, disingenuously, at her. 'Those hayrides are rough,' he said. 'See you later.' He went in and lay down on his bed. He lay stiffly, with his eyes open, and when he heard his mother and Jeff walk past his window on the way down to the hotel bar, he counted up to five hundred slowly, one by one, and then went into the living room and called his father in Hartford.

Chapter Eleven

THE car was mud-spattered when it drove up to the cottage and the wipers had made two smeary crescents on the windshield, which gleamed dully in the reflection of the headlights off the wet trees. Oliver stopped the car and sat for a moment at the wheel, resting after the long drive in the rain. There was a light on in the cottage but Oliver saw no one moving within. He got out of the car, carrying his raincoat and a small overnight bag that he had thrown into the back of the car. He went in the front door. The room was empty. The only sound to be heard was the small drip of rain from the maple whose branches hung over one side of the house. There were newspapers scattered on the table in the middle of the room and a book was lying open, face down, on the couch. There were some chessmen scattered over the chessboard and two or three of the pieces had fallen to the floor. Some petals had drifted down from a bunch of peonies in a vase on the mantelpiece and had dropped on to the rug.

Standing there, looking at the empty room, Oliver thought, whenever she's anywhere for five minutes she creates a small unimportant disorder. Sometimes it gave him a sense of pleasure, of intimacy, of indulgent understanding, when he saw a room like that after Lucy had been in it. But tonight, after the long trip, he was annoyed by it.

He took off his hat and rubbed his hands to warm them. There was no fire on the hearth. He looked at the clock on the mantelpiece. It was two minutes past eight. As always, Oliver had arrived exactly when he said he would arrive. He went into the kitchen to look for the bottle of whisky that was kept in the cupboard above the icebox. There were some dishes left in the sink from the afternoon's tea. Three cups, he noticed, three saucers, some plates with crumbs of chocolate cake. He took down the whisky and poured himself a drink. He didn't bother to put any water in it and went back into the living room and sat down wearily, sipping the drink, waiting. A moment later he heard footsteps on the porch. The door opened and Tony came in, wearing a baseball cap. Tony stopped just inside the door. He seemed almost reluctant to come into the room.

'Hullo, Tony,' Oliver said, smiling at him.

'Daddy,' Tony said. He approached Oliver as though to kiss him and stopped at a little distance from him.

Oliver took off his cap and ruffled his hair gently in a slight affectionate movement. 'You're being pretty mysterious, Tony,' Oliver said, making a little joke out of it. 'Not telling me what was wrong on the phone. Insisting that I get up here exactly at eight o'clock. Telling me not to speak to your mother.'

'You're sure you didn't call her?' Tony asked suspiciously.

'I didn't call her,' Oliver said. There was no sense in telling Tony that he had tried to telephone en route from Waterbury, but that there had been a break in the line because of the rain and he hadn't been able to get through.

'She doesn't know you're here?' Tony asked.

'No,' Oliver said. 'I came in the back way, as you said, during dinnertime. Tony,' he asked mildly, 'are you sure you're not reading too many comic books?'

'I don't read any comic books,' Tony said.

'You've had me worried all day,' Oliver said gently.

'I'm sorry.'

'Come over here and sit down.' Oliver indicated a chair close to his. Tony came slowly over to the chair and seated himself. Oliver sipped his drink. 'Now—what is it?'

'Daddy,' Tony said in a low voice, 'I want to go home.'

'Oh.' Oliver looked pensively at his glass. 'Why?'

Tony made a restless movement with his hands. 'I've had enough of this place.'

'It's done you a lot of good, Tony,' said Oliver. 'You look very healthy and brown and Mother writes me that . . .'

'I want to go home,' Tony said flatly.

Oliver sighed. 'Did you tell that to your mother?'

'No,' said Tony. 'There's no use talking to her.'

Oliver nodded indulgently. 'Ah,' he said, 'you two have had a little argument.'

'No.'

Oliver took another sip of his drink. 'With Jeff?'

Tony didn't answer for a moment. 'With nobody,' he said. 'Can't a fellow want to go home with his own father once in a while without everybody jumping on him?'

'Nobody's jumping on you, Tony,' Oliver said reassuringly. 'Only you have to expect people to ask you a question or two when you make long-distance phone calls and give all sorts of mysterious instructions. Be reasonable, Tony.'

'I am reasonable,' Tony said, sounding cornered. 'I want to go home because I don't want to be in the same place with Mother and Jeff.'

Oliver put his glass down and spoke very gently. 'What did you say, Tony?'

'I don't want to stay here with Mother and Jeff.'

'Why?'

'I can't tell you.'

Oliver glanced sharply at the boy. He was sitting with his head bent, staring at his shoes, his hands plunged in his pockets, looking resentful and embarrassed. 'Tony,' Oliver said, 'we've always been on the level with each other, haven't we?'

'Yes.'

'I've always told you what was bothering me and you've always told me, up to now,' Oliver said. 'Am I right?'

'Yes.'

'Have I ever promised you anything I didn't do for you,' Oliver asked.

'No,' said Tony.

'When you asked me questions, have I ever given you an untruthful answer?'

'No.'

'When you began to get into that habit last summer of telling fancy stories,' Oliver said, 'like saying you swam across the lake one afternoon when you couldn't swim at all and saying that old Mr. Norton invited you out to his ranch in Wyoming for a month and was going to give you your own horse. . . .'

'That was just kid stuff,' Tony said.

'I know.' Oliver nodded reasonably. 'Didn't I tell you I knew and understood? It was all right to tell me those stories and not anyone else because I knew you were just having fun and using your imagination. But other people who didn't know you the way I did might have begun to think you couldn't be trusted and that you told lies.'

'I don't tell stories any more,' Tony said. 'Not to anyone.'

'Of course,' said Oliver. 'And even about your eyes—there were a couple of times in the beginning when it was awfully hard to tell you what was wrong and what the chances were. When you get to be a father, Tony, you'll understand what it meant to me.' He stopped. 'But I did it,' he said. 'Didn't I?'

'Yes,' said Tony.

'Do you know why I did it?'

'I think so.' Tony's voice was down to a whisper now.

'Because I wanted everything to be clear and straight between us,' said Oliver. 'Because a long time from now, when you're a man as old as I am now, I want you to be able to say, no matter what else happens in your life, "There was honour between my father and me." ' Oliver leaned over and patted Tony's knee.

Then he stood up, walked over to the front door and looked out into the wet night.

Tony raised his head and stared at his father's back, his lips trembling. He waited for Oliver to say something more, but Oliver remained quiet and Tony got up and crossed and stood next to him. 'I don't know how to say it,' he whispered. 'Mother and Jeff . . . They're doing something wrong. They're doing what grownups do when they're married. I want to go home.'

Oliver closed his eyes momentarily. He hadn't known what to expect after Tony's call, but he hadn't expected this. He'd told himself, as he sat at the wheel peering through the rain all day, that it was just some child's crisis that would probably be over by the time he arrived. He wouldn't even have come up, really, if things hadn't been slow at the works this week. Now—he thought, this is something different. This is like hearing cries from the nursery and going in thinking you are going to separate two children who'd hit each other with pillows or toys and finding, upon opening the door, one child lying in a pool of blood and the other standing over him with a knife in his hand. 'Who told you that, Tony?' he asked.

'Susan,' Tony said.

'Who's Susan?'

'She's here with her mother at the hotel. Susan Nickerson. She's fourteen years old. She has three fathers. Her mother was divorced twice. She knows a lot of things.'

'Is that why you asked me to come up here, Tony?' Oliver asked. 'Is that the only reason?'

Tony paused. 'Yes,' he said.

'Tony,' Oliver said, choosing his words meticulously, 'in a place like this in the summertime there are often idle women, women of bad character, women who have nothing else to do but sit and play bridge and make up stories about their neighbours, stories that a decent person mustn't even listen to. And often little girls of fourteen who are just beginning to become interested in boys hear bits and scraps that are not meant for them and build them up into . . . uh . . . colourful fairy tales. Especially a little girl whose mother has gone from husband to husband.'

'I hit her,' Tony said. 'I hit Susan when she told me.'

Oliver smiled. 'I don't think you should have hit her. But I don't think you should have listened to her either. Tony, will you do me a favour?'

'What?' His voice was suspicious.

'Don't say anything about this to your mother,' said Oliver. 'Or to Jeff. We'll just pretend that I suddenly found out I could have some time off and I jumped into the car and came up here. Don't you think that's a good idea?'

Tony moved away as though he were in pain. 'No.'

'Why not?' Oliver asked.

'Because Susan wasn't the only one.'

Oliver put his arm around the boy's shoulders. 'Just because two or three or a hundred people gossip,' he said, 'doesn't mean they're saying the truth. Do you know what gossip is?'

'Yes,' said Tony.

'It s one of the worst things in the world,' said Oliver. 'It's a grownup disease. And one way a good man remains a child all his life is that he doesn't gossip and he doesn't listen to gossip.'

Suddenly Tony pulled away from his father's grasp. 'It's me! . . . It's me! I went down to his sister's house yesterday and I looked through the window and I saw with my own eyes.' He turned and, almost running, went across the room and flung himself into the easy chair, burying his face away from Oliver, into the wing. He was crying, racked by the effort of pretending he was not crying.

Oliver ran his hand wearily across his eyes and walked over to the easy chair and sat on the arm. 'All right, all right now.' He stroked the boy's head. 'Tony, I hate to have to do this. But I don't know what else I can do. You're very young. I don't know what you know and what you don't know. You might see something you think is very wrong and it could be completely innocent. Tony,' he said, 'you must tell me exactly what you saw.'

Tony spoke without turning his head, into the crease of the chair. 'She said she was going to the movies. But Susan was right. She wasn't in the movies. I went down to his sister's house. She's not here this week and there's nobody in the house. There're Venetian blinds on the windows. They don't come all the way down. There's a little space at the bottom and you can look in. They were in bed together and they . . . they didn't have any clothes on. And Mummy was kissing . . .' Tony swung around and faced his father. 'I want to go home . . . I want to go home.' Now he wept, inconsolably and openly.

Oliver sat on the arm of the chair, rocklike, taut, watching his son weep. 'Stop crying, Tony,' he said in a hoarse whisper. 'You haven't cried since you were a little boy.' He stood up and pulled Tony out of the chair. 'Go in now and wash your face,' he said in a colourless voice.

'What are you going to do?' Tony asked.

Oliver shook his head. 'I don't know,' he said.

'You're not going away, are you?'

'No,' said Oliver. 'I'll just sit out here for a while. Go ahead, Tony. Your eyes are all red.'

Slowly, his feet shuffling along the floor, Tony went into the bathroom. Oliver watched him go and shook his head vaguely. He walked heavily and pointlessly around the chilly room. There was a straw handbag with a bright orange scarf tossed over it that Lucy had left on a chair. He stopped in front of the chair and picked up the scarf. He put the scarf to his face and sniffed the perfume that Lucy had put on it. He bent again and opened the bag and rummaged in it. There was a small compact there and he opened it. The powder was spilled all over the mirror. He put the compact on the table and neatly took out all the other things from the bag and with absent precision arranged them on the table. There was a tiny bottle of perfume, a bunch of keys, a comb. A clipping from a newspaper of a recipe. The recipe was for angel-food cake. He took out a small coin purse. He opened the purse and took the coins out of it and made a neat little pile of the coins. They came to seventy-eight cents. Then he methodically put all the things back into the bag, one by one. He heard voices, Lucy's and Jeff's, outside the cottage, and their footsteps on the porch and he composed his face and turned towards the door as it swung open. Lucy came in, followed by Jeff. She was laughing. When she saw Oliver standing in the middle of the room, the shadow of a frown crossed her face. Then she said, 'Oliver,' sounding pleased and surprised, and ran across the room to throw her arms around him and kiss him. Tactfully, Jeff waited at the door until the embrace was over.

Oliver kissed her on the cheek. 'Hullo, Lucy,' he said pleasantly.

'What are you doing here?' Lucy bubbled on. 'Why didn't you telephone? How long are you going to stay? Have you had your dinner? What a lovely surprise! Have you seen Tony?'

Oliver chuckled. 'Easy now,' he said. 'One thing at a time. Hullo, Bunner.'

'Welcome, Mr. Crown,' Jeff said with boyish politeness, standing very straight.

Lucy took Oliver's hand and led him to the couch. 'Come over here and sit down,' she said. 'You look tired. Can I get you something? A drink? A sandwich?'

'Nothing,' said Oliver. 'I ate on the road.'

Jeff looked at his watch. 'It's getting late,' he said. 'I guess I might as well be moving on.'

'Oh, no. Please stay,' Oliver said. He wasn't sure whether Lucy glanced at him uneasily or not. 'There are a few things I'd like to talk to you about. Unless you're busy.'

'No,' said Jeff. 'I'm not busy.'

'Have you seen Tony?' Lucy asked.

'Yes,' said Oliver. 'He's inside. In the bathroom.'

'Doesn't he look marvellous?' Lucy asked.

Oliver nodded. 'Marvellous.'

'Did I tell you he swam a hundred yards this week?' Lucy asked. She seemed to Oliver to be speaking more quickly than he remembered, like a pianist who is suffering from an attack of nerves before an audience and to make up for it finds himself going faster and faster through the difficult passages. 'Way, way out on the lake,' Lucy said. 'With Jeff following him in a boat. My heart was in my mouth and . . .'

'I just talked to him for a minute,' Oliver said. He turned pleasantly towards Jeff. 'Are you taking all your meals at the hotel now?'

'This week,' Lucy broke in hastily before Jeff could reply. 'His sister's away this week and the poor boy was faced with two cans of salmon and we took pity on him.'

'Oh, I see.' Oliver smiled. 'You both look as though the summer has agreed with you.'

'It hasn't been too bad,' Lucy said. 'It's rained a lot, though. Now what about you? How'd you manage to break away? Did all those charming people at the works go on strike all of a sudden?'

'Nothing as lively as that,' Oliver said. 'I just managed to sneak some time off.'

'It's been awful in the city, hasn't it?' Lucy asked.

'Oh, not so bad.'

Lucy patted his hand. 'We missed you so. Tony asked when you could come. You're going to stay now, aren't you?'

'I don't know,' Oliver said. 'That depends.'

'Oh,' said Lucy. 'Depends.' She wandered back towards the little hall that led to the bedrooms and called, 'Tony! Tony!'

'Leave him alone, please,' Oliver said. 'I'd like to talk to you, Lucy.'

Jeff, still standing near the door, coughed, a little awkwardly. 'In that case,' he said, 'I'd better . . .'

'And to you too, Jeff, if you don't mind,' Oliver said pleasantly. 'Would you think I was rude if I asked you to wait down by the lake for a few minutes? I see it's stopped raining. I'd like to speak to my wife alone and then—if it's all right with you—I'll call you.'

'Of course,' said Jeff easily. 'Take as long as you want.'

'Thanks,' Oliver said, as Jeff went out the door.

Lucy felt her mouth get dry and she wanted to call to Jeff, 'Stay! Stay! Give me time!'

But she watched him go out, and then, trying to swallow, to restore the moisture in her mouth and throat, she made herself go over to Oliver. She was almost sure she was smiling, as she put her arms around him. The important thing, at this moment, she thought, is to be normal. What would be normal, though? She had a flicker of panic, at the impossibility of knowing what normal was.

'It's so good to see you again,' she said. 'It's been such a long time.'

Normal.

To give herself something to do, to prolong time, she made herself examine Oliver's face closely. The long, hard, familiar face, the pale, clever, knowing eyes, the set, pale mouth, so surprisingly soft when he kissed her, the hard, smooth texture of the skin. She touched, with the tips of her fingers, the marks of fatigue under his eyes. 'You look so tired.'

'Stop saying I look tired,' Oliver said with a first little flash of anger.

Lucy moved away from him. Everything I am going to do, she thought, is going to be wrong. 'I'm sorry,' she said in a small voice. 'You said your staying here depends—On what?'

'On you.'

'Oh.' Lucy clenched her hands, unconsciously, squeezing her fingers. 'On me?'

Suddenly the light was too bright in the room and everything stood out too clearly, the sharp, ugly lines of the table, the hideous yellow of the curtains, the worn drab spots on the arms of the easy chair. Everything was angular and hurtful and time was moving too fast, like a train going downhill into a tunnel. How wonderful it would be if she could faint, if she could make time for herself in darkness, prepare in a warm, protective haze for the hard thing that was ahead of her. It's unfair, she thought confusedly, the most important act of my life, and nobody gives me time to get ready for it.

'You know what I would like,' she said lightly, still almost sure she was smiling, 'I would like a drink and . . .'

Oliver reached over and took her wrist. 'Come here, Lucy.' He led her to the couch. 'Sit down.'

They sat down next to each other.

This is the millionth time, she thought, we have sat next to each other.

Lucy laughed, letting things happen, not trying to guide them. 'My, you're serious,' she said.

'Very serious,' Oliver said.

'Oh.' Lucy's voice was small, domestic, apologetic. 'Have I spent too much money? Did I overdraw at the bank again?'

There, that wasn't a bad thing to say, she thought. Just let it happen.

'Lucy,' Oliver said, 'have you been having an affair?'

Let it happen. Say the normal thing. He was sitting there like a teacher in school, asking her questions, grading her. Suddenly she realized that she had been afraid of him for fifteen years, every minute for fifteen years.

'What?' she asked, proud of the tone of amusement and incredulity in her voice. This is only temporary, she thought. Later on, when we have more time, we will talk seriously. Later on, we will lead up to the permanent truth.

'An affair,' Oliver was saying.

Lucy wrinkled her forehead, looking puzzled, as if Oliver had presented her with a riddle, but a riddle she was prepared to enjoy, once she understood its intent. 'With whom?' she asked.

'Bunner,' Oliver said.

For a moment Lucy seemed stupefied. Then she began to laugh. Somewhere inside me, she thought, there is the perfect model of an innocent wife, who makes the correct noise and gives the correct answer to all questions. All I have to do is mimic her automatically. 'Oh, my,' Lucy said. 'With that child?'

Oliver watched her closely, already almost convinced because he was so ready to be convinced. 'You must get over your habit of thinking men are children until they reach the age of fifty,' he said mildly.

'Poor Jeff.' Lucy was still laughing. 'He'd be so proud if he could hear you. Why,' she said, feeling her face frozen in the difficult lines of laughter and inventing spontaneously and without plan, 'why, all last winter he was going to dances with a girl who's still in high school in Boston. She's a cheer leader. She wears those short skirts and does somersaults at the high-school football games every Saturday afternoon and they can't go to bars when they have dates because none of the bartenders will serve them.' Listening carefully to herself with her inner ear she sought and found the proper tone of incredulous amusement. It's like a dive, she thought. Once you start, there's no turning back, no matter how high it suddenly seems, or how deep the water below, or how frightened you are or how much you regret having started. 'Is that why you came up here like this?' she asked.

'Yes,' said Oliver.

'That long, long ride all alone,' said Lucy pityingly. The middle of the dive, going through the air, balancing. 'Poor Oliver. Still, if that's the only way I can get you up here, I'm satisfied.' Then she spoke more seriously. 'Now how did you happen to get an idea like that? What happened? Did you get an anonymous poison-pen letter from one of those old hens up in the hotel? I have nothing to do with them and I suppose that annoys them. They see me and Tony and Jeff together all the time and they love to have a scandal to munch on and . . .'

'I didn't get any anonymous letters,' Oliver said.

'No?' Lucy challenged him. 'Then what?'

'It's Tony,' said Oliver. 'He called me last night. He asked me to come up here.'

'Oh,' said Lucy. 'And you didn't call me back?'

'He asked me not to,' said Oliver.

'So that's why he rushed away from dinner. So that's why you came at this odd hour,' she said sardonically. 'For the secret rendezvous of the males of the family.'

'Well, the truth is,' Oliver said, on the defensive, 'I did try to call from Waterbury, but the line was out this afternoon. He didn't tell me anything on the phone. He was almost hysterical. He kept saying that he had to see me alone.'

'I . . . I'm ashamed,' Lucy said, quoting the impeccable model within her. 'Of you. Of Tony. Myself. Our marriage.'

'What would you have done?' Oliver said miserably. 'If Tony had called you and said that I . . .'

'What have I always done?' Lucy said quickly.

'There's never been anything with me,' Oliver said. 'You know that.'

'No? Maybe not,' Lucy said. 'Who's to know? I haven't asked. Still—is that the only thing in the world? Is that the only problem that people who've been married for fifteen years have to face? Have I ever lied to you? Have I ever hidden anything from you?'

'No,' Oliver said wearily, and Lucy had the feeling that he was almost ready to let the whole matter drop.

'Suddenly,' she said, speaking swiftly, pressing her advantage, 'everything changes. Now is the time for conspiracy and secret visits and spying and the testimony of children. Why?'

'All right,' Oliver said. 'I admit—I should have called. But it still doesn't answer the question. Why did Tony tell me what he did?'

'How do I know?' Lucy said. 'I don't even know what he told you.'

'Lucy,' said Oliver gently, 'he said he saw you and the young man in his sister's house.'

End of dive.

Lucy took in her breath with a sighing noise. 'Oh. He said that?'

'Yes.'

She spoke in a flat, dead voice. 'What exactly did he say he saw?'

'I can't repeat it, Lucy.'

'You can't repeat it,' she said, her voice still lacking in timbre.

'No,' said Oliver, 'but unhappily, it was most convincing.'

'Oh . . . I'm so sorry.' Lucy bent over and he couldn't see her face and for a moment he thought she was going to confess. 'Mostly for Tony,' she said. Mistake. The dive was not over. Because it wasn't a real dive. It was a descent in a dream, whirling, grabbing handfuls of air. 'Listen, Oliver,' she said soberly. 'There're several things you ought to know about your son. Not such pleasant things. You know how he makes up stories? Let's use the exact words. Lies. How many times have we pleaded with him?'

'He's stopped that,' said Oliver.

'That's what you think,' said Lucy. 'It's just that the stories become more clever as he grows older. More ingenious, more believable, less innocent.'

'I thought he was getting over that,' Oliver said.

'That's because you don't know him. You see him a few hours a week when he's on his best behaviour. You don't know him the way I do, because you haven't been with him day and night for years.' Arson, she thought, horrified with herself. Once you light the match, there's nothing to do but stand back and watch the house burn down. And deny everything and solidify the alibi. 'That's why this has happened,' she said. 'The truth is he doesn't behave with me like a normal little boy. He behaves like a jealous, possessive lover. You said so yourself.'

'Not really,' Oliver said. 'Not seriously. As a joke maybe—'

'It's not a joke,' said Lucy. 'You know how he acts when he comes into the house and I'm not there. He prowls around, looking for me. He telephones my friends. He goes to my bedroom and stands at the window waiting, not saying a word to anyone. You've seen it dozens of times, haven't you?'

'Yes. And I never liked it,' Oliver said sullenly. 'And I thought you liked it too much. That's one of the reasons why I hired Bunner.'

'And then you told me to leave him alone more,' said Lucy rapidly. 'To let him spend more time by himself. To force him to be independent. And you told Jeff the same things. Well, we followed instructions. Your instructions. And this is the result.'

'What do you mean?' Oliver asked, confused.

'We left him alone from time to time,' Lucy said. 'We carefully avoided making him the centre of things every minute of the day. And he hated it. And this is his revenge. This sick, unpleasant little story.'

Oliver shook his head. 'No little boy can make up a story like that.'

'Why not?' Lucy asked. 'Especially now. Among other instructions you left you prescribed a course in sex for him.'

'What's wrong with that? It's about time he . . .'

'About time he could whip together his jealousy and all this interesting new information and try to destroy us with it.'

'Lucy,' Oliver said, 'are you telling the truth?'

Lucy took a deep breath, raised her head and stared directly into Oliver's eyes. 'I swear it,' she said.

Oliver turned and went to the door and opened it. 'Bunner,' he called to the boy at the edge of the lake. 'Bunner.'

'What are you going to do?' Lucy asked.

'I want to talk to him.' Oliver came back into the room.

'You can't,' Lucy said.

'I have to,' Oliver said gently.

'You can't embarrass me like that. You can't embarrass yourself. You mustn't degrade me in front of that boy.'

'I'd like to talk to him alone, please,' Oliver said.

'If you do this,' said Lucy, 'I'll never forgive you.' She said it not because she meant it, but because it was what the automatic, innocent wife would have said.

Oliver made a short gesture of dismissal. 'Please, Lucy.'

They were standing there facing each other tensely when Bunner came into the room. Oliver finally saw him. 'Oh, yes,' he said, 'you're here.' He turned back to his wife. 'Lucy,' he said, waiting. Without looking at Jeff she walked swiftly to the door and went out. After a moment, Oliver visibly braced himself, then gestured politely to Jeff. 'Sit down,' he said. Jeff hesitated, then sat on a wooden chair. Oliver walked slowly back and forth in front of him as he spoke. 'First,' he said, 'I want to thank you for the letters you've been writing every week reporting on Tony's progress.'

'Well,' Jeff said, 'since you couldn't get up here I thought you'd like to know what we were doing with ourselves.'

'I enjoyed the letters,' said Oliver. 'They were very shrewd. You seemed to know what was going on with Tony all the time and I got the feeling you really liked him a great deal too.'

'He's a rewarding little boy,' said Jeff.

'Rewarding?' Oliver repeated vaguely, as though this was a new concept of his son. 'Yes, isn't he? The letters gave me quite a good picture of yourself incidentally.'

Jeff laughed a little self-consciously. 'They did? I hope I didn't give myself away.'

'Quite the opposite,' said Oliver. 'I got the picture of a most intelligent, decent young man. I even began to feel that, after college, if you might somehow change your mind about diplomacy, I might try to find something for you in my business.'

'It's very nice to hear, Sir,' Jeff said, embarrassedly. 'I'll remember it.'

'By the way,' Oliver said, as though it would have been impolite to get to the main question too soon and he was casting about, looking for subjects of conversation, 'that girl of yours you talked about the day I met you. I even remember your exact words. I asked you if you had a girl and you said, approximately. Is she by any chance still in Boston, in high school?'

'In high school?' Jeff asked, puzzled.

'Yes,' said Oliver. 'Cheer leader for the high-school football team?'

Jeff laughed uneasily. 'No,' he said. 'I don't know any high-school girls in Boston. And certainly no cheer leaders. The girl I was talking about is a junior at Vassar and actually I was boasting. I don't see her more than five or six times a year. Why do you ask?'

'I must have gotten a little mixed up,' Oliver said easily. 'Maybe it was something in one of Tony's letters. His handwriting leaves a great deal of room for speculation.' He shrugged. 'It's of no importance. So—no cheer leaders.'

'Not a one,' said Jeff.

Oliver waited. 'How about older ladies?' he said evenly. 'Married ladies?'

Jeff dropped his eyes. 'I don't think you really expect me to answer that, Mr. Crown.'

'No, perhaps not.' Oliver took out his cheque book and pen from his pocket. 'Has Mrs. Crown paid you regularly every week?'

'Yes,' said Jeff.

'She hasn't paid you this week?' Oliver asked, with the cheque book open.

'No,' said Jeff. 'Now wait a minute, Sir.'

'This is Friday,' Oliver went on calmly, 'and the arrangement was thirty dollars for a seven-day week, wasn't it? That would be five-sevenths of thirty—well, let's say roughly twenty-one dollars as a flat sum. You don't mind a cheque, do you? I'm a little short on cash.'

Jeff stood up. 'I don't want any money,' he said.

Oliver raised his eyebrows. 'Why not?' he asked. 'You took it each week from Mrs. Crown, didn't you?'

'Yes. But . . .'

'Why should this week be any different?' Oliver sounded good-tempered and reasonable. 'Except that it's two days short?'

'I don't want it,' Jeff said.

Oliver purposely misunderstood him. 'Things being as they are,' he said, 'you don't think that you ought to stay on any longer, do you?'

'No,' Jeff said, mumbling so low that Oliver could hardly hear him.

'Of course not,' Oliver said, in a fatherly tone. He gave Jeff the cheque. 'Here, take it. You've earned it. I remember when I was your age I could always use twenty dollars. It can't be so different today.'

Jeff looked down unhappily at the cheque in his hand and started towards the door. Then he turned back. 'I suppose I ought to say I'm sorry or ashamed or something like that. I suppose it would make you feel better.'

Oliver smiled warmly. 'Not necessarily,' he said.

'Well, I'm not,' Jeff said defiantly. 'It's the greatest thing that ever happened to me.'

Oliver nodded. 'It always is,' he said. 'At the age of twenty.'

'You don't know,' Jeff said incoherently. 'You don't know her.'

'Perhaps not,' Oliver said.

'She's pure,' Jeff said. 'Delicate. You mustn't blame her. I did it. It's all my fault.'

'I don't want to take any of the glory away from you,' Oliver said pleasantly, 'but I must say that when a thirty-five-year-old woman takes up with a twenty-year-old boy I can't give him credit for anything more than being—present.'

'You . . .' said Jeff bitterly, confronting the older man. 'You're so sure of yourself. I know all about you. She's told me. Sitting back. Telling everybody what they're to do. What they're to think. The people who work for you. Your child. Your wife. Having everything your own way. Being polite and frozen and ruthless. God, even now you don't even have the grace to be angry. You come up here and find out I'm in love with your wife and what do you do? You sign a cheque.' With a melodramatic gesture he crumpled the cheque and threw it on the floor.

Oliver's air of indulgence, of amusement, did not change. 'It's one of the arguments you always hear,' he said, 'against hiring the sons of wealthy families. They don't have the proper respect for money.'

'I hope she leaves you,' Jeff said. 'And if she does, I'll marry her.'

'Bunner,' Oliver said, repressing a smile, 'if I may say so, you're behaving like a fool. You're being sentimental. You use words like love, marriage, delicacy, purity, and I know why, and I even admire you for it. You're not a brute. You want to have a high opinion of yourself. You want to think of yourself as passionate, exceptional. Well, it's natural enough, and I don't blame you for it—but I have to tell you that it doesn't square with the facts.'

'What do you know about the facts?' Jeff asked bitterly.

'This much,' Oliver said. 'You haven't had a love affair. You've had a work of the imagination. You've imagined a woman who doesn't exist, an emotion that doesn't exist.'

'Don't tell me,' Jeff started to interrupt.

'Please let me finish.' Oliver waved his hand. 'You've taken something that's routine and casual and you've larded it with roses and moonlight. You've mistaken a season for a lifetime. You've mistaken a silly, childish woman's easy conscience for passion, and finally, you'll be the one who gets hurt the worst because of it.'

'If that's the way you feel about her,' Jeff said, almost stuttering in his anger and confusion, 'you have no right to talk about her. You don't respect her, you don't admire her, you don't love her . . .'

Oliver sighed. 'When you get older,' he said, 'you'll find out that love very often has almost nothing to do with respect and admiration. Anyway, I didn't come all the way up here to talk about me. Jeff,' he said, 'let me ask you to do something fairly hard—look at things as they really are. Look at the summertime, Jeff. Look at all the hotels like this one. All the clapboard palaces with thin walls and bad dance bands and postcard lakes and lazy, thoughtless, vacationing women separated from their husbands for the hot months. Women who lie out in the sun all day, bored, restless, drinking too much, looking for amusement and finding it in travelling salesmen, waiters, hired athletes, trumpet players, college boys. The whole tribe of cheap, available males with only that to recommend them. That, and the fact that they conveniently vanish when the cold weather comes. By the way,' Oliver said conversationally, 'have you talked to Mrs. Crown on the subject of marriage?'

'Yes. I did.'

'What did she say?'

'She laughed,' Jeff admitted.

'Of course.' Oliver was friendly and sympathetic. 'The same

thing happened to me when I was just past twenty. Except that it was on a boat, on the way to France. Actually it was perhaps even more romantic than this . . .' He waved his arm to indicate the cottage, the lake, the surrounding forest. 'Boats being what they are and France being what it was right after the war. And the lady was wise enough to leave her children at home, since she was perhaps more practised than Mrs. Crown. It was very intense. It even included a two-week trip to the Italian lakes and adjoining cabins on the old *Champlain* and I made speeches to her on the boatdeck on the way back to America that I imagine were very much like some of the speeches you must have been making here on moonlit nights. And we were luckier, too. The husband never knew anything. Never appeared until we docked. Even so,' Oliver laughed reflectively, 'it took two hours to get through customs and by the time we were through the gate she was having trouble remembering my name.'

'Why are you trying to make it so ugly?' said Jeff. 'Why does that make it better for you?'

'Not ugly,' Oliver said, 'merely ordinary. Pleasant—that summer in Europe is one of the most agreeable memories I have—but ordinary. Don't be so unhappy because at a certain age you happen to have gone through an experience that other young men have had before you.' He bent down and picked up the crumpled cheque from the floor. 'You're sure you don't want this cheque?' He held it out, offering it to the boy.

'No,' said Jeff.

'Whatever you say. As you get older, you learn to treat money more carefully, too.' He smoothed out the cheque, looked at it absently, then with a sudden movement threw it into the fireplace. 'Incidentally—that gramophone is yours, isn't it?'

'Yes,' said Jeff.

'I think you'd better take it with you,' Oliver said. 'Now. And Anything else around here that belongs to you.'

'That's all there is,' said Jeff.

Oliver went over to the gramophone and snapped out the plug. He wrapped the cord neatly around the instrument and tucked the plug firmly through the twist of wire. 'I think you'd better stay away from here from now on, don't you?'

'I'm not making any promises.'

Oliver shrugged. 'It makes no difference to me. I was merely thinking of your own peace of mind.' He tapped the gramophone.

'Here we are.' He waited, smiling pleasantly. Jeff, his face set, came over and put the machine under his arm and started out. As he got to the door it opened and Lucy came in.

After Lucy had left the house, she walked blindly down towards the lake. She stopped at its edge, staring out across the water. The clouds had parted a little and there was pale, wet moonlight picking out the tips of branches, the pilings at the end of the hotel dock, a mast on one of the small sailboats tied a few feet off the end of the dock.

It was cold along the edge of the water, and Lucy shivered. She hadn't put on a sweater and she couldn't go back into the house now and get one.

She thought of what the two men were saying to each other in the living room. She tried to imagine the conversation, but it was impossible. In other times and other places, men had killed each other in situations like this. Not only in other times. She remembered a story she had read in a newspaper a month or so ago. A sailor had come home unexpectedly and found his wife with another man and had shot them both. Then he had shot himself. It had been all over the front pages for two days.

Well, nobody was going to shoot anybody. Maybe that was what was wrong with them. All three of them. Maybe something like this was only valid and worthwhile if people were willing to shoot each other as a consequence.

She turned and looked at the house. It looked exactly the same as it had looked all the summer and the summer before. The light streaming peacefully, too brightly, through the curtains of the living-room window, making the wet grass gleam on the lawn in front of the house. And several windows away, the light was on in Tony's room, shaded, from the lamp on his desk. She wondered what Tony was doing. Reading? Drawing his pictures of horses, boats and athletes? Packing, preparing to run away? Listening?

She shivered. Suddenly, she knew that the worst thing was going to be facing Tony, whether he was listening or not. She turned away from the house and looked out across the lake. How easy it would be just to walk out and keep going, out into the blackness, out into the simple blackness . . . Well, she knew she wasn't going to do that, either.

She listened to the tapping of the water against the dock-pilings, small, monotonous, familiar, the same sound as last summer, as all the summers before that. She wished it was last summer. She wished it was any time before tonight. With everything to be done over again, and done better and more wisely, not with that insane, rushing, diving, automatic, dreamlike inventiveness. Or next summer, with everything settled, forgotten, punished.

She wished that they could go back a half-hour, to the moment when she came into the house and saw Oliver standing there, and knowing it was going to be bad, and being frightened of him and at the same time feeling that sensation of warmth and gladness that she always felt when she saw him after being away from him for some time, a sensation of rootedness, familiarity, connection, a subtle, comfortable relinquishment of the responsibility of being alone. She wondered if she could ever explain that feeling to Oliver, and explain that it could exist at the same time that she was making love with another man, at the same time that she was lying to him about it, at the same time that she was pretending to be outraged and innocent.

What she should have done when Oliver sent Jeff out of the room and accused her, was to get up and say, 'Please give me fifteen minutes alone. I want to arrange everything exactly, correctly, in my mind, because this is too important to rush.' Then she should have gone into her own room, by herself, and thought it all out and come back and begged for forgiveness.

Only she hadn't done that. She had behaved instinctively, like a guilty child, in a gush and brainless female flurry of tricks, thinking only of protecting herself for the moment, no matter what losses it would mean later on. Instinctively, she thought. Well, my instincts are no damned good.

When she went back into the house, she decided, she was going to make it all up. She was going to be calm and sensible and she was going to say, 'Please forget everything I said tonight. Now, this is the way it happened . . .'

And she would also promise never to see Jeff again. She would keep the promise, too. It would be easy—because as soon as she had seen Oliver and Jeff together, in the same room, Jeff had vanished, he had become nothing, he had become once more just a nice little boy who was hired to teach her son how to swim and to keep him out of mischief for a few weeks in the summertime.

If only Oliver hadn't been so stubborn, she thought, with a little twinge of anger against him, if only he had taken her home

113

with him when she'd asked him to, in July, none of this would have happened. If he hadn't complained that night over the phone about that garage bill. Let him take some of the blame, too. Let him understand that there were consequences for him, too, in always making other people do what he wanted them to do. Let him understand that she was a human being, not a block to be pushed, a piece of material to be shaped, that her feelings were sign-posts, danger-signals, appeals, and were to be considered.

Maybe this was all to the good, she thought—this event—this, this accident. Maybe, she thought optimistically, this will shake our marriage into its proper final shape. Maybe from now on, the rights and privileges and decisions will be more equally divided.

She saw shadows moving across the light, behind the living-room curtains and she wondered what the two men were saying about her, who was attacking her, who defending, what judgments they were reaching about her, what revelations, criticisms, what plans for her future. Suddenly, it was intolerable to think of them alone together, debating her, exposing her, settling her. No matter what happens, she thought, it is going to happen in my presence.

She hurried across the wet grass and into the house.

When she opened the door, she saw Jeff standing there, in the middle of the room, with his gramophone under his arm, ready to leave. He looked small and defeated and unimportant, and she knew immediately that whatever Oliver had wanted from him he had got.

Oliver was standing on the other side of the room, impassive and polite.

Lucy glanced once at Jeff, then turned to Oliver. 'Are you through?'

'I believe so,' Oliver said.

'Lucy . . .' Jeff began.

'Go ahead, Jeff,' she said. She was still holding the door open.

Miserably, looking disciplined, Jeff went out, the bulk of the gramophone under his arm making him walk awkwardly.

Oliver watched him leave. Then he lit a cigarette deliberately, conscious that Lucy, standing rigidly near the door now, was following his every movement. 'Quite a nice young man,' Oliver said finally. 'Quite nice.'

I can't go through with it, Lucy thought. Not tonight. Not

while he's standing there, looking amused. Not while he's patronizing and in control. She felt herself shaking and she couldn't remember what she had decided to do while she was out at the edge of the lake. All she knew was that she had to get through the next ten minutes somehow, anyhow.

'Well?' Lucy asked.

Oliver smiled wearily at her. 'He seems . . . very attached to you.'

'What did he say?' Lucy demanded.

'Oh—the usual,' said Oliver. 'I don't understand you. You're pure and delicate. It was all his fault. He's glad it happened. It's the greatest thing in his life. He wants to marry you. Very gallant. No surprises.'

'He's lying,' Lucy said.

'Now, Lucy,' said Oliver. He made a tired small movement of his hand.

'He's lying,' Lucy repeated, stubbornly. 'He's a crazy boy. He was up here last summer. I never even met him. But he followed me around, watching. Never saying a word. Just watching. All summer.' She rushed on, speaking very quickly in an attempt to overwhelm Oliver, to keep him from interrupting. 'Then this summer,' she said, 'he came up just because he found out I was going to be here. Then one night I did something foolish. I admit it. It was silly. I let him kiss me. And it all came out. How he was in love with me from the first minute he saw me. How he followed me. How he wrote me dozens of letters during the winter and didn't mail them. How he couldn't bear not to be near me. All the childish, extravagant things. I was going to call and tell you about it. But I kept thinking, if I told you you'd be worried. Or you'd make a scene. Or you'd think it was a trick on my part to get rid of him. Or you'd make fun of me for not being able to handle a boy like that myself. Or you'd say it's just like her—always needing help and not being able to take care of herself like everybody else. I kept thinking, It's only for six weeks, it's only for six weeks. I kept him off. I used every trick I knew. I ridiculed him. I was bored, I was angry, I suggested other girls. But he was always there. Always saying, Eventually. But nothing happened. Nothing.'

'That isn't his story, Lucy,' Oliver said quietly.

'No, of course not. He wants to make trouble. He told me himself. Once he even told me he was going to write you and say we were lovers so that you'd kick me out and I'd have to turn to him. What can I do to make you believe me?'

'Nothing,' Oliver said. 'Because you're a liar.'

'No,' Lucy said. 'Don't say that.'

'You're a liar,' Oliver said. 'And you disgust me.'

Her defences overrun and all pretence suddenly abandoned, she walked blindly towards him, her arms out in front of her. 'No . . . please, Oliver . . .'

'Keep away from me,' Oliver said. 'That's the worst part. The lies. The unforgivable part. After a while, maybe I could forget your summertime college boy. But the lies! Especially the lie about Tony. Good God, what were you trying to do? What kind of a woman are you?'

Lucy slumped into a chair, her head down. 'I didn't know what I was doing,' she said dully. 'I'm so scared, Oliver. I'm so scared. I want so much to save us, both of us, our marriage.'

'Damn all such marriages,' Oliver said. 'Lying in his arms, laughing about me, complaining. Telling him between kisses that I was cold, I was a tyrant. With your son outside, peering through the window, because you were too eager to jump into bed to make sure the blinds were drawn properly.'

Lucy moaned. 'It wasn't like that.'

Oliver was standing over her now, raging. 'Is that the marriage you're so anxious to save?'

'I love you,' she whispered, her head still down, not looking at Oliver. 'I love you.'

'Am I supposed to be melted by that?' Oliver asked. 'Am I supposed to say now that it's all right that you've lied to me for fifteen years and all right that you're going to lie to me for the next fifteen? Just because, when you've been found out, you're brazen enough to say you love me?'

'This is the first time,' Lucy said hopelessly. 'I never lied to you before. I swear it. I don't know what happened to me. You shouldn't have left me alone. I begged you not to. You said you were going to come up and you never did. I told him I wasn't going to see him again. You can ask him.'

Suddenly Oliver picked up his hat and coat and overnight bag. Frightened, Lucy looked up. 'Where are you going?'

'I don't know,' Oliver said. 'I'm getting out of here.'

Lucy stood up, putting out her hand towards him. 'I'll promise anything,' she said. 'I'll do anything. Please don't leave me.'

116

'I'm not leaving you yet,' Oliver said. 'I have to get off by myself till I can decide what to do.'

'Will you call me?' Lucy asked. 'Will you come back?'

Oliver took a deep breath. He sounded exhausted. 'We'll see,' he said. He went out of the cottage and a moment later Lucy heard the car start. She stood in the middle of the room, dry-eyed, drawn, listening to the sound of the engine. The door from the hallway was flung open and Tony came into the room.

'Where's Daddy?' he asked harshly. 'I heard the car. Where did he go?'

'I don't know,' Lucy said. She put out her hand to touch Tony's shoulder, but he pulled away and rushed on to the porch. She could hear him running down the road, his voice growing smaller and smaller, calling after his father, and the noise of the car diminishing and then vanishing in the distance.

Chapter Twelve

FOR the next ten days and nights, Oliver kept to himself as much as he could, spending as little time as possible in his office and avoiding all his friends. He gave the coloured maid the time off, telling her that he was going to eat out, and she went down to Virginia to visit her family, leaving him alone in the house.

Each night, after coming home from the office, Oliver prepared his dinner and ate it, with austere and solitary formality, in the dining room. Then he neatly washed up and went into the living room and sat in front of the fireplace until one or two o'clock in the morning, not reading, not turning on the radio, but merely sitting there, staring at the cold swept hearth until he felt tired enough to go to sleep.

He didn't call or write Lucy. When he finally got in touch with her, he wanted to know exactly what he was going to do. All his life Oliver had come to decisions unhurriedly, after long and thoughtful examination. He wasn't a vain man, but he wasn't modest, either, and he believed in his intelligence and his ability to reach conclusions that would stand up to the test of events.

Now he had to come to a conclusion about his wife and his son and himself and he gave himself time and solitude for the process.

The process was long and more difficult than he had imagined it would be, because instead of reasoning out the problem, he kept imagining Lucy and Jeff together, the murmur of their voices, the low laughter in the darkened room, and the intolerable gestures of love. At these moments, alone in the empty house, he was tempted to write Lucy and tell her it was all over and that he never wanted to see her again. But he didn't write the letter. Perhaps in a week or two, the letter would be written, but it would come as a result of severe reflection, not as a result of self-torment. He had given himself this time to regain control of himself; when the control was re-established, complete, he would act.

His jealousy, if that was what it was, hit him harder than it might have hit another man, who was accustomed to being jealous. The jealous man secretly believes in his own betrayal. He is in a state of siege and is convinced that somehow, somewhere, the wall will be breached, and makes his pessimistic adjustments before hand to cope with his defeat. Oliver had never imagined that he might be betrayed and was unprepared for it and found himself, for the first few days, disarmed and overrun.

Curiously, he thought of what other men must have done in similar situations. After all, it was a common enough phenomenon. What were the lines of Leontes?

'There have been
Or I am much deceived, cuckolds ere now,
And many a man there is, even at this present,
Now, while I speak this, holds his wife by the arm,
That little thinks she has been sluiced in 's absence . . .'

He didn't remember the rest of the speech, but he remembered it was apposite. He got up and took down a big volume of Shakespeare's plays and opened it at *The Winter's Tale* and thumbed through the pages until he found the passage.

'Should all despair,' Oliver read,
'That have revolted wives, the tenth of mankind
Would hang themselves. Physic for 't, there's none;
It is a bawdy planet.'

Oliver closed the book. Shakespeare, for once, made it simpler than it was. *A bawdy planet*, the poet said, poetically, and that was explanation enough for him. After fifteen years of marriage, Oliver thought, this didn't explain Lucy to him. He tried to clarify for himself just what he *did* think of his wife. Reserved, devoted, moderate, he thought, anxious to please him and win his approval. Generally obedient, he thought, grinning sourly at the echo of the wedding ceremony, given only to the lesser sins of sentimentality, inefficiency, timidity.

Necessary to him.

Ten days' reflection, he thought grimly, and it comes down to that. Necessary.

I accepted her too lightly, he thought, as one reflects upon a friend who has died and whose value, too late, is suddenly appreciated. I wasn't careful enough.

He thought of what it would be like with just himself and Tony in the house. Tony, with his mother's eyes, and the same delicate cheekbones, and so many of the same gestures, roughened a little by his maleness and made cruder and a little comic by his awkwardness and adolescence. Whatever else happens, Oliver thought, I couldn't stand *that*.

He tried to think of what it must be like now up at the lake, Tony and Lucy together day and night, confronting each other, after the rainy evening ten days ago. Oliver supposed that he should have taken Tony home with him, for Tony's sake. If he hadn't rushed around like a stabbed bull, perhaps he would have done so. Only it would have made coming to a proper decision that much harder. Well, he comforted himself, let him have a rough week or so—in the long run, we'll all profit by my being allowed to figure this out, undisturbed.

Oliver got up to go to bed. He put out the light and went upstairs to the bedroom that he shared with Lucy. It was a big room with a bay window, looking out through the foliage of an oak tree at the quiet street below. Oliver made the bed each morning, turning it down so that it would be ready to sleep in at night. The room was neater than it ever was when Lucy was there, and it suddenly seemed artificial and unfamiliar to Oliver because of that.

Lucy had left her silver-backed toilet articles on the dressing table and the first morning that Oliver had done the housework, he had arranged all the things, the brushes, the combs and nailfiles, the carved hand-mirror, in a severe geometric pattern on the glass surface. Now they seemed like articles put out for sale in the shop of a man without much imagination. Oliver went over to the table and lifted the mirror. It was heavy and the silver handle was cool and he remembered the hundreds of times he had watched Lucy, getting dressed to go out, holding the mirror up, her head twisted, to see the back of her head and make sure her hair was all right, and the small, soft indefinite movements with which she pushed strands of hair in place. He remembered the mixture of tenderness and irritated amusement with which he had regarded her, pleased with her beauty, annoyed because she was taking so much time and making them late for wherever they were going, accomplishing nothing, as far as he could tell, with the hesitant, undecided movements of her hand.

He put the mirror down carelessly, changing the pattern on the table. Then he put out the lamp and sat for a long time in the dark on the edge of the bed.

Reserved, devoted, moderate, he remembered. That's what *I* thought. Shakespeare, no doubt, would have a different opinion. And what about her own opinion of herself? Lying next to him for so many years, plotting, resentful, mocking his estimate of her, cherishing other qualities, closing her eyes, turning secretly away from him in the same bed, the twisting, stubborn inhabitant of the bawdy planet.

If I were another kind of man, he thought wearily, sitting fully dressed on the side of the bed in the dark room, I wouldn't stay here alone, suffering, like this. I would drink or I would find another woman or I would do both. Then, satiated and loose, I'd arrive, sidewise, and with less pain, at a decision. For a moment, he thought of getting into the car and driving to New York and going to a hotel there. Women wouldn't be hard to find in the city, and, in fact, there were one or two whom he knew who had made it plain that all he had to do was ask. But even as he turned it over in his head, he knew he wouldn't call anyone. He doubted, even, that he could manage to take another woman. He was a passionate man; he knew he was much more avid than other men his age—but it had all been channelled into the one direction. This is a hell of a predicament, he thought, for an uxorious man.

Necessary.

What a goddamn summer, he thought, and stood up and undressed in the dark and got into bed.

The next morning, there was a letter in the mail from Lucy. Oliver was just leaving the house when the postman came, and he stood at the door, in the warm, early sunshine, turning the envelope over in his hand, conscious of his neighbours setting out to work, saying good-bye to children, hurrying to catch trains and buses, moving through the greenness of trees and lawns, against a background of flowers, moving through the bright summer morning, the men already greyed over a little, Oliver thought, by the shadows of the offices and factories that were waiting for them.

Oliver didn't open the letter immediately. He looked at the familiar inscription on the envelope—backhand, childish, not quite controlled, always a little hard to read. Where had he heard that that kind of handwriting, backhand, was evidence of repression, hypocrisy, self-consciousness? He didn't remember it accurately. Perhaps it was another kind of handwriting and he'd mixed it up. Some day, he'd get one of those books and look it up.

He opened the envelope and read the letter. It was short and without apologies. All she said was that she was going to leave him, because she couldn't bear living any longer in the same house with Tony and him. And when she signed it, she didn't say, Love, or anything like that. Just Lucy.

There was no information about how Tony was, no inquiries about him or what he had decided, no hesitation or offers. It was like no letter she had ever sent before, and if it hadn't been for the handwriting, it would have been hard to believe that Lucy had written it.

That afternoon, he called Sam Patterson and asked him to come to dinner that night. The good thing about Sam was that there never was any problem about seeing him alone. All Sam ever did was tell his wife he wasn't going to be home to dinner, and that was the end of it. Maybe Sam had the secret, Oliver thought, maybe he was the man to ask about marriage.

They had dinner at a hotel, with a bottle of wine, and Oliver found himself enjoying it and eating a great deal, after the ten days of cooking for himself. They talked lightly all through dinner, in the kind of conversational shorthand that develops between friends who have known each other many years, and it was only when the dishes had been cleared away and the coffee set down before them that Oliver said, 'Sam, the reason I asked

121

you to have dinner with me is that I need advice. I'm in trouble and I have to make a decision and maybe you can help me . . .'

Then, sipping his coffee, not looking at Patterson, Oliver told him the whole story, the call from Tony, the arrival at the lake, Tony's outburst, Lucy's denial and accusation of Tony, Bunner's confession, everything.

He spoke slowly and evenly, without emotion or shading, methodically presenting all the facts to Patterson, like a responsible witness making a deposition after an accident, like a doctor giving the symptoms of a puzzling case to a specialist who has been called in for consultation.

Patterson listened silently, showing nothing on his face, thinking, I don't know another man who would make such a dry, accurate, well-organized report out of his life's convulsion like this. He is making love, desire and betrayal sound like a paper to be read before an historical society on a minor treaty of the eighteenth century. At the same time, listening impassively, Patterson could not help feeling an unworthy twinge of jealousy. If she finally was going to choose somebody, he thought, why couldn't she have chosen me?

And mixed with all this was a helpless flavour of satisfaction. Oliver, who before this had never asked help or advice from anyone. Oliver, the most self-sufficient and reticent of men, was coming to him for aid in his moment of pain and doubt. It made Patterson feel more important in Oliver's company than he had ever felt before, and at the same time seemed to open some new gate of affection and compassion for his friend. Finally, he thought, no friendship is complete until your friend turns to you in despair.

Seated in the corner of the restaurant, their table removed from the other diners, Patterson listened carefully to the measured, fastidious voice of his friend. I must get all the facts straight, he thought, almost as if he were going into an operating room where the slightest haziness or misunderstanding might mean the difference between life and death; this is one time I must not say or do the wrong thing.

'. . . It never occurred to me,' Oliver was saying, 'that anything like this could ever happen to us. It's just unbelievable.'

Patterson smiled inwardly to himself, although no sign of it showed on his face. Friend, he thought, out of his different experience, it is never unbelievable.

122

'And the way it happened,' Oliver went on. 'The damned commonplace way it happened. With the twenty-year-old tutor! It's like a joke you hear at a smoker!'

I will warn Lucy, Patterson thought sardonically, to make it more original the next time. Pick a hunchback, or the governor of a Southern state, or a Negro drummer. Her husband has an aversion to the obvious.

'When women are ready to pick someone,' Patterson said, 'they choose from the available material. Literary precedents have very little to do with it. At a moment like that, nobody thinks of herself as a character in an off-colour joke.'

'What do you mean, ready to pick someone?' Oliver said harshly. 'Did you ever think that Lucy was ready to pick some-one?'

'No,' Patterson said honestly. 'Not until now.'

'And now . . .'

'Now, after it's happened, it's not altogether surprising.'

'What do you mean by that?' There was hostility in Oliver's voice.

'Adultery,' Patterson said mildly, 'is the upper-middle-class American woman's form of self-expression.'

For a moment, Oliver seemed angry. Then he laughed. 'I see I came to the right man,' he said. 'Okay, Philosopher. Continue.'

'All right,' Patterson said. 'Try to look at it from her point of view for a few minutes. What have you done with her since your wedding day . . . ?'

'I've done a hell of a lot,' Oliver broke in. 'I've taken care of her every minute for fifteen years. Maybe it might sound crass, and I don't suppose I'd ever say it to her, but she's lived damned well and she's never had to worry about anything and no matter how tough it was for me from time to time, I never said a word to her. Christ, she's pretty nearly the only woman in the country who hardly even knew there was a Depression. To this day she can't keep a cheque book straight or remember to pay the electric company on time. I'll tell you what I did for her—I took full responsibility for her,' he said angrily, as though Patterson were Lucy's representative and was arguing her case. 'She's thirty-five years old and she hasn't the faintest notion of how tough it is to be alive in the twentieth century. For fifteen years she's been living like a schoolgirl on a holiday. Don't ask me what I've done for her. What're you nodding about like that . . . ?'

'Exactly,' Patterson said. 'Just what I said.'

'What do you mean, just what you said?' Oliver's voice was beginning to rise.

'Now don't get angry with *me*,' Patterson said good-humouredly. '*I* haven't slept with any college boys.'

'That's a damned poor joke,' said Oliver.

'Look,' said Patterson, 'you've come to me for help, haven't you?'

'I suppose so,' Oliver said. 'Yes, of course.'

'Well, the only way I know how to help,' Patterson said, 'is to try to figure out why she finally did something like this.'

'I know why,' Oliver said angrily. 'She's a . . .' He stopped and shook his head. Then he sighed. 'No, she's not at all. Go on. I'll keep quiet.'

'You made all the decisions,' Patterson said. 'You took her away from her work . . .'

'Her work.' Oliver made a contemptuous sound. 'Messing around in a smelly laboratory for an old idiot by the name of Stubbs. You ever hear of him?'

'No.'

'Neither has anyone else. If she worked with him for twenty years, maybe they'd have produced one paper, proving that algae were green.'

Patterson chuckled.

'You laugh,' Oliver said. 'But it's true. What the hell, it wasn't like tearing Galileo away from his telescope. The human race was going to survive just the same, whether or not she went into that laboratory five mornings a week. She wasn't so different from all the other girls. She fiddled around, pretending to have a career, waiting to get married. The cities are full of them.'

'That's another thing,' Patterson said. 'I talked to her. She hated leaving New York.'

'If every woman who couldn't live in New York felt she had to betray her husband in consequence . . .' Oliver began. He shook his head angrily and drained the last of the wine from his glass. 'And what about me?' he asked. 'Do you think I wanted to come here to live?' he asked. 'Do you think I wanted to be saddled with the printing business? That was the meanest day of my life, when I came up here after my father died and looked at the books and saw that the whole thing was going to collapse if I didn't take hold. For ten years,' he said, 'every time I've gone through the gate of the works, I've felt myself growing rigid with boredom. But I haven't taken it out on my wife . . .'

'The difference is,' Patterson said gently, 'that you made the decision. And she had to follow.'

'God, it was over ten years ago?'

'You can build up a good case of regret in ten years,' Patterson said. 'You can get to feel real useless in ten years.'

'Useless!' Oliver was making little balls of bread crumbs and flicking them brusquely against the wine bottle. 'She had the boy to take care of, the house . . .'

'Would you be satisfied just taking care of a little boy and a house all your life?' Patterson asked.

'I'm not a woman.'

Patterson grinned.

'What is a man supposed to do?' Oliver asked. 'Set up a Female WPA? Interesting projects,' he said sardonically, 'for women who have nothing to do between three and five in the afternoon.' He looked at Patterson suspiciously. 'How do you know so much?' he asked. 'Has she been filling your ear?'

'No,' Patterson said. 'She didn't have to.'

'What about your own wife?' Oliver said, attacking. 'What about Catherine?'

Patterson hesitated. 'Catherine is a lost, placid soul,' he said. 'She gave up hope when she was nineteen. Or maybe she didn't. Maybe I don't know her at all. Maybe she's writing pornographic novels in the attic, or she has a string of lovers from here to Long Island Sound. We don't communicate enough for me to find out. It's a different kind of marriage,' he explained regretfully, concealing his envy of his friend. 'There's nothing she or I could do that could possibly make either of us angry.' He smiled crookedly. 'Or even mildly disturbed.'

'Why've you kept it up so long, then?' Oliver demanded. 'Why didn't you quit?'

Patterson shrugged again. 'It hardly seemed worth the trouble,' he said, almost truthfully.

'Good God,' Oliver said. 'Marriage.'

They sat in silence for a moment, gloomily, two men fixed in contemplation of complexity, waste, cross-purposes. Patterson allowed his mind to wander away from Oliver, and he remembered some of the other problems that he had been confronted with just that day, in the ordinary course of his work, in his own office. Mrs. Sayers, who was only thirty-three years old, but who had five children, and who was suffering stubbornly from anaemia and who was tired all the time; so tired, she said, that when she had to get up at six-thirty every morning, to prepare breakfast and take care of the kids, it was like climbing up on the cross, she said, and she meant it. And nothing, as far as Patterson could see, to be done about it. And Mr. Lindsay, who was a machinist, and whose hands were so crippled with arthritis that he could barely hold his tools, and the effort of trying to hide it from the foreman was so great that the sweat broke out on his face from the minute he entered the shop until long after he got home at night. And nothing to be done about it. And the woman who had come into his office three months pregnant, only her husband had been in Panama for six months. All the routine, random misery and ailments that the human race casually pushed across a doctor's desk every day of the week. And a step removed from that—the newspaper tragedies—the men who were going into battle in Spain, and who would be dead or broken by tomorrow evening, and the people being hunted down and destroyed all over Europe . . .

By any objective scale, Patterson thought, Oliver's pain must be minute and inconsiderable. Only no man calculated his agony against an objective scale, and a thousand deaths on another continent finally were likely to weigh less in a man's private balance than his own toothache.

No, Patterson corrected himself, it's not fair. There was also the question of tolerance of injury to be considered. The threshold of pain varied enormously—one man might suffer an amputation with nothing more than a stoical grunt, while another might go into shock with a crushed finger. Perhaps Oliver was a man with a low threshold of pain when the injury was infidelity.

'Self-expression,' Oliver was saying thoughtfully, staring down at his hands spread out on the table cloth.

'What?' Patterson asked, forgetting for a moment.

'Your theory,' Oliver said.

'Oh, yes,' Patterson said, smiling. 'Of course, you must remember it's just a theory and I haven't kept any scientific checks . . .'

'Go on,' Oliver said.

'Well, with a man like you,' Patterson said, 'who insists upon making all the decisions at all times, for everybody . . .'

'It's not because I want to,' Oliver protested. 'I'd be delighted

126

if other people would take the responsibility. But people just diddle around . . .'

Patterson grinned. 'Exactly. Well, after a few years like that, it seems to me that a woman'd begin to feel that the thing she wanted most, the thing she just had to do—would be to make one big important decision by herself. And you'd closed all the other fields to her—you told her where she was to live and how she was to live and how she was to bring up her son— By God, I remember now, you even told her what the menus should be for dinner.'

'I have special tastes in food,' Oliver said defensively. 'I don't see why I can't eat what I want in my own house.'

Patterson laughed, and a second later, Oliver laughed, too. 'I must have some reputation around this town.'

'Well, it is true, you're considered a man who knows his own mind, Oliver.'

'If she had so many objections,' Oliver said, 'why didn't she speak up? Nobody's under a vow of silence in our house.'

'Maybe she was afraid to. Or maybe she didn't know she had the objections until this summer.'

'Until a twenty-year-old boy came along,' Oliver said sullenly, 'who doesn't have to shave more than twice a week and who hasn't got anything better to do than lounge around a lake all summer, playing with married women.'

'Maybe,' Patterson said astringently.

'At least,' Oliver said, 'if it was a grand passion—if she was in love with him, if she was ready to make some sacrifices for him! But he told me himself—she laughed at him when he asked her to marry him! It's so damn frivolous!'

'I can't help you there,' Patterson said. 'And I think, in the long run, you're going to be glad it was frivolous.'

Oliver tapped the table impatiently. 'And then, to top it all,' he said, 'she had to be so inept. Letting the boy see her.'

'Oh,' Patterson said, 'children see worse things than that. They see their parents being cowardly, or cruel, or crooked . . .'

'It's easy for you to talk,' Oliver said. 'You don't have a son.'

'Send him away to school for a couple of years,' Patterson said, ignoring what Oliver had just said, 'and he'll forget it. Children forget everything.'

'You think so?'

'Sure,' said Patterson, being glib.

'I'll have a lot of things to forget, too.' Oliver sighed.

'Grownups forget everything, too,' Patterson said.

'You know you're a liar,' said Oliver.

Patterson smiled. 'Yes.'

'Then what're you talking like that for?'

'Because I'm your friend,' Patterson said soberly, 'and I know you want to take her back, and I want to give you all the reasons why you should, even if they're lousy reasons.'

'Some day,' Oliver said sarcastically, 'when you're in trouble, make sure to come to me for advice.'

'I'll do that,' Patterson said.

'So—what do you think I ought to do?' Oliver asked. 'Practically?'

'Go up there tomorrow and be noble,' Patterson said promptly. 'Forgive her. Take her to your bosom. Tell her you know she'll be a paragon amongst wives from now on. Tell her you'll let her arrange her own menus from now on . . .'

'Leave out the jokes,' Oliver said.

'Don't send her off in the summer by herself any more.'

'She didn't want to stay up there,' Oliver remembered. 'She begged me to take her back with me. If I let her, she'd hang around my neck twenty-four hours a day.'

'There you are,' Patterson said.

'It's so damned complicated. And what can I tell Tony?'

'Tell him it was an accident,' said Patterson. 'A grownup accident, that he's too young at the moment to understand. Tell him you'll explain everything when he's twenty-one. Tell him to be a good boy at school and stop looking through windows.'

'He's going to hate us,' Oliver said, peering down into his cup. 'He's going to wind up hating both of us.'

There was nothing to be said to this and Patterson didn't try. They sat in silence for a moment, then Oliver called for the bill. 'This is on me,' he said, when Patterson tried to take it. 'Payment for professional services.'

On the way out of the hotel, Oliver sent a telegram to Lucy, telling her to pack and be ready as he was coming for her the next afternoon.

128

Chapter Thirteen

'ARRIVING around three o'clock, tomorrow,' the telegram had read. 'Please have everything packed and be ready to leave immediately. Wish to make as much of the trip in daylight as possible. Oliver.'

Lucy had re-read the telegram a half dozen times. She had been tempted to telephone Oliver, but had decided against it. Let him come, she had thought. Let it be settled, once and for all.

After the night of Oliver's visit, Lucy had stayed in the cottage, numbly forcing herself to go through the routine of holiday with Tony, waiting, in the beginning, for something to happen, some message, some event which would push her one way or another, bring the season to a climax, disastrous, or violent if need be, but punctuating her life, finishing one section, marking the beginning of another.

But nothing had happened. Oliver had not called or written; Jeff had disappeared; the days wore on, sunny, long, ordinary. She went in to meals with Tony, she worked with him on his eye exercises, she went swimming with him, read to him, feeling that everything she did was unreal, that what she was doing she was not doing because it was useful, but because it was habit, like a ruined man going daily to his office to work over accounts that had long been closed merely because he had grown accustomed to it through the years and there was nothing else he could think of to do with his time.

She watched Tony greedily, but every day, under the cloak of custom and familiarity, she had the feeling that he was becoming more and more unknown to her. If, suddenly, he had leaped up and denounced her in the dining room, if she had awakened and found him standing over her bed with a knife in his hand, if he had disappeared forever into the forest, she would have had to say to herself, 'Of course, I expected something like that.'

He was polite, obedient, ungiving, and with the passage of each day she felt the strain becoming greater. It was as though, each night, when she put the light out in his room, and said,

'Good night, Tony,' somebody, somewhere, was turning a ratchet to which her life was attached and pulling her one notch tighter.

Ten days passed; the guests departed from the hotel, the nights turned chilly, the members of the band packed their instruments and returned to the city. Tony seemed neither happy nor unhappy. He held the door open for her politely when they went in to dinner, he came immediately out of the water when she called to him, 'You're getting cold, you'd better dry yourself now,' he asked no questions, volunteered nothing.

When she caught him watching her, his eyes seemed to her the eyes of a grown man, stubborn, unrelenting, accusing. By the end of the ten days she found that it was only by a painful act of memory that she could remember what he had seemed like earlier in the summer. And it was almost impossible to believe that so short a time ago she had considered him a little boy, loving, childish and easy to handle. Now, when they sat together on the lawn, in a stiff, artificial representation of a mother with her son on holiday, she felt herself rattled and clumsy, resenting him more and more each day, like two strangers, shipwrecked, floating across the ocean on a raft, begrudging each other the daily swallow of water from the canteen, suspicious of each movement. Soon his remoteness seemed to her to be open malevolence, his cold politeness an unhealthy and precocious vengeance on her. Finally, she thought, What right has he to sit there judging me like that? Unreasonably accepting him not as a child, but as a mature and implacable opponent, she thought, In the long run, what have I done to *him*?

And mixed with it all, there was a growing resentment of Oliver, too, for leaving her there alone with Tony for ten days, each of them using the other, she felt, to punish her.

At last, Lucy wrote to Oliver and told him that she was going to leave him. She wrote it without heat, without excuses, without disclosing her plans for the future.

Actually, she had no plans for the future. It seemed to take all her energy, all her powers, merely to wake up each morning and know that for another fourteen hours she would have to support the scrutiny of her son.

In the act of writing the letter to Oliver, she had forced herself to make certain decisions about herself. But even as she made them, she had the feeling that they were provisional, that a smile

130

from Tony, a word from Oliver, might overthrow them completely. 'I must leave you,' she had written. 'It's impossible for me and Tony to live in the same house,' and she had meant it, but as time wore on she had almost lost her belief in the validity of what she had written, as a condemned man, after months of waiting in his cell, comes to believe more in the permanence of his bars, the faces of his guards, the regularity and monotony of his diet and his hours of exercise than in the words of the sentence, which, at some distant and by now unimaginable hour, will abruptly kill him.

Then the telegram had come and broken the painful but familiar routine, the drift, the sense of being suspended in time, the feeling of being able to postpone, indefinitely, the decisions that would change her life.

She had told Tony to get ready and had helped him pack and now his bags were all neatly arranged on the porch—the telescope, the baseball bat, the fishing rod, the debris and symbols of boyhood and summer, leaning against an angle of the wall. She had packed nothing of her own. Tony had noticed it, she knew, but silent as ever, had said nothing about it. It was nearly three o'clock now and Lucy sat quietly on the porch, waiting, her eyes going again and again to the small pile of her son's belongings. It was a clear, brilliant day, with a touch of autumn in the air, and the lake had taken on a colder blue, preparing for winter.

Tony came out, dressed in the suit which he had worn for the trip up to the lake and which now, after only two months, seemed too small for him. He was carrying a small valise which he put down next to the others. 'Is that the last one?' Lucy asked.

'Yes,' said Tony.

'Did you look around? Is everything cleared out of your room?'

'Yes,' Tony said.

'You're sure there's nothing left?' said Lucy.

'There's nothing left,' Tony said.

Lucy watched him for a moment and stared out at the quiet lake and the distant, hazy mountains. 'You can almost see the autumn approaching,' she said. She shivered a little. 'It's a season I never liked. It's funny,' she said, trying to make a connection, even in this fragile way, with her son, 'it's funny not to hear the bugle any more, isn't it?'

Tony didn't answer. He looked at his watch. 'What time is Daddy coming?' he asked.

'He'll be here any minute,' said Lucy, once more defeated. 'He said he'd be here about three o'clock.'

'I think I'll go wait for him down at the gate.' Tony started off.

'Tony,' said Lucy.

He stopped. 'What?' he asked flatly.

'Come over here,' Lucy said—almost coquettishly. 'Please.'

Reluctantly Tony came back and stood in front of her. 'What do you want?' he asked.

'I want to look at you, in your city clothes,' Lucy said. 'You look so grown-up. Those sleeves are too short for you.' She touched his shoulder. 'And it's awfully tight across here, isn't it? You must have grown inches this summer. You'll have to get a new wardrobe for school as soon as you get home.'

'I'm going down to the gate,' Tony said.

Lucy made a last effort. 'Tony,' she said, smiling tremulously, feeling that this was the last possible moment, alone here with everyone else departed, the hills and the lake silently plunging into autumn, 'Tony, will you give me a kiss?'

He stood there impassively but not unkindly, studying his mother's face. Then he turned, without emotion or resentment, and started away. Lucy flushed. 'Tony,' she called sharply. He stopped once more and looked at her patiently. 'What do you want?' he asked.

Lucy hesitated. 'Nothing,' she said.

There were footsteps from around the corner of the house and Jeff came into view. He, too, was wearing city clothes, a brown tweed suit, and a carefully knotted tie. He was carrying the gramophone under his arm. That boy, Lucy thought, with an hysterical desire to laugh, makes all his entrances and exits lugging a gramophone. Jeff came up to the porch tentatively. He looked much paler than he had two weeks before, as though he had been indoors all the intervening time. He stopped without coming on to the porch.

'Hullo, Tony,' he said. 'Lucy.'

Tony said nothing. Lucy was taken aback. By an act of will, she had dismissed Jeff from her calculations long ago. Now, looking at him, she had a double sensation, a memory of past pleasure in him and present annoyance. She hid her annoyance by being determinedly casual. 'Hullo, Jeff,' she said lightly. 'I didn't know you were still around.'

'I came up again,' Jeff said uncomfortably, 'to help my sister pack. I heard you were still here and I thought . . .' He looked at the bags in a row on the porch. 'Are you leaving today?'

'What do you want?' Tony asked, ignoring the question.

'I just came to say good-bye,' Jeff said. The neat city clothes and his obvious lack of ease made him seem smaller to Lucy, seemed to push him back into awkwardness and adolescence. If he had been wearing those clothes all the summer, she thought, remembering the white T shirts, the bare feet, I would never have touched him. He put the gramophone down on the edge of the porch. He smiled experimentally at Tony. 'I thought you might like to have this, Tony. As a kind of a present. It's a pretty good little gramophone. I know you like to listen to music and I thought . . .' He stopped, floundering under Tony's unblinking stare.

Lucy broke in, moved by Jeff's embarrassment. 'That's awfully kind of you,' she said in an artificial, hostess-like voice, 'but really, it's too much. What will you do those cold winter nights up in New Hampshire when the wind howls and you're snowed in?' She looked with purposely exaggerated admiration at the gramophone. 'It *is* a beautiful little machine, isn't it, Tony?'

Tony didn't move. He stood with his legs apart, dominating them both. 'Are you giving it to me?' he asked Jeff.

'Yes,' said Jeff.

'Why?'

'Why?' Jeff asked, unhappy at the question. 'Oh, I don't know. Because we had some good times together this summer. Because I'd like you to remember me.'

'Are you going to say thank you, Tony?' said Lucy.

'It's all mine?' Tony said, ignoring her, speaking directly to Jeff. 'I can do whatever I want with it?'

'Sure,' said Jeff. 'You can take it with you to school and put it in your room. When you have parties you can dance to it and . . .' Jeff stopped and watched tensely as Tony approached the machine, looking at it, touching it impersonally. Then Tony went over to where the baseball bat was leaning against the porch wall. He came back to the gramophone, holding the bat in one hand. With his free hand he brushed the machine off the porch, on to the lawn. Then, with great deliberation, he began to swing the bat at the gramophone.

'Tony!' Lucy called. She moved over to stop him but Jeff caught her arm. 'Leave him alone,' Jeff said harshly. They

133

watched silently while Tony coldly and methodically destroyed the gramophone.

After a minute or two Tony stopped, breathing hard. He turned and faced his mother and Jeff with a look of hard, mature triumph on his face. Deliberately he dropped the bat. 'There,' he said.

'That was a brutal, wasteful thing to do,' Lucy said. 'I'm ashamed of you.' She turned to Jeff. 'I apologize for him.'

'Don't you apologize for me,' Tony said. 'Never. Not for anything.'

'It's okay—Tony,' Jeff said gently. 'If it made you feel better, it's okay with me.'

Tony looked from the broken machine, first to his mother and then to Jeff. 'No,' he said, 'it didn't make me feel better. I guess you want to talk to each other before my father comes. I told Bert I'd say good-bye to him before I left. I'll be back in five minutes,' he said threateningly, and strode away towards the docks.

Lucy and Jeff watched until he had gone out of sight. Then Jeff went over and touched the wreckage of the gramophone ruefully with his toe. 'I bet my aunt would be surprised if she ever found out what happened to her present,' he said. He stepped on to the porch and came across to Lucy. 'These last weeks,' he said, 'have been gruesome, haven't they?'

Gruesome, Lucy noted. Is that a word in vogue this year at Dartmouth? She hesitated. I'm not going to get involved, she thought. I'm going to finish him. 'Have they?' she said lightly. She chuckled.

'What are you laughing at?' Jeff asked suspiciously.

'I keep remembering what I was thinking as Tony was whacking away at the poor little gramophone,' said Lucy.

'What's that?'

'I kept remembering how carefully you worked with him,' Lucy said, 'teaching him how to swing a bat. "Step in, Tony. Keep your eye on the ball." ' She mimicked him. ' "Don't put your foot in the bucket." He certainly learned, didn't he?'

'It's not so funny,' Jeff said.

'Oh, it's not so serious,' Lucy said airily. 'Tell your aunt it was stolen and she'll give you another one for Christmas.'

'It's not that,' Jeff said. 'He hates me.'

'A lot of people will hate you before you're through. What of it?'

'What about you?' Jeff said.

'Hate you?' She managed to smile again. 'Of course not.'

'Am I going to see you again?' Jeff asked.

'Of course not,' Lucy said.

'I'm sorry,' said Jeff. He plunged his hands in his pockets. He seemed smaller than ever. 'I guess I should have stayed away.'

'No,' Lucy said. 'I'm glad you came. It was nice and generous. It was even a little brave.' Her tone was motherly, bantering. 'Don't pull such a long face. This was a nice, educational experience for you. The summer course for third-year students—a short term, compulsory for a bachelor's degree—choice of instructors.'

'How can you take it so lightly?' Jeff's face looked stricken.

'Instructors . . .' Lucy sounded puzzled. 'What's the feminine of instructor? Instructress? It sounds wrong somehow, doesn't it?'

'I made a lot of trouble, didn't I?'

Lucy made a grimace, indicating that she thought Jeff was overestimating his importance. 'People have to expect to pay a little for their fun,' she said.

'Fun?' Jeff said, shocked.

'Don't look so scandalized,' she said. 'It *was* fun, wasn't it? I'd feel awful if I thought you hadn't enjoyed it at all. If you did it just out of a sense of duty.'

'It was glorious,' Jeff said solemnly. 'It was heartbreaking . . . it was like an earthquake.'

'Oh, my,' Lucy waved her hands in a fluttery, girlish gesture, 'it's too late to be getting solemn all over again.'

The pain was clearly evident on Jeff's face. 'You're so different today,' he said. 'Why?'

'It's later in the season.' Lucy went over to the row of bags and stood there, frowning down at them, pretending to check them against some list in her mind.

'You're going back?' Jeff asked. 'Back to him?'

Lucy pretended to be puzzled. 'Back to whom?'

'Your husband,' said Jeff.

'I imagine so,' Lucy said matter-of-factly, turning towards him. There was no sense in telling him about the letter she had written Oliver. 'Don't people usually go back to husbands? That's one of the main reasons a girl gets married—to have someone to go back to.'

'Lucy,' he appealed to her, 'what's happened to you?'

Lucy walked towards the edge of the porch and stared out across the lake. 'I guess I've finally become a big, grown-up lady,' she said.

'You're making fun of me,' Jeff said bitterly. 'I don't blame you. I behaved like such a hick. Blurting out everything the minute he asked me. Going off with that damn gramophone under my arm like a kid who's just been kicked out of school because he's been caught smoking.'

'I wouldn't worry about little things like that if I were you,' Lucy said. 'Actually I'm glad he found out.'

'Glad?' Jeff asked incredulously.

'Yes,' she said. 'I'm such a bad liar. It's too much of a strain for my poor little head.' Then her tone changed suddenly, becoming serious, almost threatening. 'I found out it's not for me. Never again.'

'Lucy,' Jeff said, trying to salvage something from the summer, 'if we ever meet again, what're you going to think of me?'

Lucy turned and regarded him thoughtfully. But when she spoke her tone was more playful than ever. 'I'll think,' she said, 'What a touching young man! Isn't it strange that I once thought, for a little while, that I was rather in love with him?'

They were facing each other—Lucy obdurate, implacably frivolous, Jeff forlorn and boyish—when Oliver, whom they had not heard, came around the corner of the porch. He was dressed for travelling and the long journey had left him wrinkled and weary-looking and he moved slowly, as though his energy were low. He stopped when he saw Lucy and Jeff. 'Hullo,' he said and they turned and faced him.

'Hullo, Oliver,' Lucy said, without warmth. 'I didn't hear the car.'

'I just came to say good-bye,' Jeff said uncomfortably.

Oliver waited. 'Yes?'

'I want to say I'm sorry,' Jeff said.

Oliver nodded. 'Ummn . . .' he said vaguely. 'Are you?' He moved across the porch, looking down at the ruins of the gramophone. 'What happened here?'

'Tony . . .' Jeff began.

'It met with an accident,' Lucy broke in.

Oliver was not interested. 'An accident?' he said incuriously. 'Are you finished here, Jeff?'

'Yes, all finished,' said Lucy. 'He was just leaving.' She put out her hand to Jeff. 'Good-bye,' she said, forcing him to shake her hand. 'Walk away with a nice springy step now. Make sure you study hard and get beautiful high marks this year at school.'

Jeff tried to speak but couldn't. He tore his hand away from her and wheeled and plunged out of sight around the corner of the cottage. Watching him, Lucy felt like weeping. Not because he was going and she would never see him again, or because for a little while he had been dear to her and it was all spoiled now. She felt like weeping because he was so clumsy and she knew how it was hurting him and it was her fault.

Chapter Fourteen

WHEN Jeff was gone, Oliver turned to Lucy. 'Where's Tony?' he asked.

'He'll be back in a minute,' said Lucy.

'Oh.' Oliver looked at the row of bags on the porch. 'Where are your things?' he asked. 'Inside?'

'They're not packed,' Lucy said.

'I told you in the telegram,' Oliver said, a little of the old domestic irritation at her inefficiency creeping into his voice, 'to be ready at three o'clock. I don't want to drive the whole way in the dark.'

'I can't go home,' Lucy said. 'Didn't you get my letter?'

'I got it,' said Oliver impatiently. 'You said there were a lot of things to be cleared up between us. Well, we can clear them up just as well in our own house as here. I don't want to stay here any longer than necessary. Go in and pack your things, Lucy.'

'It's not as easy as that,' Lucy said.

Oliver sighed. 'Lucy,' he said, 'I've thought it all over. And I've decided to forget what happened this summer.'

'Oh, you have,' said Lucy, her voice curiously hard.

'I'll accept your promise that it'll never happen again,' Oliver said.

'Oh, you will,' said Lucy, the hardness now becoming metallic and toneless. 'You'll believe me if I say that?'

'Yes.'

137

'Two weeks ago you wouldn't believe a word I said.'

'Because you were lying,' said Oliver.

'How do you know that I won't lie again?' Lucy asked.

Oliver sat down, the lines of fatigue bitten into his face, his head nodding over his chest. 'Don't torture me, Lucy,' he said.

'Answer me,' she said harshly. 'How do you know I won't lie to you again?'

'Because I *have* to believe you,' Oliver said, his voice almost inaudible. 'I sat in the house, thinking of what it would be like to try to live the rest of my life without you . . . and I couldn't stand it,' he said simply. 'I couldn't do it.'

'Even though I'm a liar and you hate liars,' Lucy said, standing over him. 'Even though I disgust you?'

'I'm trying to forget I ever said those things,' Oliver said.

'I can't forget it,' Lucy said. 'You were right. It *was* disgusting. I disgusted myself.'

Oliver raised his head and looked at her. 'But you'll change now?'

'Change?' said Lucy. 'Yes, I will. But perhaps not in the way you think.'

'Lucy,' Oliver asked, and that was the first time he'd ever asked the question, 'don't you love me?'

Lucy stared at him thoughtfully. 'Yes,' she said slowly, 'yes, I do. I've been thinking myself these last ten days, about you. About how much I owe you. How much I need you. How much you've done for me. How solid you've been. How secure.'

'Lucy,' Oliver said, 'it's so good to hear that.'

'Wait,' said Lucy. 'Not so fast. You've done something else too, Oliver. You've educated me. You've converted me.'

'Converted you?' Oliver asked, puzzled. 'What do you mean?'

'You always talked so much about your principles,' said Lucy. 'About the truth. About seeing things clearly, about not fooling yourself. You even wrote a long letter to Tony about it this summer, when you were worried about his eyes.'

'Yes, I did,' said Oliver. 'What about it?'

'I am now your disciple,' said Lucy. 'And I'm the worst kind of disciple. Because the first person I've used my faith on is you.'

'What are you talking about?' Oliver asked.

'Lies offend you, don't they, Oliver?' Lucy was speaking calmly, reasonably, as though she were explaining a mathematical equation.

'Yes, they do,' said Oliver, but he sounded wary and defensive.

'Deception of any kind, by anyone,' Lucy went on, in the classroom tone, 'is sickening to you, isn't it?'

'Yes, it is,' said Oliver.

'You believe that, don't you?' Lucy asked.

'Yes.'

'And you're lying,' said Lucy.

Oliver's head jerked back angrily. 'Don't say that.'

'You're lying to me,' said Lucy. 'But most of all to yourself.'

'I don't lie,' Oliver said tightly.

'Should I prove it to you?' Lucy said, still friendly and impersonal. 'Should I prove to you that a good part of your life is based on lies?'

'You can't,' said Oliver. 'Because it isn't true.'

'No? Let's forget us for the moment,' said Lucy. 'Who's your best friend?'

'What are you driving at?' Oliver asked.

'Sam,' Lucy said. 'The good Dr. Patterson. You've known him for twenty years. He and his wife are in and out of our house every week. You play golf with him. You've lent him money. You confide in him. I wouldn't be surprised if you've even told him about this . . . this trouble between you and me.'

'It happens that I did,' Oliver said. 'I had to talk to someone. He's not only my friend. He's yours, too. He advised me to come back to you.'

Lucy nodded. 'My friend,' she said. 'And your friend. And what do you know about our friend, Dr. Patterson?'

'He's intelligent and loyal,' said Oliver. 'He's a damn good doctor, too. He pulled Tony through.'

Lucy nodded again. 'All true. But you know several other things about him too, don't you? About him and other women, for example?'

'Well,' said Oliver, 'it's always hard to be sure.'

'Now you're lying again, Oliver,' Lucy said gently. 'You see what I mean? You know about him and Mrs. Wales. You know about him and Evelyn Mueller. You know about him and Charlotte Stevens, because it started in our house two years ago and people have been talking about it right at our own dinner table ever since.'

'All right.' Oliver was cornered. 'So I know.'

'And now I'm going to tell you something else,' Lucy said

139

mildly. 'He's tried with me, too. Because that's the kind of man he is. Because he can't see a woman more than twice without making the effort. You must have known that, too.'

'I refuse to believe it,' Oliver said.

'Of course you do. And you went to his house a hundred times and invited him to ours. And all the others. The wives and husbands. The attached, the divorced, the dissatisfied, the curious, the loose . . . you knew about them all. And you were polite to them and friendly to them and laughed, the way all our friends do, when the talk turned that way, or when there was a scandal in the newspaper. But when it struck home you didn't laugh. All that tolerance, all that civilization, all that humour, it turned out, was not for use at home.'

'Stop it,' Oliver said.

But Lucy went on, inexorably. 'I've been thinking about all this, Oliver, for the last ten days, and I've decided you were right. At least what you said was right, even if you didn't live up to it.'

'We'll live any way you want,' said Oliver. 'We'll stop seeing anyone you say. We'll start with a whole new group of friends.'

'I didn't say that,' Lucy said. 'I like our friends. Part of the reason for my feeling that I've been happy for so long has been because of them. I'd hate not to see them any more.'

Oliver stood up, his face flushed. 'What in the name of God do you want, then?' he shouted.

'I want to live,' Lucy said quietly, 'so that no one will ever be able to say liar again to me. So that I'll never be able to say liar to myself.'

'Good,' Oliver said hoarsely. 'If you mean that, I'm glad all this happened.'

'Not so fast,' Lucy said. 'As usual, you're in a hurry to settle for half the truth. The pretty half. The half that you can believe in publicly. The attractive half. The half that makes you feel noble and self-satisfied. But the private half—the secret, unpleasant, harmful half—that exists, too, Oliver. From now on you're going to have to take them both together . . .'

'If you want to confess about anyone else,' Oliver said, 'about any other college boys, or doctors, or dinner guests, or people on a train—spare me. I'm not interested in your past. I don't want to hear about it.'

'I don't want to confess the past, Oliver,' said Lucy softly, 'because there's nothing there.'

140

'Then what?' Oliver asked.

'I want to confess the future,' said Lucy.

Oliver stared at her, baffled, angry. 'Are you threatening me?' he asked.

'No,' said Lucy. 'I just want to make sure that if ever I go into our house again I come in clean. If I finally come home, we start a new marriage and I want that understood.'

'Nobody starts a new marriage after fifteen years,' said Oliver.

'No.' Lucy nodded agreeably. 'Perhaps not. Well then, a different marriage. Up to now you've treated me as though I've been the same girl you met so many years ago. As though I'm still twenty, to be cuddled, protected, patronized. Finally, in any important matter, disregarded. And until now I've always accepted it because . . . Who knows why I've accepted it? Because I was lazy. Because it was easier. Because I was afraid to anger you. But now . . . now you've been so angry that there's nothing more to fear. The marriage has been broken. Maybe it will be put together again and maybe it won't. Whatever happens I see that I'll survive it. So—now—I no longer accept you.'

'What does that mean?' Oliver asked.

'When I agree with you, good,' said Lucy. 'I accept you. When I don't—I go my own way.'

'This is the damnedest thing,' Oliver said. 'You behave like a slut . . .'

Lucy raised her hand warningly. 'You mustn't use words like that, Oliver.'

'Whatever you call it. You commit the crime, the transgression . . . God, what's the polite word for it? And somehow you're the one who's laying down the terms.'

'Yes, Oliver,' said Lucy. 'Because your terms don't work any more. I've been trying to figure out these last ten days why I did what I did, after so long . . .'

'Why?' Oliver demanded.

'You're not going to like this, Oliver,' Lucy said warningly.

'Get it over with,' Oliver said bitterly. 'Get all the poison out this afternoon and we can start forgetting it on the trip home.'

'We can't forget it,' said Lucy. 'Not you and not me. In many ways you were a good husband. You were generous to me. I was warm in winter and well fed and you remembered my birthday and you gave me a handsome son whom I used to love a great deal . . .'

141

'What now?' asked Oliver sharply. 'What are you going to tell me now?'

'You treated me as a child so long,' said Lucy slowly, 'that the times when you suddenly had to treat me as a woman, when you made love to me, I had a child's reaction. Bored, embarrassed, incomplete, disgusted.'

'You're lying,' Oliver said.

'I told you I was never going to let anybody say that to me again,' said Lucy.

'But you always seemed . . .'

'Most of the time it was a performance, Oliver,' said Lucy gently. 'Not always—but most of the time.'

'For so many years?' Oliver asked dully, disbelievingly.

'Yes.'

'Why? Why did you do it?' Oliver asked. 'Why didn't you tell me?'

'Because I didn't think you could bear it,' said Lucy, 'if I did.'

'And now?'

'And now,' said Lucy, 'I'm more interested in myself than in you, I guess. That's what you did to me that evening ten days ago, Oliver.'

'I'm not going to listen to you!' Oliver was raging now. 'For five thousand years women have been excusing whatever cheap excursions they've made by wailing that their husbands were too old or too preoccupied or too inadequate to satisfy them. Do me the honour of thinking of something original.'

'Don't think,' said Lucy, 'that I'm trying to throw all the blame on you. Maybe if you'd been different, if we'd been different together, it wouldn't have happened. Nothing would have happened. But,' she explained honestly, 'it wasn't only that. I wanted him. For a long time I wouldn't even admit it to myself. But after it was over I was sorry I'd been so foolish and waited so long.'

'What are you trying to tell me?' Oliver asked. 'Are you going to see him again?'

'Oh, no,' said Lucy lightly. 'He has his own . . . inadequacies. He's too young. He'll be inconsequential for another ten years. He served a useful purpose but it's back to school for the children now.'

'A useful purpose,' Oliver said sardonically.

'Yes,' said Lucy. 'He made me feel what a delightful thing it was to be a woman again. He was nothing—but at the age of thirty-five he made me see what pleasure was to be found in men.'

'That's a whore's philosophy,' Oliver said.

'Is it?' Lucy shrugged. 'I don't think so and I don't believe you think so. Whatever it is, that's the way I feel and you might as well know it.'

'What are you trying to tell me?' Oliver asked.

'I'm trying to tell you that it's probably going to happen again.'

'You don't mean it. You're just saying it. You're revenging yourself on me.'

'I mean it,' Lucy said.

'We'll see,' Oliver said desperately. 'We'll see.'

'We won't see,' said Lucy. 'Why are you so shocked? You've been in locker rooms, bars, smoking rooms. Isn't that what all the conversation amounts to? And if you could listen in on ladies' luncheons and teas . . . The only difference is that after fifteen years my husband has made me tell the truth about myself and to myself.'

'No marriage can last like that, Lucy,' said Oliver.

'Maybe not,' Lucy said. 'That would be too bad.'

'You'll wind up as a lonely, forgotten old woman.'

'Maybe,' said Lucy. 'But at the moment I think it will be worth it.'

'I can't believe it,' said Oliver. 'You're so changed. You're not the same person you were even two weeks ago.'

'You're right. I *am* changed,' said Lucy. 'Not for the better. Honestly, I believe that. Much for the worse. But it's me now. It's not a reflection of you. It's not one unimportant, timid, pale, predictable fifth of your life. It's me, uncovered. My own owner. My own self.'

'All right,' Oliver said sharply. 'Go in and pack and let's go home. I'll get hold of Tony and tell him to get ready.'

Lucy sighed. Then, surprisingly, she laughed. 'Oliver, darling,' she said, 'you're so in the habit of not listening to anything I say that I could tell you your clothes were on fire and you wouldn't catch on until they'd burned right off . . .'

'Now, what do you mean by that?'

Lucy spoke very seriously. 'I wrote you I wasn't going home with Tony. Didn't you read my letter?'

Oliver made an impatient gesture. 'I read it. I read it,' he said.

'It's absurd. You obviously were in a state of nerves when you wrote it and . . .'

'Oliver,' Lucy said warningly.

'Anyway,' Oliver said, 'it's only for a few days. He'll be going to school by the end of the month and then you'll get a chance to calm down. You won't see him again until Thanksgiving and . . .'

'I'm not going to see him for a few days,' Lucy said. 'And I'm not going to see him at Thanksgiving. And I'm not going to see him at Christmas. And I'm not . . .'

'Lucy, stop that damned chant,' Oliver said harshly. 'And don't be a fool . . .'

Lucy closed her eyes wearily and waved her hand gently, dismissingly. 'Why don't you go home, the both of you,' she said, 'and leave me alone?'

'I thought we settled that,' Oliver said.

'We haven't settled anything. You said you wanted me back, and I said I wanted to come back. On certain conditions. One of the conditions is that I don't have anything more to do with Tony.'

'For how long?' Oliver asked hoarsely.

'Forever.'

'That's melodrama,' Oliver said. 'It doesn't make any sense at all.'

'Now listen carefully,' Lucy said, standing directly in front of Oliver, controlling her voice with effort. 'I mean every word I've said and every word I'm going to say. He hates me. He's my enemy . . .'

'A thirteen-year-old boy . . .'

'He's the witness against me,' Lucy said, 'and he'll never forget it, and neither will I. Every time he looks at me, he's looking through that window that rainy afternoon. He looks at me and he's judging me, prosecuting me, condemning me . . .'

'Don't be hysterical, Lucy.' Oliver caught her hands, soothingly. 'He'll forget.'

'He won't forget. Ask him. Ask him yourself. I can't live in the same house with my judge like that! I can't be made to feel guilty twenty times a day!' Her voice was shaken now and she was close to sobbing.

'You must try,' Oliver said.

'I have tried,' Lucy whispered. 'I did everything I could to heal

144

us. Even when I wrote you that I couldn't come back with him, I still hoped . . . I didn't really believe it, even while I was writing it. Then, this afternoon, he did this . . .' She pulled her hands away and pointed to the broken gramophone. 'With a baseball bat. But it wasn't a machine he was destroying. It was me. He was murdering *me*!' She was shouting crazily now. 'Murder!'

Oliver seized her and shook her, sharply. 'Stop that! Control yourself!'

Sobbing, not trying to free herself, she said, 'He'll poison everything. What'll we turn out to be after five years like that? What sort of man will he be at the end of it?'

Oliver dropped his hands. They stood next to each other for a moment, without moving. Then Oliver shook his head. 'I can't do it,' he said.

Lucy took in her breath in a long sigh. She bent her head and absently put her hands across her breast to her shoulders, stroking the spots where Oliver's hand had gripped her. When she spoke her voice was flat. 'Then leave me alone. Take him away with you and leave me alone. For good.'

'I can't do that, either,' Oliver said.

In the same flat and toneless voice, still touching her shoulders gently, Lucy said, 'You'll have to do one or the other, Oliver.'

Oliver turned and went over to the edge of the porch, his back to Lucy. He leaned against a pillar, staring out across the quiet lake. *And I was sure I had it all figured out*, he thought. He felt defeated and incapable of further plans or decisions. *What I should have done*, he thought, with bitter hindsight, *was pack everybody up the night I was here and get us all home together. Now, everybody's had time to dig in.*

He heard a movement behind him and he turned quickly. Lucy was opening the door of the cottage, on her way in.

'Where're you going?' he asked suspiciously.

'Tony's coming.' She pointed towards the hotel, and Oliver saw Tony walking swiftly towards the cottage. 'I think it'd be a good idea if you talked to him.'

She went inside, the screen door tapping lightly behind her. Oliver watched her shadowy figure disappear.

He shook his head and made himself smile before he turned to face Tony. He walked out on to the lawn a little way to greet him. Tony approached warily, his face grave and watchful, and stopped before he reached his father.

'Hullo, Daddy,' he said, waiting.

Oliver went over to him and put his hand around Tony's shoulders and kissed his cheek. 'Hullo, Tony,' he said. Still with his arm across the boy's shoulders, Oliver walked back to the porch.

'I'm all ready to go,' Tony said, pointing to the bags on the porch. 'Shall I start carrying things to the car?'

Oliver didn't answer. He dropped his arm from Tony's shoulders and walked slowly over to a rattan armchair. He sat down heavily, like an old man, staring at his son.

'I thought we were supposed to get out of here by three o'clock,' Tony said.

'Come over here, Tony.'

Doubtfully, as though fearing punishment, Tony walked across the porch and stopped in front of the chair. 'Are you sore at me, Daddy?' he asked in a low voice.

'No. Of course not. Why should I be?'

'For calling you that night,' Tony said, looking at the floor. 'For telling you what . . . what I saw . . .'

Oliver sighed. 'No,' he said. 'It wasn't your fault.'

'I had to tell you, didn't I?' Tony was pleading now.

'Yes,' Oliver said, after a pause. He stared at his son, wondering how much of this day the boy was going to remember. Children forget everything, Patterson had said. He had also said, Grown-ups forget everything. But none of it was true. Tony was going to remember clearly, accurately, painfully, and his life was going to be built on the memory. It would be simpler and less painful to slide past this moment, to make an excuse for taking the boy home alone, for packing him off to school alone. It would be easier to put him off temporarily if he asked about Lucy, to be vague and tricky when he wrote from school about coming home for the holidays, to let him discover slowly, by himself, over a period of time, that he had been put outside the boundaries of the family. It would be simpler, less painful, and finally, and with justice, as a grown man, Tony would despise him for it.

Oliver reached out and drew the boy to him, putting him on his lap, holding his head against his shoulder, as he had done long ago, when Tony had been small.

'Tony,' Oliver said, and it was easier to talk this way, with the boy's weight against him, and the bony feel of his legs, and his head averted, 'listen carefully. I wish this hadn't happened. I

146

wish, if it had happened, you never knew about it. But it happened. You found out about it. And you had to tell me.'

Tony said nothing. He sat tensely, imprisoned in his father's arms.

'Tony,' Oliver said, 'I'd like to ask you a question. Do you hate your mother?'

Oliver felt the boy stiffen in his arms. 'Why?' Tony asked. 'What did she say?'

'Answer the question, Tony.'

With a sudden movement, Tony wriggled out of his father's arms, and stood in front of him, his hands clenching and unclenching. 'Yes,' he said savagely. 'I hate her.'

'Tony . . .' Oliver started painfully.

'I'm not going to talk to her,' Tony said, speaking rapidly, his voice high and sharp and childish. 'She can say anything she wants. Maybe I'll say yes or no once in a while, when I have to, but I'm not going to talk to her.'

'How would you feel if you never saw her again?' Oliver said.

'Good!' He stood there, shoulders hunched, chin out fiercely, like a boy challenging another boy to cross a line drawn in the dust before him.

'She doesn't hate you,' Oliver said gently. 'She loves you very much.'

'I don't care what she says.'

'But she's afraid of you . . .'

'Don't believe her. Don't believe anything she says.' Now he didn't sound like a little boy at all.

'And because she's afraid of you,' Oliver went on, conscientiously, but without hope, going to the end of every argument, 'she says she doesn't want to take you home with us. She doesn't want to live in the same place with you, she says.'

For a moment, Oliver thought that Tony was going to cry. He ducked his head and he rubbed his hands jerkily against his thighs. But then he raised his head and looked squarely at Oliver. 'That's okay with me,' he said. 'I'm going to school anyway.'

'Not only school,' Oliver said, persisting. 'She never wants to see you, she says. She doesn't even want to let you come into the house. Not on Christmas. Not on holidays. Never.'

'Oh.' Tony's voice was so soft that Oliver wasn't sure he had said anything. 'What if you said, "It's my house, I'll take in anybody I want."'

'Then she'll leave me,' said Oliver flatly. 'This afternoon.'

'Oh.' Tony glanced, measuringly, at his father. 'Don't you want her to?'

'I'm afraid not.'

'Why not?'

Oliver sighed and when he spoke, he didn't look at Tony, but above his head, at the blue sky, cold with its premonition of autumn. 'It's hard to explain to a thirteen-year-old boy what a ... a marriage is like, Tony. How a man and a woman become— locked—with each other. I miscalculated on myself. Do you know what that means?'

Tony thought for a moment. Then he nodded. 'Yes. You thought you were a certain way and you turned out to be another way.'

'A certain way.' Oliver nodded. 'It turns out that I was wrong.'

'All right,' Tony said harshly. 'What do you want me to do?'

'I'm going to leave it up to you, Tony. If you say the word, I'll call your mother out here and tell her you're staying with me. And we'll say good-bye to her and that'll be the end of it.'

Tony's mouth quivered. 'And how'll you feel than?'

'I ... I'll feel like dying, Tony,' Oliver said.

'And if I say I'll go away?'

'I'll take you home and start you in school and I'll come back for your mother,' Oliver said, still looking over Tony's head at the cold sky. 'I'll visit you on holidays and in the summertime we could go on trips together. To the Rockies, to Canada, maybe even to Europe.'

'But I never could come home?' Tony asked, like a man at a ticket window in a railroad station asking all possible questions, to make sure there would be no mistake about the train he was to take.

'No,' Oliver whispered. 'Not for a long time.'

'Never?' Tony asked harshly.

'Well, in a year or two ...' Oliver said. 'Right now your mother's rather hysterical, but in time, I'm sure ...'

'Okay!' Tony turned away, presenting his back to Oliver. 'What do I care?'

'What do you mean, Tony?' Oliver stood up and walked over behind Tony, but didn't touch him.

'Call her out here. Tell her you'll come back for her.'

'Are you sure?'

Tony wheeled around and stared bitterly at his father. 'Isn't that what you want?'

'It's up to you, Tony.'

Tony shouted now, out of control. 'Isn't that what you want?'

'Yes, Tony,' Oliver whispered. 'That's what I want.'

'Okay,' Tony said recklessly. 'What're we waiting for?' He ran over to the door and threw it open and shouted in. 'Mummy! Mummy!' Then he turned back to his father. 'You talk to her.' Moving very quickly, his hands fumbling, he started to pick up his valises. 'I want to put these things in the car!'

'Wait.' Oliver put out his hand to restrain him. 'You've got to say good-bye. You can't just go off. Maybe, at the last minute she'll change her mind . . .'

'I don't want anyone to change their mind,' Tony shouted. 'Where's my telescope?'

The door opened and Lucy came out. She looked pale, but composed, her eyes going from Oliver to Tony and back again.

'Oliver . . .' she said.

'I'm taking Tony with me now.' He tried to sound routine and matter-of-fact. 'I'll call you. I'll be back for you some time next week.'

Lucy nodded, her eyes on Tony.

'We might as well get started now,' Oliver said, with shaky briskness. 'It's pretty late as it is. Tony, are these all your things?' He pointed at the two valises.

'Yes,' Tony said. He avoided looking at his mother, and gathered up the bat, the telescope, the fishing rod. 'I'll carry these.'

Oliver picked up the two valises. 'I'll wait for you in the car.' His voice was choked and muffled. He tried to say something to Lucy, but nothing seemed to come out. He walked off hurriedly, carrying the bags.

Tony stared after him for a moment, then, still avoiding looking at his mother, peered around him, as though making sure he wasn't leaving anything behind him.

'Well,' he said, 'I guess I got everything.'

Lucy went over to him. There were tears in her eyes, but she wasn't crying. 'Aren't you going to say good-bye?' she asked softly.

Tony fought with the movements of his mouth. 'Sure,' he said gruffly. 'Good-bye.'

149

'Tony,' Lucy said, standing close to him, but not touching him, 'I want you to grow up into a wonderful man.'

With a childish cry of anguish, Tony dropped the things he was carrying and threw himself into Lucy's arms. They held each other tight for a long time, but they both knew they were only saying good-bye and that it wasn't going to do any good. Finally, Lucy stepped back, resolutely.

'I think it's time to go,' she said.

Tony's face stiffened. 'Yes,' he said. He bent and picked up the bat and the telescope and the fishing rod and started after Oliver. He stopped at the corner of the porch, and Lucy felt that for the rest of her life that was the way she was going to remember him, in the suit that had grown too small for him during the summer, stiff-faced, holding the implements of childhood, outlined against the ruffled blue lake. 'If we happen to just see each other,' he said, 'you know, just by accident, like people do, on a train or in the street, I mean—what do we say to each other?'

Lucy smiled shakily at him. 'I . . . I guess we say hullo,' she said.

Tony nodded. 'Hullo,' he said thoughtfully He nodded again, as though satisfied, and disappeared around the corner of the porch, following his father.

Lucy stood still. After a while she heard the car start and drive off. She didn't move. She just stood there, looking out at the lake, with the wreckage of the gramophone at her feet.

And that was the summer.

Chapter Fifteen

'WELL, Mr. Crown,' the headmaster was saying, 'as in most cases of boys his age, there's a little of everything to report.' The headmaster raised the bottle of sherry inquiringly, but Oliver shook his head. Where Oliver had been at school he was sure that his headmaster had not offered sherry to the fathers of the pupils before lunch. Oliver realized that this was a sign that education had become more relaxed since he was a boy, but he also realized that if he accepted a second glass, a minute demerit would be

150

entered, at the back of the headmaster's mind, against the Crown family.

The headmaster put the bottle down ceremonially. His name was Hollis, he was surprisingly young, and he moved delicately in the cheerful library-like room, as though to reassure the parents of the boys entrusted to his care that the developing souls would not be harmed by any sudden or uncalculated movement on his part.

'What I mean,' Hollis went on, smiling boyishly, expertly taking the sting out of judgment, 'is that he has his problems, even as you and I did at his age, I'm sure.'

'When I was his age,' Oliver said, purposely frivolous, to keep from being lectured, 'my one problem was that I could only chin forty-three times. I'd set my heart on fifty, by my sixteenth birthday.'

Hollis smiled dutifully, accustomed to many generations of fathers. 'Of course,' he said, 'the physical thing cannot be altogether discounted. Because he can't join in all the games with the other boys, the team games—although I do hear he plays rather good tennis—it's possible that his—uh—leaning towards solitude, towards going-it-alone, has been somewhat accentuated. Although the school doctor is quite satisfied with his physical condition—we give him very careful over-all examinations once a month, you know. In fact, the doctor has privately expressed the opinion to me that Tony, if he wished, could indulge in a great deal more group activity than he actually does.'

'Maybe he just doesn't like the group,' Oliver said. 'Maybe if the group was different, he'd plunge in up to his neck.'

'Perhaps,' Hollis said. The tone was mollifying and polite, but there was a chilly blink of the eyelids over the candid, clever blue eyes. 'Although we do have a fine group of boys here, if I say so myself. Most representative.'

'I'm sorry,' Oliver said, knowing that he had been too brusque to this harmless, conscientious man only because it was impossible to explain anything to him. 'I'm sure it's Tony's fault.'

'Well'—Hollis spread his hands forgivingly—'fault is a harsh word. Taste, perhaps. No doubt he'll change as he gets older. Though, as the twig is bent . . .' He shrugged and smiled at the same time, administering a warning and a caress at the same moment. 'He does particularly well at one thing,' Hollis went on, happy to be able to uncover treasure. 'He does the cleverest cartoons for the school paper. We haven't had a boy as gifted as that in many years. They're surprisingly mature. Rather acid, I must say . . .' Again the soft apologetic smile, to put the gloss of manners on the necessary and rather unpleasant truth. 'I, myself, have heard some grumblings in certain quarters about the sharpness of some of his caricatures. But, of course, he must have sent them to you, you've seen them yourself . . .'

'No,' Oliver said. 'I haven't seen them. I didn't know he did them.'

'Ah.' Hollis regarded Oliver curiously. 'Really?' He bent his head and shuffled through some papers on his desk, then spoke more quickly, tactfully getting away from the subject. 'He does fairly well in biology and chemistry. Which is all to the good, of course, since he means to take a pre-medical course. He's—uh—negligent, I'm afraid, in most of the other subjects, although I'm told he does a great deal of reading on his own. Unfortunately,' again the understanding, practised, headmaster's grimace, 'almost none of the reading has anything at all to do with his class work. And if he wants to get into a good college in two more years . . .' Hollis left the sentence hanging, mildly and ominously threatening, like the first delicate puff of wind on a still, dark day.

'I'll talk to him,' Oliver said. He stood up. 'Thank you very much.'

Hollis stood up, too, framed against the window, behind which, in the distance, the grey Gothic buildings of the campus glittered dully in the autumn sun. He held out his hand, a spry, intelligent young man in a soft blue shirt, knowingly representing solid, grey-stone tradition, discreetly tempered by progress. The two men shook hands and Hollis said, 'I suppose you've come up to take Tony back to Hartford with you for the holiday?'

'We don't live in Hartford,' Oliver said.

'Ah?' Hollis said. 'I thought I remembered . . .'

'We moved almost a year ago,' Oliver said. 'We live in New Jersey now. In Orange. I had a chance to sell my works in Hartford and buy a larger and more up-to-date one in New Jersey,' he explained, giving all the false reasons.

'Do you like New Jersey better?' Hollis inquired politely.

'Much,' Oliver said. He did not explain that he would have liked any place in the world better than Hartford, any place to which he and Lucy came as strangers, any place in which they had no friends to ask curious questions about Tony and to fall

152

into strained silence whenever the subject of children came up in conversation. He did not explain, either, that for the last six months of their stay in Hartford, Lucy had refused to see any of their old friends, with the exception of Sam Patterson. Sam Patterson knew most of what there was to be known, and there was no need to lie to him. With all the others, the weight of speculation had finally been too much to bear. 'It's no good any more,' Lucy had said. 'After an evening with them, I feel as though I've been with a group of cryptographers who've been working with all their might to crack a code. And the code is me. I've had enough of it. If you want to see them, you go yourself.'

'Well,' Hollis was saying, 'Orange isn't so far. Are you driving Tony home today?'

'No,' Oliver said. 'This Thanksgiving my wife and I are going down to South Carolina. It's my one chance to play some golf before the winter sets in. I just came up to have lunch with Tony.'

'Oh.' A noncommittal blink of academic eyes. 'I'll arrange to have Tony in to our house for Thanksgiving dinner. I'll tell Mrs. Hollis.'

'Thanks,' Oliver said. 'Will there be many boys here?'

'A few,' Hollis said. 'We have a boy whose parents are in India, and there are always one or two from—uh—broken families . . .' He shook his head deprecatingly, smiling, deploring and forgiving the ways of the modern world. 'Though most of the boys who live too far away, or who don't go home for one reason or another, usually are invited by friends.' He paused, dutifully, permitting a parent to understand that his son was not the sort of boy who was invited by friends. 'Don't worry,' he said heartily. 'Tony will be well fed.'

He escorted Oliver to the outside door, and stood there, in the cold autumn wind, his bright necktie blowing, watching Oliver get into his car and start off towards the hotel where he was to meet Tony.

Oliver went to the bar of the hotel to wait for Tony. He ordered a whisky to take the taste of the academic sherry out of his mouth, and thought over what the headmaster had said, the gentle warnings, the unfavourable judgments, the delicate avoidance of comment on the fact that Tony's mother, in all the two years that the boy had been at the school, had never put in an appearance. Well, that was one of the things a teacher was for—to show you your son in the light that others saw him, to prepare you for what he was probably going to be like as a man. Staring sombrely into his whisky glass, Oliver realized that, as kindly as possible, the headmaster had been trying to tell him that he foresaw Tony as a lonely and unpopular man, with no great taste or aptitude for work, and an unpleasantly sharp and mocking attitude towards the people around him. Oliver sipped his whisky, resenting the headmaster and his confidence in his own judgment and his sense of prophecy. All these people, Oliver thought defensively, are wrong most of the time. That's why they became teachers in the first place. When he had been Tony's age, his own teachers, he knew, had predicted vague but glittering glories for him. He had been a tall, handsome, easy-going boy who hardly had to study at all to get the highest marks in his class, who had been a leader in all games, a captain of teams, a president of clubs and classes, a precocious and graceful squire of young ladies. Well, Oliver thought grimly, hunched over his glass, they ought to come and take a look at me now.

Thinking again of Hollis, he wondered what made him so confident of himself. Having a small, definite, achievable aim, and achieving it early? Being surrounded by the grey, unchallenging, semi-failures who made up the faculties of small, country schools? Dictating, with affable severity, to hundreds of boys who passed out of his life before they became old enough seriously to oppose him, and whose later estimates of him would never come back to him? Living always by a comfortable curriculum that hardly changed from one year to the next—so many hours for Latin, so many for sport, so many for the neat, adolescent adoration of God and the laying down of proper, devout rules? Thou shalt honour thy mother and thy father, thou shalt learn to recognize the ablative absolute, thou shalt not cheat on examinations, thou shalt prepare thyself for Harvard. And, along with all these solid foundations and secure passageways, having a pretty, buxom young wife who had come to him with a little money of her own, and who saw him always in a position of command, and who, because of his job, worked with him daily, almost hourly, so that each year their interdependence became cosier and more useful and intimate. Maybe the next time Oliver went into that cheerful office and shook that hearty hand, he would murmur, delphically, 'Remember Leontes . . .'

All goes well, Teacher? Oliver thought, grinning at his own vulgarity. Try sending your wife to the mountains for a summer.

He was about to order another whisky when through the open doorway of the bar he saw Tony coming into the lobby of the hotel.

Tony hadn't seen his father and Oliver watched him for a few seconds, as Tony peered, a little near-sightedly, through his glasses, around the hotel lobby. He wasn't wearing an overcoat and his tweed jacket was too short in the sleeves for him and he was carrying, rather clumsily, a large square of drawing board under one arm. He was taller than Oliver remembered, although he had seen him only six weeks before, and he looked thin and undernourished and cold from the sharp November wind. His hair was long and fine, in contrast to all the other close-cropped students whom Oliver had passed on the campus, and he seemed to hold himself nervously and challengingly. He had a big head, too large for his thin shoulders, and his features had fined down and his nose seemed too long for the rest of his face and to Oliver he seemed to have the air of some queer, half-timid, half-dangerous bird, solitary, ruffled, uncertain whether to fly or attack.

Looking at his son, Oliver had a strange double image. In the long nose and the fair hair and the large grey eyes, even behind the glasses, he could see Lucy's inheritance, and the broad, slightly domed forehead and the big, firm mouth made him remember, confusedly, photographs of himself when he was in school. But none of it seemed to hang together. The air of challenge, the feeling of suspicion, almost, that Tony brought with him, seemed to keep the elements of his face and body from fusing.

Then Tony saw him, and waved, and when he was up close and shaking Oliver's hand, familiarity wiped out the fragmentary impressions, and it was just Tony, grave, polite, well known.

They went into lunch and after the first ten minutes in which they discussed what they wanted to have and Oliver asked the usual questions about how Tony felt and how things were going in class and if he needed anything, and Tony gave the usual answers, the periods of silence grew, as usual, longer and longer and harder for each of them to bear. Oliver was sure that if he never came to see Tony, both he and Tony would be happier for it. But that was out of the question, although it would be hard to say why.

Observing Tony across the table, Oliver noted that the boy ate

155

politely, spilled nothing, moved his hands deftly and with precision. He kept his eyes down, and only once or twice during the meal, when Oliver for the moment had looked away and then suddenly turned back, did he catch Tony watching him, thoughtfully, without malice or love. When Tony caught Oliver's glance, he lowered his eyes, without haste, and continued eating, calmly and silently. It was only when they were eating dessert that Oliver suddenly realized that there had been something about the boy's appearance that had been bothering him ever since they had shaken hands. A heavy, long, blond fuzz had come out on Tony's upper lip and chin and there were isolated tufts of fine, curly hair along his jaws. It gave him a shaggy and unkept look, like a puppy that has walked through a puddle.

Oliver didn't say anything about it for a while, but he kept staring at the uneven, fine beard on his son's face. Of course, he thought. He's almost sixteen.

'Mr. Hollis,' Oliver said, 'told me that he was going to invite you to Thanksgiving dinner at his house tomorrow.'

Tony nodded, without pleasure. 'If I have time,' he said, 'I'll go.'

'He's a pretty good fellow, Mr. Hollis,' Oliver said heartily, glad of a subject for conversation, avoiding, with a twinge of guilt, asking what other plans Tony might have for the holiday. 'He's been watching you pretty closely. He says you have a lot of talent. The cartoons, I mean, for the paper . . .'

'I draw most of them in his class,' Tony said, neatly spooning up his chocolate ice cream. 'It keeps me from falling asleep.'

'What does he teach?' Oliver asked, avoiding a more searching question about Tony's estimate of Mr. Hollis.

'European history. He's crazy about Napoleon. He's only five feet four inches tall, so he's crazy about Napoleon.'

Was I that mean, Oliver thought, was I that observant, when I was fifteen years old?

'I'd like to see some of the drawings,' he said. 'If you happen to have any around.'

'They're nothing,' Tony spooned away at his ice cream. 'If anybody with any real talent came into this school, they'd never even look at mine.'

One thing this boy really can do, Oliver thought ruefully, is choke off conversation. He glanced around the room, to avoid looking at his son's burgeoning beard, which, unaccountably, was beginning to get on his nerves. There were several boys eating with their parents at other tables, and directly across from the table at which Oliver and Tony were sitting, there was a handsome blonde woman who didn't look more than thirty-five, and who had gold bracelets on both sleeves that sounded all over the room when she moved her hands. She was sitting across from a tall, heavy-boned boy, who was obviously her son, with the same straight nose, the same direct, happy look of carefully tended health. The son had fair hair, cut very close, and his well-shaped head rose on a powerful, thick neck from a fullback's broad shoulders. Oliver noticed that he was very polite with his mother, smiling often and listening eagerly, quick at passing the butter and pouring water, holding her hand unselfconsciously on top of the tablecloth as their voices mingled in quiet, friendly murmurs. American youth, Oliver thought, advertisement.

He became acutely conscious of the impression that he and Tony must give in contrast. Tony, with his long, unfashionable hair, his thin shoulders, his glasses, his fragile neck, and the puppy hair on his chin and jaws. And he himself stiff and obviously ill-at-ease, trying, as must be plain to all the room, to strike up a conversation with his taciturn and unfriendly son. As he stared across at the mother and son at the other side of the room, the woman saw him, and smiled warmly, in parental convention, at him. She had shining, even white teeth, and when she smiled she looked much less than thirty-five. Oliver smiled back and nodded. He nodded again when the boy, following his mother's silent greeting, saw Oliver, and gravely stood up and made a little, reserved, respectful bow.

'Who's that?' Oliver asked curiously.

Tony glanced at the other table. 'Saunders,' he said, 'and his mother. He's captain of the ice-hockey team, but he's yellow.'

'Why do you say that?' Oliver felt that he had to protest, although he wasn't quite sure whether he was protesting on the part of the boy or on the part of the mother.

'I've seen him,' Tony said. 'He's yellow. Everybody knows it. He's the richest boy in school, though.'

'Oh, is he?' Oliver glanced once more at the couple at the table, noticing more carefully the golden arms. 'What does his father do?'

'Chases chorus girls,' Tony said.

'Tony!'

'Everybody knows it.' Tony methodically cleaned off the plate of ice cream. 'His father isn't so rich. It isn't that. Saunders makes the money himself.'

'Oh, does he?' Oliver regarded the large handsome boy with new respect. 'How?'

'He lends money at interest,' Tony said. 'And he has a copy of the last chapter of *Ulysses* and he rents it out for a dollar a night. He's the president of the sixth form.'

Oliver was silent for a moment. Confusedly, he remembered reading *Alice in Wonderland* and *Just So Stories* to Tony when he was six years old. A chapter a night. After Tony had his bath and his supper and was in his slippers and bathrobe, ready for bed, smelling of soap, sitting on the edge of the armchair, his feet on Oliver's knees, so that he could see the illustrations in the lamplight.

'What do you mean, the last chapter?' Oliver asked, certain that there was some childish misunderstanding or desire to shock here.

'You know,' Tony said patiently, 'Mrs. Bloom in bed, and the tenor and the soldier in Gibraltar. Yes, yes, yes. All that stuff.'

'Have you read it?'

'Of course,' Tony said. 'It's worth a buck.'

'This is a hell of school,' Oliver said, forgetting, for the first time during the meal, the constraint that had made conversation so difficult for him. 'I think maybe I'd better let Mr. Hollis know about this.'

'What's the difference?' Tony shrugged. 'Everybody in the whole school's read it by now.'

Oliver stared, baffled, at his son, sitting two feet away from him, shaggy, with the pimples and fuzz of puberty on his face, and a cold, unafraid, measuring light in his eye, removed, mysterious, unpunishable.

'Well,' Oliver said, more loudly than was necessary, 'one thing we're going to do before we leave here is shave that damned beard off your face.'

When they left the dining room, Mrs. Saunders smiled again, radiantly, shaking her golden bracelets. Saunders, immense, smooth-cheeked, bull-necked, smiling with the gravity of a young senator, stood up and made his mannerly, serious bow.

They walked to a drugstore and Oliver bought a heavy gold-plated safety razor, the most expensive one in the shop, and some shaving soap. Tony watched him impassively, asking no questions, standing there with the clumsy piece of drawing board under his arm, glancing from time to time at the covers of the magazines that were displayed near the soda fountain. Then they went to Tony's room, walking side by side, as other fathers and sons were doing, across the dying grass, cold and wet through the thin soles of Oliver's city shoes. Some of the fathers lifted their hats in salute and Oliver did the same, but he noticed that the greetings between Tony and the other boys, with or without their parents, were always curt and unenthusiastic. Oh, God, Oliver thought, as he followed Tony's narrow back up the stairs of his house, what have I got here?

Tony had a room of his own, a sombre cubicle with greenish walls, one window, a narrow bed, a small desk, and a battered wooden cupboard. It was severely neat. There was an open wooden box on the desk, with a stack of papers, evenly clipped together, in it, and the books on the desk were lined up in an orderly row by two granite bookends. The bed didn't have a wrinkle on it and no clothing was hanging in sight anywhere in the room. Automatically Oliver thought, I ought to send Lucy here to take lessons in housekeeping.

On the wall above the bed was a large map of the world, with little coloured pins stuck into it, here and there. And hanging from a string from the ceiling, in front of the cupboard, was a yellowed human skeleton, wired together, with several important bones missing. On the desk was Tony's telescope.

This was the first time that Oliver had been in Tony's room, and he blinked, taken aback, at the skeleton. But he didn't speak about it for the moment, telling himself, with nervous reassurance, that it probably showed commendable zeal in a boy who was preparing for the study of medicine.

'I thought everybody here shared a room with another boy,' he said, unwrapping the razor and slipping in a blade.

'That's the idea.' Tony was standing in the middle of the room, staring reflectively at the map on the wall. 'I had a room-mate, but my cough drove him out.'

'Your cough?' Oliver asked, puzzled. 'I didn't know you had a cough.'

'I don't.' Tony grinned. 'But he was a nuisance and I wanted to be alone. So I used to wake up every night at two o'clock and cough for an hour. He lasted just over a month.'

159

Oh, Lord, Oliver thought despairingly, Hollis is earning his money keeping *him* in school. 'Take off your shirt, so you won't get wet,' he said, opening the tube of shaving cream.

Without taking his eyes from the map, Tony began slowly to unbutton his shirt. Oliver looked more closely at the map. There was a pin stuck in the city of Paris, and a pin stuck in Singapore and pins in Jerusalem, Assisi, Constantinople, Calcutta, Avignon, Beirut.

'What're those pins for?' he asked curiously.

'I'm going to live in each of those places three months,' Tony said matter-of-factly, 'after I get out of medical school. I'm going to be a ship's doctor for ten years.' He took off his shirt and went over to the cupboard and opened the door, making the skeleton swing out into the room, with a dry, unpleasant clatter of loose bones. Tony hung his shirt neatly on a hook and closed the cupboard door.

Ship's doctor, Oliver thought. What an ambition! He kept his eyes off Tony and stared at the map. Paris, Calcutta, Beirut. Distance, he thought.

'And where'd you get the skeleton?' Oliver asked.

'In a pawnshop on Eighth Avenue,' Tony said. 'In New York.'

'Do they let you go to New York by yourself?' Oliver asked, beginning to feel that it was hopeless to try to keep up with the plans and movements of his son.

'No,' Tony said, thoughtfully touching the skeleton. 'I tell them I'm going home for the week-end.'

'Oh,' Oliver said lamely. 'I see.' For a moment, he had a vision of his wife and his son, unknown to him, unknown to each other, standing on opposite corners of the same avenue, waiting for the lights to change, crossing, in the crowds, close enough to touch, never touching. With a sense of revulsion, he watched Tony, naked from the waist up, thoughtfully fingering the skeleton. 'How much did that cost?' he asked.

'Eighty bucks.'

'What?' Oliver couldn't stifle the tone of surprise. 'Where'd you get that much money?'

'I won it at bridge,' Tony said calmly. 'We have a regular game. I win three out of four times.'

'Does Mr. Hollis know about this?'

Tony laughed coldly. 'He doesn't know about anything.' He raised his arm and touched the base of the skeleton's skull. 'The

160

occipital bone,' he said. 'I know the names of all the bones.'

A more normal father, Oliver thought, with a more normal son, would praise him for such proof of industry. But the sight of the bare, smooth adolescent torso, vulnerable, slender, balanced and neatly shaped, next to the yellowed sticks of the pawnshop skeleton was suddenly unbearable to Oliver.

'Come over here,' he said brusquely, going to the basin in the corner of the room, 'and let's get this over with. I have to be in New York by six o'clock.'

Tony gave the skeleton one last, affectionate pat, which started once more the dicelike clacking of the bones. Then, obediently, he walked towards the basin and stood in front of Oliver.

'First, wash your face,' Oliver said.

Tony took off his glasses and turned the water on and washed his face. He did it thoroughly, meticulously. Then he dried his hands and turned towards Oliver, the fuzz on his cheeks darkened and flattened by the water.

Oliver rubbed the shaving cream carefully on to Tony's face, feeling the sharpness and delicacy of the cheekbones under his fingertips. Tony stood patiently, unblinking, without moving. Like an old blasé horse being shod, Oliver thought.

Oliver used the razor a little uncertainly, in small, tentative strokes. He had never shaved anyone else before and it was different from shaving yourself. As he worked, he remembered, sharply, the day that his own father had shaved him for the first time. It had been the summer when he was fourteen, in the big house at Watch Hill, facing the ocean, and his father had come up for the week-end and had squinted at him for several hours, much as he himself had squinted at Tony during lunch. Only, at the end of it, his father had burst into laughter and had roughly mussed Oliver's hair and had marched him up to the old, dark mahogany bathroom, shouting through the halls for the entire family to come and watch.

Oliver's elder brother wasn't there that week-end, but his mother and his two sisters, aged twelve and ten, a little disturbed by the unaccustomed boisterousness of their father, had appeared at the doorway of the bathroom, where Oliver was standing, grinning uneasily and stripped to the waist, while Oliver's father methodically stropped his ivory-handled, straight-edge razor.

As Oliver cautiously made narrow swathes in the shaving

cream on Tony's cheek, he remembered, with total clarity, the exact, flat, pleasing, rhythmic noise that the razor in his father's hand had made against the leather strap that hung next to the marble basin in the bathroom on the seashore in 1912. He remembered, too, the dry smell of the shaving soap, the feel of the badger-hair brush, the mixed smell of his father's bay rum and his mother's lavender that always hung in a thin, mysterious perfume in the bathroom. He remembered the feel of the ocean salt on his bare shoulders from the morning swim, and his mother in a blue organdie dress and his sisters, bare-legged and grave, at the door of the bathroom.

'Come in, come in,' his father had said. 'Watch the initiation of a man, ladies.'

His mother and sisters had stood there in the doorway, while his father had worked up the lather on his face, but when his father had taken the razor and had flipped it three or four times on the palm of his hand, his mother had tapped the shoulders of her daughters and had said, 'This is no place for us, girls. This is for the males of the tribe.' She had been smiling, but the smile had been a funny one, one that Oliver had never seen on his mother's face before, and she had firmly led the girls out and closed the bathroom door before Oliver's father had made the first stroke with the razor. Oliver's father had watched silently, gravely, for several long moments after the door had closed. Then he had chuckled, and holding Oliver's chin with one hand he had shaved him, swiftly, accurately, with assurance. Oliver still remembered the feel of his father's fingers on his jaw, firm, strong, gentle—and, he realized much later, after his father was dead, full of love and regret.

With his own hand on his son's chin, conscious that his movements lacked the assurance of his father's at that distant, similar ceremony, Oliver was obscurely oppressed by the recurrence of rites, with their different weight of love and gaiety. Remembering, for the first time in many years, vanished summers, almost-forgotten children, unvisited rooms, his robust and sure-fingered dead father, Oliver had the feeling that when Tony, in his turn, looked back from the vantage point of maturity on this half-comic, half-solemn moment, in the bare, neat dormitory room, with its flaking skeleton and its map marked with the coloured pins of escape, he would have reason to complain of his father.

None of this showed on his face, Oliver was sure, as he matter-of-factly scraped the thick white cream from Tony's jaws and chin. He finished, taking the last bit of fuzz off the boy's upper lip, and stepped back. 'There we are,' he said. 'Now wash your face.'

Tony bent over the basin, cupping water in his hands and splashing himself vigorously. Oliver looked at the bent, naked back, thin, but with a wiry shape of muscle that the ill-fitting jacket had belied. The skin, Oliver noted suddenly, was exactly the same colour and texture as Lucy's, soft, very smooth, very white, with a healthy glowing flush of blood near the surface.

When Tony straightened up and dried his face, he looked, for the first time, into the mirror above the wash-basin. Staring at himself, he touched, with one hand, the new smoothness of his cheeks. Oliver, standing behind him, met Tony's eyes in the mirror. With the glasses off, they were exactly Lucy's eyes, large, deep grey, shadowy, intelligent. Suddenly, examining his son's scrubbed, lean, adolescent face in the mirror, Oliver realized that Tony was going to be a spectacularly handsome man.

Almost as if he had divined what was going on in his father's mind, Tony grinned at Oliver in the mirror. 'Boy,' he said, embarrassed and pleased with himself, 'we're going to kill them.'

Then they both chuckled. And then Oliver knew that it was going to be impossible to leave Tony to the Thanksgiving dinner of the Hollises, to the headmaster's hearty, paid-up hospitality, and his regretful misgivings, to the mournful prophecies he would make to his buxom wife about the future he foresaw for young Crown, to the company of the deserted boys whose parents were in India or who came from broken homes and had failed to get invited for the holidays to homes that were not yet broken.

'Pack your bag, Tony,' Oliver said crisply. 'I'm taking you home for the week-end.'

Tony remained motionless for a second, searching his father's face in the mirror. Then, without smiling, he nodded, and put on his shirt, and unhurriedly and efficiently packed his bag.

On the drive towards New York, just as they neared the city limits, Tony asked, 'How is Mother?'

'Fine,' Oliver said.

It was the first time they had mentioned Lucy between them in two years.

Lucy came to the Pennsylvania Hotel bar five minutes before

six. Keeping an obscure and unvoiced bargain with herself, she was always on time now and never kept Oliver waiting when they went out together or had an appointment to meet each other. The bar was full of men on the way home catching a last drink or two before getting their trains to New Jersey or Long Island, and there was a sign that announced that unescorted ladies would not be served at the bar. She found a table in a corner and ordered a whisky.

She sat modestly in her corner, waiting for her husband, looking from time to time without shyness at the men who crowded around the bar, not lowering her eyes when they glanced at her. They looked grey and worn by the day's work, and they drank greedily, as though they needed the liquor to face the journey home and the evening ahead of them. Freshly bathed and dressed herself, prepared for holiday, she felt a touch of pity and contempt, observing them in their drab, office-staled clothes. She was looking forward to the dinner with Oliver in an Italian restaurant nearby that they both liked. And after that, the night on the train together. She had a childish love of trains and felt cosy and important sleeping in a compartment, listening to the sound of the wheels. And Oliver was a good traveller, attentive and much more talkative and light-hearted when he was away from home.

Then she saw Oliver coming towards her, moving among the crowded tables. She smiled and waved at him. He didn't smile back. Instead, he halted for a moment, to allow someone who was walking behind him to come abreast of him. The two figures stood there, some thirty feet away, in the narrow aisle between the tables, cigarette smoke drifting lightly around their heads.

Lucy blinked, and shook her head. Impossible, she thought.

Then the two figures advanced towards her and, without realizing what she was doing, she stood up. What a place to see him, she thought. In a bar like this.

Oliver and Tony stopped across the table from her. They stood that way, confronting each other silently.

'Hullo, Mother,' Tony said, and she heard that his voice had changed.

'Hullo, Tony,' she said.

She looked from one face to the other. Tony seemed wary, but not uneasy or embarrassed. Oliver was regarding her closely, his expression watchful, vaguely threatening.

Lucy sighed, gently. Then she moved out from behind the table and put her arms around Tony and kissed his cheek. He stood there, his hands at his sides, permitting himself to be kissed.

He looks awfully tall and old to be my son, Lucy thought, conscious of the commuters watching the family scene.

'We're not going South,' Oliver said. 'We're all going home for the week-end.'

It was more than a statement, and she knew it. It was a demand, a question, an assertion of change, a warning.

Lucy hesitated only a moment. 'Of course,' she said.

'You two stay here,' Oliver said. 'I'll go across the street and turn in the tickets. I'll be right back.'

'No,' Lucy said, panicky at the idea of being left alone, so abruptly, with Tony. 'It's terribly noisy and smoky here. We'll all go together.'

Oliver nodded. 'Whatever you say.'

In the station she stood close to Oliver at the ticket window while he wrangled with the man behind the wicket. She kept talking, in a voice which sounded, even to her, high and unnatural and artificially animated. 'Well, this changes everything, doesn't it? We have a huge amount of planning to do. The first thing is to make sure we have something to eat in the house for Thanksgiving dinner tomorrow. You know what we'll do . . . we'll go down to those wonderful Italian shops on Eighth Avenue, because all the stores'll be closed tomorrow at home, and we'll buy a turkey and sweet potatoes and cranberry sauce and chestnuts for the dressing . . .'

'By God,' Oliver said to the man behind the window, 'I'm giving you four hours' notice. That's enough for any railroad. When you buy a ticket you don't make a contract for life, do you?'

The man grumbled and said he had to talk to the night manager and he left and could be seen talking, bent over, to a grey-haired man behind a desk, who occasionally glanced up bleakly at the window at which Oliver was standing.

Tony stood silently, listening to his mother, scanning the crowds moving through the station.

'And we'll go into Schrafft's,' Lucy went on, still in the high, nervous voice, 'and get a pumpkin pie and a mince pie, and we'll buy some bread for cold turkey sandwiches for tomorrow night. And do you know what I think we ought to do tonight, Oliver . . .' She paused, waiting for him to answer, but he was glowering at the clerk and the manager and he didn't reply. 'Tonight, let's eat in Luigi's, with Tony. Do you like Italian food, Tony?'

Tony turned slowly and looked at her, across the gap of the two years, across the gap in which knowledge of each other's tastes and manners and idiosyncrasies had disappeared. 'I like it all right,' he said, speaking a little more slowly than usual, as if he understood that his mother was going on at a rate and a pitch that was not normal for her and as if, by his own sobriety, he hoped to tone her down.

'Good!' Lucy said, with too much enthusiasm. 'It's your father's and my favourite restaurant,' she said, offering it to him, offering him, in the same sentence, a picture of shared tastes, marital harmony, friendship. 'And then, after that, Oliver, do you know what I think we ought to do with Tony?'

'It's about time,' Oliver said to the clerk, who had just come back to his station and was counting the money for the exchanged tickets.

'We ought to go see a show together,' Lucy said. 'Do you like the theatre, Tony?'

'Yes,' Tony said.

'Do you go often?'

'Once in a while.'

'Maybe we can get into a musical comedy,' Lucy said. 'What do you think, Oliver?'

Oliver turned away from the ticket window, after a disapproving grunt of farewell for the clerk. 'What's that?' he asked.

'I was saying,' Lucy said, talking swiftly, as though by the continual froth of her conversation she could keep any of them from taking stock of themselves and each other, 'that we could take Tony to a musical comedy. Since it's a holiday evening and we're all here in town together and . . .'

'What about it, Tony?' Oliver asked. 'You want to go to the theatre?'

'Yes, thank you,' said Tony. 'But if it's all the same to you, not to a musical comedy. There's a play I heard about . . . *Thunder Rock*. I'd like to see that, if we can get tickets.'

'*Thunder Rock*,' Lucy said, making a little grimace. 'I heard it's terribly morbid.'

'There's no sense in wasting time on a musical comedy,'

166

Tony said firmly. 'It'd be different if I lived in New York and got to the theatre all the time.'

'Oliver . . .' Lucy said doubtfully. She was afraid of the effect on them of a grim play, afraid of the moment when they came out of the theatre, wary and uncertain of each other, and disturbed by two hours of dark emotion. A musical comedy, inconsequential and pretty, would make things easier.

'It's Tony's party,' Oliver said, as they walked towards the steps leading out of the station. 'The first thing we'll do is go into the hotel and see if they can get us the tickets.'

Lucy fell silent, walking between her husband and her son. He's beginning to make everybody's decisions again, she thought resentfully.

She conducted the shopping tour through the crowded, holiday-eve markets with an extravagant and almost hysterical open-handedness, piling her purchases indiscriminately into Oliver's or Tony's arms, talking steadily, adding to the morrow's menu, her eyes roving across the hanging rows of turkeys, the piled pyramids of oranges, apples, tangerines, grapefruit, the displays of South American melons and pineapples, the bins of potatoes and chestnuts. Then they were late and they dumped their purchases into the trunk of the car and hurried to the restaurant, where Lucy drank too much, without realizing what she was doing, and where they had to cut the meal short to get to the theatre on time. As she shopped, and rattled on, and nervously ate and drank, Lucy was conscious only of a need for postponement. Dazed by the sudden appearance of Tony, uncertain whether it was an ambush or a reinforcement to her happiness, too unstrung to be able to see what signals either Oliver or Tony were putting up, she fought confusedly to keep from making any decisions herself in those first hours or permitting the others to make any decisions on their own part.

In the theatre, she was drowsy and only listened intermittently to what the actors were saying on the stage. Between the acts she said she was too tired to go out, and sat numbly by herself when Oliver took Tony across the street for a Coca-Cola. And on the long trip home, she sat in the back of the car, not quite awake, not trying to hear what Tony and Oliver were saying to each other in the quiet darkness in front of her. When they got home, she stumbled going up the front steps and said, quite

167

truthfully, that she couldn't keep her eyes open another minute. She kissed Tony good night, briskly and without emotion, as though the two years had not intervened, and left Oliver with the job of settling the boy down in the guest room.

It was a retreat and she knew it and she was sure that Oliver, at least, and probably Tony, too, understood it, but she was too tired to care. When she got into bed and turned out the light, she had a little weary flicker of triumph. I got through the whole evening, she thought, and nothing happened. Tomorrow I'll be refreshed and I'll take hold.

As she drifted off to sleep, she heard the voices of Oliver and Tony, low, friendly, intimate, on the other side of the bedroom door and the male tread of their footsteps going down the hallway to the guest room at the back of the house. They walk so heavily, she thought. Both of them.

She wondered whether Oliver would come into her room to sleep tonight. And if he did, for whom would he be doing it? Himself? Her? Tony?

She folded her arms across her breasts and held her shoulders, because she was shivering with cold.

She was asleep when Oliver came into the darkened room, and the careful sounds he made as he undressed and got into the bed didn't awaken her.

Usually she awoke fairly early, but on this Thanksgiving morning, she slept till past ten o'clock, and when she woke she felt heavy and hangover-ish. She moved slowly as she washed and combed her hair, and she dressed with more care than she ordinarily took in the mornings. Whatever opinion he has of me, she thought grimly, at least he's going to admit that his mother is not bad looking.

She heard no sounds in the rest of the house and she took it for granted that Oliver and Tony were either in the living room or the breakfast room, off the kitchen, downstairs. But when she went down she saw that the house was empty, shining in the morning sunlight, with two sets of breakfast dishes neatly washed and left in the wire frame on one side of the kitchen sink to dry.

There was a note on the kitchen table in Oliver's handwriting, and she hesitated before picking it up and reading it, disturbed by absurd fears that there would be news in it of departures, discoveries, denunciations. But when she picked it up and read it, all it said was that they'd had their breakfast and they hadn't wanted to wake her and that since it was such a fine morning they were going to a high-school football game in town that was to start at eleven o'clock. They would be back, the note went on, in Oliver's precise and authoritative handwriting, not much later than one-thirty and they would be ready for the turkey. Love, Oliver, it ended.

She was grateful for the respite and she bustled around the kitchen, cleaning the turkey, putting the cranberries up to cook, roasting and shelling the chestnuts, moving swiftly and automatically about her chores, glad that the maid had been given the week-end off and that she had to do the work herself and that she had the house all to herself to do it in. When, during the morning, flushed from her work and the heat of the oven, she thought of Tony, it was almost carelessly. It all seemed so normal —In how many homes throughout the country was the son of the house back from school for the holiday and out watching a football game with his father while the mother prepared the standard feast. And if Tony had not been wildly affectionate the evening before, that was to be expected. He hadn't been antagonistic, either. His attitude, if it had been an attitude, could be described as neutral. A little warmer and better than neutral, Lucy corrected herself, basting the bird. She hummed comfortably to herself in the sunny kitchen. After all, two years is a long time, she thought, especially in the life of a boy. A lot of things are forgotten in two years—or at least blurred over and softened. She herself, she thought comfortably, setting the table, couldn't remember clearly just what had happened two years ago and it had all flattened out and lost the power of damaging her. At this distance it was hard to remember just why everybody had made such a crisis out of it.

Looking at the table, with the linen white, the glasses shining, she regretted for an instant that it was only going to be the three of them for the meal. It would have been nice to have some other families in, and other boys and girls Tony's age. She imagined what the table would look like, with the grownups at one end and five or six boys and girls, scrubbed, in their best clothes, the girls at that marvellous, shining age when from moment to moment they teetered back and forth between being children and young women.

169

For Christmas, Lucy decided, I'm going to arrange something big. Standing there, looking at the glittering table and thinking about Christmas, she was happier than she had been for many years.

She glanced at her watch, went into the kitchen to take a last look around and sniff, luxuriously, all the warm and pungent smells of the dinner. Then she went upstairs and took a long time surveying the dresses hanging in her wardrobe, trying to decide which one might please Tony best. She chose a soft blue dress with a wide skirt and a high neck and long sleeves. Today, she thought, he'd probably prefer me to look motherly.

Oliver and Tony came back at a quarter to two, both of them flushed from the cold and entertained by the game they had seen. Lucy was waiting for them in the living room, in her motherly dress, proud that everything had been efficiently prepared, with fifteen minutes to spare, and that they could find her sitting in the orderly, bright room, calm, leisurely, ready for them. She heard them coming in through the front door and the pleasant male mumble of their voices, and when they entered the room she smiled at them, observing that while he was undoubtedly Oliver's son, his resemblance to her, the wide brow, the long grey eyes, the fine fair hair, was overwhelmingly strong.

'It smells good in here,' Oliver said. He had obviously enjoyed his morning and he was smiling and full of energy and the nervousness and sombre watchfulness of the night before had vanished. He only glanced at her but she could tell that he was pleased with her. Perhaps it wasn't all quite real—perhaps it was all prepared and staged, his glance told her, but it was well staged.

'We met Fred Collins and his daughter at the game,' Oliver said, standing in front of the fire, 'and I invited them up here for a drink on the way home. They'll be here in a minute. Is the ice out?' He looked over at the silver ice bucket on the sideboard that they used as a bar.

'Yes,' Lucy said, satisfied with herself because she had thought of that, too, because today she was thinking of everything. She smiled up at the two of them, standing side by side in front of the fire, in their tweeds and flannel trousers, the boy almost as tall as the father, filling the room with a sense of the crisp holiday outdoor morning. Tony looked at home, as though he was familiar with every corner of the room, as though he had lived here a long time and could move about the house carelessly and without strangeness.

'Did you like the game?' Lucy asked.

'It was a pretty good game,' Tony said. 'There's a full-back who's going to go places in college, if they don't break his neck for him first.'

'Do you like football?' Lucy said.

'Uhuh,' said Tony. 'As long as I'm not expected to cheer for anybody.'

Oliver gave Tony a swift, searching look, and Lucy thought, I must stop asking him direct questions about himself. The answers always are a little queer, and not what you would really want to hear from your son. Disturbed, she stood up and went over to the bar and fussed, getting out glasses, with her back to Oliver and Tony. She was relieved when the doorbell rang and Oliver went to the front hall to let in Fred Collins and his daughter.

There was a kind of roaring at the front door because Fred Collins talked like that. He came from Oregon and he had the notion that the way you demonstrated the virtues of the primitive and open-handed West was to talk at the top of your voice at all times. He was a big man with a crushing handshake and he still affected a wide-brimmed, vaguely Texan kind of felt hat and he drank a good deal and organized poker games and he was always taking Oliver off to go hunting for deer and birds. Twice a year he discovered prizefighters who would make everybody forget Joe Louis and he had once taken Oliver all the way out to Cleveland to watch his current discovery get knocked out in three rounds by a Puerto Rican. Although she had never seen him put to the test, Lucy believed that he was generous and good-hearted and she was grateful to him for taking Oliver off so many evenings of the year and on the protracted trips to hunting camps and distant arenas.

He had a pretty, rather washed-out-looking wife whom he called Sweetheart and whom he treated with the cumbrous gallantry of a bear in the zoo. His daughter Betty was only fifteen years old, small, honey-coloured, confident of herself, coldly coquettish, and, as Lucy described her privately, ripening daily into wickedness. Even Oliver, who was among the least susceptible of men, confessed that when Betty Collins came into a room, she made him uncomfortable.

171

'I'm telling you, Ollie,' Collins was saying, his words clearly discernible in the living room, 'that boy is a find. Did you see the way he cut back when they piled up in front of him at the tackles? He's a natural.' In the autumn, Collins supplemented his discoveries of fighters who would make everybody forget Joe Louis by discoveries of backs who would make everybody forget Red Grange. 'I'm going to write my old coach at Oregon and tell him about this boy, and maybe get to him with an offer. We could use him out there.' Collins had left college more than twenty years before, and he hadn't been back in Oregon for more than a decade, but his loyalty never wavered. He was also loyal to the American Legion, of which he was an officer, several secret societies, and to the New Jersey State Republican Committee, which was at the moment rocking under the hammerblows of the Roosevelt dynasty. 'Don't you agree, Ollie?' Collins asked, invisible but loud. 'He'd really be something in Oregon, wouldn't he?'

'You're absolutely right, Fred,' Lucy heard Oliver murmur, approaching down the hall. Collins was the only person who ever had called him Ollie. It made Lucy wince every time she heard it, but Oliver hadn't ever complained about it.

The men came into the room, herding Betty in front of them. Betty smiled at Lucy and said, 'Hullo, Mrs. Crown,' in the voice that, as much as anything else about her, made men uncomfortable in her presence.

Collins stopped melodramatically at the doorway. 'By God,' he roared, spreading his arms like a wrestler preparing to grapple an opponent. 'What a vision! Now, here's something *really* to be thankful for! Ollie, if I was a churchgoing man, I'd go to church this afternoon and praise the Lord for making your wife so beautiful.' He advanced on her, rolling archly. 'I can't resist it, Ma'am, I just can't resist it,' he shouted, taking her into his arms. 'You're getting prettier every day. Son,' he said to Tony, who was standing at the doorway, watching carefully, 'with your permission I'm going to kiss your mother, because it's a holiday and because she's the loveliest lady this side of the Mississippi River.'

Without waiting for an answer from Tony, Collins gripped her tight, the wrestler coming to close quarters, and kissed her loudly on each cheek. Almost smothered by the man's bulk, Lucy laughed, a little uneasily, permitting herself to be kissed, because if you allowed Collins into the house you had to take him with

172

all his noise and all his rough-hewn and boisterous gallantry. She had a glimpse, past Collins' head, of Tony. Tony wasn't looking at her now, but had turned and was watching Oliver with an expression of scientific interest on his face.

Lucy couldn't see Oliver, and Collins pressed her heartily to his barrel-like chest once more, crying, incomprehensibly, but with the best will in the world, 'Venus! Venus!' Then, winking broadly and rolling his head lewdly, he said, in a loud stage whisper, 'Baby, my car is waiting, with the motor running. Just say the word and off we go. The first night of the new moon. Watch out for me, Ollie, boy, watch out for me. She brings out my tiger blood.' He roared with laughter and let her go.

'That's enough, now, Fred,' Lucy said, knowing how ineffectual it must sound in the midst of all that bellowing and lip-smacking. She looked over again at Tony, but his eyes were fixed on his father, coolly, expectantly.

But Oliver didn't seem to notice. He had seen so much of Collins in the last year that the noise and confusion that surrounded him by now seemed normal, as the sound of a waterfall finally seems almost like silence to people who live next to it.

Collins finally released her and sank expansively on to the couch, pulling his daughter down beside him and fondling her hand in his. 'Ah, these cushions feel good,' he said. 'Those benches at the game are awfully rough on the derrière.' He beamed with coarse benevolence at Tony. 'He's a fine-looking boy, Lucy. A little stringy so far, eh, Son, but that's the age for it. When I was your age you may not believe it, but I only weighed a hundred and thirty-five pounds, soaking wet.' He laughed loudly, as though what he had said had been irresistibly witty. 'We're glad we finally met the young Crown prince, aren't we, Honey?' He peered lovingly into his daughter's eyes.

Betty looked consideringly at Tony, using her lashes. 'Yes, Daddy,' she said.

'Yes, Daddy,' Collins mimicked her in a quivering falsetto. 'Oh, the volumes that're concealed in those two simple words. Yes, Daddy.' He leaned over and kissed her cheek, entranced with his own vision of his daughter. 'Beware this girl, Son,' he said. 'She has her eye on you. I recognize the signs. Consider yourself lucky and beware! The whole senior class of the high school would give up their next year's allowance for that little Yes, Daddy.'

'Now, Daddy, stop . . .' Betty said, tapping her father's hand reprovingly.

'When we went through the stands to our seats this morning,' Collins said, booming, 'you could hear the sigh of desire sweeping across the cheering section like the wind through a field of wheat.' He laughed fondly, proud, overt, simple-minded.

Oliver, who was standing by the fire now, next to Tony, laughed, too. Tony looked at him, unamused, icily puzzled.

'Say, Betty,' Collins said, 'aren't you going to a dance tonight?'

'Yes,' the girl said.

'Why don't you take Tony along with you?' Collins said. 'If he's half the man his daddy is, I'll bet he'll be able to show you a thing or two.'

Nervously, Lucy glanced at Tony. He was peering at Collins studying him, as though Collins were an animal he had never seen before and which he was trying to place in its proper category.

'Well, I'd love to,' Betty said, smiling at Tony, using her medium artillery. 'I honestly would. But I promised Chris I'd let him take me and . . .'

'Chris, Chris!' Collins waved impatiently. 'You know you have no use for him. We can't let Tony just mope around with the old folks on his holiday. Let 'em both take you.'

'Well, of course, that would be lovely,' Betty said, and Lucy was sure the girl was calculating secretly the impact of the moment of her arrival at the dance with a boy on each arm. 'If Tony would like to . . .'

'Of course Tony would like to,' Collins said. 'You be at our house at nine o'clock tonight, Son, and . . .'

'I'm sorry, Sir,' Tony said. 'I'm busy this evening.'

He spoke very quietly and it cut into the booming torrent of Collins' sound, coldly polite, uninterested, a rebuke to the loud and foolish father and the coquettish and triumphant daughter. There was nothing boyish or hesitant about it. It was an adult and chilly snub, fastidiously administered. Betty did not mistake it. She glanced thoughtfully at Tony, annoyed and interested, her face open for a moment, revealed. Then she dropped her eyes, covering up.

Where did he learn to behave like this, Lucy wondered. What has he had to do with girls in the past two years that makes him so sure of himself? And seeing Collins now through Tony's eyes,

174

she realized, painfully, that as recently as a year ago, Oliver would never have permitted either the man or his daughter to enter the house.

Collins didn't miss it either. He narrowed his eyes, measuring Tony, understanding antagonism. The room was uneasily silent, the atmosphere strained. Only Tony, of all of them, Lucy felt, was undisturbed. Then Collins patted his daughter's hand protectively.

'Well,' he said, 'you had your chance, Son.' He turned to Oliver. 'Didn't you say something about a drink, Ollie?'

'Oh, I'm sorry,' Oliver said. 'What'll it be?'

'Martinis,' Collins said. 'It's the only drink for Thanksgiving.'

Oliver started to put the ice into the shaker and opened a bottle of gin. They all watched him with exaggerated interest, trying to ignore the breach that Tony had opened between them.

'No, no, no,' Collins said, jumping up. 'You're drowning it in vermouth, lad.' He went over to the bar and took the shaker from Oliver's hand. 'You'll ruin the holiday, Ollie! Here, let me make it, let the old martini-master get to work.'

'If you want.' Oliver relinquished the gin bottle, too. 'We usually drink whisky and I . . .'

'It's all in the wrist, all in the wrist, my boy,' Collins said, pouring elaborately, squinting with one eye. 'I learned it from an old Indian out in the big woods . . .'

'I'll do it.' It was Tony. He had moved, unhurried, between the two men, and he took the shaker from Collins' hand.

Collins stood there, his mouth open foolishly, his hand still curved in the position it had been in when he was holding the shaker.

'In this house, Mr. Collins,' Tony said, 'we supply our own bartenders.'

Calmly, Tony poured the gin and the vermouth and began to mix the drink, staring at Oliver, rebuking him silently and pitilessly.

'Sure, sure . . .' Collins said. He shrugged, disciplined, wanting to react, not knowing just how. He went back to the couch and sat down, dismissed.

Tony stood next to the bar, stirring, ignoring Collins, looking steadily and contemptuously at his father. Oliver met his eye briefly, smiled uncomfortably, and moved away. 'Well,' he said, more loudly than was necessary, 'that's the advantage of sending your son to a good school. They teach him to make martinis.'

He laughed, falsely, and Lucy felt she couldn't stay in the room a moment longer. She sprang up from her chair. 'If you'll excuse me,' she said, 'I have to go and see that the dinner isn't burning up.'

She fled into the kitchen, making sure the door was shut tight behind her, so that she wouldn't hear what they were saying in the living room. She worked distractedly, uselessly, not paying attention to what she was doing, wishing that the day was over, the week-end, the year . . . Oh, God, she thought, the accidents! Why did they have to meet Collins at the game? Why couldn't it have been raining, so that they would never have left the house? Why did Oliver have to invite him over? Why did I let him kiss me? Why does Oliver let him call him Ollie?

She put the turkey on the platter and the sweet potatoes around it and the gravy in a boat and the cranberry sauce in a bowl. Then she sat down next to the window, staring out at the greying afternoon, her hands folded desolately in her lap, waiting until she heard the voices die down in the living room, and a few minutes later, the sound of Collins' car going off down the street.

Then she carried the holiday turkey into the dining room, smiling almost correctly, crying, 'Dinner, dinner,' knowing that nothing was going to be any good.

Tony hardly talked during the meal and Oliver talked too much, drinking almost a whole bottle of wine, and making a rambling speech about politics and taxes and the possibility of war, speaking with his mouth full of food, looking over their heads, not waiting for answers.

After the meal was over, Oliver said he had promised Collins he was going to walk over to his house for a brandy. He asked Tony and Lucy if they wanted to go with him and seemed relieved when Tony said, 'No,' and Lucy said that she was tired and wanted to take a nap.

Oliver went out of the house, humming, loudly, a march that the high-school band had played between the halves that morning. For a moment, left alone at the cluttered table with Tony, Lucy thought that, finally, she could talk to him, and, by saying the exact, right word, cure them all. But Tony's face was still and removed and she got up from the table and said, 'Leave everything, I'll clear it up later,' and went up to her bedroom without looking back.

She lay down on the bed and dozed a bit, pursued by dreams, and doors seemed to open and close in her dreams and there were steps in a shadowy, distant hallway and a final soft thud of a faraway door shutting.

When she woke, unrefreshed, she went down to the living room and it was without surprise that she saw the note on the library table. She picked it up and took the note out of the envelope and read, still unsurprised, in Tony's handwriting, that he had decided that it would be better if he went back to school.

'I despise what you have done to my father,' he wrote, 'and what you have made him turn into and I don't want to see him again in this house with you and with the kind of friends you have driven him to.'

There was something that had been heavily scratched out at the end of the letter and for a while she didn't bother to try to decipher it. She sat wearily in the dimming November afternoon light, the letter in her hand, oppressed by accident and failure.

After a while she turned on a lamp and looked more closely at the scratched-out sentence that ended the note. She puzzled over it, holding it directly under the lamp light, and after a minute or two she saw what Tony had put there.

'I repudiate you,' he had written, and she wondered why he had taken the trouble to cross it out.

Chapter Sixteen

AND the next time she saw him was through the cigarette smoke at the bar in Paris, with the noise of the piano behind her and the Negro singing 'Le piano des pauvres' with a broad Harlem accent, and the college boy holding her hand among the beer-glasses on the table.

How many years between the sombre November twilight and the club proprietor saying, 'Let me advise you, Madame, to telephone first. Mr. Crown is married. To a beautiful and charming lady'? Sixteen years. And a war won and lost; Oliver dead; age accepted or nearly accepted; everything repaired, or almost repaired; revisions accomplished; pain and loss misted over by habit, dimmed in the memory, incapable, one had thought, of causing further harm.

She slept very little that night, in the high-ceilinged, old-fashioned hotel room, the wide, lumpy bed crowded against the wall by a huge, dark wardrobe whose door she couldn't quite close and which creaked gently and warningly from time to time in the darkness, disturbed by the wind that came in through the slit of the iron shutters at the window.

She lay in the bed, listening to the obscure complaints of the wardrobe door, on the edge of sleep, changing her mind a dozen times, deciding to leave the next morning, deciding to go to the address the man had written down for her at the bar, deciding to act as though she had never seen Tony, and go sightseeing the next day, as she had planned, the Louvre, Versailles, the walk along the river, deciding to jump up immediately and call him on the telephone and say . . . what? 'This is your mother. Do you still hate me?' or, 'I happened to go into a night club a few hours ago and guess who I saw standing at the bar . . .'

She fell asleep, remembering his face, so much like the other face, dead and almost forgotten, remembering the child's face from which it had been formed, narrow, soft-skinned, with the speckled grey eyes which were so much like hers.

It was early, not much past eight o'clock, when she woke in the morning, with the sound of the Vespas and motor-bikes and trucks coming in off the street. She lay still, listening uncomfortably, not remembering for an instant, but conscious that something had changed, feeling no longer like a tourist, but like a victim, in the strange, shaded room.

Then she remembered and understood why she felt that way. She made herself get out of bed and look at the clock. She regretted that she had not slept later, because if she had, she would have been able to tell herself that it was too late, he undoubtedly would be out of the house, at work . . .

She bathed, in cool water, to try to wake herself up, and dressed hurriedly and mechanically, anxiously looking at the clock, like a woman with a train to catch. She looked in the mirror before leaving the room. She stared curiously at herself, wondering what he would see when they met. Even in the daylight, she realized without vanity, even with so little sleep, she didn't look so bad. Her eyes were clear, the skin smooth, she didn't need any make-up except a little lipstick because she was tanned, the dark blonde of her hair was highlighted by the strawy streaks that always came out in it when she stayed in the sun.

She put on a hat and started out, then stopped and took the hat off and threw it on the bed. She didn't wear a hat except on ceremonial occasions, and she didn't want this to be a ceremonial occasion. She brushed her hair nervously once more, then, on a sudden impulse, went over to where her valise was lying open on its stand and reached into the pocket under the top lid and took out a wrinkled, crumbling envelope. Carefully, she put the envelope into her bag and went out of the room.

Downstairs, she hailed a taxi, and managed to make the driver understand the address in only two tries. As she settled on the seat in back, and the taxi started off down the cool, tree-lined street, she had a small feeling of triumph. Perhaps it's an omen, she thought. Maybe today I can communicate with everybody.

Bouncing on the rough springs of the taxi seat, moving swiftly along the foreign streets, she didn't know exactly what she wished to communicate to her son. It was difficult, even, to know just why she was going to see him or what she expected from the visit. She just knew that it had to be done. It was like opening a door to a long corridor in a dream and feeling that for some reason that would never be clear, before the dream ended it would be necessary to go to the end of the corridor.

The taxi stopped in front of an apartment house on a quiet street and she got out and paid the driver, trying to control the slight shaking of her hands. Before going in, she looked at the face of the house. It was of anonymous grey stone, rather shabby and weatherbeaten, one of those buildings which have very little beauty in themselves but which combine, somehow, in Paris, with the similar buildings around them, to make a soberly pleasant pattern on street after street of the city.

At home, she realized, people who lived in a house like that would move to another neighbourhood as soon as they could manage it.

She went in and said clearly to the fat blonde woman in the concierge's room, 'Monsieur Crown, s'il vous plaît.'

'Troisième, à gauche,' the concierge said, looking at her sharply, suspecting everything.

Lucy translated laboriously for herself and pushed the button in the lift for the third floor. The hall was dark when she got out and she fumbled for more than a minute before she found the button of the doorbell, to the left of the lift shaft. She heard the bell ring inside the apartment, and the muffled sound of a vacuum cleaner somewhere else in the building, insistent and annoying.

The door did not open, and Lucy rang again, hoping guiltily that there was no one home, that she could make her way down the dark stairway and into the street and away from the building without having to come face to face with her son. She was just about to turn away when she heard steps within and the door opened.

A young woman stood there, in a pink wrapper, a young, small woman with short dark hair, outlined against bright sunlight that poured into the hallway behind her. Lucy couldn't see her face, just the small, slender silhouette against the light.

'Mrs. Crown?' Lucy said.

'Yes.' The woman stood there, with the door thrown carelessly wide open.

'Is Mr. Crown in?' Lucy asked.

'No.' The woman made a quick, inquisitive movement of her head, as though she was trying to get a better look at Lucy.

'Will he be back soon?' Lucy asked.

'I don't know,' the woman said. Her voice was cool and unfriendly. 'I don't know when he'll be back. Who shall I say called?'

'My name is Crown,' Lucy said, feeling ridiculous. 'I'm his mother.'

They stood silently for a moment, facing each other. Then the woman laughed.

'Come in,' she said, taking Lucy's arm. 'It's about time we got to know each other.'

She led Lucy down the hall and into the living room. The room was cluttered and a breakfast tray was set on a low table in front of the couch, with a half-drunk cup of coffee, a smouldering cigarette, and the Continental edition of the *Tribune*, turned back to the editorial page.

'Well, now,' the woman said, turning towards her, smiling a little. 'Welcome to Paris.'

It was hard to tell whether the words and the smile that went with them were derisive or not, and Lucy stood there, waiting, cautious, uncomfortable, on foreign and uncertain ground.

'First,' the woman said, staring directly at Lucy, 'I suppose I ought to introduce myself. Or do you know my name?'

'No,' said Lucy, 'I'm afraid I . . .'

'Dora,' the woman said. 'And I know yours. Won't you sit down? And can I get you a cup of coffee?'

'Well,' Lucy said, 'if Tony's not here . . . I wouldn't like to interfere with your morning.'

'I have nothing to do with my morning,' the girl said, 'I'll go get another cup.'

She left, walking lightly, the pink wrapper floating through the beams of sunlight that came in through the open windows. Lucy sat down on a straight chair, looking around her at the room. It was a room that had seen better days. The paint was old and dirty, the rugs threadbare. It gave an impression of rented furniture, things slightly out of repair, a provisional and careless existence. Only two large, brilliant paintings on the wall, abstract and nervous, gave the feeling of personal choice, ownership.

They must be poor, Lucy thought, or nearly poor. Where did all the money go?

Dora came back, carrying a cup and saucer. While she was pouring the coffee, Lucy examined her obliquely. She was very young, with deep black eyes, and a heavy mass of dark hair pulled back from her forehead with attractive austerity. She had a pointed small face and a wide, full mouth, whose sensuality was accentuated and made somehow disturbing by the paleness of her skin. With a cigarette hanging from her lips, squinting a little, bent over the low table as she poured out the coffee, Dora's face seemed marked by resignation and a permanent dissatisfaction.

Maybe it's the style for the young married set this year, Lucy thought, accepting the cup and saucer. Maybe this year they have decided to look dissatisfied.

'Well, now, at last,' Dora said, seating herself directly across from Lucy. 'I'm sorry Tony isn't here to do the honours.'

'Has he gone out already?' Lucy asked.

'No,' Dora said, without expression. 'He hasn't come in yet.'

'Does he work at night?' Lucy asked, confused.

'No,' said Dora.

'I mean . . . I saw him at two o'clock, in a bar . . .' Lucy stopped, embarrassed.

'Did you?' Dora said, without interest. 'How was the reunion?'

'I didn't speak to him. When he left, I got the address from the manager.'

'Was he alone?' Dora tilted her head back, finishing her coffee.

'Yes.'

'Fancy that.' The tone of the girl's voice was still flat, automatic.

'I'm sorry,' said Lucy. 'I don't want to meddle . . . Perhaps I'd better go. If you want, when he gets back, you can tell him I'm in Paris and I'll leave the telephone number of my hotel and if he . . .'

'Don't go, don't go,' the girl said. 'You're not meddling. And he's liable to come in any minute. Or any week.' She laughed drily. 'Oh, it's not as bad as you think,' she said. 'Or anyway, I like to tell myself it's not as bad as people think. He has a studio near here and sometimes when he's working hard or when he can't stand domesticity any more, he stays there. If you saw him at a bar at two o'clock, I guess he wasn't working very hard last night, though.'

'A studio?' Lucy asked. 'What does he do in a studio?'

'Don't you know?' Dora asked, sounding surprised.

'No. The last time I heard from him was during the war, when he got the news that his father had been killed,' said Lucy. 'He wired me that he didn't intend to come to the funeral service.'

'That sounds like him.' The girl looked amused. 'He can't stand ceremonies. If our own wedding had lasted another five minutes, he'd have run like a deer.' She paused, grimacing a little, lighting another cigarette, looking up at the ceiling over Lucy's head, as though remembering the wedding. 'I don't suppose you knew he was married, either, did you?'

'No.'

'Well, he is,' the girl said. 'For his sins. For the moment, he's married. No guarantees go along with this purchase.' She chuckled briefly.

She's not as hard as she wants me to think she is, Lucy thought, studying the pale, youthful, bitter face. Perhaps that's the style, too. Or she has learned to put it on to live with her husband.

'You wanted to know what he does in a studio,' Dora said. 'He's a cartoonist. He draws funny pictures for the magazines. Didn't you know that, either?'

'No,' said Lucy. It seemed like an improbable profession for a son of hers to be following. Naïvely, the word cartoonist made her think of clowns, comedians with funny hats, simple and light-hearted young men. The glimpse she had had of Tony the night before had suggested none of these things. And certainly, when he was a boy he had been serious enough. 'It's true, he used to cover all his school books with little drawings. They weren't terribly good, though.'

'I imagine he's improved a bit,' the girl said. 'In that direction, anyway.'

'But I've never seen his name . . .'

'He doesn't draw under his own name. I think he's ashamed of it. If he could do anything else, he'd quit.'

'What does he want to do?'

'Nothing. Or at least nothing that he's ever told me.'

'Does he do well?' Lucy asked.

'Well enough,' she said. 'We eat. If we went back to America, he probably could make a lot of money. He's not very interested. His tastes are simple. Awful but simple.' She smiled bleakly. 'And he never showed any desire to shower his wife with mink.'

'Why doesn't he want to go back to America?' Lucy asked, hoping for an answer that would not damage her.

Dora looked at her coldly. 'He says he got used to living in exile when he was young, and he'd feel uncomfortable changing the pattern. And he says he likes living in France best of all, because the French are in despair and he admires that.'

What conversations must have gone on in this shabby room, Lucy thought, what hurtful, desolate interchanges!

'Why does he talk like that?' she asked.

The girl looked at her levelly. 'You tell me,' she said.

Lucy hesitated. 'Some other time,' she said. 'He sounds like a terribly difficult man.'

Dora laughed. It sounded as though it had been choked out of her. 'Lady,' she said, 'what a gift for description you have.'

She is not my friend, Lucy thought. Whatever else she may turn out to be, she is not my friend.

'Ah, I shouldn't talk like that,' Dora said. 'I make him sound like a monster. And he's not a monster. We've been married five years and he's given me some rough times, and there's always the chance he'll come home one day and tell me we're finished—in fact, I'm sure it's going to happen eventually—and yet, I wouldn't change it, I wouldn't change any of it. It's been worth it,' she said, as though challenging Lucy to deny it. 'No

183

matter how it ends, it's been worth it.' Then, with an obvious effort she checked herself. 'Oh, you'll see for yourself,' she said lightly, 'when you talk to him. Inside of twenty minutes, he'll probably charm you into feeling that he's the most devoted and loving son who ever lived. If he wants, he'll convince you that he really has been trying to reach you on the telephone for twenty years, only you just happened to be out the times he called . . .'

'I doubt that,' Lucy said. She felt nervous and unlucky and she had to hold her hands together to keep them from fidgeting. Bad luck, bad luck, she thought. Tony not there, when she had herself all prepared, finally, to confront him—and instead, this hostile, unhappy, cynical, pathetic girl, with her disturbing revelations about him, with her little anthology of her husband's bitter aphorisms on exile and despair, her challenging, open devotion in the face of neglect, or worse than neglect.

'Oh,' the girl was saying, suddenly polite and hostess-like, 'that's enough about me. I'd love to hear something about you now. You look so young . . .'

'I'm not so young,' Lucy said.

'I knew you were beautiful. Tony told me,' the girl said, sounding genuine and artless, her eyes smiling, looking directly at Lucy, unexpectedly approving of her, as though she had decided to observe her objectively, with no reference to her history, no reference to what was behind the smartly cut dark blonde hair, the wide, deep eyes, the large, youthful, pleasant mouth. 'But it just never occurred to me that you could look like this—that when I saw you, it would still all be there like this . . .'

'It really isn't still all there, my dear,' Lucy said.

'You ought to see *my* mother.' Dora chuckled mischievously. 'Garden-club type. Light-heavyweight division. When she decided to let herself go, she took the longest cruise that was being offered.'

The two women laughed together, a gossipy, feline, comfortable laugh.

'You must hang around,' Dora said, 'and teach me the trick. I never've been able to stand the idea of growing old. When I was sixteen, I made a holy vow to myself—to commit suicide on my fortieth birthday. Maybe you can save me from that.'

The trick, Lucy thought, smiling at her daughter-in-law, but feeling something sober and shadowy within her, the trick is to suffer and be alone and never be certain enough of anything to fall back comfortably and know that someone is there to catch you. The trick, if you're interested, is to struggle constantly.

'It's a shame it isn't afternoon,' Dora said. 'We ought to have a drink to celebrate meeting each other, after all these years.' She looked inquiringly at Lucy. 'Would you think it was sinful to have a drink at this hour of the morning?'

Lucy looked at her watch. It was nine-thirty-five.

'Well . . .' she said doubtfully. She had known several women who were constantly looking for excuses to drink at all hours of the day and night. Maybe that was it, that was why Tony kept away from his home so much . . .

The girl giggled. 'Don't look at me like that,' she said, understanding. 'I've never had a drink before noon in my whole life.'

Lucy laughed again, pleased with the girl's perceptiveness. 'I think it would be a wonderful idea,' she said.

Dora stood up and went over to a small, marble-topped table against the wall, on which stood some glasses and bottles. She poured Scotch and a little soda into two glasses. Her movements were precise and graceful and she looked like a serious and slender child with her head inclined to one side, measuring out the drinks. Watching her, Lucy felt a sharp twinge of dislike for her son, for causing pain to a girl like that, who, because of her beauty, must have expected, ever since her first look in a mirror, that kindness, forbearance and love would be the constant climate of her life.

Dora offered her a glass. 'At French festivals, in little towns,' she said, 'they often drink in the morning. A lot of people are invited and they advertise it in the local newspaper as the Verre d'Amitié, or the Coupe d'Honneur. That's the glass of friend-ship,' she translated conscientiously, 'or the cup of honour. What should we call this?'

'Well, let me see,' Lucy said, 'how about a little bit of both?'

'A little bit of both.' Dora nodded and raised her glass, and they drank. Dora rolled the liquor around on her tongue, con-sidering it. 'Now I know why people drink in the morning. It tastes so much more significant in the morning, doesn't it?'

'Yes, it does,' Lucy agreed. The flavour of hostility had vanished and she was beginning to feel very much at home with the girl and approving of her son, at least in this one respect, for having chosen her.

'Now,' Dora said, between sips, 'I've talked enough about

185

myself and Tony. How about you? What're you doing here? Touring?'

'Only partly,' Lucy said. 'I work for an organization in New York that's attached, more or less unofficially, to the United Nations. It devotes itself to children. We sort of meddle all over the world, making politicians uncomfortable if they don't take a proper stand on child-labour and voting credits for schools and making sure all the little citizens are vaccinated and eligible for a few pints of milk a year. And we're very stern about illegitimate children getting full rights before the law. Things like that.' She spoke lightly, but her pride in the work she was doing and her fundamental seriousness about it were not disguised. 'And a lot of money comes our way from people in America, and we decide how it's to be spent. I've been roaming around Europe for five weeks now, looking solemn at meetings and taking notes and patting small dark heads in Greece and Yugoslavia and Sicily. I had a conference last night and everything had to be translated into three languages and it didn't end till after one A.M. and I was famished when I got back to my hotel, because I missed my dinner. That's how I happened to go into that place and see Tony . . .'

'You sound like a very important person,' Dora said, youthfully impressed. 'Do you give Press conferences and all that?'

'Occasionally.' Lucy smiled. 'I'm very strong on birth control.'

'I never did anything,' Dora said absently, twirling her glass. 'I didn't even finish college. I came over here for a vacation and I met Tony and there went college . . . It must be a wonderful thing to feel useful.'

'It is,' Lucy said soberly, meaning it.

'Maybe when Tony finally leaves me,' Dora said matter-of-factly, 'I'll take steps to become useful.'

The door from the dining room was slowly pushed open and a small boy's head appeared, poking out behind it. 'Mummy,' the boy said, 'Yvonne says this afternoon is her day off and if you say all right she'll take me to visit her sister-in-law. Her sister-in-law has three birds in a cage.'

'Come in here, Bobby,' Dora said, 'and say hullo.'

'I have to tell Yvonne,' the boy said. 'Right away.' But he came into the room, shyly ignoring Lucy, straight-backed, sturdy, with thoughtful grey reminiscent eyes and a domed, long head. His hair was cut close and he was wearing shorts and a knitted shirt and his bare arms and legs, scarred by the usual mishaps and antiseptics of childhood, were straight and surprisingly strong-looking.

Lucy watched him, feeling dazed, forgetting to smile, remembering what Tony had looked like at that age. Why didn't she tell me they had a son, Lucy thought, aggrieved and mistrustful once again, feeling that somehow Dora had purposely and with some ulterior motive held back this key piece of information.

'This is your grandmother,' Dora was saying, smoothing the boy's hair gently. 'Say hullo, Bobby.'

Silently, his eyes still averted, the boy came over to Lucy and put out his hand. They shook hands gravely. Then, unable to resist it, and at the risk of frightening or offending the boy, Lucy took him in her arms and kissed him. Bobby stood politely, waiting to be released.

Lucy held on to him, not because she wanted to prolong the kiss, but because if she let him go, she was afraid that he would see her crying. Now, suddenly, with her arms around the bony shoulders, with the soft, firm child's skin under her fingers, the sense of loss, of wasted years, which until then had been only abstract and theoretical, became real, painful, sadly and powerfully fleshed.

She bent her head and kissed the bristly, little-boy's hair, smelling the dry, fresh, forgotten smell of childhood. She was conscious of Dora watching her.

She took a deep breath and held back the tears. She released the boy, making herself smile at him. 'Robert,' she said, 'what a nice name! How old are you?'

The boy went back and stood next to his mother, silent.

'Tell your grandmother how old you are, Bobby,' said Dora.

'My grandmother is fat,' the boy said.

'That's your other grandmother,' Dora said, 'that's the one who was here last year.'

'Four,' the boy said. 'My birthday is in the winter.'

There was the sound of a key in the lock and footsteps in the hallway. Then Tony came into the room. He stopped when he saw Lucy, and looked, puzzled, politely, not recognizing her for the moment, from her to Dora. He was in the same clothes that he had been wearing the night before and they looked as if he had slept in them. He seemed tired and he needed a shave and he blinked once or twice, coming out of the darkness of the lift

187

shaft into the bright sunlight of the living room. He was carrying a pair of smoked glasses in one hand.

'Daddy,' the boy said, 'Mummy says I can go with Yvonne this afternoon to her sister's. She has three birds in a cage.'

'Hullo, Tony,' Lucy said. She stood up.

Tony shook his head, quickly, two or three times. 'Well, now,' he said softly. He didn't smile.

'Your mother and I have been having a visit,' Dora said.

Tony's eyes travelled from their faces to the whisky glasses set down before them. 'So I see,' he said. He smiled. But the smile was chilly and withdrawn. 'What a nice idea,' he said. He put out his hand and Lucy took it formally. Then he turned to the boy. For a moment, he stood in silence, seeming to be studying his son, puzzled, intense, loving, as though searching for some minute, hidden secret in the soft, pleased, welcoming child's face.

That's something she neglected to tell me, Lucy thought. How much he loves his son.

'Robert,' Tony said gravely, 'how would you like to be a messenger this morning?'

'It depends,' the boy said cautiously, sensing dismissal.

'How would you like to go in and tell Yvonne that your father would like some bacon and eggs and a large pot of coffee?'

'Then can I come back here?' the boy asked, bargaining.

Tony looked at his wife, then at Lucy. 'Of course,' he said. 'In fact, we insist that you come back in here.'

'That's what I'm going to tell Yvonne,' the boy said. 'In fact, you insist.'

'Exactly,' Tony said.

The boy ran out of the room towards the kitchen. Tony watched him soberly as he went through the door, then turned back towards Lucy and Dora.

'Well,' he said, 'where do we begin?'

'Look,' Dora said, 'I think I'd better get out of here. I'll dress and take Bobby with me and . . .'

'No,' Lucy said, more loudly than she wanted to speak. The idea of staying alone with Tony in the shabby, provisionally furnished room, waiting for Dora and the boy to leave, was unbearable to her. She needed time and neutral ground. 'I think, if you want to see me, Tony, it'd be better if we made it later.'

'Whatever you say,' Tony said agreeably.

'I don't want to interfere with your schedule . . .'

'My schedule today,' Tony said lightly, nodding pleasantly at her, 'is to entertain my mother. Still . . .' He looked around him. 'I don't blame you for wanting to get out of here. I'll tell you what. There's a bistro on the corner. If you don't mind waiting a half hour or so . . .'

'Good,' Lucy said hurriedly. 'That'll be fine.' She turned towards Dora. 'Good-bye, my dear.' She wanted to kiss the girl in farewell, but she couldn't bring herself to make the gesture under Tony's watchful gaze. 'Thank you so much.'

'I'll take you to the door,' the girl said.

Clumsily, feeling more awkward than she had felt since she was a young girl, Lucy picked up her bag and her gloves and, leaving Tony standing in the middle of the room, looking tired, and coldly amused, she followed Dora into the hallway.

Dora opened the door and Lucy hesitated, half in, half out. 'Do you want to tell me anything?' she whispered.

Dora thought for a moment. 'Be careful,' she said. 'Be careful of yourself. Maybe it would be a good idea if you weren't waiting in the bistro when he gets there thirty minutes from now.'

Impulsively, Lucy leaned over and kissed the girl's cheek. Dora didn't move. She stood there, motionless, waiting, no longer friendly.

Lucy pulled back, and nervously started putting on her gloves.

'You have to walk down,' Dora said. 'It's a French lift. It only carries passengers going up.'

Lucy nodded and started down the steps. She heard the door close behind her and she walked carefully down in the darkness, her heels making a cold clatter on the stone steps. The vacuum cleaner was still being used somewhere in the building and the jittery, throbbing noise, like giant insects in a dream, pursued her until she reached the street.

Chapter Seventeen

SHE walked aimlessly for fifteen minutes, looking at the shop windows without really seeing what was in them, then hurried back to the corner of the street in which Tony lived. The bistro was there as he had said and there were several tables on a little terrace outside, under an awning, and she sat down and ordered coffee, to give herself something to do while waiting.

The scene in the apartment had unnerved her. Through the years, she had thought, of course, from time to time, of seeing Tony again, but in her imaginings of the encounter, it had usually been at a moment of drama—with her on her deathbed and Tony summoned to her side, youthful, gentle, forgiving in the face of the ultimate farewell. Then there would be the final expression of love, a last, healing kiss (although the face to be kissed had always stubbornly remained a thin, thirteen-year-old face, browned by the sun of that distant summer)—and then a miraculous recovery and a lasting reconciliation and friendship after it. She had also had a recurrent dream, less frequent in recent years, of Tony standing at her bedside, watching her sleep, saying, in a harsh whisper, 'Die! Die!' But the way it had actually happened had been worse than either the bitter dream or the naïve deathbed fantasy. It had been so accidental and confused and unpromising. She hadn't really been certain that she had recognized him at the bar and she had been embarrassed because she was sitting at a night-club table with two college boys whom she had allowed, however innocently, to pick her up. And then there was the unhealthy impression of the shabby apartment and the disappointed wife, with her confession of unhappiness and her despair for the future. And there had been the unexpected ache of seeing the little boy, with the almost familiar face, the mild, grave, inherited eyes, in a confusion of generations, seeming to condemn her once more across the years, putting a new and heavier burden of responsibility on her all over again. And then Tony himself—prematurely grey, prematurely weary, unpleasantly distant and careless with his wife, incuriously polite, unmoved and cool with herself. It was true, Lucy warned herself, that she might have been influenced by the unappetizing and perhaps distorted picture of Tony that Dora had given her before he came in. There was a good chance that Dora, nursing wifely grudges, especially after a night which her husband had spent away from home, might have misrepresented the case considerably. But even so, and making all allowances for Dora's possible exaggerations, the impression Tony had made on her was a disturbing one.

190

And mixed up with it all was the image of her grandson, hopeful and vulnerable, caught between the failures and animosities of his parents, still too young to understand the bitter currents that were twisting his life, but inevitably to be shaped and damaged by them. God, Lucy thought, what will *he* be like finally? How long does the punishment go on?

Suddenly the memory of Tony's smile in the dishevelled living room, standing there between his wife and mother, his mouth pulled to one side in cynical amusement, seemed hateful and terrifying to her. It seemed to mock her and belittle her and endanger everything she had so carefully built up for herself since the war—the sense of purpose and accomplishment in her work, the feeling of having at last matured, of having come to honourable and rigorous terms with herself, the pride in having overcome accidents, in not being swamped by her faults, of having come into her sixth decade whole, robust and useful. Now, remembering Tony's smile, all that was shaken, and once more she felt as she had at the end of the summer on the lake— uncertain, ashamed of herself, unloving. Some way, some way, she thought, I must get him to stop smiling like that.

She felt rushed and inefficient and she was frightened of the meeting that was ahead of her. What could she hope to accomplish here, in a few minutes, over a cup of coffee? There was a lifetime to be explained, an abyss to be bridged, and these things were not to be done in a half hour at a bistro table. She needed time, all the time she could get, and an atmosphere different from this ugly little café, with the stained waiters banging glassware in the background and a young man, who needed a shave and who looked as though he were hiding from the police, working on a racing form a couple of tables away.

Nervously, she opened her bag and took out a small mirror to examine her face. It looked anxious to her, and artificial, not her real face, not natural for the occasion. She put the mirror away, and was about to close the bag when she saw the letter she had taken from her valise in the hotel. She took the letter out of the bag, a plan slowly beginning to form in her brain.

She pulled the letter out of its envelope, four sheets of flimsy paper, thin and almost transparent at the folds. She hadn't read it for years, and she had only put it in her baggage at the last moment when she left America, not really understanding the impulse behind it, thinking, confusedly, Well, as long as I'm going to be in Europe . . .

She opened the letter and started reading.

'Dear Mrs. Crown,' the letter began, 'I am in the hospital and I take this opportunity of writing to you about your loss.' The paper was stamped with the sign of the Red Cross and the handwriting was cramped, semi-literate, painful. 'I suppose you have been notified by the War Dept. about the Major but I was there with the Major and I know that people feel easier in their minds when something like this happens if they hear exactly what took place at the time from someone that was on the spot. The name of the town was Ozières, if the censor don't cut it out, you never know what they will pass, and I will remember it for a long time because I got hit there, too, excepting that I was lucky since I am a short man and the Major, as you remember, was a very tall man, and the machine gun must of been traversing on the same elevation and while I only got it in the shoulder and the neck (two 30 calibre) the Major, being taller, got hit in the lungs. If it is any consolation, he never knew what hit him. There was a Frenchman, too, but he was very quick and he jumped into the ditch and he never even got scratched. I have been reading the papers from back home since I been in the hospital and they make it sound as though it was a parade after the breakthrough, but take it from someone who was in it, it was no parade. I was in a reconnaissance squadron, attached to Corps, we had some half-tracks but mostly jeeps, and we were all over the place in those days because nobody knew where anybody else was and there were pockets of Germans, some of them hostile and some of them just looking to give themselves up. There was no telling what you were going to run into until you moved in and they opened fire. Then you could run and maybe call back on the radio for help if you were lucky, which was our job. I'm not complaining, since I guess that it is the only way it could be done. As you probably know, the Major was attached to G2 at Corps and a man couldn't ask for a safer or more comfortable job than that in the ordinary run of things, but the Major was not like the usual officers you find at Corps, though I am sure they have their jobs to do back there and they do them to the best of their ability. But he was always poking around where there might be trouble, seeing for himself, and his jeep became a very familiar sight to us and he engaged personally with us in quite a few little actions of one kind and another and I am happy to say that as old as he was, he was a brave and as fearless as the day is long and cheerful and democratic. If he had a fault, it was that he exposed himself sometimes when it wasn't one hundred percent necessary. Well, on the day he was killed, we were at a couple of farmhouses about five miles from Ozières, and there was nothing doing there and we were taking a break. A Frenchman, a farmer, came up to us and he said he was from outside Ozières, and there was a bunch of Germans maybe 18 or 20 hiding there that wanted to give themselves up. So the Major took the Frenchman along with him and another jeep with four more guys and we took off. If you happen to be in France and see Ozières, you will see, coming in from the north, there is a crossroads 200 yards outside the town and when we got near there, the Major stopped the jeeps and he said we better go in on foot. He cut off a stick from a hedge and he had a white towel in the jeep and he tied it on to the stick and he said to the Frenchman in French You come with me and he said to me Sergeant you better come along too and he told the other boys to turn the jeeps around in case there was any trouble and to spread out a little and to try to cover us if anything went wrong. The town was all buttoned up. They got shutters on the windows in France and they were all closed and there wasn't anybody moving anywhere and it was so quiet and peaceful you would think you were back in Iowa. The Frenchman and the Major and myself started walking up the road, with the Major in the middle and there was no sign that anything was going to happen and the Frenchman was talking in French to the Major and the Major was answering him, he said he was in France a long time ago, before the war, and that is how he picked up the language, when all of a sudden, just as we got to the crossroads, without any warning, the machine gun opened up. As I said above, I was hit in the shoulder and neck, but I managed to roll over into the ditch alongside the road just the same and the Frenchman did the same on the other side. In case you think the Frenchman was not one hundred percent on the level, let me tell you it came as much as a surprise to him as to me, and I could hear him crying and swearing in French in the other ditch all the time we were laying there. The Major was out in the middle of the road and I looked up out of the ditch at him after awhile and I saw that there was nothing to be done for him. After the one burst, the Germans shut up and they were never heard from again. Anybody tells you the Germans play according to the rules of the Geneva Convention, you refer them to me, and I will show them the two holes in my shoulder and neck. Although you never can tell, they might really of wanted to give themselves up and then maybe some crazy officer showed up in town and gave them a pep talk. Anyway, the boys back at the jeeps fired a few rounds over our head at the town to show the Germans there would be trouble if they tried to come for us and one of them took one of the jeeps back to the farmhouses for the Lieutenant and he showed up in record time and he came and got us, right out in the open, without paying any attention to whether the Germans might open fire again at any moment. I heard the Lieutenant say He never knew what hit him while he was looking at the Major, as I said above and that is something. They put a field dressing on me and they got me back fast and I could not ask for better treatment. In case you want to correspond with the Lieutenant, his name is Lieutenant Charles C. Draper and he was very close to your husband almost like Father and Son, except that I have heard a rumour back here in the hospital that the Lieutenant was ambushed in Luxembourg, but it is only a rumour.

Yours truly,

(Sgt.) Jack Mc Cardle.

'P.S. They tell me I am going to get a medical discharge and a partial disability pension.

(Sgt.) Jack Mc Cardle.'

Lucy folded the letter carefully and placed it in its envelope and dropped it back into her bag. Then she saw Tony coming towards her, on the shady side of the street. At least he turned out handsome, she thought, watching him approach, at least that. He walked deliberately, as though he planned each step. There was none of the exuberance or thoughtless grace of an athlete in the way he walked, but rather the feeling of a city man who has made a conscious decision long ago to be private to himself, not to allow himself to be swept up into the tempo of the crowds around him. He was wearing his dark glasses and they seemed like an affectation, because it was a cool day and there was no glare. They seemed like a further, conscious barrier that he was putting up between himself and the world, the stage props of a carefully guarded and unrelenting austerity.

194

He stopped at the table and Lucy saw that he had shaved and put on a clean shirt and a pressed suit, sober and well-cut and expensive-looking, which he carried easily and well, making Lucy remember the care and taste with which Oliver had always dressed. Tony's expression was polite, but there was still the small, enigmatic twist at the corner of his mouth.

Lucy smiled up at him, making no claims of familiarity with the smile.

'You found it all right?' Tony said, seating himself beside her. 'The bistro?'

'No trouble at all,' Lucy said, noting that Tony's voice was softer and deeper than Oliver's had been.

Tony nodded and signalled a waiter and ordered two coffees, without asking her whether she wanted another or not. 'Dora told me you saw me in the bar last night,' he said. 'You should have come over.'

'I wanted to think about it,' Lucy said, not telling him that she hadn't been sure it was he.

'We could have had a bottle of champagne to celebrate,' he said. 'A meeting like this would have been more fitting in the middle of the night.' He spoke mildly, his accent generalized American and hard to place, and Lucy couldn't tell whether he was making fun of her or not. 'Well, we'll have to make do with coffee. Dora told me what you're doing here in France. It sounds most impressive.'

'It's not as impressive as all that,' Lucy said, searching for mockery and hurrying to turn its edge if it was there.

'Protecting the new generation all over the world,' said Tony. 'They can use some protecting, can't they? What did you think of Bobby?'

'He's a beautiful little boy.'

'Yes, isn't he?' Tony said objectively, admitting a fact. 'He'll change, though, before it's too late.' He smiled. 'When you left, he wanted to know where you'd been all this time.'

'What did you tell him?'

'Oh, I said you'd been busy,' Tony said lightly. 'That seemed to satisfy him. You know the new theory about children, I'm sure. Tell them the truth, but only as much as they seem to want at the moment. No overload of truth at the age of four, the books say.'

The waiter came with their coffee and Lucy watched Tony

stir the sugar into his cup. He had long hands, with the nails carelessly, manicured and she remembered that until he was eight he had bitten them so badly that the cuticles had often bled. Now, the psychiatrists said, that was a sign of insecurity, a fear of being left alone, of being unloved. What the hell was he insecure about when he was eight? she thought. Maybe I'll start biting *my* nails tonight.

She raised her cup and tasted the coffee. 'It's surprisingly good,' she said, like a well-mannered guest at her host's favourite restaurant. 'After everything you hear about French coffee.'

'When you visit a country,' Tony said, 'you find that no one has ever told the truth about it.'

He took off his glasses and rubbed his eyes gently, in what looked like an habitual assuaging gesture. Without the glasses, his eyes, deeply fringed with dark lashes, seemed thoughtful and gentle and the air of restraint and austerity vanished from his face.

'Do you still have to wear those dark glasses?' Lucy asked.

'Most of the time.'

'The eyes are no better?'

'No.'

'Have you tried doing anything about it?'

'Not for a long time,' Tony said, putting the glasses on again, giving Lucy the impression of a flat, impenetrable barrier being raised against her. 'I tired of the medical fakes,' he said. Listening to his slow, unaccented deep voice, with its undertone of weariness and scepticism, Lucy remembered the rushed, shrill confusion of his speech when he was a boy. *We saw a deer*, she remembered, in the high adolescent tones. *He came down to the lake to drink* . . .

'Tony,' Lucy said, impulsively, 'what's the matter? What's wrong with you?'

He looked surprised. He hesitated for a moment, twisting his cup in its saucer. 'Ah,' he said, 'I see that Dora didn't waste her time.'

'It isn't only Dora. Anybody can see in a minute that . . .'

'Nothing's wrong with me,' Tony said harshly. He shook his head, irritated. Then he smiled and resumed the tone of formal good manners. 'By the way, what did you think of her? Dora . . .'

'She's very pretty.'

'Isn't she?' Tony said pleasantly.

'And very unhappy.'

196

'That's the way it goes,' he said, his voice flat.

'And afraid.'

'Who isn't afraid these days?' Tony asked. Now he sounded flippant and impatient and Lucy had the feeling that he was on the verge of getting up from the table and running off.

'She's afraid you're going to leave her,' Lucy went on stubbornly, hoping that perhaps by disturbing him, questioning him, wounding him, to make a connection between them.

'It probably would be the best thing in the world for her,' Tony said, smiling. 'It's not so serious. Everybody we know leaves everybody else we know all the time.'

'Tony,' Lucy said hurriedly, moving away from that subject, 'why do you live in Europe?'

Tony glanced at her, amusedly. 'You're so American,' he said. 'Americans think it's somehow immoral to live in Europe.'

'It's not that,' Lucy said, thinking of the shabby, characterless, uncomfortable apartment, so obviously furnished only for brief passages and people without roots. 'It's just that you're not at home here . . . and your wife and child.'

Tony nodded. 'Exactly,' he said. 'That's the great thing about it. It takes away most of the feeling of responsibility.'

'How long is it since you've been back home?'

Tony looked as though he were considering this. He tilted his head back and half-closed his eyes, the sun glittering on the dark glasses. 'Eighteen years,' he said.

Lucy felt herself flushing. 'I don't mean that,' she said. 'I meant since you were back in the States.'

'Five, six years,' he said carelessly, bringing his head forward again, and pushing his cup thoughtfully a little distance away from him on the table, like a man making a move on a chessboard.

'Do you ever intend to go back?'

Tony shrugged. 'Maybe,' he said. 'Who knows?'

'Is it a question of money?'

Tony grinned. 'Ah,' he said, 'I see that you've caught on that we're not the richest young Americans in Europe.'

'What happened to all the money you got when the will was settled and the business was sold?' Lucy asked.

Tony shrugged again. 'The usual,' he said. 'False friends, riotous living and bad investments. Easy come, easy go. I wasn't particularly anxious to hold on to it. It made me uncom-

197

fortable.' He peered at her closely. 'How about you?' he asked. 'Do you feel comfortable with it?' His tone was not censorious, merely inquisitive.

Lucy decided to ignore the question. 'If you ever need any money . . .' she began.

Tony waved, interrupting her. 'Be careful,' he said, 'this may be costly.'

'I mean it.'

'I'll remember it,' he said gravely.

'Dora says you're not particularly happy with your work . . .'

'Did she actually say that?' Tony sounded surprised.

'Not exactly,' Lucy admitted. 'But she said you used another name and . . .'

'I'm not good enough to make it really worth while,' Tony said thoughtfully, seeming to be talking for himself rather than for her. 'And, after that, it's just a grind. A rather pointless, depressing grind.'

'Why don't you do something else?' Lucy asked.

'You sound like my wife.' Tony smiled. 'It must be a general female optimism—that if you don't like what you're doing all you have to do is close up shop and start something else the next day.'

'What happened to the medical school?' Lucy asked. 'I heard you were doing very well, until you quit . . .'

'I dabbled among the corpses for two years,' Tony said. 'I had a light touch with the dead and my professors thought highly of me . . .'

'I heard,' Lucy said. 'I know a man from Columbia and he told me. Why did you stop?'

'Well, when the estate was settled it seemed foolish to be slaving fourteen hours a day with all that money in the bank, and suddenly the idea of travel seemed very attractive. Besides,' he said, 'I discovered I wasn't interested in healing anybody.'

'Tony . . .' Lucy said. Her voice sounded strained inside her head, and muffled.

'Yes?'

'Are you really like this, Tony? Or are you putting it on?'

Tony leaned back and watched two girls in black dresses crossing the street diagonally in front of them. 'I don't know,' he said. 'I'm waiting for someone to tell me.'

'Tony,' Lucy said, 'do you want me to go and leave you alone?'

He didn't answer immediately. He took off his glasses slowly and put them on the table with great care. Then he looked at her soberly, his face exposed, not defending himself, the deep, familiar eyes sad, considering. 'No,' he said finally, and he reached out and touched her hand gently. 'I couldn't bear it.'

'Will you do something for me?'

'What?' Now his voice was guarded again.

'Will you come with me to Normandy today? I want to see the town where your father was killed, and the cemetery in which he's buried. I have a letter from a man who was with him when it happened and I know the name of the town . . . It's Ozières.'

'Ozières,' Tony said, putting his glasses on again, restoring the barrier, as though he was already regretting the moment of softness. 'I've passed through there. I saw no plaques.' He laughed sourly. 'What a place to get killed in!'

'Didn't you know?'

Tony shook his head. 'No. You sent me a telegram that he'd been killed. That's all.'

'Did you ever hear how it happened?'

'No.'

'He heard there were some Germans in the town who wanted to surrender,' Lucy said, 'and he walked in under a white flag and five minutes later he was dead.'

'He was a little old for things like that,' Tony said.

'He wanted to get killed,' said Lucy.

'Read the papers,' Tony said. 'The world is full of people who want to get killed.'

'Didn't you get that feeling from him when you saw him during the war?'

'I didn't see him much,' Tony said, staring past Lucy, obviously not wanting to talk about it. 'And when I did see him the only feeling I got from him was embarrassment that I wasn't in uniform.'

'Tony!' Lucy said. 'That wasn't true.'

'No? Perhaps not. Perhaps he was only embarrassed that I was alive.'

'Don't talk like that!'

'Why not?' Tony said harshly. 'I made up my mind a long time ago I wasn't going to lie about the way we felt about each other, my father and I.'

'He loved you,' Lucy said.

'Under a white flag,' Tony said, as though he hadn't heard her. 'I suppose there're worse ways for fathers to die. Tell me something . . .'

'Yes.'

'Did you really just see me by accident at that bar last night, or did you come to Paris knowing you were going to look for me?' He was watching her quizzically, his face ready to disbelieve her.

'I didn't even know you were in Europe,' she said. 'And when you went out and I asked the man if he knew where you lived, I think I was hoping he wouldn't know and I wouldn't be able to find out.'

Tony nodded. 'Yes,' he said, 'I can understand that.'

'I knew that, one day, we would have to meet somewhere,' Lucy said.

'I suppose so,' Tony said. 'I suppose if you have a son you must eventually see him . . .'

'I would have arranged it differently,' Lucy said, remembering her fantasies, the deathbed, the kiss, 'if I was arranging it.'

'Still,' said Tony, 'this will have to do. So now you want to visit the grave . . . Well, that's natural enough. I don't say we should do it, but it's natural enough. Tell me,' he said conversationally, 'did you notice how vulgar he became towards the end?'

'No,' Lucy said.

'Of the dead only good.' Tony smiled harshly. 'Of course. Loud and empty, full of officers' club jokes and patriotic editorials and speculation about chorus girls. He was always asking me if I had enough money to have a good time. He winked when he said it. I always told him I could use an extra hundred.'

'He was a generous man,' Lucy said.

'Maybe that was what was wrong with him.' Tony looked up at the sky. It was clear and blue, burning out whitely towards the south. 'It's a good day for a trip to the country. I have a date for lunch, but I guess I can explain about dead fathers and returned mothers and things like that. I'll explain I have to travel to a battlefield, under a white flag.'

'Don't,' Lucy said thickly, standing up. 'Don't come with me if you feel like that.'

'Tell me,' Tony said, without moving, still staring up at the hot sky, 'why do you want to do this?'

Lucy held on to the table to steady herself. She felt exhausted.

She looked down at the tight, back-thrown face of her son, with the dark glasses casting a sharp, smoky shadow on the taut skin of his cheekbones.

'Because we destroyed him,' she said dully. 'You and I. Because we must not forget him.'

Then she saw that Tony was crying. She watched, unbelievingly, clutching her gloves, as the tears rolled down from under his glasses. He bent forward in a sudden movement, covering his face.

He's crying, she thought. There's hope. He's crying.

Chapter Eighteen

THEY drove in silence, through the brilliant noon light, in Tony's small, black two-seater. The top was down and the wind, blowing gustily across them, would have made it difficult to speak, even if they had wanted to. Tony drove carelessly and too fast and chickens went scurrying off the road before them as they passed the old stone farmhouses and in the towns people stared at them, reproaching them for being Americans and for travelling so fast. Black and white cattle grazed in the green fields and for long stretches the road curved between tall graceful parentheses of poplars that sent back the noise of the car's passage as a soft, repetitious whoosh, like cloth-muffled drums being played nervously, in an obsessed rhythm, in a distant room.

There is no need to hurry, Lucy wanted to say, sitting uncomfortably in the wind, her hair wrapped in a scarf, feeling that she was too old for such a vehicle and that much speed. No need to hurry. He has been there for eleven years, he can wait another hour.

They passed family groups picnicking along the roadside, seated on chairs at collapsible small tables with cloths on the tables and wine bottles and tiny vases of flowers next to the long loaves of bread. From time to time they passed through shell-marked villages, where ruined walls stood, softened by the weather, looking as though they had been that way for hundreds of years. Lucy tried to think of what the houses had looked like before the shells had hit them and what it must have been like at the moment of impact, with the stone flying and the smoke and the people calling to one another from under the collapsing walls. But she couldn't manage it. The ruins looked permanent, peaceful—the picnickers, with their wine bottles and carnations and tablecloths looked as though they had never missed a summer. Where was I, she thought, when this belfry toppled into this stone square? I was preparing lunch in a kitchen three thousand miles away. I was walking across the linoleum to the electric toaster and opening the refrigerator door to take out two tomatoes and a jar of mayonnaise.

She looked across at her son. His face was expressionless, his eyes set on the road. He paid no attention to the picnickers or to the residue of war. If you live in Europe, Lucy thought, I suppose you become accustomed to ruins.

She felt exhausted. Her forehead ached from the repetitious, liquid blows of the wind and her eyelids kept drooping heavily over her eyes. Her stomach felt knotted and the top of her girdle bit into her flesh and it was difficult to move enough in the small leather seat to relieve the pressure. From time to time there was the taste of nausea, induced by weariness, in her throat, and when she looked over at Tony he seemed to be swimming minutely at the wheel.

There is something I should be able to say, she thought, to change him from a stranger into a son, but I am too tired to think of it.

She closed her eyes and dozed, passing swiftly between the fresh fields and the weathered ruins.

Well, now, Tony kept thinking, well, now. Here she is at last. If you have a mother it is too much to hope for that she will not finally put in an appearance.

He glanced over at her. Sleeping comfortably, he thought, happily digesting the day's emotion, placidly nourishing herself on death, reunions, tears and guilt. Still pretty, even in the scarf and the harsh light, still—at fifty-three, fifty-four?—with that sliding hint of sex and invitation that he hadn't recognized when he was a boy, but which in retrospect, and after knowing so many other women, he now could recognize so well. Still robust, with firm shoulders and a shapely bosom and clear skin and those

202

damned long grey Eastern eyes. How long would she stay, he wondered, before going home again. A week, two weeks? Long enough to damage him and to try her hand at the French, to whom a woman in her fifties, especially one who looked like her, was interesting game. Long enough to open wounds, demand grief, claim kinship, visit graves, produce tears, disturb security, flirt in a new language, sample foreign beds . . .

We sat at my father's grave and made the summer air over the crosses ring with stories. We stopped the sports car at the spot where the bullet hit him and remembered that he was a fool. It is the height of the tourist season and all over the Continent, Mama and Mama's boy are visiting the monuments. To the left we have Mont Saint Michel. To the right, observe disaster. Diagonally, at a point close to the interesting fourteenth-century Norman church, which unfortunately was hit in an air raid, notice the ditch into which Papa rolled when the machine gun hit him. He was a firm believer in the Geneva Convention, Papa, who should have been wiser about conventions.

Regard Mama's boy at the wheel. The car is smart, though inexpensive, and is used extensively by photographers who wish to make pictures of people on holiday. In a pinch, it is suitable for funerals, if the funerals have taken place long enough ago in the past. The expression on the face of Mama's boy is also smart, although, unlike the automobile, it did not come cheaply.

Lucy opened her eyes. 'Are we nearly there?' she asked.

'Another two hours,' Tony said. 'Go back to sleep.'

Lucy smiled tentatively, half-awake, then closed her eyes again. Tony glanced across at her again momentarily, then stared once more at the road. It was narrow and humped in the middle and its surface had been roughly repaired many times and the car jolted as it hit the filled-in places. There was a smell of tar, melting stickly at the road edges in the sun.

How easy it would be, Tony thought, squinting at the heat waves rising from the middle distance, to speed up just a little more and, with one turn of the wheel, slam off the road into a tree. How easy. How definite.

He grinned, thinking of his mother sleeping trustingly at his side. That would teach her, he thought, not to pick up rides with strange men. He stared at the heat waves, shimmering and oily on each small rise of the road, disappearing like mist as the car rushed on.

The grave waits, he thought. The scene of the death is two hours away by small, open car. This is the spot on which my father was killed . . . But is it, really? Or was he killed long before he reached the crossroads, on another continent, except that the deed was done quietly and none of the participants, including the victim, admitted to it until a long time later? It isn't as simple as it seems, Tony thought, to fix the point in time and space in which a father dies.

His eyes on the road ahead of him, Tony thought of the last time he saw his father.

He was twenty years old and it was in New York, and the evening started at a bar near Madison Avenue, and his father was standing with a glass in his hand, looking fit and soldierly in his uniform, with the ribbon from the First World War on it.

It was about seven o'clock and the room was full, with many uniforms and well-dressed women with fur coats who looked as though they were pleased there was a war on. It was cold and rainy outside and people came in rubbing their hands, hurrying a little, showing how happy they were to be in a warm place, with a war on and a drink coming up. There was a pianist in a corner, playing songs from *Oklahoma. Pore Jud is daid*, he played, singing it softly.

Oliver had called Tony at the dormitory about an hour before, sounding jovial and a little mysterious, saying, 'Tony, you better drop everything and come and have dinner with your old man. It may be the last chance you get.'

Tony hadn't known that his father was anywhere near New York. The last he'd heard Oliver had been down South somewhere. After he had received his commission in Intelligence, because the only thing he'd been offered in the Air Force had been a desk in Washington, Oliver had wandered inconclusively around training camps for two years, appearing on leaves from time to time in New York, without warning, for a dinner or two, then disappearing once more to some new station. When he thought of it, Tony was sure that his father would never get out of the country, but would greet the armistice foolishly and uselessly in an officers' club in the Carolinas or in a troop train heading slowly towards the Middle West.

They shook hands when Tony came in. Oliver put an excessive amount of force into his grip, as though almost automatically these days, in all situations, he felt that he had to prove that the uniform made him more youthful and potent than he looked. The Army had slimmed him down a bit and the belt of his tunic was flat across his stomach. His dark hair was shot with grey and cut short. From a distance, with his weatherbeaten face and the rough, sturdy hair and the flat-stomached tunic he looked almost like the drawings of senior officers that were filling the advertising sections of the magazines. He was not a senior officer however. He wore major's leaves (he had had only one promotion since he had been commissioned) and when you came up close to him you saw that there were greyish puffs under his eyes, which were unhealthily yellowed, and which had the nervous searching expression of the man who is too vain to wear glasses, or is afraid to admit to his superiors that his eyes are not as sharp as they should be. His face, too, which at a distance seemed healthily conditioned-down, was, when examined closely, more haggard than muscular, and there was a hidden muddy tone of fatigue under the skin.

He smiled widely as he shook Tony's hand. 'Well,' he said. 'It's good to see you. What're you drinking?'

Tony would have preferred to decline, since he didn't like to drink. But he thought, I'm not in uniform, the least I can do is drink with him. He looked at his father's glass. 'What're you having?' he asked.

'Bourbon. Good old Kentucky Bourbon,' Oliver said. 'Stocking up.'

'Bourbon,' Tony said to the bartender.

'The best in the house,' Oliver said. He waved jovially and vaguely to the bartender and Tony wondered how long he had been drinking.

'Yes, sir,' said the bartender.

'You look fine, Son,' Oliver said. 'Just fine.'

'I'm all right,' Tony said, wincing a little at the 'Son.' Until Oliver had gone into the Army, he had always called him by his name. Tony wondered what obscure military motivation had effected the change.

'A little thin,' Oliver was saying judiciously, 'a little pale. You don't look as though you're getting any exercise.'

'I feel all right,' Tony said defensively.

'You'd be surprised,' Oliver said, 'how many boys are rejected every day. Young boys. You'd think they'd be in A-number-one

205

condition. The widest variety of ailments. City living,' Oliver said. 'The soft life. White bread. No manual labour.'

'I could be built like Joe Louis,' Tony said mildly, wanting to get off the subject, 'and they'd still reject me.'

'Of course, of course,' Oliver said hastily. 'I wasn't talking about you. I was talking generally. I wasn't talking about particular cases. The results of accidents. Things like that.' He was embarrassed and Tony was relieved when the bartender put his glass down in front of him on the bar and they could move off the subject. Tony lifted his glass.

'To victory,' Oliver said solemnly.

Tony would have liked it better if his father had picked something else to drink to, but he clinked glasses, feeling a little melodramatic in the softly lit bar, in the civilian suit, with the pretty women in furs and the man at the piano.

'I heard about a steak place,' Oliver said. 'On Third Avenue. A little on the black-market side.' He grinned. 'But what the hell! Nothing's too good for the troops. Where I'm going there'll be damn few steaks.'

'Are you going overseas?' Tony asked.

Oliver looked around slyly. 'I wouldn't say yes and I wouldn't say no.' He clapped Tony's shoulder and laughed. 'Anyway, I can give you a hint. Take a good long look at your old man. You won't see him again for a long, long time.'

He wasn't like this, Tony thought wearily. No matter how young I was, I couldn't have been that wrong.

'Maybe it'll be over soon,' Tony said.

'Don't you kid yourself, Son,' Oliver said. His voice dropped to a whisper and he leaned closer to Tony. His breath had an afternoon's whisky on it. 'This is a long, long job, Son. If you'd seen what I've seen. If you'd heard some of the things . . .' He shook his head portentously with morbid proprietary satisfaction for his inside information about the duration and future miseries of the war. 'Bartender,' he said. 'Two more.'

'One, please,' Tony said to the bartender. 'I'll string along with this for a while.'

'When I was in college,' Oliver said, 'we only refused a drink when we dropped below the level of the bar.'

'I have a lot of work to do tomorrow.'

'Sure, Sure.' Oliver nervously wiped his mouth with his hand, suddenly conscious of his breath. 'I was only kidding. I'm glad to see you're serious. I mean that. It makes me feel that maybe, with all the mistakes, maybe I didn't do too bad a job with you. Too many boys these days . . .' He wavered, because Tony had ducked his head and was playing with his glass. 'What I mean is, too damned many boys these days . . . Well, all they think of is drinking and screwing and having a good time and the hell with the future.'

Every single damn time he sees me, Tony thought, he uses that word. If he does it once more, I'm getting out. I don't care where he's going.

'Not that I'm against it, you understand,' Oliver said, with the wide, vague, jovial movement of his arm. 'Far from it. Does a boy good. In its place. Talk about wild oats.' He laughed and drained his drink as the bartender came up with the new one. 'I was one of the leading wild-oat sowers of my time. You can imagine. A young lieutenant in France after the Armistice.' He shook his head and chuckled. Then he suddenly grew serious, as though at the back of his head, beyond the fumes of whisky, past the moment and the recent memory of barracks, a distant light was shining. 'But I'll say one think for myself. Most men— they sow their wild oats when they're young and then, by God, they're in the habit, and they're pinching the nurse on their deathbed. Not me. I did it. I don't deny it and I don't say I'm ashamed of it. And I stopped.' He snapped his fingers. 'Like that. Once and for all.'

He peered down at his glass, holding it in both hands, his eyes reflective and serious and no longer clownish, his cheeks drawn and unmilitary.

The pianist had switched songs now. *Many a new face will please my eye*, he was singing softly, *many a new . . .*

'Your mother,' Oliver said, still playing with the glass with his roughened hands. 'Have you heard from her?'

'No,' said Tony.

'She's doing a big job, now, you know . . .'

'Is she?' Tony said politely, wishing Oliver would stop talking about her.

'In the laboratory at the hospital at Fort Dix,' Oliver said. 'All sorts of blood tests and work on tropical fevers and things like that. When we got into the war she decided that it'd be a shame to let her training go to waste, and I agreed with her. She'd forgotten a lot and she had to work like the devil to get back to it, but she didn't stint herself. She has six assistants working under her now. You'd be proud of her.'

'I'm sure,' Tony said.

'You know,' Oliver said, 'we could call her and she could be here in two, three hours . . .'

'No,' said Tony.

'On a night like this,' Oliver said, without looking at his son. 'I know it would please her.'

'Why don't we go get those steaks?' Tony asked.

Oliver glanced at him and sipped at his drink. 'I haven't finished this yet,' he said. 'There's no hurry.' Then he looked at Tony again. 'You're a tough boy, aren't you?' he said quietly. 'You look like a squirt in a size-fourteen collar who doesn't have to shave more than once a week, but you may turn out to be the tough one in the family.' He chuckled a little. 'Well,' he said, 'there ought to be one in every family. By the way, did I tell you I ran into Jeff the last time I was in New York?'

'No,' Tony said.

'Lieutenant in the Navy,' said Oliver. 'Just in from Guadalcanal or Philippeville or some place like that and very salty. I saw him in a bar and after a while I said what the hell and we sat down and had a drink together. He asked how your eyes were.'

'Did he?' Oh, God, Tony thought, this evening is going to be the worst. The very worst.

'Yes. He turned out very well, I thought. Calmed down a bit. We decided to let bygones be bygones. Shook hands on it. After all, it was a long time ago, and we're all in the same war together.'

'Except me,' Tony said. 'Come on, Father, I think we ought to eat.'

'Sure. Sure.' Oliver took out a wallet and put a five-dollar bill on the bar. 'Bygones,' he said vaguely. He flattened the bill out carefully. 'A long time ago.' He laughed. 'Who remembers it? Ten countries have fallen since then. All right. All right.' He put a hand restrainingly on Tony's arm. 'I have to wait for my change, don't I?'

But before they could leave, two second lieutenants came in with their girls and it turned out that they had been with a head-quarters that Oliver had been attached to in Virginia, and they were good boys, according to Oliver, the best damn boys you could hope to find, and they had to have a drink, and then an-

208

other, because they were the best damn boys you could hope to find, and everybody was moving off mysteriously to secret destinations, and then they remembered Swanny, who had transferred to Armour and who, somebody said, had been reported missing in Sicily, and they had to have another drink to Swanny because somebody said he was missing in Sicily and by that time one of the girls was looking directly and provocatively at Tony and putting her hands on him when she talked and was saying, 'Look, a pretty civilian,' and Oliver, as usual, rushed in to tell about Tony's eyes, and the heart murmur, and Tony, who had been forced to have another drink in the flood of martial comradeship, and who was feeling it, said, 'I'm going to have a sign painted and hang it on my chest. "Do not scorn this poor Four F," the sign is going to read, "He has patriotically volunteered his father on all invasions." ' Everyone laughed, although Oliver did not laugh heartily, and a moment later Oliver said, 'Well, I promised the boy a steak,' and he put down another five-dollar bill and they left.

The steak restaurant was crowded and they had to wait at the bar and Oliver had another drink and his eyes were beginning to have a dense, opaque shine to them, but he didn't say anything, aside from muttering once, staring at the diners, 'Goddamn black-marketeers.'

Before they were seated, a girl whom Tony had taken out several times came in with an Air Force Sergeant who wore glasses. Her name was Elizabeth Bartlett and she was very pretty and she couldn't have been more than eighteen and her parents lived in St. Louis and she was working at something that was not arduous or time-consuming in New York and she was making the most of the war. Each time Tony had gone out with her he had left her, exhausted, with the sun coming up over the rooftops, because part of living through a war for Elizabeth consisted of staying up all night four or five times a week. The Sergeant was no longer young and had the lugubrious air of a man who had done very well before the Army and who suffered keenly every time he looked down and saw the stripes on his sleeve.

Tony had to introduce Elizabeth to Oliver, and she said, throatily, '*Major* Crown,' when she shook his hand. Then she introduced the Sergeant, who said, 'Hi,' indicating that he was off duty. Oliver insisted upon buying them a round of drinks and said, 'You're a damn pretty girl,' in a fatherly way to Elizabeth, and, 'I don't mind admitting, Sergeant, that it's the sergeants who keep this man's army going,' to the Sergeant.

The Sergeant did not react warmly to this. 'I think it's idiocy,' he said, 'that keeps this man's army going, Major.'

Oliver laughed democratically and Elizabeth said, 'He was an industrial chemist and he's peeved that they put him in the Air Force.'

'I hate aeroplanes,' the Sergeant said. He looked bleakly around the restaurant. 'We'll never get a table,' he said. 'Let's go somewhere else.'

'I've been thinking about steak all day,' Elizabeth said.

'Okay,' The Sergeant nodded gloomily. 'If you've been thinking about steak all day.'

Then the headwaiter came over and told Oliver that there was a table ready for him in the corner and Oliver invited the Sergeant and Elizabeth to join them, which made the Sergeant look unhappier than ever. But it turned out that the table was too small and it was impossible to squeeze four people around it. Oliver and Tony, carrying their drinks, left the couple at the bar, and Tony heard Elizabeth saying, 'My God, Sidney, you *are* a pill.'

Tony, as he sat down, was sorry they hadn't joined his father and himself. He was not particularly interested in either Elizabeth or the Sergeant, although Elizabeth had her uses, but he didn't want to be alone with his father for a whole evening. For so many years now he had sat through these random, uncomfortable dinners with Oliver, in hotel dining rooms in the country towns where Tony had gone to school, in roadside restaurants during vacations when Oliver had dutifully toured the national parks with him when he was a boy, here in the city when Oliver had had his leaves. Sometimes it was worse than others, especially when Oliver was drinking, but there wasn't a single dinner that Tony remembered with pleasure. And Oliver was certainly drinking now. He insisted upon continuing through the meal with whisky. 'I understand Churchill does it,' he said, when Tony suggested wine. 'What's good enough for Churchill is good enough for me.' And he'd looked at Tony proudly and fiercely, linked momentarily with greatness.

There was something strange about Oliver's drinking this night. He was not a drunkard, and even on the other occasions when he'd had one or two too many, it had seemed almost accidental. But tonight he went at his glass with purposeful intensity, as though there was something to be done before the evening was over that could only be achieved after a certain excessive intake of alcohol. Tony, who had returned to water, watched him warily, hoping to be able to get away before Oliver collapsed completely. Deuteronomy, he remembered, enjoined fathers not to show themselves naked before their sons, but that was before the invention of Bourbon.

His father ate noisily, taking bites that were too large for him, eating fast.

'Best steak in the city,' he said. 'They smear it with olive oil. Italians. Don't believe what you hear about the Italians. Damn good boys.' He spilled some salad on his uniform and brushed it off carelessly with his hand, leaving an oily stain. When he was a boy, when he still lived at home, Tony remembered, he had resented his father's insistence on fastidiousness at the table.

Oliver ate in silence for a while, nodding with approval over the steak, eating with compulsive rapidity, emptying half a glass of whisky at a time, mixing the food and drink in his mouth. He chewed strongly, his jaw making a small, regular clicking sound. Suddenly, he put his fork down. 'Stop looking at me,' he said harshly. 'I'll be goddamned if I'll have anybody looking at me that way.'

'I wasn't looking at you,' Tony said, flustered.

'Don't kid me,' Oliver said. 'You want to disapprove of me, do it some other time. Not tonight. Understand?'

'Yes, Father,' Tony said.

'The low, slavering beast,' Oliver said obscurely, 'munching on his bloody bones.' He glowered at Tony for a moment, then put out his hand and touched him, gently. 'I'm sorry,' he said. 'I'm feeling funny tonight. Don't pay it any attention. The last night . . .' He stopped inconclusively. 'Some time,' he said, 'it might be a good idea if you wrote me a full report. "My Impressions of Father." ' He smiled. ' "Father Drunk, Sober and Mistaken." Something like that. Leaving out nothing. Might do us both a lot of good. Might get that strangled look off your face the next time you see me. Christ, you're an unhappy-looking boy. Even if you had good eyes, the Army'd probably turn you down on grounds of morale. You'd infect a whole regiment with melancholy. What is it? What is it? Ah, don't tell me. Who wants to know?' He looked around the room vaguely. 'We should have gone to a musical comedy tonight. Leave the country singing and dancing. Only all the goddamn tickets are sold out. You got anything to say?'

'No,' Tony said, hoping the people at the next table weren't listening.

'Never anything to say,' Oliver said. 'Made a big speech at the age of thirteen that astounded his listeners with its brilliance and maturity, then shut his mouth for the rest of his life. That girl is smiling at you with all two eyes . . .'

'What?' Tony asked, confused.

Oliver gestured obviously towards the door. 'The Sergeant's girl,' he said. 'She's on her way to the latrine and she's signalling to you like a sailor on a mast.'

Elizabeth was standing at the door and she was smiling and gesturing to Tony with her finger. The room was L-shaped and the Sergeant was seated around the bend of the L and couldn't see her. He was slouched in his chair, morosely eating a breadstick.

'Excuse me,' Tony said, glad of an excuse to get away from the table. 'I'll be right back.'

'Don't hurry on my account,' Oliver said as Tony stood up. 'We don't sail until the wind changes.'

Tony crossed the room to Elizabeth. She laughed as he came up to her and pulled him out into a little vestibule. 'Are you prepared to be wicked?' she said.

'What about the Sergeant?' Tony asked.

'The Sergeant is only on pass until eleven,' Elizabeth said carelessly. 'Can you get away from Papa?'

'If it kills me,' Tony said grimly.

Elizabeth chuckled again. 'They're a riot,' she said. 'Fathers.'

'A riot,' Tony agreed.

'He's pretty cute, though,' said Elizabeth. 'In his soldier suit.'

'That's the word,' said Tony.

'The Village?' Elizabeth asked.

'Okay.'

'I'll be at the bar in Number One at eleven-fifteen,' she said. 'We'll celebrate.'

'What'll we celebrate?'

'We'll celebrate that we're both civilians,' Elizabeth said. She smiled and pushed him back, out of the vestibule. 'Go ahead back to Papa.'

Tony went back to the table, feeling better. At least the whole evening wouldn't be wasted.

'What time are you meeting her?' Oliver said as he sat down.

'Tomorrow,' Tony said.

'Don't mislead the troops,' said Oliver. He smiled mirthlessly and stared at the door through which Elizabeth had disappeared. 'How old is she? Twenty?'

'Eighteen.'

'They begin earlier and earlier, don't they?' said Oliver. 'Poor sod of a Sergeant.' Oliver looked over at the Sergeant, safely behind the bend of the wall, and laughed, without pity. 'Paying five bucks a steak and losing his girl at the toilet door to the pretty young man.' Oliver leaned back in his chair and studied his son gravely, while Tony kept his mind on eleven-fifteen that night. 'It's pretty easy for you, isn't it?' Oliver said. 'I'll bet they heave themselves at you.'

'Please, Father,' Tony said.

'Don't be ungrateful,' Oliver said, though without heat. 'Maybe the best thing in the world is to be handsome. You're halfway up the hill to begin with. It's unfair, but it's not your fault, and you ought to make the most of it. I wasn't a bad-looking young man, myself, but I didn't have that thing. Women could constrain themselves in my presence. When you're older, write me about it. I've always wanted to know what it would be like.'

'You're drunk,' Tony said.

'Of course.' Oliver nodded agreeably. 'Although it isn't a polite thing to say to a father on his way to the wars. When I was a young man fathers were never drunk. That was before Prohibition, of course. A different world. Yes,' he said, 'you've got what your mother has . . .'

'Please, Father, cut it out,' Tony said. 'Have some coffee.'

'She was a beautiful woman,' Oliver said oratorically, using the past tense as though he were speaking of someone he had known fifty years before. 'She couldn't come into a room without having every head turn her way. She had a modest, apologetic way of walking into a room. It came about because she was frightened, she was trying to make as little impression as possible, but it had a funny result. Provocative. Frightened . . . That's a funny thing to say about your mother, isn't it?' He stared at Tony. 'Isn't it?' he asked, challengingly.

'I don't know.'

'Frightened. For many years. For long, long years . . .' Oliver was almost chanting now and by this time the people on both sides of their table were hushing and listening to him. 'Long, long years. I used to make fun of her for it. I kept telling her how beautiful she was because I wanted to give her confidence in herself. I thought I had so much myself that I could spare some, without feeling it. Confidence . . . Nobody has to give you any. You have it, and I'm happy for your sake. You have it and you know how you got it?' He leaned forward belligerently. 'Because you hate everybody. That's pretty good,' he said, 'that's pretty lucky—at the age of twenty to be able to hate everybody. You'll go a long way. If they don't bomb New York.' He looked around him fiercely and the people at the other table, who had been listening, suddenly began to talk loudly among themselves. 'Wouldn't that be a laugh,' he said. 'All these fat ones sitting here, saying, "I'll have it rare," and all of a sudden hearing the whistle and looking up and seeing the ceiling fall in on them. God, I'd like to be here to see that.' He pushed his plate away from him. 'Do you want some cheese?'

'No.'

'I do,' Oliver said. 'I want every damn thing I can get.' He waved to the waiter, but he wouldn't order coffee. He insisted upon another whisky.

'Father . . .' Tony protested. 'Go easy.'

Oliver gestured at him with good-humoured impatience. 'Quiet, quiet,' he said. 'I've simplified my tastes. All that crap about cocktails before dinner, two kinds of wine, brandy later . . . We live in a state of emergency. Streamlining is the order of the day. Even the Army's done it. The streamlined division. Triangular. Eliminated the brigade, just the way I've eliminated wines and liqueurs. Great step towards winning the war. Don't look disapproving. There are two or three things I intend to tell you before disappearing, and that's one of them. Don't look disapproving. It's . . . it's platitudinous.' A look of satisfaction spread over his face because he had thought of the word. 'You're too smart for stuff like that. The attempt should be in the direction of originality. Love your father. Where could you find something more original than that in this day and age? You'd be the talk of the academic world. A new phenomenon in psychological studies. Biggest thing since Vienna. The Cordelia complex.' He laughed, pleased with his wit.

Tony sat there looking at the tablecloth, wondering when the wild, unexpected monologue would end, yearning suddenly for all the old, stiff, silence-studded meetings of other years, when his father had always been so polite, awkwardly restrained, painfully searching for subjects to talk about with Tony in the two or three hours a month that they spent together.

'My father, for example,' Oliver said expansively, 'killed himself. That was the year you were born. He walked into the sea at Watch Hill and just went and drowned himself. That was a fashionable place to commit suicide in those days, except, of course, nobody mentioned the word suicide, what they said was he had a cramp. Maybe he caught me looking at him that morning and he said, "That does it—this is the day for it." We never found the body. Rolling somewhere to this day in the Gulf Stream, maybe. The insurance was respectable. It was a windy day and there was a big sea. My father was always very careful of appearances. It's a family characteristic and I can see it's come down to you. Have you any theories on why your grandfather drowned himself at Watch Hill in 1924?'

Tony sighed. 'Father, I have to get up early tomorrow and you've probably got a big day ahead of you . . . Why don't we get through here and go home?'

'Home,' Oliver said. 'My home is Room 934 in the Shelton Hotel on Lexington Avenue, but I'll go there if you come with me.'

'I'll take you in a taxi,' Tony said, 'and drop you.'

'Oh, no.' Oliver put his finger slyly along his nose. 'None of that. I'm not buying any of that. I have a lot of things to talk to you about, young man. I may be gone thirty years and we have to plan out the plan. Ulysses' final instructions to Tele—Telemachus. Be good to your mother and keep a running count of the guests.' He grinned. 'See—I'm just a simple soldier—but there are still relics of a former and more gracious life, before the Hotel Shelton.'

Tony looked at his watch. It was a quarter past ten already. He looked across at Elizabeth. She and the Sergeant were at their coffee already.

'Don't worry,' Oliver said. 'She'll wait. Come on.' He stood up. The chair teetered behind him, but he didn't notice it, and finally, it settled back without falling. Elizabeth smiled at them as they went out, after Oliver paid the bill, and Tony tried to make his

215

face express his resolution to get down to the Number One Bar as close to eleven-fifteen as possible.

When they stepped out of the lift on the ninth floor, Tony opened the door, because Oliver couldn't get the key into the lock, and put on the light in his father's room. The room was a small one, littered with gear, a Valpack sprawled open on the floor, a greenish raincoat on the bed, a pile of laundered khaki shirts in a rumpled heap on the dressing table, some newspapers on the desk, hastily flipped together by a maid.

'Home,' Oliver said. 'Make yourself comfortable.' Without taking off his cap or trenchcoat he went over to the dresser and opened a drawer and brought out a bottle of whisky. 'This is an amazing hotel,' he said, holding the bottle up to see how much was left. 'The maids don't drink.'

He went into the bathroom and Tony heard him humming *Pore Jud is daid* while he ran some water into a glass. Tony went to the window and pulled back the curtain. The room was on a court and on all sides blind windows looked back at him. The sky was an indeterminate black distance above him.

Oliver came back cuddling his glass and poured some whisky in it. Then, still in cap and coat, he sank into the one easy chair.

He sat there, slumped deep in the chair, sunk in his trenchcoat, with his cap back on his head, holding his glass in his two hands, looking like an ageing soldier just returned from a defeat, caught for a moment in an escapable posture of exhaustion and despair. 'Ah, God,' he said. 'Ah, God.'

Outside the door, down the hotel corridor, the lift shafts howled softly, ominous and jittery in the metropolitan night.

'A son,' Oliver said, mumbling. 'Why does a man have sons? Ordinarily, you don't ask yourself a question like that. If you lead an ordinary life, if you sit down to dinner with him every night, if you crack him across the ears once in a while because he's annoying you, you take it for granted. What the hell, everybody has sons. But if the whole thing is torn apart, ruptured, departed'—he drawled out the verbs of division and farewell with mournful pleasure—'that's another story. Another story.' Oliver sipped at his drink, deep in the chair, mumbling. 'You ask yourself—why did I do it? What was in it for me? You want to hear? You want to know what I decided?'

Tony turned away from the window and moved soothingly

216

over towards the chair and stood in front of his father. 'Do you want me to help you get ready for bed?' he asked.

'I don't want to get ready for bed,' Oliver said. 'I want to tell you about sons. Who knows—one day you might have some of your own and you might be curious on your own hook. You have a son to renew your optimism. You reach a certain age, say, twenty-five, thirty, it varies with your intelligence, and you begin to say, "This is for nothing." You begin to realize it's just more of the same, only getting worse every day. If you're religious, I suppose you say to yourself, "The goal is death. Hallelujah, I hear them tuning the golden harps, my soul is in training for glory." But if you're not religious—if you say, "That's more of the same, only it includes Sunday," what have you got? A bankbook, unpaid bills, the cooling of the blood, what have we got for dinner, who's coming to dinner—Last week's menu, last year's guests. Take a train full of commuters on their way home at six o'clock any evening in the week and you'll have enough boredom collected in one place to blow a large-sized town off the face of the map. Boredom. The beginning and end of pessimism. And that's where a child comes in. A little boy doesn't know anything about pessimism. You watch him and listen to him and he's in a fury every minute he breathes. He's in a fury of growing, feeling, learning. There's something in him that tells him it's worthwhile to get bigger, to learn to communicate, to learn to eat with a spoon, to learn to go to the lavatory, to learn to read, fight, love . . . He's on that big wave, pushing him ahead —anyway he thinks it's ahead—and it never occurs to him to look back and ask, "Who's pushing me? Where am I going?" You look at your son and you see that there is something in the human race that automatically believes in the value of being alive. If you had a father who walked into the waves at Watch Hill, that can be a damned important consideration. When you were three years old I used to watch you sitting on the floor trying to learn how to put on your own shoes and socks, working hard, and I would roar with laughter. And while I was sitting in your room, among the boys, laughing like a farmer at the circus, I was on the wave with you, I leached away some of the optimism for my own uses. I was grateful to you and I treasured you. Now . . .' Oliver sipped his drink and grinned cunningly at Tony over the rim of the glass. 'Now I don't treasure you at all. More of the same. A young man with a grudge who reminds me of myself when I was younger, who reminds me of a pretty woman I happened to marry, who reminds me we screwed up the whole works . . .'

'Father,' Tony said painfully, 'there's no need for all this.'

'Sure,' Oliver said, mumbling into his glass. 'Sure there's a need. Last will and testament. On the way to the wars. The wars help, too. You can't have a son, have a war. That's another wave. No time to look back and say who's pushing me, where am I going. An illusion of purpose, of accomplishment. Take a town. Don't ask what town. Don't ask who's in it. Don't ask what they're going to do after you've passed through. Don't ask if it had to be taken. Just hope the war lasts long enough and the supply of towns holds out and that you don't come back . . .'

'You wouldn't talk like that if you weren't drunk,' Tony said.

'No? Maybe not.' Oliver chuckled. 'That's a good reason for being drunk. You don't remember, because you were too young, but I used to have a high opinion of myself. I thought I was God's own combination of intelligence, honour, industry and wit. Ask me anything in those days, and I'd come up with the answer, quick as the Pope or an electric brain. I was solid as the Republic and none of the wires was crossed and certainty was my middle name. I was certain about work and marriage and loyalty and the education of children and I didn't care who knew it. I stared out at the world with a clear and lunatic eye. I was the product of a solid family and a suicide father. I had prosperity behind me and a good college and a proper tailor and lightning couldn't crack me if it hit me between the eyes on the Fourth of July. And then, in fifteen minutes in a little stinking summer resort beside a lake, the whole thing collapsed. I made the wrong decision, of course. But maybe the only right decision was to take you and hang you by the heels and drown you in the lake, and of course my social position wouldn't permit that. Abraham and Isaac would never go down in Vermont no matter what angels were on the premises. What happened, of course, was that I turned the knife on myself, although I'm sure you have a different opinion. What the hell,' he said belligerently. 'How bad was it for you? You left home a little earlier than usual and you were lonely on a couple of holidays, that's all.'

'Sure,' Tony said, bitter now and remembering the seven years. 'That's all.'

'As for me,' Oliver said, ignoring his son, 'I merely turned up dead. Later on, when I looked back on it, knowing I was guilty, I said it was sensuality that did it. And maybe it was. Only after a little while there wasn't any sensuality left. Of course, we pretended, because when you're married there's a certain obligation to politeness in that department, but by that time there were too many other things in the way, and finally we just about dropped the whole thing.'

'I don't want to hear about it.'

'Why not? You're twenty years old,' Oliver said. 'I hear you have a rising career as a collegiate stud. I'm not raping any virgin ears. Know Thy Father and Thy Mother. If you can't honour them, at least know them. It's not the next best thing, but it's a thing. The war has made me virile again. I had an affair with a waitress in the town of Columbus, North Carolina. I outlasted a warrant officer and two captains from the Adjutant-General's office on the crucial week-end. It was a hot week-end and all the girls were going around without stockings. If I were a Catholic, I would seriously think of taking orders. You are my priest,' he said, 'and my favourite confessional box is located on the ninth floor of the Hotel Shelton.'

'I'm going,' Tony said, moving towards the door. 'Take care of yourself and let me know where I can write you and . . .'

'For absolution,' Oliver said. 'Three slugs of Bourbon. Where's the bottle?' He asked peevishly. 'Where's the goddamn bottle?' He felt around on the floor next to the chair and found the bottle and poured himself a third of a tumbler full of whisky. He put the bottle down again and, closing one eye, like a marksman, flipped the cork across the room into the wastebasket. 'Two points,' he said, with satisfaction. 'Did you know that I was an athlete in my youth? I could run all day and I was deft around first base, although the best first basemen are all left-handed. I also hit a long ball, although not often enough to make it finally worthwhile. I also had leanings towards being a military hero, because a great-uncle was killed in the Wilderness, but the First World War cured me of that. I spent all my six months in France in Bordeaux and the only time I heard a shot fired in anger was when an MP fired at two Senegalese who were breaking the window of a wineshop on the Place Gambetta. Don't go yet,' he pleaded. 'Some day a son of yours might ask you, "What are the great moments in the family history?" and you'll be sick at heart that you didn't stay another five minutes and soak in the old traditions. On our shield are the three Great Words—Suicide, Failure and Adultery, and I challenge any red-blooded American family to do better.'

'You're raving now,' Tony said, not moving from the door. 'You're not making any sense.'

'That's a court-martial offence, Son,' Oliver said gravely, from his chair. 'Charity begins at the Hotel Shelton.'

Tony opened the door.

'Don't,' Oliver cried. He struggled out of the chair, rocking a little, carefully holding his glass. 'I have something for you. Close the door. Just five more minutes.' His face worked painfully 'I'm sorry. I've had a hard day. Close the door. I won't drink any more. See . . .' He put the glass shakily on the dresser. 'The ultimate sacrifice. Come on, Tony,' he coaxed, his head lolling. 'Close the door. Don't leave me alone yet. I'm getting out of the country tomorrow and you'll be free of me for God knows how long. You can spare five more minutes. Please, Tony, I don't want to be alone just yet.'

Reluctantly, Tony closed the door. He came back into the room and sat stiffly on the bed.

'That's it,' Oliver said. 'That's the boy. The truth is I drank today for your sake. Don't laugh. You know me—I'm not a drinking man. It's just that there're so many things I wanted to tell you—and I haven't been able to communicate with you for so long . . . Those goddamn dinners . . .' He shook his head. 'First of all, I want to apologize.'

'Oh, Christ.' Tony put his head in his hands. 'Not now.'

Oliver stood over him, wavering a little. 'We sacrificed you. I admit it. The reasons looked good at the time. How did we know they wouldn't hold up? If what you're looking for is revenge, look at me and you've got it.'

'I don't want anything,' Tony said. 'I'm not interested in revenge.'

'Do you mean that?' Oliver asked eagerly.

'Yes.'

'Thank you, Son.' Suddenly Oliver reached over and took Tony's hand with both of his and shook it crazily. 'Thank you, thank you.'

'Is that all you wanted to say?' Tony lifted his head and looked up at his father, standing, half-bent, unsteady and bleary-eyed, above him.

'No, no.' Oliver dropped his hands and spoke hastily, as though he were afraid that if he stopped talking for one moment he would be left alone in the room. 'I told you I have something for you.' He went over to the open Valpack and got down, with a thump, on his knees in front of it and began rummaging in the interior. 'I've been meaning to give this to you for a long time. I was afraid the proper occasion might not come up and . . . Here it is . . .' He pulled out a little package wrapped in tissue paper, with a rubber band around it. Still on his knees, he tore clumsily at the paper. He dropped the paper, now in shreds, on the floor and held up an old-fashioned gold watch. 'My father's watch,' he said. 'Solid gold. I've always carried it for luck, although really I prefer a wristwatch. He gave it to me two weeks before he died. Solid gold,' Oliver said, squinting at it in the lamplight and turning it over slowly and shakily. 'An old Waltham. It's over forty years old, but it keeps perfect time.' He stood up and came back to Tony, still admiring the watch. 'You don't have to wear it, of course, it's terribly out of date, but you could keep it on your desk, something like that . . .' He held it out, but Tony didn't take it.

'Why don't you hang on to it?' Tony said, with a twinge of superstition. 'If it's brought you luck.'

'Luck.' Oliver grinned painfully. 'You keep it for me. Maybe the luck'll work better that way. Please.'

Tony put his hand out slowly and Oliver dropped the watch into his palm. The watch was surprisingly heavy. It was thick and the gold of the case was elaborately chased and the face was yellowed a little and marked with thin, old-fashioned Roman numerals. Tony looked at it and noticed that it was after eleven. Damn it, he thought, I'm going to miss Elizabeth. She'll never wait.

'Thanks,' he said. 'I'll give it to my son, when the time comes.'

Oliver smiled anxiously. 'That's it,' he said. 'That's the idea.'

Tony put the watch in his side pocket and stood up. 'Well . . .' he began.

'Don't go yet,' Oliver said. 'Not yet. There's one more thing.'

'What's that?' Tony tried to keep his impatience with his father, with the evening, with the sad and littered little room, out of his voice.

'Wait. Just wait.' Oliver made a wide, mysterious gesture with his hand and went over to the telephone. He sat down on the bed, still in his cap and trenchcoat, and picked up the phone. He clicked the instrument impatiently. 'I want Orange 7654,' he said. 'That's in New Jersey.'

'Whom're you calling?' Tony asked suspiciously.

'That's right,' Oliver said, into the phone. 'Orange.' He turned to Tony, holding the instrument to his ear. 'You knew we moved to New Jersey a few years ago?'

'Yes,' Tony said.

'Of course. You were there. Happy Thanksgiving. It turned out it wasn't really practical to live in Hartford any more,' Oliver said. 'And in one way, it turned out very well. The plant was obsolete, anyway, and I had a chance to buy in New Jersey and we expanded enormously. The move made a rich man out of me.' He laughed. 'The romance of business,' he said vaguely. 'I could even afford to be a patriot and join up when my country called. Operator, operator!' he said impatiently into the phone.

'Whom're you calling?' Tony asked.

'Your mother.' Oliver's face was tight, almost as though he might cry, although it was probably only the whisky, and his eyes were full of pleading.

'Oh, come on now,' Tony said. 'What's the sense in that?'

'Just once,' Oliver said. 'Just this last night. Just for the both of us to say hullo to her, together. How much harm can that do—just to say hullo?'

Tony hesitated, then he shrugged. 'Okay,' he said wearily.

'That's fine,' Oliver said happily. 'That's a sport.'

That's a sport, Tony thought. The vocabulary of my father.

'Come over here.' Oliver waved to him vigorously. 'You take the phone. You speak to her right off. Come on, come on.'

Tony walked over and took the phone and put it to his head. He heard the regular distant ringing sound in the receiver. His father was standing close to him, liquorish-smelling, breathing fast, as if he had just run a distance. The phone rang and rang.

'She's probably asleep,' Oliver said anxiously. 'She hasn't heard it yet.'

Tony didn't say anything. He listened to the ringing.

'Maybe she's taking a bath,' Oliver said. 'Maybe the water's running and she can't hear it . . .'

'There's no answer,' Tony said. He started to hang up, but Oliver grabbed the phone from him and put it to his own ear, as though he didn't trust Tony.

222

They stood still, the thin, mechanical double sound surprisingly loud in the quiet room.

'I guess she went to a movie,' Oliver said, 'or she's playing bridge. She plays a lot of bridge. Or maybe she had to work late. She works very hard and . . .'

'Hang up,' Tony said, 'she's not home.'

'Just five more rings,' said Oliver.

They waited for the five more rings, then Oliver hung up. He stood staring at the phone on the shabby bed-table scarred with cigarette burns and the marks of wet glasses.

'Well, isn't that too bad?' he said, very low, shaking his head, staring at the phone. 'Isn't that just too bad?'

'Good night, Father,' Tony said.

Oliver didn't move. He stood looking at the phone, his face serious, reflective, not especially sad, but remote and thoughtful.

'I said good night, Father.'

Oliver looked up. 'Oh, yes,' he said flatly. He put out his hand and Tony shook it. There was no force in his grip.

'Well . . .' Tony said uncomfortably, suddenly feeling the weight and embarrassment of saying good-bye to the wrong member of the family who was going to the war. 'Good luck.'

'Sure. Sure, Son,' Oliver said. He smiled remotely. 'It's been a nice evening.'

Tony looked hard at him, but his father obviously had nothing further to say. It was as though he had exhausted all his interest in him. Tony crossed to the door and went out, leaving his father standing next to the telephone.

He took a cab down to Number One, hoping that Elizabeth hadn't gone. She wasn't at the bar when he went in and he decided to have one drink and wait fifteen minutes and then, if she hadn't arrived, go home.

He ordered a whisky and idly put his hand in his pocket and felt the watch. He took it out and stared at it. It was like having 1900 in your hand. A fat man was standing in a spotlight next to the piano, singing a song called 'I Love Life.'

Tony turned the watch over. It was almost dark at the bar, but if he held the watch down low on the bar a beam of light from a small lamp behind the bottles struck it. The lacily engraved gold gleamed in his hand. There was a little catch on one side of the watch and Tony flicked it and the back snapped open. There was a picture in it and Tony bent over to look at it. It was a photograph of his mother, taken when she was very young. Her hair was in a funny dowdy bun, but it didn't matter, she was beautiful just the same, staring out of the ageing photograph with wide, candid, rather shy and smiling eyes in the slanting, furtive light that the barman used to mix his drinks while the show was on at the piano.

Oh, God, Tony thought, what did he want to do this for?

He looked around for a place to throw the photograph, but at that moment he saw Elizabeth making her way among the tables towards the bar. He closed the watch and put it in his pocket, thinking, I'll do it when I get home.

'Wicked, wicked,' Elizabeth whispered, and squeezed his hand. 'Is Papa safely in bed?'

'Yes,' Tony said. 'Safe and sound.'

Chapter Nineteen

THE road sped smoothly under the tyres, the car passing through flickering bands of shade thrown by the rows of trees on each side, the kilometre stones, with the Norman names, going past with streaming regularity. Tony sat straight at the wheel, driving automatically, remembering the night in New York, realizing that for many years he had tried, with a conscious effort, to forget it.

The last time you see your father before he dies, he thought, you should know it, there should be a sign, a warning, a *Nevermore*, so that you can say an appropriate word, so that you do not hurry from a bare hotel room, worrying that you are late for a rendezvous at a bar with a girl who has come to the city at the age of eighteen, to enjoy a war.

He was conscious of his mother seated beside him, her eyes closed, the wind picking at the loose ends of her scarf. What would it have been like, he wondered, how would everything have been changed if she had been home that night, if she had come to the telephone and he had heard her voice after Oliver had said, 'That's fine. That's a sport'?

224

Sitting in the cramped little seat, half-dozing, with the wind in her ears, rushing towards the grave she had never seen and whose meaning she still did not truly understand, Lucy was thinking, too, of the last time she had seen Oliver. It had been nearly three o'clock in the morning and she knew that Oliver had seen Tony earlier and that he had tried to call her, because he told her later, in the cold, empty, echoing house in New Jersey, after she had come in, weary and unsatisfied, turning the young soldier away from the door . . .

'No,' she said to the lieutenant, barring the way, not turning the key in the lock, 'you can't come in. It's too late. And don't send the taxi away. Go home, like a good boy. Tomorrow's another day.'

'I love you,' the boy said.

Oh, God, she thought. He means it, too. It's the war. A couple of sad, clutching hours in a shabby roadhouse room, to console the wounded, and they say I love you. Why do I do it? she thought, exhausted, remembering that she had to be in the laboratory at nine in the morning. I must have pity on myself, too.

'Don't talk like that,' she said.

'Why not?' The boy put his arms around her and tried to kiss her.

'Because it makes everything too complicated.'

She let him kiss her briefly. Then she pushed him away.

'Tomorrow night?' he said.

'Call me in the afternoon,' she said.

'I'm being shipped out in three more days,' he said, pleading. 'Please . . .'

'All right,' she said.

'It was wonderful,' he whispered.

Payment, she thought wryly. A polite well-brought-up boy, who has carried his manners over with him into the war.

'Are you sure you don't want me to come in?'

She laughed and waved him off and he smiled sadly and went down the steps towards where the taxi was waiting at the curb. He looked sorrowful and lonely and rather frail, even in his officer's overcoat, and too young and polite for what was ahead of him. Watching him, Lucy felt confused, uncertain about the value of what she had done that night, and which until that moment she had thought was an act of generosity and pity. Maybe, she thought, it will only make him sadder in the long run.

She put on the light in the hall and started towards the stairs, in a hurry to get to bed. Then she stopped and sniffed. There was a strong smell of cigarette smoke, coming from the living room. I must talk to the cleaning woman, she thought, irritated, about smoking while she works. Then she remembered that the cleaning woman only came in twice a week, on Mondays and Thursdays, and this was not a Monday or Thursday.

Lucy hesitated. Then she went into the living room. From the doorway, in the dark, she saw the glow of a cigarette and the shadowy bulk of someone sitting in a chair that had been pulled into the centre of the carpet. She turned on the light.

Oliver was sitting there, with his coat on, smoking, hunched deep in the chair, facing her. She hadn't seen him for five months and she noticed that he was thinner than the last time and that he seemed much older. His eyes were sunken in their sockets, and his mouth was twisted with fatigue.

'Oliver,' she said.

'Hullo, Lucy.' He didn't stand up. His head rolled a little and he licked his lips and she realized that he had been drinking.

'Have you been here long?' she asked. She took off her coat and threw it on a chair. She felt uncomfortable and a little afraid. It wasn't like him to arrive unannounced or to drink too much, or to sit like that, in his coat, brooding and obscurely threatening, in the dark, in the chair that seemed to have been deliberately aimed at the doorway.

'A couple of hours,' he said. 'I don't know.' He spoke slowly, his voice a little thick and deliberate. 'I called from New York but you weren't home.'

'Can I get you anything?' she asked. 'A drink? A sandwich?'

'I don't want anything,' he said.

'Are you on leave?' she asked. 'How much time do you have?'

'I'm shipping out tomorrow,' he said. 'Overseas.'

'Oh,' she said. Everybody is shipping out this week, she thought. The entire Army. If I weren't so tired, she thought, I would undoubtedly feel something else besides this.

She shivered a little. 'It's cold in here,' she said. 'You should've turned the heat up.'

'I didn't notice,' he said.

She went over to the thermostat on the wall and turned it up, to the point at which it said 80 degrees, Summer Heat. She didn't do it because she expected the heat to come up fast enough to do any good, but to keep herself busy, to avoid the direct, examining stare of her husband.

'I'm hungry,' she said. 'I think I'll go see what's in the icebox. You sure I can't bring you something?'

'I'm sure,' he said. He doused his cigarette into the ashtray on the arm of his chair and watched her as she went out towards the kitchen.

In the kitchen, she dawdled, staring into the icebox, not wanting anything, but not wanting to go back and face Oliver again, annoyed with herself for being afraid of him, after so many years. She wondered if he was going to sleep in the house that night and if he was going to insist upon sleeping in the same bed with her. Before he had gone into the Army, they had had separate rooms, and there had been long periods when he hadn't touched her at all. Then, suddenly, and for no particular reason or stimulus that she could ever discover, he would move into her room and stay with her three or four nights in a row. Then he would be as passionate, almost, as in the first days of their marriage, except that mixed with the hunger and the pleasure she would sense a hidden melancholy and regret.

Once he had gone into the Army she had volunteered to come down to see him at the various camps where he had been stationed, but he had refused to allow her to do it, saying that the work she was doing was too important to be sacrificed. He wrote her, dutifully, once a week, affectionate letters much more like the urbane and confident man he had been in the first years of her marriage than the abstracted and harried businessman he had become since they left Hartford.

From time to time, after the Thanksgiving on which he had brought Tony home, she had thought of leaving him. If, among the men she knew, there had been one she could have persuaded herself she loved, she would have asked Oliver for a divorce.

Then the war came and Oliver went away. He was too old, really, to join up, and she was sure that he had done it to get away from her and the insoluble, continuing problem she presented to him, and she had allowed everything to slide, telling herself that when the war was over some final decision would have to be reached.

Standing in front of the refrigerator, looking in at the almost-bare shelves, she sighed, thinking about all this. It's not much of a marriage, she thought wryly, but it's a marriage. Probably it's no worse than most.

There were some bottles of beer in the icebox and a piece of Swiss cheese, but she decided against them, although now she realized she was thirsty and would have liked the beer. She took out a bottle of milk instead, and poured herself a glass. Then she took a box of crackers from a shelf and carried it, with the glass of milk, into the living room. Let that be his last image of his wife to take to the wars with him, she thought, amused at her female slyness, innocently and girlishly sipping at a glass of milk at three o'clock in the morning.

Oliver hadn't moved. He was still sitting, planted low in his chair, staring down at the carpet, a new cigarette hanging from his lips and the collar of his trenchcoat turned up around his ears.

Lucy sat down on the couch, putting the milk and crackers on the coffee table in front of her. From where she was sitting she saw Oliver in profile, and the lines of his face were unaccustomedly sharp and aquiline, stripped down by fatigue.

'You should have let me know you were coming,' she said, sipping at her milk.

'I didn't expect to come,' Oliver said. 'I only had the one night in New York and I decided to spend it with Tony.' His voice was low and a little hoarse, as if he had been shouting orders outdoors, in bad weather.

'How is he?' Lucy asked, because she felt Oliver expected her to ask.

'No good,' Oliver said. 'No damn good at all.'

She didn't reply, because there was nothing to say. She sat tensely on the edge of the couch, watching his profile, worn, coinlike, memorial, against the lamplight, sensing the double reproof, of himself and of her, in his judgment on their son.

He twisted his head slowly and peered at her, regarding her with a tipsy, scholarly gravity. 'That's a pretty dress,' he said surprisingly. 'Have I seen it before?'

'Yes,' she said.

'Did you choose it yourself?'

'Yes.'

He nodded approvingly. 'You were always a marvellous-looking woman,' he said, 'but you wore the wrong clothes. You underplayed yourself. Now you've learned how to dress. I like that. It makes no difference, but I like it.'

He turned his head again and leaned back against the chair and didn't speak for more than a minute. His breathing was steady and Lucy wondered if he was falling asleep.

'We called you from New York, Tony and I,' he said suddenly, out of his immobility. 'He was willing to talk to you. He'd have come out here with me, I think, if you'd have been home.'

'I'm sorry,' she said in a low voice.

'This one night,' Oliver said. 'Why couldn't you have been home this one night?' He stood up and faced her, a bulky, almost shapeless figure in the creased trenchcoat, with the belt dangling open. 'Where were you?' he asked, his voice flat and unaccented.

Finally, Lucy thought, making herself look up candidly at him. 'I was out,' she said. 'I had an appointment.'

'You had an appointment.' He nodded, drunkenly agreeable. 'An appointment to do what?'

'Now, Oliver, be reasonable,' Lucy said. 'If I had known you were going to call, I certainly would have stayed at home. It was just bad luck . . .'

'Just bad luck,' he said, plunging his hands in his pockets, lowering his head, his chin resting on his chest. 'I'm tired of the bad luck. When does the good luck begin? I asked you a question —an appointment to do what?'

'I went out to dinner,' Lucy said calmly. 'With a soldier, a young lieutenant I met at the hospital. A pilot.'

'Dinner with a pilot,' Oliver said. 'You ate slowly. It was past three o'clock when he left you at the door. What else did you do?'

'Now, Oliver . . .' Lucy began. She stood up.

'What else did you do?' Oliver repeated in the same flat, unemotional voice. 'Did you let him make love to you?'

Lucy sighed. 'Do you really want to know?'

'Yes.'

'He made love to me. Yes.'

Oliver nodded, still agreeable. 'Was it the first time?'

Lucy hesitated, tempted to lie. Then she rejected the idea. 'No,' she said.

'Do you love him?'

'No.'

'But you enjoy going to bed with him?'

'Actually, no.'

229

'Actually, no,' Oliver said gravely. 'Then why did you do it?'

Lucy shrugged. 'He was hurt when he was in Africa. Badly hurt. And he's terribly frightened because he's going out again, to the Pacific . . .'

'Oh, I see,' Oliver said reasonably. 'It's a form of patriotism.'

'Don't make fun of me, Oliver,' Lucy said. 'I pitied him. That's understandable, isn't it? He's young and frightened and damaged. It seemed to mean a great deal to him . . .'

'Of course, I understand,' Oliver said, speaking gently. 'Of course, in a hospital these days, there are hundreds of boys who are young and frightened and damaged. I, of course, am not young and I'm not frightened. But I guess you could say I'm damaged. Do you want to go to bed with me?'

'Oliver . . .' Lucy made a move towards the door. 'You're in no condition to talk right now. I'm going to sleep. If you insist on ploughing through all this, I'll answer any questions you want in the morning.'

Oliver made a gesture with his hand, stopping her. 'I won't be here in the morning. And I'm in marvellous condition for a talk like this right now. Drunk, insomniac and on the way out. When a man goes to war, there's certain things he likes to leave in order behind him. His will, his memory, the exact status of his wife. Tell me,' he said conversationally, 'there've been others haven't there?'

Lucy sighed. 'A long time ago,' she said, 'I told you I wasn't going to lie to you any more, Oliver.'

'That's exactly why I'm asking,' he said. 'I want the true bill to take away with me.'

'Yes, there have been others,' Lucy said. 'So?'

'When you stayed in the city overnight after the theatre,' Oliver said, 'it wasn't only because you didn't want to come home alone so late on the train?'

'No.'

'Have you loved any of them?' Oliver peered at her closely now and took a step nearer her.

'No.'

'Do you mean that?'

'I regret to say it, but I haven't,' Lucy said.

'Why not?'

'Maybe because I'm incapable of loving,' Lucy said. 'Maybe because I love you. I don't know.'

230

'Then why do you do it?' Oliver asked, standing in front of her, barring the way to the door. 'Why the hell do you do it?'

'Maybe because it makes me feel important and ever since I was a girl I felt unimportant. Maybe because I feel empty. Maybe because for a few minutes each time it seems as though it's going to mean something, as though there's a puzzle I'm finally going to find the answer to. Maybe because I'm disappointed in myself and in you and in Tony. Maybe because I'm worthless or my mother left me alone one night when I was two years old.' She shrugged. 'Maybe because it just happens to be the style these days. I don't know. Now I'm going to sleep.' She took another step towards the door.

'One more question,' Oliver said, his voice low, hollow with fatigue. 'Are you going to keep on?'

'I suppose so,' Lucy said wearily. 'There must be an answer to the puzzle somewhere.'

They stood facing each other, Lucy rigid and defiant, Oliver stooped a little, thoughtful and questioning and rumpled in his dangling, stained coat. 'Tell me, Lucy,' he said, and his voice was kindly, almost elegiac, with a tone of tender farewell in it, 'are you happy?'

'No,' she said.

He nodded. 'That's the unforgivable thing,' he said, 'not to be happy.'

He moved close to her, his hands hanging at his sides, staring deeply into her face, searching.

'You're a clumsy, frivolous woman,' he said quietly.

Then he hit her. He hit her hard, with his closed fist, as though he were hitting a man.

She fell back a little, against the wall. She didn't cry out and she made no move to defend herself. She stood there, straight, her back supported by the wall, looking steadily into his eyes. He sighed and took another step nearer her. Then he hit her again, heavily, punishing her, punishing himself.

She felt the blood come to her lips and the lights of the lamps began to dance redly before her eyes, but she still didn't try to defend herself. She stood with her chin up, watching him impersonally, with the blood dripping from her mouth, waiting. He had never struck her before, but it didn't seem strange or unjust that he was doing it now. And even as he rained blows on her, heavily, soberly, with the ceremonial inevitability of a sentence

231

being carried out, she kept staring into his eyes, forgivingly, understandingly.

It had to happen, she thought, with the roaring in her ears and the numbing pain of the blows, it was all arranged a long time ago.

When she slid down to the floor at the base of the wall, the pretty black dress splashed with blood and rumpled around her knees, Oliver stood above her for a moment, looking down at her, his face gentle and lost, framed by the upturned warlike collar of his coat.

Then he turned and went out of the house.

She lay there for a long time, long after she heard the door close behind him. Then she stood up and with housewifely thrift turned out all the lights in the living room, and switched the heat down before she went up to her room.

She didn't leave the house for ten days after that because the bruises took that long to heal.

Chapter Twenty

IT was getting late and Ozières was still an hour away and Tony decided to stop for lunch. The graves of unloved fathers, he thought, are better visited on a full stomach.

He pulled the car into the driveway of a small hotel which stood by itself in open country. There was an arbour of plane trees with tables set under it, in the shade, and there was the usual collection of signs at the entrance to the hotel to indicate that various organizations, representing the gluttons of France, had put their mark of approval on the restaurant.

He stopped the motor and sat for a moment, stiff from the ride, with his forehead burning from the glare of the sun and the rush of wind. He looked over at Lucy, waiting for her to open her eyes. Her face was calm and there was a little smile on her lips, as though she had been dreaming of happy evenings, dances in her youth, secret pleasures of the past. Tony felt a flicker of annoyance. She oughtn't to look like that, he thought. On a day like this, there should be some hint in the way she looks that her memories are touched by sorrow and include suffering. Resilience, he thought, is a recessive characteristic in the Crown line, transmitted only to the females of the family.

Lucy opened her eyes.

'Lunch time,' Tony said.

She looked at the hotel and the arbour of the restaurant and the apple orchard beyond it. 'What a pretty little place,' she said, masquerading as a tourist.

They went into the garden and Lucy said, 'You order for me, please. I want to freshen up a bit.' Tony sat at a table, watching his mother walking across the washed gravel between the tables, noticing the straightness of her back and the surprisingly youthful shape of her long legs and the smart, high-heeled shoes which she had worn, because when she left her hotel that morning she hadn't known she was going out into the country. There were two men sitting at another table, eating langouste, and Tony saw them stop eating for a moment and follow Lucy with their eyes, approvingly, until she disappeared into the hotel. How long have men been looking at her like that, Tony wondered. More than thirty years? And what has it done to her?

The waitress came over and he ordered trout and salad for them both, and a bottle of white wine. At least, he thought, I might as well have a good lunch out of this day.

He was sorry he had come now. He had been surprised into it, and he had been curious, and his natural inclination at all times was to be polite, to seem to be agreeable and do what people asked him to do. But now he was disturbed and uncertain and the memories that his mother had brought with her were hurtful and shameful ones. And, somehow, she made him feel old and reminded him that by the age of thirty he had wasted a great portion of his life. Without saying anything about it, it was as though they had joined in the ride up into Normandy to judge the man he was today against the possibilities of the boy he had been the last time they had been together. And the judgment, on his side as well as on hers, was a disapproving and negative one.

She has come a long way, he thought, to give me pain.

The thing that troubled him most about his mother, he realized, had been the expression on her face just before she awoke, when they drove up and stopped in front of the restaurant. That soft, secret, reminiscent female smile. It made him remember the moment when he had looked through the slit in the blinds as a boy and had seen her in Jeff's arms. Her head had been turned towards the window, her eyes closed, her lips parted slightly in the kind of smile he had never seen on anyone's face before that, selfish, devouring, impervious to any other claims but the claims of her own pleasure, shocking in the power of its relished emotion and its egotism. That smile had haunted him, and it had become for him the sign and danger signal of the entire sex. Whenever he was with a woman he kept looking for that smile, or a hint or hidden indication of it, like a gambler watching for a marked card or a soldier searching for a mine. It had made him reticent and cold, an observer rather than a participant, and had prevented him from giving himself completely in any relationship. The women he had known had sensed this quality of watchful aloofness. None of them had understood exactly what it was or what was behind it but he had been accused, in varying tones of hysteria, of being suspicious, frozen, incapable of love. Looking back at his connection with the female sex, it now seemed to him like one long and bitter arraignment, in which the accusers changed from time to time, while the accusation, grave and damning and unanswerable, remained always the same.

None of the women whom he had once been intimate with remained his friends and he had grown accustomed to seeing a set and vengeful expression on their faces when they met him anywhere by accident. He had left America in 1947 because a girl whom he had loved, he thought, very much, had refused to marry him. 'I love you,' the girl had said, 'but I'm afraid of you. You're not all present, at any time. Even when you're kissing me, you seem to be making some sort of qualification about me. There've been times when I've caught you looking at me, and some of them have been damn queer times, too, when the look on your face has chilled my blood. I never can get over the feeling that you're always on the verge of moving off. I can't get hold of you, and I'm sure, in my bones, that one morning I'd wake up and you wouldn't be there. You're an escaper and it isn't only from me or from women, either. I've watched you with men, too, and I've talked to them about you, and finally, everybody has the same feeling. There isn't a man I know who can honestly say that you're his friend . . .'

The girl's name was Edith, and she had had long blonde hair, and she had married a man who lived in Detroit and she had had two children and been divorced twice since then.

234

An escaper. He had denied it bitterly when Edith had charged him with it, but he had known it was true, just the same. He had escaped the love of his mother and the pity of his father; he had escaped the war and the desires of women and the affection of men. He had escaped the profession he had almost prepared himself for and the country in which he was born. His wife was sure he was preparing to escape her, and in a way she was right. With his studio in another part of the city, and his trips and his nights away from home, he was already half-departed. He had married her soon after Edith had broken off their engagement. He had married her mostly because she had been very young, gay, innocent, and insistent, and it had looked at the time as though the marriage would not impose heavy claims upon him. But then the boy had been born and the gaiety and innocence had gone and only the insistence had seemed to remain and there were long periods when only the responsibility for his son kept a kind of surface and hurtful marriage in being.

At what birthday, he thought, do I escape my son?

He looked up across the bottle of cold wine that the waitress had set on the table and saw Lucy coming out of the restaurant, her hair in order, her scarf trailing from her hand. He noticed the two men watching her again, interested, involuntarily and automatically pleased with the sight of the tall, handsome, well-dressed woman, freshly combed and washed, falsely youthful in the flattering summer light and shadow of the arbour, moving towards the table at the end of the garden at which a young man awaited her. Wreathed in lust, Tony thought sardonically, garlanded everlastingly with desire, my mother approaches.

He stood up and helped her with her chair and poured them both a glass of the wine. They made no toast as they took the first sips.

'Well, now, that's better,' Lucy said, drinking thirstily, feeling the wine working at the dust of the road in her throat. She looked across at Tony and was conscious again of the grimace of amusement, the twist of irony and rejection on his lips that had disturbed her so profoundly in the living room of his apartment that morning. It froze her and made it impossible for her to speak naturally, and her plan of being easy and matronly and superficial, waiting for a sign of compassion or affection from him before making any demands on him, now seemed naïve and hopeless to her.

She was uncomfortable and ate quickly, without speaking or noticing what was placed before her. Nervously she drank most of the wine herself, unaware that Tony was keeping her glass full, with the solicitous and humorous malice of a roué debauching a child.

The wine was cold and dry, and her thirst seemed unquenchable and she was grateful when Tony ordered another bottle. It was very light, and aside from making everything about her stand forth with pleasant clarity, she was sure it was having no effect on her.

By the time they were halfway through another bottle, she seemed to be floating off at a little distance, viewing the scene coolly, seeing a mother and son, linked by their good looks, gravely polite with each other, sitting in a Norman garden, enjoying each other's company, civilized and reticent, decently on their way, long after the guns had been silenced, to pay their respects to their dead. Only, if you blinked a little, and pushed back the wine, and looked a little more closely, there was something wrong with the scene. The fixed smile on the man's face, which at a distance would pass for an expression of indulgence and filial attentiveness, dissolved upon inspection into mockery, opened a gulf, denied love, was a tortured grin from the darkness of an abyss.

'Intolerable,' she said, putting her glass down, staring at him.

'What's that?' Tony asked, surprised.

'Tell me,' she said, 'what's your opinion of me?'

'Now, really,' he protested, 'I haven't had the time really to form one.'

'You've had the time,' she said, her tongue slippery and a little thick with the wine. 'I can see it in your face. You have a good, big, interesting opinion, and I'm interested to hear it.'

'Well . . .' Tony leaned back in his chair, deciding to humour her. 'I must say I've been admiring you all day.'

'Admiring me?' Lucy asked harshly. 'Why?'

'For remaining so young and beautiful and lively,' he said, smiling at her. 'It's very clever of you.'

'Clever,' she repeated, knowing that he meant to hurt her with that 'clever,' and knowing that he had succeeded.

'I can't help wondering how you've managed it,' he said, his tone light.

'Your wife asked me the same question.'

236

'I must ask her what you told her,' he said.

'I didn't tell her anything,' Lucy said. 'You tell her. I'm sure you have a theory about it.'

'Perhaps I do,' he said. They were staring across the table at each other, hostile, ready to do harm.

'Tell *me*,' Lucy said. 'Maybe the right answer will do me a lot of good in the next twenty years.'

'Well,' Tony began, thinking, She asked for it, she came here, she dug it all up again, she yearned to see the grave, let her hear it. 'Well, I was thinking along rather old-fashioned lines, I'm afraid. The wicked thrive, I was thinking. Youth lingers for the hard of heart. Sin and flourish. Remain untouched and families can crumble around you, empires crash, and not a hair in your head will turn grey.'

'Untouched.' Lucy shook her head dazedly. 'So that's what you've been thinking, all these years.'

'Only in the figurative sense, of course,' Tony said.

There was silence at the table for a moment, while they both were caught in the chilly echo of Tony's gibe.

'You miscalculate yourself, Tony,' Lucy said gently. 'You think of yourself as a mean and unpleasant man and, naturally, you try to live up to that picture of yourself. I don't believe you really are, though. I know what you were like as a boy and the boy couldn't have vanished completely, no matter what's happened. I know about miscalculation, Tony, because I've spent the last ten years of my life trying to repair the damage I did by being all wrong about myself. All wrong. All wrong . . . Accidents and errors,' she said, her voice loose and musical and a little thick from the wine. 'Accidents and errors. If that nasty little girl hadn't been at the lake that summer, if she hadn't been bored on a grey afternoon and decided to take a walk through the woods—if the sun had come out and she'd gone swimming, or if you'd just arrived a half hour later—we wouldn't be here like this today. If you hadn't been sick and nearly died your father would never have thought he had to hire a young man to take care of you . . . If he hadn't gone into a garage one morning and found out that I hadn't paid a bill that I thought I'd paid, and if he hadn't called me up to scold me about it and made me feel rebellious and small . . . Nothing would've happened. Nothing.' She shook her head, seeming to wonder at the complex and malicious windings of fate which had overthrown her life. 'But it was a grey day and

237

there *was* a nasty little girl and there *was* a young man and you didn't arrive a half hour later. So something that might have been only a single, rather foolish, unnecessary excursion—the sort of thing that happens to millions of women, and finally fades away into a harmless secret that they look back at indulgently in their old age—turned into a disaster. A watershed. To divide my life and yours, and your father's.'

'That's too easy,' Tony said, hating his mother for remembering everything so clearly 'You're letting yourself off too easy.'

'Oh, no,' she said. 'Don't think that. Never think that. Everybody's responsible for his own accidents and I stand behind mine. Only nobody avoids accidents, of one kind or another. You mustn't expect that you're going to get off without them. It's what you do with them, how you come out of them, how you repair the damage, that's important. Well, I did the worst possible thing. I made my accident permanent. I made every mistake in the book. After fifteen years of marriage, I enjoyed a young man for a couple of weeks in the summertime, so I decided I was a sensual woman. Well, it turned out I wasn't. I was afraid of your father and I lied to him and the lie was an ugly one and I was caught in it, and ashamed of it, so I decided that from then on we could only survive by candour. Well, we didn't survive. You were the witness and you were hurt and you had hurt us, so I decided to make the hurt irreparable. Your testimony was too painful to listen to that year so I sent you away. And your absence testified against us, more and more damningly, every year . . .'

'Do you think it would have been better to keep me with you?' Tony asked, without belief.

'Yes,' she said. 'We would have endured. A family is like flesh and bone. When it's wounded, if it's given a chance, it knits and heals. But it doesn't heal if the wound is kept open. We made an institution of the wound, we built our marriage on it, our life, and we paid for it.'

'Paid for it,' Tony said flatly, looking across the table at the robust, healthy, preserved woman, with her unlined face and her youthful mouth, her skin delicately and prettily flushed now by the wine and the sun. 'Who paid for it?'

'I know what you think,' she said, nodding. 'You think that you've paid for it. That your father paid. And that I got off free. But you're wrong. I paid, too,'

'I can imagine how you paid,' Tony said, unrelenting.

'Yes, you're right,' Lucy said wearily. 'I paid in many beds. But that was a long time ago, and it stopped one night, when your father came home to say good-bye before going to the war.' She closed her eyes, shutting out the sight of her son, remembering herself, bloody and punished, lying against the wall at four o'clock on a winter morning, and the sound of the door closing behind the husband she was never going to see again. 'But that wasn't the only way I paid. I paid in guilt and loneliness and envy.' She opened her eyes and looked across at Tony. 'I thought I was all paid up, too, but I see I'm not. Not yet. No matter what you think of me, finally, I suppose you can believe in the guilt and loneliness. But maybe the envy was the worst of all. Because I envied everybody. I envied the women who had placid, uneventful marriages and the women who had uproarious ones, with fights and separations and reconciliations. I envied the women who were thoughtlessly promiscuous and who could take seven men a week and accept them easily and forget them as easily. I envied the women who knew they wanted to be faithful for all the years of the war and never wavered and I envied the women who were swept away by love or by lust and would sacrifice anything, fight anyone, with any weapon, for the men they'd chosen. I envied the women who took it hard and the women who took it easy, because I didn't know how to take it at all. At the hospital there were a lot of women and there was a joke they passed among them. They said they belonged to a club that had started in England, because the war had started earlier there. The club was called the M.Y.O.V.A., and the letters meant Making Young Officers Very 'Appy and it was good for a laugh in all circles from 1940 to 1945. I laughed with them and I envied them. And most of all I envied myself. The myself that I had been and the marriage I had had until that summer on the lake. It wasn't that I had a sentimental view of myself or a false memory of the marriage. There were a lot of things wrong with it and if your father didn't tell you what they were, listen to me and I'll tell you now. Your father was a passionate and disappointed man. When he was young, he had high hopes for himself. He loved aeroplanes and the people who made them and flew them and the business he'd started was full of promise and I suppose he saw himself as a pioneer and experimenter and a power in the land. Then his father died and he had to go back to the printing works and the town he'd been trying to escape for ten years and he saw himself as a nobody, a failure, and all the passion and disappointment of his life he centred on me. And I was inadequate to it, and I knew it and I resented him and finally I made him suffer for it. He frightened me and he expected too much from me and he directed every move of my life and a good deal of the time he didn't satisfy me. But I loved him, and, looking back on it now, I see that the marriage balanced out, although I didn't see it then. I was timid and uncertain and vengeful and I had a low opinion of myself, so I went out looking for a good opinion of myself in the arms of other men. At first I told myself I was looking for love, but it wasn't so. I didn't find love and I didn't find a good opinion. And it wasn't as though I didn't try.'

She stopped and rocked a little in her chair, and leaned forward and put her elbows on the table, supporting her chin on the backs of her crossed hands, staring past her son's head into a confusion of shadowy faces, seeming to hear, in the Norman garden, a hidden murmuring of men's voices, importuning, laughing, sighing, whispering, weeping, calling her name, saying, 'Lucy, Lucy,' saying, 'Dearest,' saying, 'I love you,' saying, 'It was wonderful' and 'Write to me every day' and 'I'll never forget you' and, in the obscurity of spent and darkened rooms, 'Good night, good night . . .'

'All manner and conditions of men,' Lucy said, her voice low and without emotion. 'There was a lawyer who wanted to give up a wife and three children to marry me, because he said he couldn't live without me, but he lived without me all right and he has five children now. There was a gay young man who was football coach at Princeton and who drank applejack old-fashioneds and I sent a silver cake dish to his wedding. There was an antique dealer who took me to chamber-music concerts all over New York and wanted me to live with him to prevent him from turning homosexual, but I didn't live with him and he's living with a Mexican boy now. There was a movie writer on a train and I slept with him because I was drunk and we were getting off the next morning, anyway. There was even a boy who was in your class at Columbia and he told me that you were brilliant and you had no friends and he didn't think you'd amount to much, in the long run. There was a deck officer of a ship that made cruises of the Caribbean in the wintertime, and he had the body of a dancer and he'd learned a great deal from the ladies who went cruising in those warm waters, and the one time I was with him, while it was happening, it seemed to me that that was what I had been searching for all that time— But when he got up to leave he took too long admiring himself while he was putting his tie on in front of the mirror. I looked across at him, whistling and grinning and snub-nosed and sweating with cheap male confidence in himself, and I knew I was never going to see him again, because he had debased me. He wasn't a lover preparing to say good-bye, he was a professional athlete, tipping his cap to the public as he crossed home plate. And after that,' she said flatly, 'I knew it wasn't for me. Sensuality is for sensualists and I had made a mistake about myself.

'Then, of course,' she said pitilessly, 'there was the Army, the Navy, and the Air Force. Only by that time I wasn't looking for anything any more. I was dispensing charity. But it takes talent to be charitable, too, and in the long run, as was to be expected, my amateur benevolence did more harm than good. I hurt the wounded and I left the disconsolate unconsoled. I was a whore for pity, and I insulted men who were on their way to die, because they weren't looking for whores. They wanted tenderness and reassurance and all I could give them was brisk professional accomplishment. And I insulted myself, because that wasn't the métier for me and it warped me into something I hated. I became callous and tricky and a liar on the telephone and a coquette in bed and a counterfeiter who squandered all her real wealth in forging bills that no one finally would accept.

'And at last,' she said, flooding on, not giving Tony a chance to interrupt her, intent, like someone adding a long column of figures, in toting up the account and getting the sum right before turning to other things, 'when the moment came to make the big decision, the salvaging decision, when perhaps I could have saved your father and myself with one word, the word I said was the wrong one. Naturally. You have to prepare yourself carefully, for years, you have to understand yourself, to say the right word in a crisis. And I didn't understand anything and I wasn't prepared for anything. He was waiting for me in the dark before he sailed for England. It was after three o'clock in the morning and he'd just come from seeing you and he must have heard something of what the lieutenant was saying to me at the door, but not much. And he asked me if I'd let the boy make love to me and I said yes. And he asked me if there had been others and I said yes. And he asked me if there would be others and I said yes. I was proud of myself because I thought I had become strong enough to be honest. But it wasn't honesty, it was revenge and self-approval. In any case, it wasn't the "yes" of honesty that was needed between your father and me, it was the "no" of charity. Only I'd run out of charity by that time, and your father beat me for it, as he should, and went off and got killed.'

She stopped and for a few seconds the only sound in the arbour was the buzz of a bee dipping erratically over a basket of plums on the table. She licked her lips and picked up her wine glass and drained it. 'Well,' she said, 'there's your mother, who got off free. I've had a long time to think about all this and I never said it to anyone and you might as well be the first to hear it. And if you're interested, I've never touched another man from that morning to this. It wasn't hard and I don't claim much credit for it, because I was only tempted once, and then not really seriously.'

She flicked with her napkin at the bee and it left the plums and darted up a beam of sunlight towards the leaves above their heads. 'When I got the news that your father was dead and you wired that you wouldn't come to the funeral service, I went through it myself. And after it, I sat alone in that damned house in New Jersey where your father and I had ground ourselves down into hatred and despair, and I decided that I had to rehabilitate myself. I had to be able, finally, to forgive myself. And I felt that the only way was through being useful and loving. And I was sure that I wasn't going to be able to love another man, because I'd tried all that, and I fixed on children. Maybe you came into that, too. I'd botched you so badly I wanted to prove to myself that if I had another chance, I could do better. I applied to adopt two children, a boy and a girl, and while I was waiting I roamed the streets and the parks, staring at children, playing with them when their mothers and nurses would let me, making great plans about how for the next twenty years I would devote myself completely to turning out glorious, sunny young people, who would behave faultlessly, with gentleness and courage and intelligence, in every situation of their adult lives. Only the people who had charge of putting children out for adoption had other ideas. They weren't so pleased with the notion of a single woman well over forty taking on two babies, and they investigated me quietly and they heard a few things. Not all. But enough. And they turned me down. The day they said no, I went walking in the meadows at Central Park, staring at little boys running across the grass and little girls playing with balloons and I knew what those poor women must feel who steal babies out of carriages. I wasn't bitter at the people from the society. The actions of ten years must have their consequences. You can't expect people to believe you if you go to them and say, "I'm changed. I'm a different woman. From today on I plan to become a saint." They have other things on their minds besides making it easy for a widow with a bad reputation to forgive herself.'

She reached over and took the bottle of wine and poured what was left into her glass. There wasn't much and she didn't drink it immediately, but sat looking at the glass between her fingers on the chequered tablecloth, not wanting or expecting any word from Tony, using him merely for the bitter and salutary pleasure of having a listener to involve in her self-denunciation.

'Still,' she said reflectively, turning the stem of the glass, 'that was when I began to have some hope for myself. Do you remember Sam Patterson?' she asked abruptly.

'Yes,' Tony said. 'Of course.'

'I hadn't seen him for years, but he'd come to the funeral, and after that, from time to time, he'd visit me or ask me to meet him for dinner when he came to New York. His wife had divorced him just before the war, fifteen years too late for both of them, and he was easy to be with because he knew all about me and I didn't have to pretend about anything with him. Once, long ago, when he was drunk at a dance, he'd put his arms around me and almost said he loved me.' She smiled sadly. 'Saturday night at a country club. Only it turned out he meant it, and when I went to him and told him that I couldn't have the children, he asked me to marry him. That way, he said, married, we'd be sure to be able to adopt all the children we wanted. And he said he'd loved me from the beginning, even though it had only slipped out that one drunken time . . . And I nearly said yes. He was a good friend, maybe the only friend I had, and I'd liked him and admired him from the first time I met him. And it wasn't only the children. It was a promise of pardon from loneliness. You have no idea what the loneliness of an ageing woman, husbandless and without a family, can be like in a city like New York. Maybe it's the real loneliness, the ultimate, naked meaning of the word in the twentieth century. But I said no.

243

And I said no because he loved me and wanted me and all I felt I could love was a child and all I wanted was not to be alone, and I'd disappointed enough men in my life. When I'd said it and he'd gone away, I began to feel that, finally, I was going to be able to forgive myself. Don't think I didn't regret it later, and don't think that I didn't nearly call him up ten times in the next few months to tell him I'd changed my mind—but I didn't. For once, I calculated correctly, and I stuck to my calculation. And even so, it was Sam Patterson in the long run who saved me. He'd heard about this committee that was being formed in connection with the United Nations, to do what they could for all the children who were left starving and homeless by the war, and he got me an interview and he got me hired and he made me stay with it when it all seemed pointless to me. Because, it isn't the same thing, you know, caring for a million children you'll never see, and worrying about tons of wheat and cases of penicillin and powdered milk. It's not like watching a child grow in your own hands, and whatever victories you may win are terribly cold and abstract. And I'm not an abstract woman. But I worked twelve hours a day and I put as much money of my own into it as I could, and if I wasn't satisfied and if I'm still hungry and lonely, well, what could I expect? And there're other rewards. I'm not satisfied—but I'm necessary. That will have to be enough for this year. I'm thankful to those million unknown children whom I don't love and who will never love me.'

She picked the wine bottle up and looked at it critically. 'I suppose it's too late to order another,' she said.

Tony looked at his watch. 'Yes,' he said. He felt stunned and suddenly incapable of judging the woman who had exposed herself so painfully to him for the last hour. Later on, he knew, he would have to judge her, because now all the facts were in. But for the moment it was impossible. All he could do was look at his watch and say, 'We'll never get back to Paris tonight if we don't leave here now.'

She nodded and tied the scarf around her head, to hold her hair in place against the wind, and in the soft warm shade of the arbour, the lines of her face were soft and calm, and she reminded Tony of girls he had seen driving in the summertime in open cars on the way to the beach. He took out his wallet and reached for the bill, which was lying on a plate next to him, but Lucy bent over and picked up the slip of paper and squinting, a little near-sightedly, to see how much it was, said, 'This lunch is on me. The pleasure's been mine.'

Chapter Twenty-One

THEY drove in silence through the lengthening shadows of the afternoon. They went very fast, sweeping around the turns of the humped, narrow road, the tyres squealing. Tony was tight over the wheel, and he seemed to Lucy to be driving fast and dangerously for a purpose, to keep himself so intent and concentrated on passing cars and managing curves that there was no chance of thinking about anything else.

She did not try to talk to him. I am expended, she thought dully. There's nothing further I have to say.

They were approaching a village. It was still a quarter of a mile off, in a little declivity, a huddle of bluish slate roofs over grey stone, clustered around a church steeple.

'There it is,' Tony said.

Lucy stared through the windshield. The town lay quietly in the sunshine, surrounded by its green fields, with the road running straight into the middle of it, looking like a dozen other villages they had gone through.

'Well,' Tony asked, 'what do you want to do?'

'It happened at a crossroads,' Lucy said. 'I got a letter from a man who was with him and he said they were coming in from the north and there was a crossroads just outside the town.'

'North is on the other side,' Tony said.

They were silent as they drove through the village. The street was narrow and winding and the buildings were right along the edge, with boxes of geraniums in bloom under the windows. The shutters were closed on all the windows and Lucy had a sudden picture of all the inhabitants lurking within, balefully spying on the strangers rushing through their town in their noisy machines, breaking the centuries-old peace of the place, reminding them of their poverty and their bitter roots in this peasant soil, and of the hard lives they led.

Lucy remembered the Sergeant's letter, and thought, distractedly, He crossed an ocean to take this empty place. And he never even reached it.

They were almost through the town by now and they still hadn't seen a single person. The broken shutters on the windows absorbed the glare of the sun and the single petrol pump on the edge of the town was locked and unattended. It was almost as though, for her benefit, the town had remained exactly as it was, asleep and dangerous, on the day eleven years before when her husband had walked up the road towards it with a white towel on a stripped branch.

Tony was frowning as he drove through the town, as though he disapproved of the place. But it might only have been the effect of the sun, reflecting off the flaking stone walls. They pulled slowly out to the other side of the village and Lucy saw the crossroads. Looking at it, the two narrow country roads, thick with white dust, intersecting each other in a meaningless small widening of their surfaces. Lucy had a sense of recognition that was almost pleasurable. It was like searching for something that you have lost, that has nagged you with its loss for many years, and suddenly coming upon it.

'Here,' she said. 'Stop here.'

Tony pulled the car a little to one side, just before they reached the crossroads, although he couldn't get all the way off the road because of the ditch that ran alongside it. The ditch was almost three feet deep and was overgrown with grass, powdered with the dust of the road. There were no trees, although there was a row of hedge a few yards back from the road.

Tony leaned back in his seat, stretching and working his shoulders.

'This is the place,' Lucy said. She got out of the car. Her legs were stiff and cramped and the sun beat down, very hot on the unshaded, bright road, now that they were no longer moving. She took off her scarf and pushed her hand through her hair and walked to the crossroads, the dust rising in little chalky puffs around her heels. The countryside slumbered all around them, empty and stretching and anonymous, without emotion, sending up a grassy, thin aroma.

In the distance there were several clusters of roofs and church steeples, other towns lost under the open sun. Only to the north, on the side away from the town, was the landscape broken. There was a rise about a hundred feet away and trees along the edges of the road which came down towards them in a gentle, direct slope, and Lucy could imagine, from the Sergeant's letter, the jeeps parked facing in the other direction, just under the rise, and the four men in helmets lying there, rifles ready, their eyes just over the crest of the ridge, watching the town, watching the three figures walking through the hot naked sunlight in the white dust, coming up to the crossroads, outlined there for a moment in the blank and meaningless swelling, then starting on the other side towards the silent walls . . .

She paced slowly down the centre of the road, thinking, I am treading on the spot. This is the place he was looking for, this is the place he was travelling to. Why did I come here? It is just a place, like any other. A back-country road, marked by cartwheels, in a part of Europe that looks as though it might be anywhere, Maryland, Maine, Delaware, with no sign any place within the horizon that a war ever passed this way, that armed men ever died here.

She shook her head. She felt empty and at a loss. There was no possible ceremony at this nondescript, vacant crossroads with which to dignify the moment or bring it to a climax. There were no symbols or monuments, just meaningless roads without history. She was conscious of Tony behind her, brooding and implacable, and suddenly resented his presence there. If she had been alone, or with someone else, anyone else, she thought, she would have been able to find significance in the moment, give way to sorrow or relief. I'm here with the wrong man, she thought.

Despite herself, she found herself wondering, How long should I stay here? Will it be decent to leave in ten minutes? Fifteen? Should I drop a flower, weep a tear, scratch a name on a stone?

She looked back at Tony. He was still sitting at the wheel of the car, his hat pulled down in front, so that the sun was kept from his eyes. He wasn't watching her, but was staring incuriously across the empty fields. It occurred to Lucy that he had the air of a chauffeur waiting for his employer to come out of a shop, not caring what she was buying, how long she would stay, where the next stop would be, waiting with a remote, hired, unconnected patience, earning his salary, thinking of six o'clock, when he would be free.

She walked over to the car. He turned his head towards her. 'What a place to get killed,' he said.

Lucy didn't answer him. She went round to the other side of the car, being careful not to slip into the ditch, and opened her bag, which was on the seat. She took out the Sergeant's letter, and carefully removed it from its envelope. The paper was cracked and flaking with age at the edges and when she opened it she could see little holes along the creases.

'Here,' she said. 'You might want to read this.'

Tony glanced at her suspiciously, the chauffeur wary of being involved in the secrets of his employer. Then he took the letter, spreading it against the wheel, and began to read.

Lucy went around to the back of the car and leaned against the baggage rack. She didn't want to watch Tony reading the letter. She didn't want him to feel that it was necessary to put any kind of expression on his face for her, pity or amusement at the Sergeant's grammar or sorrow for the event of the distant afternoon. She became conscious of the silence, so different from the crowded music of the American countryside, and she realized that she missed the sound of birds. That's right, she remembered, the French shoot everything, the birds are dead or they have learned to keep quiet.

She heard Tony rustling the letter, putting it back in the envelope, and she turned around. He was being very careful with the frail paper and tucking the edges in neatly. He tapped the envelope reflectively against the steering wheel several times, then sat still, staring out at the road. Then he climbed out of the car, putting the letter in his pocket. He went out into the middle of the road and stopped, scuffing the dust with his shoe.

'Making mistakes right up to the last minute, wasn't he?' Tony said, pushing the dust, smoothing it out with the sole of his shoe. 'Always so sure people were going to surrender.'

'Is that all you have to say?'

'What do you want me to say? Should I make a speech about our heroic dead? He was just taking a walk.' He came back towards her. 'He should have stayed back at Corps, as the Sergeant said.'

'The Sergeant didn't say that.'

'He intimated as much. All the others—the sensible ones—stayed there. They weren't fearless and cheerful and democratic . . .' Tony smiled grimly. 'And they're back home today.'

He swung around and looked at the crossroads. Then he bent into the back of the car, under the lowered canvas top, and felt around for a moment and came up with a thin, pointed jack handle. He straightened it out and locked the joint. It had a curved end and now it looked like a cane in his hands. He leaned over again and he came up this time with a bottle in a straw jacket. He took the jacket off and Lucy saw that it was a bottle of brandy, still sealed.

'For cold nights and thirsty travellers,' Tony said, tossing the straw jacket into the ditch, and holding up the bottle. 'Do you happen to have a corkscrew on you?'

'No.' Lucy watched him, puzzled and suspicious.

'That's a mistake,' he said. 'One should not be caught out in France without a corkscrew.' He went to the middle of the road and stared down at the surface. Then, with the jack handle, he began to write in the dust, slowly and carefully. Curiously, Lucy came up behind him to see what he was doing.

Oliver Crown, he was printing in the dust in wide, evenly spaced letters. *Husband. Father.* He hesitated, the jack handle poised. Then he added one more word. *Negotiator*, he wrote. When he had finished, he stepped back a little, cocking his head to one side, like an artist criticizing his own work. Then he stepped up again and drew a box around the inscription. 'That's better,' he said. He went over to the side of the road and bent down and knocked off the head of the brandy bottle against a stone and came back and carefully poured out brandy, in a series of little spurts, along the lines of the letters.

'To make it stand out,' Tony said, 'for all the world to see.'

The brandy smelled strong and sweetish in the heat and when Tony had finished with the letters he had enough left over for the frame. For a moment, the memorial looked permanent and sensible, darkly outlined in the glittering dust.

When he finished, Tony straightened up. He looked at Lucy, his face strange, sad, pulled into a tortured grimace. 'Something had to be done,' he said, standing there with the jagged-throated bottle in his hand.

Then Lucy heard the sound of footsteps, many footsteps, shuffling in a rough irregular rhythm, growing stronger and stronger. She looked up. Over the edge of the rise a banner was showing, small and triangular, carried on a staff. A second later, uniformed men appeared over the rise, marching in a column of twos, coming out of the shade of the trees, moving swiftly. Lucy blinked. I'm imagining things, she thought, they stopped marching a long time ago.

The columns came closer and then she began to laugh. The uniformed men coming sweatily over the rise, with their banner before them, were boy scouts, in khaki shirts and shorts and packs, led by a scout master in a beret. Lucy went over and leaned against the car and laughed uncontrollably.

'What's the matter?' Tony followed her and peered at her closely. 'What're you laughing about?'

She stopped. She stared at the approaching columns. 'I don't know,' she said.

She and Tony stood against the car, off to one side, as the boys came up. They were between thirteen and sixteen, red-faced and thin, long-haired and knobby-kneed and serious under their packs. They looked like the sons of barbers and musicians. Without paying any attention to what was under their feet, they marched over the inscription in the dust, on which the brandy had already dried. They raised a small cloud as they passed and their boots and stockings were powdery grey. They stared admiringly from their sweating, unformed faces at the pretty little car and smiled gravely at the foreigners. The scout master saluted solemnly and said 'Bonjour' and looked curiously at the bottle in Tony's hand.

Tony said 'Bonjour,' and all the boys answered him in chorus, their voices high and choirlike over the scuffling sound of their boots on the road.

They marched purposefully against the walls of the town and after they had gone a little distance down the straight white road, they were no longer children, but soldiers again, weary and lonely in the hot sun, but determined and potent under their packs, with their banner in the van. Tony and Lucy stood silently watching them until they disappeared into the town, which received them in silence.

Then Tony tossed the bottle away, into the hedge.

'Well,' he said, 'I guess we're through here.'

'Yes,' said Lucy. In utter weariness, her feet shuffling through the dust, she started back towards the passenger's side of the car. There were some loose rocks on the edge of the ditch and her high heel turned on one of them and she stumbled and fell, heavily, on her hands and knees, into the dust of the road.

Stunned, feeling the pain begin in her knees and the palms of her hands, and the shock spreading dully up her spine and into her brain, she stayed that way, her hair hanging down over her eyes, panting, like an overburdened and exhausted animal.

For a moment, Tony looked down incredulously at his mother, awkward and in pain, fallen at his feet. Then he bent forward and put his hand on her shoulder to pick her up.

'Let go of me,' she said harshly, not looking at him.

He stepped back, listening to the dry, tearless sobbing of her breath. After a while she put out her hand to the car bumper and slowly and heavily pulled herself up. Her palms were bleeding and she rubbed them on her dress, leaving dusty red smears on it. Her stockings were torn and a little blood was seeping from the broken skin of her knees. She pushed at herself with blind, clumsy movements of her hands, and suddenly she seemed old, bereaved, pitiable, struggling to hold on to the last remnants of her courage and endurance.

He made no move to help her, but kept staring at her, his face set, as the new image of his mother, bloody, vulnerable, stained with dust, took possession of him. Watching her straightening her dress with ungainly, sexless, unwomanish movements, and bending over heavily to scrape the blood off her knees, he had a vision of her old age and her death, and remembered, in a wave of pity for them both, the night he had slept out under the stars on the glider on the porch and had listened to the owl and had decided to become a doctor and invent a serum against mortality. His eyes blurring with tears, he heard again the owl's call, and remembered the deathless monkey, and his selection of candidates for everlasting life, his mother, his father, Jeff, himself. And somehow, in the confusion of memory and the final overrunning of long-held defences, it was not only himself in the glider, but his son, too, magically thirteen, and his twin, dispensing immortality in accordance with the stern rules of love and watching his mother, light-footed, soft-voiced, cherished, coming across the misty lawn from her lover's bed to kiss him good night.

He went slowly over to her and took her hands, one after the other, and carefully brushed the dirt from the wounds. Then he pushed her hair back from her forehead and with his handkerchief wiped the sweat from her drawn and ageing face. Then he led her to the car door and helped her in. He stood over her briefly, as she looked up at him, the pain draining out of her eyes.

He touched her cheek lightly with his fingertips, as she had touched him so often when he was a boy, and said, 'There's no need to go to the grave any more, is there?'

He could feel her skin tremble minutely under his fingers. She shook her head gratefully. 'No,' she said.

It was nearly midnight when they got back to Paris, and Tony drove directly to his mother's hotel. He helped her out of the car and walked with her to the hotel entrance. They stopped there, oppressed by the difficulty of saying good-bye.

'Tony,' Lucy said, 'I'm only going to be here another day. I wonder if I might come by your apartment tomorrow some time. I'd like to give your son something. A toy.'

'Of course,' he said.

'Don't think you have to be there, Tony,' she said anxiously. 'It's not necessary.'

'I know,' he said.

'Good,' she said quickly. 'I'll come in the afternoon. What time does he get up from his nap?'

'Three o'clock, I think.'

'I'll be there at three o'clock,' she said.

Then he knew he couldn't leave her like that. With a smothered, childish cry, he threw his arms around her and held her tight, feeling the years, with their weight of memory and error, lift convulsively from his shoulders as he clung to her, forgiving her, mutely asking for forgiveness for himself, clutching at her, clutching at whatever might be left to them in the waste of love they had made around them.

She held him to her consolingly, patting his arm, oblivious of the people who passed them curiously on the dark, foreign street.

'Mother,' he said, 'do you remember—when I went off at the end of that summer and I asked you what we would say if we happened to see each other—do you remember what you said?'

Lucy nodded, remembering the quiet afternoon and the dark autumn blue of the mountain lake and the boy in the suit that had grown too small for him in the summer. 'I said, I guess we say hullo.'

Tony pulled gently back from his mother's embrace and stared into her eyes. 'Hullo,' he said gravely, 'Hullo, hullo.'

Then they smiled at each other and they were like any other mother and grown son placidly parting after a day in the country.

Lucy looked down at her torn and rumpled dress, at her ripped stockings and scarred knees. 'My,' she said, 'what a sight! God only knows what the people in the hotel will think I've been up to today.' She laughed. Then she leaned over and kissed him matter-of-factly on the cheek, as though she had been kissing him good night every night for twenty years. 'Sleep well,' she said, and turned and went into the hotel.

He watched her for a moment, going through the lobby towards the desk, a tall, heavy woman, lonely and showing her age, solid and reconciled and without illusions about herself. Then he got into the car and drove home.

The apartment was dark when he let himself in and he went into the child's room and stood over his bed, listening to the steady breathing. After a moment or two, the boy awoke and sat up.

'Daddy,' he said.

'I just came in to say good night,' Tony said. 'I just left your grandmother and she's coming here tomorrow to see you after your nap.'

'After my nap,' the boy said drowsily, fixing it against the forgetfulness of sleep.

'She's going to bring you a toy,' Tony said, whispering in the dark room.

'I want a tractor,' the boy said. 'No, a boat.'

'I'll call her in the morning,' Tony said, 'and she'll bring you a boat.'

'A big boat,' the boy said, lying back on his pillow. 'For long voyages.'

Tony nodded over the bed. 'A big boat for many long voyages,' he said.

But the boy was already asleep.

Tony went into the bedroom he shared with his wife. Dora was sleeping, too, on her back, breathing steadily, her head thrown back and her two hands up in front of her face, as though she were defending herself. Tony undressed quietly in the darkness and slipped into bed. He lay still for a few moments, thinking, Another day in my life.

Then he turned on his side and gently drew his wife's hands down from her face and took her in his arms and slept.

RICH MAN, POOR MAN
by Irwin Shaw

From the author of THE YOUNG LIONS and TWO
WEEKS IN ANOTHER TOWN comes the greatest novel
to appear in post-war America. Truly global in the scope
of its humanity and passion, RICH MAN, POOR MAN is
the story of a generation at war with the values of its past,
the hypocrisy and tension of its present and the
terrifying inevitability of a shipwrecked future.

Rudolph is the romantic, who learns to live with doubt
and make a fortune at 30. His brother Tom is the brute,
whose acid-scarred American dream is coloured with
boiling blood. Their sister, Gretchen, seduced by the small
town's leading citizen, is the beauty in urgent search of a
man – the only man – who can save her from herself.

'By the end of it we know America from coast to coast.'
— Daily Telegraph

NEW ENGLISH LIBRARY

From the author of *Rich Man, Poor Man*

EVENING IN BYZANTIUM

Irwin Shaw

An epic novel of the film industry ... and one man's struggle to survive.

Jesse Craig is a forty-eight-year-old film director who hasn't made a film for five years. In the luxurious, decadent setting of the Cannes Film Festival he ponders his last five years of apparent failure and starts to think about the possibility of another film, a fresh start ... It is there that he meets a young girl reporter, who seems to know more about him than he knows himself –

And then he realises the reason for his mission in Cannes – to save his life!

'In the finest narrative tradition ... always solid, well made, dependable ... A really professional writer ... '
New York Times Book Review

NEW ENGLISH LIBRARY

NEL BESTSELLERS

Crime

T031 306	UNPLEASANTNESS AT THE BELLONA CLUB	*Dorothy L. Sayers*	85p
T031 373	STRONG POISON	*Dorothy L. Sayers*	80p
T026 663	THE DOCUMENTS IN THE CASE	*Dorothy L. Sayers*	50p

Fiction

T029 522	HATTERS CASTLE	*A. J. Cronin*	£1.00
T030 199	CRUSADER'S TOMB	*A. J. Cronin*	£1.25
T031 276	THE CITADEL	*A. J. Cronin*	95p
T029 158	THE STARS LOOK DOWN	*A. J. Cronin*	£1.00
T022 021	THREE LOVES	*A. J. Cronin*	90p
T032 523	THE DREAM MERCHANTS	*Harold Robbins*	£1.10
T031 705	THE PIRATE	*Harold Robbins*	£1.00
T033 791	THE CARPETBAGGERS	*Harold Robbins*	£1.25
T031 667	WHERE LOVE HAS GONE	*Harold Robbins*	£1.00
T032 647	THE ADVENTURERS	*Harold Robbins*	£1.25
T031 659	THE INHERITORS	*Harold Robbins*	95p
T031 586	STILETTO	*Harold Robbins*	60p
T033 805	NEVER LEAVE ME	*Harold Robbins*	70p
T032 698	NEVER LOVE A STRANGER	*Harold Robbins*	95p
T032 531	A STONE FOR DANNY FISHER	*Harold Robbins*	90p
T031 659	79 PARK AVENUE	*Harold Robbins*	80p
T032 655	THE BETSY	*Harold Robbins*	95p
T031 594	THE LONELY LADY	*Harold Robbins*	£1.25
T032 639	EVENING IN BYZANTIUM	*Irwin Shaw*	80p
T033 732	RICH MAN, POOR MAN	*Irwin Shaw*	£1.35

Historical

T023 079	LORD GEOFFREY'S FANCY	*Alfred Duggan*	60p
T024 903	THE KING OF ATHELNEY	*Alfred Duggan*	60p
T032 817	FOX 1: PRESS GANG	*Adam Hardy*	50p
T032 825	FOX 2: PRIZE MONEY	*Adam Hardy*	50p
T032 833	FOX 3: SIEGE	*Adam Hardy*	50p

Science Fiction

T029 492	STRANGER IN A STRANGE LAND	*Robert Heinlein*	80p
T029 484	I WILL FEAR NO EVIL	*Robert Heinlein*	95p
T031 462	DUNE	*Frank Herbert*	£1.25
T032 671	DUNE MESSIAH	*Frank Herbert*	75p

War

T027 066	COLDITZ: THE GERMAN STORY	*Reinhold Egger*	50p
T025 438	LILIPUT FLEET	*A. Cecil Hampshire*	50p
T026 299	TRAWLERS GO TO WAR	*Lund & Ludlam*	50p

Western

T031 284	EDGE 1: THE LONER	*George Gilman*	50p
T032 671	EDGE 2: TEN THOUSAND DOLLARS AMERICAN	*George Gilman*	50p
T024 490	ADAM STEELE 1: THE VIOLENT PEACE	*George Gilman*	35p

General

T033 155	SEX MANNERS FOR MEN	*Robert Chartham*	60p
T023 206	THE BOOK OF LOVE	*Dr David Delvin*	90p
T028 828	THE LONG BANANA SKIN	*Michael Bentine*	90p

NEL P.O. BOX 11, FALMOUTH TR10 9EN, CORNWALL:

For U.K.: Customers should include to cover postage, 19p for the first book plus 9p per copy for each additional book ordered up to a maximum charge of 73p.

For B.F.P.O. and Eire: Customers should include to cover postage, 19p for the first book plus 9p per copy for the next 6 and thereafter 3p per book.

For Overseas: Customers should include to cover postage. 20p for the first book plus 10p per copy for each additional book.

Name ....

Address ....

....

Title ....
(MAY)

Whilst every effort is made to maintain prices, new editions or printings may carry an increased price and the actual price of the edition supplied will apply.